PROLOGUE

The Ways of Love

The Ways of Love

June Barraclough

ROBERT HALE · LONDON

Typeset in 10.5/12.75 Times
Derek Doyle & Associates, Liverpool.
Printed in Great Britain by
St Edmundsbury Press Ltd, Bury St Edmunds, Suffolk.
Bound by Woolnough Bookbinding Ltd.

Prologue

A portrait entitled *Mother and Son* hangs in one of the high-ceilinged ground floor rooms of Cliff House, a mansion in Yorkshire. The picture was painted just before the outbreak of the Great War when the boy was about twelve.

Neither demolished, nor turned into council offices, as were many such houses, Cliff House, built in the late eighteenth century, can still be found in the village of Lightholme. Ground floor rooms at the side were at one time fitted up as a small school, with added bay windows, the interior of the house having already been transformed into two apartments.

In the nineteen thirties, when she was a small child on holiday with her grandparents at Cliff House, Viola used to enjoy looking at the portrait of her father and grandmother.

Her grandmother would point to another picture on the opposite wall. 'That's the portrait of my own mother. I never knew her – she died not long after I was born. I remember looking at her for hours when I was a child. My father often used to stare at it too, poor man.'

Viola, who had been given Mary as her second name, after her grandmother, would think how awful it must be never to know your own mother. When she was about eight, she expressed this thought to her grandmother, who said with a smile, 'I was lucky, you see, because I had a very kind young woman looking after me.'

Another time, she said, 'I think you look a bit like my mother as she is on the portrait – though you also look very much like a relative of your father's.'

Unlike her father and grandmother, Viola was never to have her portrait painted. Instead, she had many tiny wartime photographs of herself and her brother James taken at Cliff House when they

7

were evacuated there from London.

Viola grew up, married, and had a daughter, Marie-Hélène. When her marriage failed in the nineteen seventies, Viola decided to move back North, found work in Leeds, and bought a small house in Lightholme for herself and her daughter.

Now it was Marie-Hélène who enjoyed looking at the portrait, whenever she visited her Uncle James and his family who still lived in one half of Cliff House. The pictures had stayed in the same place.

Marie-Hélène decided she looked very like her Uncle James and her grandfather, who were both tall and fair. Her mother, Viola, looked quite different, being very dark and very pretty. Marie-Hélène's Yorkshire school-friends said she was 'exotic.'

Perhaps she looked more like her grandmother?

Viola laughed when she heard what her daughter's friends had said. It was a Sunday and they were having tea at Cliff House with Uncle James and his wife.

'Yes, I do probably look *very* like my grandmother,' she said.

Uncle James added mysteriously, 'Blood will out,' and he laughed.

What a strange thing for him to say, thought Viola's daughter.

PART ONE
CHILDHOOD

... The childhood shows the man,
As morning shows the day...
      (Milton: Paradise Regained Book 4)

CHAPTER ONE

1876

It was a dark February afternoon. The year-old baby, Mary Ellen Settle, had been asleep on the young woman's warm aproned lap, but now she was stirring. She opened her eyes suddenly and began to wriggle.

'Oh, won't you snuggle back in the cot now?' said Jemima Field, 'I'm not ready to take you out yet.'

She could hear wind outside, and the sky through the square window was dull. The child had woken before in her cot and Jemima had taken her up to cuddle. Then Mary had fallen asleep again on her lap. This time Mary protested when Jemima scooped her up against her shoulder, got up and pulled the cot's side down.

'Just for a minute, Baba – you can have Percy if you let me finish my ironing.'

Mima smelled so nice, much nicer than the cot, but Mary decided to smile when the brown-plush monkey was put down beside her. If she could have voiced her feelings clearly she might have said, *I'd rather stay where I was, but I'll cuddle Percy and watch you if you promise to take me out very soon.* At her age had she had no idea of time, and so she said 'Mima,' which was her name for Jemima, and watched the nursemaid folding sheets.

Jemima sighed, but said soothingly, 'Play with Percy now and I'll take you out for a walk in a minute to see the horse. You'd like that.'

Mary had heard that sound 'horse' before and it apparently conveyed a cheerful image for she laughed out loud. She liked the sound of Jemima's voice. There was a peaceful silence for a few minutes whilst Jemima busied herself around the room. Then, suddenly wanting more contact, Mary shouted, 'Mima! Mima!' and threw Percy out of the cot. Jemima Field sighed again. She wanted to go out herself, but first she had to finish the cot sheets.

11

Mary pulled herself up by the bars of her cot and watched, whilst Percy lay neglected on the floor. She began to chant to herself as she stood there, swaying slightly to the sound of her own voice.

Soon she'll be walking, thought Jemima. If she let her out now she'd crawl all over the floor and hold them both up from their walk. She whistled as she put clean clothes in a wicker basket.

Whistling was a favourite occupation of hers and one she did rather well. Mary stopped her chant and listened, not sure if she liked the sound. Then she started to wail, one way of attracting attention. Jemima was patient, wiped her hands, then picked up Percy and put him back in the cot. Mary watched her hang some small garments over what Jemima called a 'winteredge.'

The wailing subsided when at last Jemima took Mary out of the cot and wrapped her in her woollen cloak. She'd take no chances. Mary must have fresh air, but must not catch cold. Mrs Demaine was very insistent about fresh air; Mr Settle worried more about the child catching cold.

Ever since she had come to take over the little girl Jemima had religiously taken her out every afternoon, sometimes on the lane and right to the edge of rougher land near the fields where grazed the old brown horse. She'd take her today in the basket perambulator. A walk would do them both good.

It was not cold, but coolish and windy. An odd sort of afternoon for February, she was thinking, when she eventually walked down the path. You became used to frequent wind and rain in Yorkshire, and often you didn't get much summer either.

Mary was sitting up against her pretty lacy cushion, looking ever so nice and clean and bright, though she did say so herself. She would often pretend she was the bairn's own mother. Looking after Mary was a joy. Hard work, but right rewarding – especially when Mary smiled at her, or clapped her hands, listening to some of the little rhymes Jemima's Nan had sung to Jemima twenty years ago – *Little Boy Blue* and *Baa Baa Black Sheep* and *Littel Miss Muffet*. Nan had known heaps.

After the death of her mother, Mary Settle's babyhood might have been difficult or unhappy but because of Jemima Green, who was devoted to her, it was not. Whether she would ever remember the mother who had looked after her until she was six months old was uncertain. Jemima had come and Jemima had

12

stayed, and the other one had gone.

The bond between the young woman and the child was to grow ever stronger. Clara Demaine – 'Aunt Demaine' – observed it, and was thankful. Babies had never been her province.

William Settle was relieved. The sudden death of his young wife had stunned him, but he always said work had been his saviour. Every morning, before leaving for work, he would look up at the portrait of his wife, dark and young and beautiful, painted only a few years ago. Maria sitting in a meadow, wearing a lilac-coloured dress, her hands folded in her lap. He wanted to remember her like that, in her finery, black velvet flounces on the full violet skirt and bustle, and lace peeping from under the sleeves and in frills around the décolleté neck. He did not want to remember her pale and sweating in the agony of a 'growth' that had invaded some private part of her female body only just recovering from childbirth, and that had so quickly gnawed her to death.

His widowed sister Clara Demaine had helped him to get through it all: Clara, and the Mill. His sister had found Jemima Green from the village to look after his daughter, whom they had christened Mary Ellen: Mary for her mother Maria, and Ellen after William's own mother. Clara had stayed to take over the reins of his household. Yes, Clara and the business had saved him from despair. Somehow, the infant had not at first appeared to be connected to him at all. Would Maria have died if she had not had that longed-for child after eight years of waiting?

William was now used to the fact of his daughter's existence and was even quite fond of her, though he had no idea how to look after her. He confessed to himself that he did not know much about babies, and was not very interested in them. At present Mary was too young, he thought, to communicate with him. Perhaps she might realize who he was when she could talk. If he was home in time to pay an evening visit to the nursery, which was not very often, he would do so in the line of duty, though he always felt awkward and out of place there. Fortunately, babies were the province of the fairer sex and could be safely left to their ministrations. Perhaps one day he would have time to get to know her better, take her by the hand and go for a walk in the garden. He had a pleasantly confused picture of a future lissom young woman, looking much like her mother but calling him Papa. For the time being, though, he left all decisions about the child's upbringing to his sister Clara. He paid for the upkeep of the nurse as he paid for that of his household. Clara managed the housekeeping money and had her own little sitting-room.

Clara had some money of her own, left to her by her deceased husband Demaine, about whom people knew very little. The couple had lived abroad for most of their marriage, apart from a year or two in Surrey. By no stretch of his imagination could William regard Clara's living with them in Lightholme as a sacrifice. It was not good for women, even if they were widows, to live alone, and by living at Cliff House Clara would save money. He was satisfied with himself for giving Clara a home, though the reason had been tragic. It was a fact that single women and widows often began to act peculiarly when they were approaching forty.

Clara's penchant was for spas, especially those abroad. She loved travel and her brother imagined she regarded spas as performing a spiritual cleansing at the same time as one for the stomach or the lungs and joints. She had however promised him to stay and oversee her little niece. No exact number of years had been specified. She had an old friend living in Woolsford so she would not be lonely.

William was a man who adored balance sheets. Not ungenerous, he yet could not help drawing up pros and cons, profit and loss, and it gave him a good deal of pleasure to think that he was doing the right thing for his daughter and at the same time giving his sister a better life. The balance at the bottom of the page was in his favour.

Clara saw things somewhat differently. She had insisted right at the start, after poor Maria's death, that if she were to come over to live in Lightholme, 'for the time being', she must have a month free every year. This month she would spend on holiday with her friend Hannah Hardcastle, and William must make other arrangements. He had been obliged to concur but had said he hoped this did not mean that she and her friend would go on holiday abroad. That would be too difficult. What if the child ailed? On whom was he to call?

'I would hope, for the time being,' replied his sister with emphasis, 'to be able to spend two or three weeks each year in Ilkley or Harrogate, or on the coast. The trains from Woolsford are quite quick and reliable. Who knows, one day Hannah and I might take your daughter and Jemima Green on holiday to the coast.' Scarborough of course was the most fashionable watering-place, and there were many families of their sort who spent their summer holidays in hotels there, though it was said that Bridlington was becoming a pleasant place for children.

'They let private dining-rooms out to families with children – you might even like to accompany us one day *en famille*, William?'

She tried her best to interest him but it was hard work.

'Very well, I am resigned to your going – but I shall have to find someone to replace you when you go away . . .'

He was about to say it would be very inconvenient but bit that back. He *was* grateful to Clara. As for the future, he did not see himself taking a holiday with a nursemaid and his sister, not to speak of an infant.

'As a matter of fact I think you will not need anyone but the nurse when I am away. Jemima Green is most competent. I have observed her and can find no fault in her. I am here only to supervise, you know, William, and I think you might be able to manage a little supervision yourself occasionally.'

He knew his sister was eccentric, knew that she loved 'abroad'. Perhaps the spas and the coast were only an excuse for a rest, so he held his peace. He had never investigated Jemima's working activities, knew only that the baby appeared contented. Babies did cry sometimes, but in a house with good thick walls that was not too troublesome. This was how matters stood during the first two or three years of little Mary's existence.

Clara had read a good deal, as well as travelled with that 'foreign' husband of hers, who was English but was an artist, so regarded as foreign. Clara had been interested in recent ideas about the role of women. Things were in the air; some new forces might one day alter female arrangements. They were at present only a faint presence in the lives of London literary people, not yet acknowledged by the wives of wealthy manufacturers. Clara however had moved at one time with her husband in literary and intellectual circles, and was rather jealous of women who had had a better education than she had had herself. William had no idea of these notions and would not have understood them if he had.

What Clara did not reveal to her brother was her own great fear that Jemima would one day leave them, and then where would they all be? So long as she stayed until Mary was able to have a governess, it would be enough. Nursemaids did leave; for one thing they had a habit of getting themselves wed. This apprehension came to her occasionally in the middle of the night when she could not sleep. But, sufficient unto the day. She knew how lucky they were to have a good young woman to do the donkeywork in bringing up a baby.

15

Jemima Green understood that she was indispensable to her employers but she did not use this as any form of bargaining counter. She loved little Mary and would be as unhappy to leave her when she was at a tender age as the child would undoubtedly be whenever she left.

And yet . . . she did want to get wed one day.

Mary soon made her own voice heard. By the time she was fourteen months old she was taking pleasure in walks where they might see animals and birds, and Jemima enjoyed showing her such things. Many had been the walks, at first with the perambulator, to the nearest farm where dogs barked and cats sunned themselves and ducks sailed on a pond.

It was quite remarkable, thought Clara Demaine, how Jemima always appeared to know how to talk to Mary as she grew and changed. At first, to Jemima's 'What do the ducks do?' the answering quack was repeated over and over, and even Clara began to take pleasure in evidences of humanity in little Mary's speech. The farm cats came in for a similar treatment and Mary knew she could make her aunt smile by her imitation of their miaows.

'I wonder if she will ever say "Mama",' she wondered rather sadly to Jemima one rainy afternoon during a visit to the nursery on one of her attempts to 'supervise'.

'Oh, all bairns say Mama,' replied Jemima unselfconsciously, 'She calls me that sometimes.'

Mary was on the floor playing with a doll given to her by a relative, an unsuitable toy for such a young child, thought her aunt. Clara did not reply to the revelation about 'Mama'.

Jemima noticed, and went on to say, when Clara was silent, 'I tell her I am Jemima, ma'am, not her mama, and so she calls me My-ma.'

Clara supposed that the syllables *ma-ma* must be common early ones, seized upon by real mothers to use as their name.

Mima, pronounced 'My-ma', sounded rather similar.

'Papa' came a little later. At first Mary looked puzzled when he began to visit her in the nursery.

'She doesn't know any men,' said Jemima wisely. But there came a day when she reported proudly to Clara: 'She spoke the word "papa" yesterday. Mr Settle must hear her!'

'I will tell him,' said Clara getting up to go, 'I am sure he will be very pleased.'

She doubted he would realize its significance. Mary was actually more concerned with 'up' and 'down' than with the complications of relationships. The stairs were 'up-down' according to her. She connected candle with 'up there', the stairs to the new night nursery, showed much dexterity screwing and unscrewing jars, and had also begun to know the names for most of the objects and items in the house and nursery, especially those for food and clothes.

She had a good appetite and her favourite food was jam, which word she repeated monotonously. She knew what a 'hat' was and could put her own hat on if Jemima asked her. She attempted to put her little boots on, knew where her hair was and now tried to brush it, had long understood toes and head, 'clap clap and 'bye bye'. Mary was a happy child, even though eventually she learned how to shake her head and say 'No!' Jemima called her Baba but on hearing this Clara asked her to call her by her name. This puzzled Mary at first but she soon cottoned on.

'She understands a lot more than she can say,' said Clara to her brother. 'I think she is a bright child, you know.'

She could now follow 'Where is it?' and 'who is that?' and would cackle with delight at Jemima's games of hiding objects underneath blankets for her to 'find'.

How did Jemima know what games to play with her? Clara would muse. Were all young women thus gifted? Surely not all nursemaids would bother to invent games and tell stories and repeat rhymes and songs? Much roaring of laughter and giggling could be heard when Mary and Jemima were around. Mary loved attention and Jemima rewarded her often with 'Clever girl!' and clapped her. Soon Mary began to reward herself with delighted claps.

Her acquaintance with the farm cat was followed by her making friends with the dog, and she would wait expectantly for Jemima to imitate its bark, and shriek with laughter when it came. 'Dog' was one of her first words, followed by 'apple'. Having already eaten a chopped-up apple, the first time she saw an apple tree she pointed to the fruit and shouted 'Apple! Eat it!'

Clara experimented with saying certain words, waiting for the child to imitate them. Really, she thought, the way little Mary learned new words was quite magical. At first she might not understand the significance of the word but would still repeat it, sometimes saying words nobody knew she had heard. As soon as a word meant something to her, she used it. Clara surprised herself in finding all this so intriguing. She had always imagined she was not interested in children.

'Show me the toast, Mary,' said Clara one day on a visit to the nursery at teatime.

Mary obediently held up her 'soldier', since she was eating a soft-boiled egg at the time. Milk and mug followed, and then the touching of various parts of the face and body.

As time went on, Clara decided to go out occasionally with Mary and Jemima, who took her employer's interest philosophically. Clara told herself she needed the exercise. One afternoon, as an experiment, she pointed to the pond with an enquiring look. Mary followed her finger.

'What is it Mary?' asked her aunt.

'It's a pond,' said Mary, and laughed. Jemima clapped her hands.

'She likes us to be pleased,' she explained.

Clara was silent. Jemima was always right. Had her own mother taken this kind of interest in her childhood? She doubted it. Had Jemima's own parents? How had they found the time?

William would not be interested in such a question. He had not invited Clara to share his household in order for her to revolutionize his ideas on the upbringing of children, so she approached him stealthily, drawing his attention to little things in the nursery when he was at home. He spent so much time away from the house you could not expect him to take an immediate interest in nursery matters. She wondered, not for the first time, how businessmen spent their time. Her own husband had been so different, had passed much of his time abroad in coffee-houses discussing the wider world with his friends. She had been lucky, although those years of her marriage had been so short.

By the time she was sixteen months old, many more words had been added to Mary's vocabulary – ball and sky and honey and swing and bricks; bread and cheese and finger – and what Jemima called 'bits of other people'. Jemima having pointed to her own nose and ears and mouth, Mary soon got the idea and they played the game of Touch Baba's ear and Touch Jemima's ear, or nose, or mouth. Soon she was pointing out pictures and words in the new alphabet book Clara had bought. Her favourite word was banana. Babies and stars also elicited her attention.

Emboldened by Clara's interest Jemima ventured to say 'Touch Yeranty Clara's arm.' Clara was not at all annoyed. She had hopes of making Jemima into a New Nanny if not a New Woman, if she was not one already.

'I suppose it is like a dog,' she said on hearing Mary's reaction to the word 'walk' mentioned in a casual conversation.

The child loved going out more and more and would look around her with great interest in the garden or on the lane. As she grew a little older she would notice things that Jemima and Aunt Demaine missed. She knew the direction of their walk and if Jemima varied it too much she would say imperiously 'Trees!' or 'Gate!' and Jemima would alter their path. Once she was old enough to walk part of the way herself she would run along the path and turn round to laugh. 'Bye-bye!' she would shout in a teasing voice. She certainly had a sense of humour. Clara taught her to say 'Sorry' and 'Please' and was at first amused when Mary called her 'Yeranty', which was what Jemima always called her when talking about her.

Soon the rain and the book and the bath joined the bed, and the milk that could be either cold or hot. She quickly learned to do as she was asked, 'giving the book to Auntie' or to Mima, and not long afterwards learned to ask other people to do things, indeed could become peremptory in her demands. 'Sit there, Yeranty!'

Clara was amused but said, 'Do call me Aunt Clara, Mary.'

Mary had a big rag book with illustrations of nursery rhymes from which Jemima would read to her.

'Where did you learn to read, Jemima?' asked Clara.

'At Sunday School, ma'am.'

Sometimes Jemima would accompany the rhymes with a tune, or would sing hymns to her, and Mary loved this. By the time she was eighteen months old she was singing herself or finishing off the line of music started by Jemima. 'To wrap my baby Bunting in' was echoed: 'buntin' in' with a loud laugh and clap. Clara decided to play a few tunes for her on the old piano in her sitting-room and this became a special treat, which was supposed to reward good behaviour. There was also behaviour that was frowned upon, like walking in puddles or shrieking. Mary could make plenty of noise but was frightened of sudden loud noises from others. A neighbour's dog terrified her for some time, unlike the farm dog whose bark had not frightened her, but she loved the new kitchen cat, Mewer. She knew the cat was allowed by Cook to drink from a saucer and would sometimes offer her own mug to the animal, even once offering the cat an orange from the table in the nursery.

19

As week followed week and month followed month and Mary had her second birthday her vocabulary had grown so extensive that there was almost nothing she could not say or imitate. She had a repertoire of nursery rhymes and songs, and at about the time when each evening William Settle would arrive home from business, Mary would listen for the sound of the parlour-maid opening the door in the hall, and look up enquiringly, 'Papa' on her lips.

William's life was a busy one. It was a worrying time also for the worsted trade, which he had inherited from his father. He had had a good education but was of the opinion that knowledge was useful only insofar as it was of use in the practicalities of living, such as making money. He was amused by his sister's transformation into what he called a Rousseau enthusiast, and was pleased that Mary appeared to be quick and intelligent. If only she had been a son. Her intelligence would be wasted on overseeing a household, he thought, quite forgetting that his intelligent sister had never exactly done that before she came back North. He had a vague idea of Clara's travels and her clever friends in London, but had never taken any interest in the details of his deceased brother-in-law's life. Giles Demaine had been as odd as Clara, in William's opinion. It was a good thing they had had no children to drag about France and Italy.

Before she was two and a half, Mary's sentences had become longer and longer. Once she had begun to talk she could not stop. She knew her way around the house, and Jemima's vigilance formerly kept so constantly on the toddler's comings and goings began to relax slightly once she knew the child was safe near staircases and windows.

The baby had become a toddler, and soon became a little girl. There was so far no overt sign of any imminent departure by Jemima. When Mary was four she was taken by Yeranty, her friend Hannah, and of course 'Mima' to spend two weeks in summer on the Yorkshire coast. Mima enjoyed the seaside as much as Mary did and was always to remember her first sight of the sea. Mary was too young to have anything but a vague memory of the waves and the sands and the donkeys on whose backs she would ride in a special wicker cage.

It was during the autumn following their return home that a young blacksmith called Sam Sutcliffe began to court Jemima.

*

Cliff House, the mansion William Settle and his bride had moved into when they married in 1868, had been built of local stone in about 1780. William had bought it at auction when the owner, Mr Walker, who was about to retire elsewhere, had sold off much of the land and houses. The Walker family had been in the district for hundreds of years, but new business could now better afford the style of life the older generation's capital could no longer encompass.

After his wife's death William had considered moving to a more modern stone villa in the village. But he liked having the space, and enjoyed being regarded as 'gentry'. There were few real gentry around. Apart from the old landowner, there had not been any in the district for many years though there were plenty of rich families in a county of industry where fortunes were made from mills.

Cliff House was not by any means the largest or most impressive house in Lightholme, at that time a place for the comparatively rich, and boasting several seventeenth century houses. One, Sholey Hall, had an eighteenth century front, others were left more or less as they had always been, yet others had turned into farms, or been divided into cottages. Smyth House and Barnabas House were low-fashioned mullioned-windowed seventeenth-century houses that amazingly still stood. The three or four nineteenth-century mansions in the village, Holme House and New End and The Grange, all within a mile of each other were all occupied by the new rich, who drowned their drives in shrubbery, but the largest house in the district and nearest neighbour to Cliff House, only a quarter of a mile away, was 'The Nest', a vast, grand, handsome mansion built in the mid-eighteenth century.

Cliff House itself was a square, solid-looking house with five windows on the two sides that faced the gardens. It had originally been surrounded by a large park, and there was still a drive leading up to a porch with a pediment at the front. Round the back, another less picturesque drive wound round from the kitchen quarters to a lane that led to the turnpike road.

'The Nest' was occupied at that time by a family called Crowther, whose daughters, Lydia and Matilda, Mary was yet to meet. When Mary was a little older, thought Clara, there would be the parties and dancing-classes local families like the Crowthers arranged for their infants. There were similar households in Lightholme with women of

Clara's age if she herself wished to make new friends, but Clara felt she had little in common with them. Only one old woman who had inherited The Grange and lived there for the last fifty years was to her taste, and she was now very deaf. Clara liked space round her both physically and metaphorically and liked the village so long as she need not join it too closely.

What Jemima Green called 'The Moor' was just rough farmland with dry-stone walls and a little valley. It was true that real moors were not far away from the village, and every little town seemed to have its 'moor', but farms and pastureland were spread around the village and other villages like it. Lightholme and its neighbours had many areas of woodland, too, that had once been all one great wood, partially cleared in medieval times.

As she grew older Mary loved it all, but above everything else she loved her own Cliff House and its big garden.

The older poorer folk lived as best they might, often as their ancestors had lived, with a pig in the yard and a cow in the field, though the old cottage handloom had usually disappeared. The young poor – whose number was growing – journeyed to the encroaching mills in the nearest town, or worked the delfs.

Cliff House was lit with gas-mantles, with a gas chandelier in the drawing-room. There was no electric light until later, though by the time Mary was seven, people were talking about a private house 'down South' that was lit by electricity. Mary did not find it a cold house; there were many coal fires, one in the nursery and even one at night in the night nursery if she was unwell. Not that she was often ill. Aunt Clara however complained of the cold in the further reaches of the rooms and said she did not wish to huddle by the fire like an old cottager. Even in summer the wind could wuther down the chimneys, and the warmest place was always the kitchen, which Mary would often visit, until called back by Jemima.

Water came to the kitchen from a tap and also from a well-spring in the back yard, which was always covered. There was a strong prohibition against going close to it and Mary soon imagined that it was the well into which pussy had been put by little Tommy Thin. The water in the closet and the bathroom came from a pipe, but if you wanted hot water it was heated in kettles and brought up to the bedroom by a dumb waiter.

The day would come, when Mary was seven, when a new cast-iron bath was delivered to the house. But by then she had lost Jemima, and it had fallen to one of the maids or occasionally Aunt Clara to give her a weekly bath.

She had grown into a bonny child with marked eyebrows like her father's, heavy-lidded dark eyes, a full mouth, a snub nose and hair that waved slightly. She was still talkative but also quite happy to be by herself looking at a picture book. When Clara read to her, which she enjoyed doing, again somewhat to her own surprise, she realized that the child could already point out certain words which by virtue of their repetition she had noticed. Before she was five she was reading very well by herself. All in all she was an attractive child, and Jemima had taught her good manners.

Jemima had given them loyal service: they had a lot to be grateful for.

CHAPTER TWO

Until Mary was six she had always thought of Jemima as a person who was as much a part of the family as herself and her father and her Aunt Clara. Maids lived in their house too, of course, and a gardener and boot boy, but Jemima was not a maid. She was just Jemima. Before her sixth birthday however, Clara tried to tell her that Jemima might not be there always.

The reason was that Jemima had approached her several weeks earlier, in tears. It appeared that she had had a young man for almost a year, and he wanted to marry her.

'And you, er, share his sentiments?'

Jemima looked blank so Clara tried again, 'I mean – you want to get married to this man?'

Clara was really worried. What she had tried to forget might happen one day was apparently about to happen.

'I don't want to leave Mary,' said Jemima, 'And I never would, and he wishes he could find work in Lightholme, but he's a blacksmith and he's been offered work over in Lancashire and wants to move over there within the year. He's a good man.'

This all came out in such a rush that there was a long silence whilst Clara digested it all.

Jemima stood there, the picture of torment, not giving the impression at all of a happy young woman who'd been proposed to by a good man.

'It won't be for a while yet but I've promised to think it over and I thought it best to say now—'

'You did quite right,' said Clara. 'I shall have a word with my brother.'

This was catastrophe indeed.

To her credit, Clara tried a few times the following week to tell her

24

niece that Mima might have to go away one day.

The first time: 'You know that Mima is not your mama?' she began, which was perhaps a mistake for Mary replied only:

'I know. I pray for my mama,' and left it at that.

Next time, she said, 'Your Mima will not be able to stay with us for ever, Mary.'

Mary looked baffled but said nothing.

Clara summoned Jemima. 'You will have to explain it yourself,' she said, 'and you must decide in good time when you will give in your notice. I have warned Mr Settle.'

William had said, 'Well, she's growing up – I expect she soon won't need a nurse in any case, will she?'

It was no good trying to tell him that Jemima Green was the child's substitute mama.

The day of Mary's sixth birthday came along, and after tea when she had blown out the candles on her cake and opened her presents, Jemima said:

'I have something to tell you, love.'

Mary waited. Perhaps it was another present? Aunt Clara was there in the nursery as well, and Mary thought she looked a bit cross. Was it because the night before, when she had been asked what she would like for her birthday, she had said:

'I'd like a sister, please?'

Aunt had looked surprised at first and been silent. At last she had said, 'Wouldn't you like a doll with clothes like yours?' Mary had thought, well, yes that would be nice, but perhaps Aunt didn't understand about what she meant about a sister?

'Like Tilly has,' she had added.

Tilly and Lydia Crowther were the sisters she had seen once or twice in the distance. Their father was the owner of The Nest, the nearest house to their own, over the lane and down a long drive. The Crowthers had many children, of whom the two youngest were girls about the same age as Mary. She had seen them walking down the lane to The Nest, and thought they looked nice. Mima had met their old nanny and reported that the girl the same age as Mary was called Matilda.

'Your aunt could arrange for us to invite her to tea, I expect,' said Mima. But so far nothing had come of it. Since then Mary had often begged Jemima to go for a walk near The Nest in case they might meet her friend.

'Oh dear, this is going to be difficult,' murmured Clara, and got up saying to the nurse, 'I'll leave you to it – bring her to me when you're done.'

Then, and Mary would never forget what happened next, Jemima burst into tears.

'What is it? What's the matter, Mima?'

Jemima took a big breath, swallowed and said, 'Sit on my knee.'

Mary did so.

Whatever could be the matter? It was her birthday and she didn't think she had been naughty.

'I'll buy you a present, Mima,' she said.

'I should have told you before,' said Jemima.

Mary waited.

'Well you see – you know when you were a baby I came to look after you because your mama had gone away?'

Mary had been told this story very often. 'I know,' replied Mary.

'Well, love, I was going to stay with you till you were four – I once told you that?'

'Yes, I know. But I'm six now,' said Mary proudly.

'I know – and that means you are growing up and you won't need me so much. I wasn't going to stay for ever and ever and just last month my young man asked me to marry him. I've known him for a long time – he's a nice lad – and so I've said yes – and that means I shall go and have a home of my own. . . .'

Mary said, 'But – you will come back?' as if marriage was like a day out.

'On receiving no reply, Mary went on, 'You can bring the – the nice lad – to live here? Papa wouldn't mind, I am sure.'

'Well, Mary, when lasses get wed they make a home – if they're lucky – and my young man – he's called Sam – has found a job and a little house and he wants me to get wed soon.'

'But Mima, where will you have a little house?'

'I shall have to go over the hills – but I can come back and see you—'

'You mean you have to go away?' Suddenly she understood what she was being told. 'I can come with you then,' she said firmly.

She would have said, I am your little girl, if she had thought of herself in that way. Mima was Mima. She knew she was not her mama but she was like her mama, wasn't she?

Mary had only just begun to understand that things could change.

She was only six, but she was an intelligent child. This, though, was unimaginable, impossible. She wanted to be reassured that it was not true what Mima had said.

How could she go away?

How could she stop her?

'I won't let you go,' she wailed. She sounded furious and determined.

'I don't want to leave you, love – but, you see I want to get wed. When you're married you do have a house of your own, and . . .'

She was going to say you can have your own bairns, but she could not. She changed tack, saying instead, 'You've got Yeranty and your pa and you'll have new friends – you might get to know those bairns at The Nest better. And you'll have a lady come to teach you, or you might even go to school.'

When Mary said nothing but stood clutching the rag doll Mima had made her, christened Griselda by Yeranty, she went on:

'You heard me speak of The Nest nanny, Nanny Crowther – Ida Ormondroyd – well, as they are big girls now she has decided to retire. They'll miss her a bit, I'm sure, but they don't really need a nanny any more. They'll be all right. And so will you.' But they've got a mother, she thought. Not like little Mary.

'I'm not going just yet,' she added. 'And I shall come back and see you.'

Mary felt no longer angry but terribly puzzled, and upset, with an ache in her stomach. Mima had always been there at Cliff House.

'If you don't want to leave me, why are you going away?' she asked sensibly, and then burst into tears.

It was all too much, thought Jemima, looking at the tear-stained face and wishing she could take Mary away with her. Life was so unfair. But she loved Sam Sutcliffe, he was a good lad, and she was twenty-six last birthday. Oh, she felt so awful though, even if it wouldn't be for some months that the wedding would take place and she'd be going across to Burnley where Sam had found the smithy job, a real opportunity.

But in spite of the tears she was that relieved she'd got round to telling Mary. She'd dreaded the day, ever since she'd got serious about Sam. She'd not wanted to tell her on her birthday but Mrs Demaine had thought it best.

'The child will be thinking about something else and so it might pass without too much upset. She'll have time then to get used to the idea.'

Mary stood there, and then hurled herself into Jemima's lap and sobbed her heart out. Griselda fell on the floor.

'There, there – it won't be just yet,' soothed Mima, cuddling Mary on her lap like a baby.

Mary was sick in the middle of the night. Aunt Clara said it was the rich birthday food.

Clara Demaine now felt almost as bad as the child. She was torn between being glad for Jemima's sake but angry she was going to leave. Oh, she was glad the girl had found a future husband but on the other hand she felt cynical about marriage for working-class women. There'd eventually no doubt be hordes of babies. Perhaps she was cynical about marriage in general as well, but she knew to keep that sentiment well hidden up here in Lightholme. She herself had not had a bad marriage, but then Giles Demaine had been an unusual man. For one thing, neither of them had wanted children. At least, she had thought she did not. Now she wondered why.

One thing was certain: her brother William would not know how to go about comforting his daughter and it would all fall upon her.

The following day Mary appeared at first to have forgotten what had been said the previous afternoon and played with her new jigsaw very quietly. After tea, however, before Jemima came to put her to bed she said, 'Mima – couldn't Yeranty get married instead of you?'

Jemima was both taken aback and amused. This was one thing she could not report to Mrs Demaine.

'Yeranty was married, Mary love. Her husband died.'

'Like Mama did?'

'I suppose so.'

Did Mary understand that people didn't live for ever? Or did she just think they 'went away'?

Mary was thoughtful, then she said, 'If you died – like Mama – I wouldn't like that.'

'Well, I'm not going to die – I'm getting wed.' Jemima tried to sound brisk and commonsensical.

Mary was confused. Mama had 'got wed', and then she had died, and that meant that she had gone away. Mary had been told about her mama, but Clara had drawn the line at the child visiting the grave. There would be time enough for that later.

Mary was now thinking: Yeranty had 'got wed' but she had not died. And now Mima was to wed.

'Do ladies have to – to "get wed"?' she asked.

'Oh no, most do – but some don't. You see . . .'

Jemima hesitated. This was perhaps not the moment to introduce the idea of babies – and in any case it might not be her place to do so. 'Yeranty' might be cross.

'I shan't, ever,' said Mary.

She must have been thinking it all over, for the next day, during a walk to the village, she said suddenly:

'Mama had me, and she died, but Yeranty didn't have a little girl, did she?'

'No, Yeranty has no bairns.'

'And when you get married you won't die?'

'Of course not.'

Mary was thinking, but if Mima has 'bairns', (as Mima always called them) she will die. Like Mama did. Better she doesn't have any, then. In her prayers that night she asked for Mima to be like Yeranty and not have a little girl.

Clara thought, Mary is getting over the initial shock, so said no more about Jemima's impending departure. They were not yet sure in any case when the young woman would have to leave. The wedding was not yet fixed as it depended upon her young man's taking over in Burnley.

Although Mary had for the time being settled the matter of marriage and 'bairns', she refused to think about Mima really leaving her.

Cook had once told her that her mam had had a baby who had 'gone away', but she called it 'Going to Jesus.' That was apparently a final departure. Mary thought that the baby must have had to 'go away' instead of Cook's mother.

Although she appeared to Clara to have managed the problem on the surface, Mary had still not let herself believe that Mima really was going to leave her one day. She pushed the terrible feeling it gave her right down inside herself. The feeling resurfaced one afternoon when she heard Annie the parlour-maid discussing Jemima's wedding with Mrs Akroyd, a woman who sometimes came in to help clean the silver.

It was Mima's afternoon off and Yeranty was busy, so Mary had gone down to the drawing-room with her doll and was sitting on the floor behind the sofa. The drawing-room was not forbidden but she was not encouraged to linger there. Usually, Mary was quite an obedient child and Yeranty thought she was in the garden, getting fresh air. But Mary had crept back into the house.

At first she did not pay much attention to the two women who were sitting at their ease polishing various small items of silver – the sweet dish and the small tea tray and several candlesticks. When she heard the name Sam Sutcliffe Mary remembered this was the man Mima wanted to wed.

'They say Jemima Green wants to wed in church, not chapel. 'Course it's not till the back end but they say the wedding'll be at Sholey. His mam is right determined to come over from Warley and they want to have the ham tea at Lower Wynteredge – Mrs Pearson will help Mrs Green, I suppose.'

'Oh, I love a wedding,' breathed Annie. 'Do you think she'll ask for our little Mary to be bridesmaid?'

Jemima Green, thought Mary, that was Mima.

But, 'in church'?

'I don't think she'd think it quite right – though I do remember when Colonel Turner's lad wed, his old nanny was there as guest.'

'It's a lovely church. Let's hope it'll be before the snow comes – it's a right pull getting up that hill in winter.'

Mary knew that Jesus lived in that church because Mima had told her. She herself had been there with Mima once or twice. The Settles were not especially pious people, though the dead Maria had been. Cook and one of the maids went to chapel and they said there was a Sunday school she could go to, which was like going to church. Cook said she was a 'Methodist'.

But if Mima was to wed in a *church*, did that mean she was 'going to Jesus'? They said Mama had gone to Jesus.

She crept away without the women catching sight of her and went up to Yeranty's sitting-room where Clara Demaine read her books and wrote her letters.

By the time she got there she was out of breath and it was with a catch in her voice that, after having knocked at the door as she had been taught to do, she burst into the room. Before her astonished aunt she came out in a rush with:

'Annie says Mima is going to wed in church. Is she going to Jesus? Will Sam go as well? Can I go?' She burst out in ragged sobs.

Clara was nonplussed. She had the presence of mind, however, to say, 'Come and sit down and tell me – slowly – what is the matter.'

Mary sat down on the edge of the horsehair sofa. Clara hated this piece of furniture, but there it was in her room, so she usually placed the books she was reading on it.

How did you make a child comfortable?

Oh dear, she was going to have her work cut out when Jemima Green left them.

Mary's sobs very slowly subsided into hiccups and then more or less stopped, but she continued to sit on the edge of the sofa. Clara hesitated to ask her to sit on her own lap. It was on her beloved Mima's lap that Mary usually sat.

'Now tell me what is all this about Our Lord? About Jesus?'

'They said Mima is going to wed in church. And – and Mima told me that Jesus is in the church – and Mama went to Jesus and she didn't come back – and Mima won't come back, will she?'

Clara found this argument from a child of six and a half a remarkably logical progression. But if she did not say something the sobbing would begin again. This might be the opportunity she needed to convince Mary that Jemima was going away for good but would not be all that far away, certainly not 'with Jesus'.

'You know your Mima is going to get married?'

'They said getting wed – is that it?'

'Yes, Mary, the people round here say that – but it means the same thing – a lady and her husband go and live in a new house – they do not go to Jesus. Jesus is in heaven and Jemima is not going to heaven'.

At least not yet, she thought, for if ever there was a saint that young woman was one.

'Jemima told me that my mama is in heaven.'

'Your Mama, yes, but Mima, although she will leave our house, is only going to live in Lancashire – perhaps she will come back to see you one day – or perhaps when you are older you will go to see her. Even if she stayed here in Lightholme she could not go on living here.'

'Lancashire?' said Mary faintly.

'It is not far away.'

'But she will never come back here to live with me?'

'No, once she is married I'm afraid she will live with her husband.'

This occasioned a fresh outburst of sobs.

Clara had seen the hurt in Mary's eyes. Although she was not a very imaginative woman, Clara Demaine was possessed of quite a sharp original mind; in this situation however she was forced to try to enter into the mind, or rather heart, of her little niece. What should she say to comfort her? What could she say? She knew of families where the children were not told of the imminent departure of a beloved nanny and that offended her sense of justice. There was no way of making life whole again for Mary but at least the truth might be alleviated. Keep it low key, she said to herself. Make it ordinary.

'I believe your Mima's friend is called Sam Sutcliffe,' she said.

'The nice young lad?' sniffed Mary.

'Er yes – that would be Sam Sutcliffe. Well, Mary dear – Mima is very pleased to get married. If you are fond of her you want her to be happy, don't you? I'm sure she will miss you but nannies do not stay with little girls for ever—'

'Annie once told me that mothers stay for ever but mine didn't.'

'No, your poor mother was unlucky – but, Mary, Jemima is not going to Jesus. She is just going to ask the blessing of the church on her future life. That is what weddings are for. People go and watch and join in and wish the new husband and wife well.'

'Can I go then? Can I go and watch?'

Thank goodness, the child had been presented with a new idea. Clara had already wondered about this. Would it be too much for Mary to attend her Mima's wedding? Too much like a wake? She had discovered an unsuspected well of sympathy in herself, whilst helping – or at least she imagined she had helped – to bring up her little niece.

'Now run along and have your tea. I'll tell Annie to bring it to the nursery as usual on Mima's afternoon off. And, Mary – no good comes of listening to servants' conversations.'

'I didn't mean to hear – I was just there.'

'We will think about whether you are invited to the wedding when the date is decided.'

Mary slid off the sofa. She thought, if Mima did go to Jesus I would go to church and tell him to send her back. That would be better than a prayer. Mima had taught Mary the Lord's Prayer and 'Thank you for the world so sweet', and to thank God for all his blessings, and told her you could ask for things you wanted to happen and if you were very good they might happen.

She was reassured that there was no question of what had happened to her mother happening to Mima.

Even so, what was the difference for a child of six between death and a parting, Clara was thinking. She knew she was unpopular in the village for her forthright opinions and she was also aware that some rich families did not treat their nursemaids quite so well. Others must worry about their children's welfare, not to mention their happiness, when beloved nannies left. But worrying and doing something about it were two different matters. Mary would need a change if she were not to become too withdrawn after Mima Green went away.

After dinner that night Clara said to her brother, 'I have tried my best to explain to Mary that her nanny is going for good. But I am afraid she confused her going away with her dying. I do think the child will need a proper governess very soon. She is intelligent – and I'm afraid she has picked up some of the servants' expressions. She talks like a village girl with her "bairns" and her "getting wed" and her "young lad".'

She smiled. William would be more bothered about that than she would, but he might now bestir himself to find a governess for his daughter.

'I could make enquiries of the Crowthers – there could be the possibility of their sharing, perhaps?' she said. Nothing like striking whilst the iron was hot.

In bed that night, though, Clara thought, I am fond of the little thing. I don't even mind being called Yeranty in the house – but she had better not repeat it elsewhere.

Mima's departure would mean that Mary left her first childhood and began to learn from others. Mary of course was far too young to appreciate this. Some of the things she had said had been startling, but that was because she was obviously intelligent.

After her aunt's explanations, for long periods Mary appeared to forget Mima's eventual departure. Then, suddenly, Clara would notice that the child held on to the nanny's hand longer than usual or that she appeared reluctant to let her out of her sight. Maybe Mary imagined that if she did not keep an eye on her, Mima might disappear. Mary's feelings clearly lasted from week to week, and six years old was not too young to constantly recall a fear or look forward to a joy.

In fact the wedding was not to be until November. Jemima had decided not to ask Mary to be a bridesmaid, since her mother thought Mr Settle would consider it 'inappropriate'. Poor people did not have big weddings and if she needed an attendant, there was her Cousin Susan's little girl. Jemima wanted as little fuss as possible and in this sentiment her faithful Sam agreed with her.

Clara thought it better if they could avoid emotional farewells. Mary and her aunt were going to attend the actual wedding ceremony and they could wave Jemima and her husband off in a horse-drawn carriage after the service. The 'ham and drink' was now to take place in town because the helpful Mrs Pearson had been 'taken badly'. Jemima's aunt had offered her house instead of the nearer farm.

Before all this, at the end of October, Clara had a brilliant idea. She would ask Jemima if she would like to take Mary on a Tuesday afternoon to the village fair that came round every year. The future husband might like to go too – everyone took time off for the annual fair. She would give them two whole shillings to spend there; then Jemima could intimate to Mary that she would be leaving in two weeks. Clara had now met the 'young lad' and thoroughly approved of him. William Settle thought his sister rather mad making such a fuss of them both.

The fair, or 'feast', as the villagers called it, had sideshows, and stalls selling toys, nuts, brandy-snap and cheap jewellery, along with a coconut shy, shooting galleries, a steam roundabout and swings. There was also a booth where photographs could be taken.

'I don't know much about the sort of thing young people like to do now,' said Clara to her friend Hannah Hardcastle who was over on a visit from Woolsford. 'Apart from the Literary and Philosophical Society I don't know what goes on in town.'

'Well, your nanny is hardly likely to want to attend that,' replied Hannah.

'No – I meant, would they like to go to the fair, or is it only for children?'

'We never went, did we? Weren't allowed,' replied Hannah who, like Yeranty, had been a young girl in the district thirty years earlier, but who had never left the area. 'Do you remember in the old days,' she went on, 'when we went to listen to hear Dickens read from his Christmas Carol?'

'Yes – we missed Thackeray, though, didn't we? But there was that ladies' French class – that came in very useful when I left. I wonder whether it's still going on?'

They often reminisced in this way. Clara had been married and Hannah never had, but they had been girls together and that meant they had much in common.

The day of the feast dawned fair and bright. Mary was excited. She had never been to a 'feast', nor had she met Mr Sutcliffe except one evening, looking out of her window in the dark, she had thought she had seen Mima walking back down the drive to the house with a tall young man.

This time Sam Sutcliffe came up to the back door and raised his cap as they both came out of the kitchen entrance.

They all left the house together. Sam said if she was tired Mary could ride on his back. At first she held on tight to Mima, but slowly Sam's jokes won her round and she prattled to him. It was quite a long walk to the fair, which was held in a big field at the top of the road that led out of the next village and ended – eventually – in Woolsford.

The merry-go-round was already whirling to hurdy-gurdy music and there were heaps of children running up and down.

'Mind the mud,' said Mima. 'I've got two shillings from Yeranty so you'll have to decide what you want to spend it on.'

What big swings they were! Like boats. And the big merry-go-round looked frightening. There was a smaller one though, and Mary said, 'I'd like to go on that, please.'

You sat in a carved chair or in a seat like a ship and other children shouted and screamed. Mary sat there quietly, watching Mima and Sam watch her. So this was the 'young lad' Mima was going to stay with for ever. With a stab at her heart she realized it all over again.

Sam was nice though and after the roundabout he bought her a bag of liquorice. Then he said to Mima, 'Let's have our likenesses taken! Me and you, then you and the little one.'

'How much is it?' asked Mima worriedly. Mary might like to do something different.

'This one is on me,' said Sam.

Mary knew what a photograph was because there was one of her mama at home. She looked at Sam as they waited in a long line of people who wanted a photograph. He was a big man, dark with curly hair and very tall, and he had big strong hands.

'I'd like a picture of you, Mima,' she said.

When they got inside the booth there was a little platform at the back on which there stood an armchair. Behind the chair hung a large painted sheet showing a palm tree and an urn of flowers.

'Come in, ladies and gents . . .'

'We want two, please – one of me and the lady and one of the little lass and the lady.'

'No time for that, lad, today – there's folks waiting – if you want more than one you'll have to go into town Saturday. I'll do the lady in the chair and the little lass at her feet and you stand behind them.'

'But it's not my little lass,' objected Sam, feeling this procedure would not be the 'done thing'.

'That or nowt,' said the big man.

'Let's have it,' murmured Mima, so they took their places as he had ordered them. Sam took his cap off and Mima straightened her skirt and made sure Mary's hair ribbon was puffed out. The man put his head under a black cloth and told them to stay still, not move a muscle. Mary at Mima's feet wanted to sneeze but managed to suppress it.

'Ready, steady, go!' said the man. Then he clicked the big camera and after a few minutes took off the cloth with a flourish.

'Ready next week,' he said. 'Collect 'em from Toothill's shop.' Sam handed over two whole shillings!

'We'll have just you and me in a fortnight,' said Sam to Mima as they left the booth.

Sam then sampled the coconut shy and knocked one down.

'Hurrah!' cheered the crowd of onlookers.

'You've still got a shilling,' said Mima to Mary, 'What would you like?' They were passing the stall with glass jewellery.

Mary said, 'I want to buy you a ring.'

'Wouldn't you like a toy animal? They've got ducks and lambs,' said Mima.

'No – please let me buy you a ring, Mima.'

Sam had given Jemima a little silver ring that had been his grandmother's and she was wearing it.

'Do you mind?' she asked him, suddenly thinking he might be jealous of the child's affection.

'Aye, lass – buy her a ring – she'd look right nice with one on her other hand,' he replied.

Mary considered. There were rings with blue glass and rings with red glass and rings with green glass. 'You choose,' said Mary. Jemima chose one with a tiny yellow stone.

'And now you choose,' she said to Mary. 'Fair's fair!'

'I'd rather have a necklace, if doesn't cost too much money,' said Mary.

'You go ahead,' said Sam.

Mary chose a little child's necklace with tiny beads of different colours.

It was time to go home, beginning to get dark now. As they looked back they could see men beginning to light the naphtha flares.

On the way home Sam put her on his shoulders. It was quieter on the lane down to the crossroads. From her perch she saw that Mima and the man were holding hands. It gave her a queer sad feeling.

'You know your Mima's going to marry me?' he said.

'Yes,' she whispered.

'Well, don't you fret – she'll be all right with me – and one day she'll come to see you. But she has to go away soon. You're a big girl now and you don't need to be babied.'

Mary was too sleepy to argue.

Clara Demaine decided that the nursemaid's departure from Cliff House would take place the week before the wedding. She would see to it that Jemima did not miss her wages for that week. Goodbyes need not be formal. They would tell Mary that Mima was going home to get ready for her wedding and that Mary would be able to see her and wave to her on that day. Clara dreaded displays of emotion, though she conceded the need to help her little niece get over Jemima Green with as little pain as possible. It might be Mima herself who would be the most affected, but she had enough to think about. Mary had already given her the little silver ring, as Clara well knew, since Jemima had showed it to her. The photographs were not ready and Sam doubted they would ever see them.

For once, a November afternoon was sunny, so that when they came in from their walk, Mary did not realize that it was the dreaded 'goodbye' when Jemima said,

'I'm off now, Mary, love – going home to get ready. I shall look out for you at the wedding next week!'

They hugged each other.

'Have you got my present?' asked Mary.

'You can be sure of that,' said the young woman, choking back tears.

'I'll wave to you from the window,' said Mary, who had often done this when Mima had been going off to the shops in the town for Yeranty.

She waved from the nursery window. Mima waved back and then

got into the pony and trap driven by Sam, who had brought it round to the back of the house. The portmanteau with all her worldly possessions was already roped on. She turned and waved again before she mounted the cart, and then they were off.

Mary found Yeranty in the kitchen when she went down for her tea.

'Today you can have your tea with me,' said that lady.

'Why did Mima have a big case with her?' asked Mary.

'Got her wedding things, I expect – you'll see her a week on Saturday.'

Such a date meant very little to Mary but she appeared thoughtful. Only, waking in the night she suddenly thought, Mima isn't here. Not that Mima had slept in the same room as Mary for ages, now that she was no longer a baby, but it was nice to know that she would come if you didn't feel well. She consoled herself, thinking Mima would come back soon, pushed all her anguish down, and cuddled the doll Griselda that Mima had given her so long ago.

The anguish was to come welling up later, but, true to Clara's plan, the actual moment when Mima left in the carriage did not appear important at the time, and Mary had unconsciously decided not to believe that she had 'gone for ever'.

The wedding was quite a short ceremony, much to Yeranty's relief. The church was full of Mima's relations and she and Mary were seated on the bride's side, almost at the front. Mary did not at first recognize Mima in her long dress, carrying a bunch of flowers, but when it dawned upon her, she did not cry out, as Clara had feared she might.

Afterwards, when the happy couple had signed the register and walked down the aisle, people let Yeranty and Mary go in front of them so that Mary had a ringside seat. Some women were throwing confetti but Yeranty had not brought any, disapproving of the practice. Suddenly, Jemima, surrounded by her close family, saw them both, waved, and blew Mary a kiss. She looked happy, and Sam, thought Clara, looked relieved.

'She is going to throw you a flower from her bouquet,' said Yeranty unexpectedly, 'So you must try to catch it, and then it will be you who gets married next.'

'To Sam?' asked Mary. Yeranty laughed.

'No, not to Sam – and not for ages, I hope, but I expect you will get married one day.' She sighed.

They stood there, not knowing anyone except for the vicar, who came up and shook hands. Then, when Mima and Sam came up to them, Yeranty said, 'Now you can kiss the bride!'

Mary felt shy but Mima bent down to the child's height and said, 'Wish me luck, love.'

Mary thought how pretty she looked, but not really like Mima, and Mima thought, Mary looks pale, I hope she's not sickening for anything. They kissed each other quickly, and Sam bowed, and then it was over.

The couple moved away, waving, and everyone said, 'They'll be off now.'

The little carriage that was to take them to the town came up and they got in. At the last minute Jemima looked round and threw a flower from her small posy in Mary's direction. Everyone stared but when Mary missed it they laughed. An old lady clapped. Yeranty picked it up and said, 'Here you are – you can press it into your Alice book.'

Several horse-drawn carts came up then to follow the principal actors down the steep hill.

With a swift glance at her niece, Clara said, 'She will come back to see us one day.'

Mary said nothing. She felt too ashamed about not catching the flower.

'Look, there's Papa's carriage,' said Clara.

On the way back, Mary said, 'I shall write Mima a letter but I don't know her address.'

'It would be very nice to write her a letter but wait a little – she will be on her honeymoon. I have her new address.'

Sam Sutcliffe had decided on Blackpool for the weekend. The wedding had cost his bride quite a lot – she usually saved most of her salary for her mother. He had paid the vicar, and the 'ham an' all' was to be at her uncle's, so the honeymoon would be his responsibility.

Clara tried her best before Mary's bedtime to talk about other things but when it came to kissing her goodnight, she said, 'Mima told me to tell you she has sent you another kiss and says you must sleep well and then she will have good luck.'

This was a shameless lie, but Mary believed it and fell quickly asleep, exhausted.

CHAPTER THREE

Clara had a long talk with her brother about whether they ought to look for a new nursemaid for Mary. She had asked Hodgson to help dress the child, a time-consuming job. At least Mary did not wear stays and she could manage most of her dressing and undressing by herself except for all the buttons on sleeves and boots. Clara was of the opinion that a new nursemaid would be too much of a dislocation for her niece and for the household in general and she knew her brother wanted to cut down on wages for staff who lived in. There were many problems at present connected with his worsted-weaving factory, and trade in general.

'I don't see the need for another nanny so long as we can find a governess for the child,' she began. 'You will remember we did discuss it?'

William, she could not help noticing, appeared relieved. Usually he contradicted her suggestions – to begin with at least.

She went on, 'So long as one of the maids helps with her clothes and meals and takes her out now and then, I am willing to do more myself. I can't take the place of Jemima Green – nobody can.'

'I agree,' he replied after a pause, 'If you don't think it will be too much for you.'

Such consideration was unusual.

'It's true there are many problems at present in the trade,' he added heavily. 'Nothing disastrous – yet – but we could soon be in a bad way. Any reduction in our expenses will help.'

She knew all this but wished he would not talk like a balance sheet. Whenever had there been upturns in textiles? As far as she knew there had always been problems. It was like the Yorkshire weather.

'But you will have to pay for her to have some school lessons,' she began.

'Yes, yes – I know – and perhaps we can find a school when she is a little older – unless you yourself—'

'I am quite willing to continue overseeing Mary's reading and writing,' she said, thinking, *and you could enlighten her about arithmetic.* 'But a school might cost quite a lot. For the present I think a governess would be a good idea. Have I your permission for the time being to ask the Crowthers about Mary joining theirs? She's a Miss Hartley from Woolsford and seems a competent woman.'

'Certainly. What a good idea. How is little Mary? Has she got over Green's going?'

She was surprised, had not thought he would attach so much importance to it. And if he did, why had he not tried to comfort the child? She may never get over it, she thought gloomily.

Mary had not yet thrown any dramatic tantrums, and appeared to have reconciled herself, but Clara knew the child cried in her sleep. When she had occasionally crept in to see if Mary was asleep, her cheeks had often been damp. She found it hard to know what to say to comfort her. Maybe if Mary could deal with this, it might help her when she was older to cope with change?

Only one thing had bothered her. Mary had asked her the week after the wedding, 'Did Mima want to leave me?'

'No, of course not – but she wanted to get married, dear, and there was no work for her husband here with us.'

Mary was quiet. At last she said, with wisdom beyond her almost seven years,

'I expect, when she looked after me when I was little, Mima wasn't quite grown up?'

'Why do you say that?' Clara waited for an answer.

Mary struggled with her thoughts and then she said, 'She did love me, she did!' There were tears in her eyes. 'But now she loves Sam more than me.'

'Mima still loves you, Mary – but when you are grown up you can love other people as well. I'm sure you will yourself one day.'

Was there always a conflict for children who wanted to be loved by their mother more than she loved anyone else? Would Mary have been jealous of her father if Maria had been alive? That sort of jealousy sorted itself out when more children came along, didn't it? Mary must have been thinking about it all more than appeared on the surface.

If only William would be more demonstrative. He did love his daughter but found it hard to show it.

She left matters where they were.

She would get in touch with the Crowthers about sharing their Miss Hartley.

The nearest neighbours to the Settles of Cliff House were the Crowthers of The Nest. You went through a little piece of parkland that had been taken out of one or two of the farmer's fields in the late eighteenth century, and then landscaped. You crossed the old lane with its high walls on the far side, and if you followed them round they led to a pair of gates. But if you were a child or a young person you scrambled up a little slope further on, climbed over the wall and then ran down a gentle slope to the house.

The Nest was much larger than Cliff House, yet it always appeared crammed with people. The Crowthers were a large family. 'Crowded with Crowthers' was one of Aunt Clara's dry phrases.

There were two older daughters, and then a bunch of boys, and lastly the two youngest, Lydia and Matilda, or 'Liddy and Tilly', of whom the youngest, Tilly, was exactly Mary's age. They would both have their seventh birthdays the following February.

It was Christmas, only a few weeks after Mima's departure, and Mary had been invited to a party at The Nest. This would be her first real party and she was extremely excited at the prospect. It should have been Mima accompanying her; she had always been the one to take Mary on visits the few times they had been invited into people's houses, but this time Mary would be left by Yeranty to be collected at half past six.

Clara was hoping that Mary could soon join the little class taken by Miss Hartley, a lady in her early forties, about Clara's own age, but whose family had fallen upon hard times. She travelled daily to The Nest to impart the first principles of reading, writing and arithmetic, as well as nature study and drawing, to Liddy and Tilly and one or two others who came and went, including the son of the village doctor.

The very first time Mary had met any of The Nest children had been with Mima when they had been walking on the lane by the high walls. Mary and Tilly Crowther had taken to each other straight away. They had had a long chat whilst Mima talked to the maid who was accompanying them. Mary had heard something about Miss Hartley from Tilly and also learned that Lydia, the sister who was walking on ahead, was two years older than Tilly, who was her age. In the manner of little girls they had then immediately fallen to discussing their dolls. The doll Mary loved most was still Griselda, but she also had a porcelain doll, Lucy, who had arrived the previous Christmas from Santa Claus. Tilly's doll was lying wrapped up in a blanket in a little perambulator much admired by Mary.

'What's her name?' asked Mary.

'It's Annabella.'

'Oh what a lovely name!' breathed Mary, looking closely at the doll.

'She's got a cold today,' added Tilly, 'so she has to stay under the blanket – you can see her another day.'

Their respective servants had to get home in time for dinner and called the girls, who went on talking until they almost had to be dragged from each other's company. Mima had thought it a good sign that Mary could so easily make a friend. She told Aunt Clara.

'We must invite them to tea,' said that lady. But before she could get round to this Mima left and then there came for Mary an invitation to a Christmas party at The Nest.

'Can I take Lucy to the party?' Mary asked her aunt. It was a few days before Christmas and her hair was being brushed, her best black pumps put on with their black laces going up her legs, and her new tartan taffeta dress carefully arranged.

'No dear, I don't think there will be time for you to play with her this afternoon – there'll be games, I expect, and you can play with your little friends.'

'Well, can I wear my new necklace, then?'

This was the necklace of coloured beads Mima had bought her at the fair and Clara had not the heart to refuse, though it did not match her taffeta dress.

It was a chilly, windy, afternoon. Clara had intended to walk to The Nest with her charge but at the last minute decided on the pony and trap.

'Hodgson will go with you,' she said, 'And I shall come for you myself at half past six.'

The invitation said three o'clock and as they got down from the vehicle Mary saw that others were doing the same from their own carriages or traps, and were all following each other through the big wide doors at the front.

Where was Tilly?

'Will you come right in with me?' she asked. Hodgson was a thick-set, slow-moving girl.

'Nay, miss, they said leave you here, and Yeranty will come for you when you're finished.'

Hodgson deposited her in the big room that opened straight from the door. There was an enormous Christmas tree, and the smell of wood. Indeed the whole floor was of polished wood.

Mary was left all alone. Not for long though. She felt dreadfully shy. Mima would have taken her by the hand and led her to Tilly but as she was hesitating a lady came up to her.

'Ah, is it Mary? Put your cloak in the room at the back. You're in good time. . . .'

She took her guest to the cloakroom and left her there. A crowd of little girls and a few boys were standing around awkwardly. Some of the girls were eyeing each other's clothes. Mary was wearing a cloak made up for her from an old one of Yeranty's, as she did not yet possess a party cloak. It was quite pretty but looked plain when seen with the velvets and silks of some of the other girls. All were changing into dancing-shoes but Mary was wearing those already.

A Nest maid took her cloak and said,' Do you want me to brush your hair?'

'Why? No.' replied Mary. Yeranty had just brushed it. Just then Tilly and Liddy erupted into the room. Would Tilly notice her? Behind them was their old nanny, the one who had met Mima. She was older than Mima, a lot older, and had already retired. Having given sterling service to the Crowthers for many years she had returned to help with the mêlée. Tilly came forward and took her by the hand.

'Hello. I'm glad you could come.'

Mary was never so grateful as she was then, as Tilly led her back into the big room. The lovely smell was there again and now she noticed a big light hanging from the ceiling. Boys were already galumphing round, whooping and shouting. But then a big man came into the room and clapped his hands.

'That's my uncle,' said Tilly.

'Right, I want all of you in a circle holding hands with both your neighbours.' Then, to two boys, he boomed, 'Stop that you two!' He cleared his throat. 'Start to walk round to the left when the music starts and whoever is opposite me when the music stops falls out of the circle. Right?'

It took some time to organize everybody holding hands in a circle and even longer to get them to walk step by step to the left. Mary clung on to Tilly's hand on one side and on the other to that of a girl she didn't know, wearing a lovely white dress. Mary hoped she could fall out first. There was a lovely fire at the far end of the room and she longed to sit by it. Then a piano struck up, played by a tall thin lady on the other side of the vast room.

When it stopped it was Liddy Crowther who was facing her uncle and she dropped out with no more than a little pout. Seeing that some girls were being dragged uncomfortably along, the uncle shouted, 'Now drop hands, turn round – and march!'

The music began again, this time a marching song, and the circle of children began to move faster and faster. The uncle wiped his fore-head. The music stopped again, and this time it was Tilly who had to go. Oh dear! With the two of them gone how could Mary manage? She was clutching the hand of a boy now, a big strapping boy with ginger hair who pulled her along. On the other side the girl in the white dress was squealing. Mary made a dash to be opposite the uncle when the music stopped, not difficult as the boy in front of her was determined not to be 'out'.

Unfortunately the uncle moved a little and it was the girl in white who was 'out'. Now Mary was between two boys. She could never keep up with them, and the boy on her left was yanking her along when suddenly her necklace fell to the ground and all the beads broke.

Her necklace, her lovely necklace that Mima had given her.

When the music stopped she pulled away and bent down to the floor, ignoring the others.

'It's my necklace!' she shouted and began to pick up the beads that were rolling around.

'I'll help you,' said a boy, and began to search with her.

The uncle waited. 'You can have another look when the game is finished,' he said to Mary, having grasped what had happened. 'Ready?'

Tilly ran up to her and dragged her away. Mary was managing to hold her tears back but it was all too much. She wanted Mima. Only Mima would do. But she went on suppressing her panic, watching anxiously as the game continued. It was over at last. Then she darted back to the floor, Tilly following, and they began to search. Another lady came up with a little bag.

'Now put them in here my dear. Don't worry – you can have them restrung. Are they valuable?'

'Oh, yes!' said Mary.

The girl in the white dress who was looking on said, 'Pooh! They're only old beads.'

'Don't take any notice of *her*,' said Tilly. Mary heard the lady say to the uncle, 'I think something a little less rough, Cyril, don't you?'

'We've got hunt the slipper and musical chairs before tea,' he replied.

The boy who had offered to help in the first place had been bending down to look on the floor and now he came up to Mary.

'Here you are,' he said and gave her two beads. Then Mary spied another and another and collected them all in the bag. There were still a lot missing.

Tilly found the string.

'Mama said we shouldn't have boys,' said Liddy, 'they're too rough. It wasn't your fault.'

Mary said, 'Can I sit down and see if I can find some more?' Somehow she hated people feeling sorry for her. Then another lady came up, and this time Tilly said to her, 'This is Mary and we want to sit down and restring her beads.'

The lady put out her hand.

'Good afternoon, Mary. Tilly, I think you should introduce me to Mary. Then we can sit down over there because they are bringing in the lemonade.'

'This is Miss Hartley, our governess,' said Tilly.

The music had stopped and the children were milling round. Tilly's mother was nowhere to be seen but Tilly kept pointing out her brothers and older sisters.

The nice boy came up. 'Good afternoon, Miss Hartley,' he said politely.

'This is Edwin, Mary,' said Miss Hartley.

Mary looked at Edwin from under her eyelashes. When he smiled she tried to smile back.

'Have you found them all yet?' he asked, as if he really minded.

'No, I don't think so. . . .'

Mary's lip trembled. His being so nice to her made her even more miserable. Mima would have said that was silly. She often imagined what Mima would have said.

'We shall take another a look after the party,' said Miss Hartley briskly. 'Meanwhile, I will look after the ones in the bag for you. I think you should all go and join in with the rest.'

Tilly squeezed Mary's hand as they joined the circle once more. This time it was musical chairs. A row of chairs had been placed at the top of the room and they all had to march one behind the other to the music, winding round past the chairs. If the music stopped you had to sit on a chair. The one who didn't was 'out'. Mary hoped once again that she would soon be 'out'.

The music started, the bigger boys pushed and shoved and not surprisingly all were lucky when the music stopped.

Miss Hartley said something to the uncle and he whispered something to the lady who was playing the piano, which made her look round as she was playing and stop the music when at least one of the bigger boys was far away from the chairs. But this did not seem to help. Some boys flew up to the chairs as if on booted wings, and one even ousted Lydia off one. She shrugged her shoulders. Mother had said you let your guests win, and anyway she didn't want the prize because she knew what it was.

'Now, now! Just go more slowly this time,' barked the uncle.

Mary walked along to the suddenly dirgelike music as slowly as she could but hesitated when she came to the first chair. The music did not stop just then, finished only as she rounded the line of chairs.

Tilly was behind her and pulled her back. 'No – you sit there – I want to look for my beads,' said Mary and thankfully left the game.

If this was a party it was not much fun. But then a maid came in with a big tray on which were several tall jugs of lemonade. There were glasses on the table at the other end of the room, and once a boy called Reginald had been presented with his prize for the chair game they were all given straws and glasses of lemonade.

'There'll be presents round the Christmas tree at the end,' whispered Lydia. Mary, who had just found another bead, did not reply. She sat on a chair next to Miss Hartley, put the bead into the bag and then sipped some lemonade through a straw. Looking above at the ceiling she noticed there were garlands of evergreen hanging from the hooks up there.

'We'll have a Yule log tomorrow,' said Tilly. 'Father is bringing it in.'

Edwin, who had joined the little party round the governess, said to Lydia, 'Will you have Santa Claus come this afternoon?'

'You mean – now?' Mary asked.

She had heard of Santa but had never seen him. Mima had told her he only came at night when you were asleep.

'Haven't you ever seen him? He brings the presents . . .'

'Yes, I know – but only at night.'

Edwin looked as if he was going to say something, but did not.

Just then the uncle barked again in a commanding voice,' All into the next room for cake.'

'Mrs Crowther decided the drinks and the cake should be consumed separately,' said Miss Hartley to the piano lady who had joined them. This lady sighed, saying:

'Liddy! Tilly! Go and look after your other little guests.'

'Who is that?' asked Mary. 'Is that a new nanny?'

'No, that's our Aunt Alice,' said Lydia, 'We'd better go – we'll all come back here for the tree.'

Mary did not want to leave the room where she was sure some of the beads were still lying hidden under chairs.

'Please, will you keep looking after the little bag?' she whispered to the governess. Miss Hartley was, she felt sure, a kind lady.

'It will be safe with me,' she replied.

'Miss Hartley, Miss Hartley,' petitioned Tilly as they followed her into the next room where most of the children were now already assembled, shepherded by the aunt and uncle and sitting at a long table, 'Can we take Mary up to the nursery and show her our doll's house?'

'Tilly – I'm sure one day you can show Mary your doll's house, but not today. Today is your party and there are all the other children who are your guests whom you must look after.'

'But I don't want to take *them* to see my toys!' said Tilly rebelliously.

'Now Tilly – I promise that if you ask your mama to ask Mary's—' she paused, recollecting Mary's semi-orphan state just in time '– Mary's aunt – if she will allow her to come and play with you, you will be able to show her your toys. For the present, no!'

Mary had expected that Tilly's and Liddy's mama – she knew they had a mama – would be there, but Miss Hartley and the aunt and uncle were the ones in charge. Just then a small rather fat lady appeared from behind the tea urn from which a maid was distributing cups of tea to the grown-ups.

'That's our mama,' said Liddy.

'Mama, Mama,' shouted Tilly.

The lady looked up and waved a hand and then disappeared again.

It was all very confusing and Mary did not feel very hungry. But Tilly was really kind.

'Will you be my best friend?' she asked Mary, her mouth full of Christmas cake. Miss Hartley did not appear to notice. Mima would have noticed, for you were not supposed to talk with your mouth full. Mary thought, I suppose there are so many of them that nobody notices much what they do. Except Miss Hartley, who wants Tilly and Liddy to be nice to everyone. I *would* like to be Tilly's best friend.

She had never had a best friend before.

'Yes, I will,' she said.

Edwin, on her other side, said, 'Would you like to be my best friend too?'

'Don't be silly,' said Liddy. 'Boys aren't friends with girls! And boys don't have best friends anyway.' Edwin did not look crushed, but rather amused.

'I can be Tilly's best friend and your friend as well,' said Mary tactfully.

'Edwin doesn't have any sisters,' said Miss Hartley, overhearing.

'Not like us!' groaned Liddy.

'I haven't any brothers *or* sisters,' said Mary.

'Lucky thing,' said Liddy, but Mary didn't think she meant it.

'I need your help, girls,' said Miss Hartley, getting up. 'Come along with me.'

Liddy and Tilly went off to do what Miss Hartley asked of them and Mary was left alone with Edwin.

'I found another of your beads,' he said and fished in the pocket of his velvet knickerbockers. He handed over a green glass bead. 'Is it very precious?' he asked her.

Mary did not quite understand what he meant.

'Is it very valuable?' he asked.

'Oh, er, yes,' she answered.

Then they were all taken back to the big room where the Christmas tree had miraculously grown parcels at its foot. The din was deafening. Mary followed Edwin who went on talking as if nothing exciting was going to happen.

'Are you coming to learn with Miss Hartley?' he asked. 'My pa said you might. He knows your pa. My pa's a doctor.'

'Is your father *Doctor* Horsfall?' asked Mary. Now she came to think of it she had seen a man Yeranty called the Lightholme doctor going up to Papa's room only last week. Papa had had a dreadful cough.

'Yes, that's right. I say, if you want to restring these beads, Miss Hartley will do it, I'm sure.'

Mary thought what an unusual sort of person he was, but nice. Thinking about the beads however made her feel so miserable.

'How many were there? Can you count?' asked Edwin.

'Of course I can count! I'm nearly seven, like Tilly. There were twenty-four.'

Their conversation was interrupted by a general shout: 'There's Santa Claus!' The din was once more deafening.

Mary fervently hoped there were to be no more games. She followed Edwin who still went on talking. Some children banged into them both in their excitement.

The Christmas tree parcels looked exciting. Tilly and Liddy were standing on each side of a big figure in scarlet.

'Now, not all at once, please,' shouted the uncle. Mrs Crowther suddenly appeared, looking anxious.

Organized by the governess, the children advanced one by one. The boys were given a small parcel, the girls a knobby-looking one. As quickly as the parcels were distributed they were torn open. Boys had a whistle on a lanyard and girls a skipping-rope.

'Three cheers for Santa Claus!' shouted the uncle.

'Happy Christmas!' said Santa Claus and disappeared through a doorway.

'He's gone to his reindeer,' said a fat girl about Mary's age whom she had not noticed before.

'Can we go now?' asked a boy rudely.

'Goodbye everyone and happy Christmas,' said Mrs Crowther in a quiet voice.

There was a general rush for the cloakroom. Tilly and Liddy came up to Mary and Edwin, closely followed by the girls' mother.

'This is Mama,' said Lydia.

'Is this Mary?' Mrs Crowther asked kindly.

Mary wondered whether should she drop a curtsy. Some girls did, Yeranty said. But she was too late. Mrs Crowther did not appear to expect one, for she went on, 'When they have all gone, Tilly and Liddy will have another look for your necklace.' Miss Hartley must have told her.

The governess came up. 'Your aunt is here for you, Mary,' she said.

'But I haven't found all my beads yet.'

'Don't worry – we'll find them all,' Tilly said.

'And we'll keep them in the bag and send them over with Marshall.' Mary wondered who Marshall was.

Edwin reappeared in his wool coat, the lanyard round his neck. He said, 'Thank you for the party.'

'It's nice to see some people have manners,' said Miss Hartley.

Mary heard her and quickly said, 'Oh, thank you.'

Liddy and Tilly took her by the hand and danced out with her to the room with the coats. There was Yeranty already waiting. Mrs Crowther came up behind.

'I'm so sorry to keep you waiting. You should have come in.'

Mary had not realized that Yeranty knew her. 'Your little one has lost her necklace,' Mrs Crowther went on.

'It broke,' said Mary.

Would Yeranty be cross with her? No, she looked really upset, and said; 'Oh, I am sorry, Mary.'

'Was it valuable?' asked Tilly's mother. They all asked that, thought Mary.

Yeranty hesitated, and then said, 'To her it was.'

'Our Miss Hartley will have a good look with the girls before she goes home,' said Mrs Crowther comfortably. 'Don't worry, dear.'

'Say thank you for the party, Mary,' said Yeranty.

'I have,' said Mary.

Once they were in the carriage she could hold back the tears no longer.

'They banged me and a boy knocked the beads – I shall never find them all again,' she got out between sobs.

'We can restring them,' said Yeranty. She knew how much the necklace meant to her niece even if it was not all that Mima had given her. There had been other, more important things.

It had occurred to her when she had seen Mrs Crowther that Mary did not now miss having a mother. If she could join the Crowthers for lessons with Miss Hartley, all would be well. Miss Hartley had appeared to her more in charge than the girls' mother, as she had heard from the cloakroom whilst waiting for her charge. The governess, however, did not 'live in'. Yeranty wouldn't have wanted to be a governess herself, but she certainly would prefer to be a governess rather than the mother of a large brood like the Crowthers.

'Tell me about Santa Claus,' she said, and Mary between

occasional hiccups, told her about the big man and the tree and the presents, and about Edwin who had been very kind. Then she was packed quickly off to bed, exhausted.

In the morning a man knocked at the kitchen door of Cliff House with a little bag, which Cook took in. Mary emptied the beads that morning and counted them.

Nineteen. Only nineteen.

'It can't be helped,' said her aunt, and took her needle and a piece of strong thread to string them all together again. 'We shall need a new clasp,' she said. 'I expect the others will turn up. Keep them in the bag for the present and I will see what I can do tomorrow at the jewellers' in town.'

Mary went to sleep that night clutching the bag. When she thought of Tilly and Edwin, though, she felt a little less miserable. Ought she to write to Mima about it? The honeymoon must be finished now, but she felt ashamed that she had broken Mima's present, even though she knew it was not her fault.

Yeranty was as good as her word and bought her a new fastener for the necklace. But Mary knew it would never be the same.

'Never mind if I can't restore it completely – it will still go round your neck,' said Yeranty. 'It was rather too long before.'

Mary kept on hoping, but no further beads turned up, despite Miss Hartley and her pupils' renewed efforts.

'If I were you, I'd put it away safely in your drawer,' said Yeranty. 'It's too precious to risk wearing it again just for now.'

Mary agreed. She no longer wanted to wear it. Perhaps when she was grown up she might. She wrapped the now shorter necklace in her best handkerchief and put it in the top drawer of the small chest of drawers in her bedroom.

Over Christmas the weather turned colder and it never stopped raining. Mr Settle ordered an enormous Yule log to keep the family warm in the drawing-room.

The servants put up mistletoe in the kitchens. Last year it had been Mima who had put up a tree in the nursery and decorated it with red and green ribbons, but Aunt Clara did not decorate anything upstairs. With the help of Hodgson, however, she wreathed holly and ivy over the drawing-room picture rails. Even William Settle said it all looked very festive.

'Mary saw the tree at The Nest. Nothing I could do would match that,' said Clara.

'Next year we must have a proper tree here,' he replied expansively.

On Christmas Eve the town wassaillers called at Cliff House and Mary was allowed to come down to listen to them singing the old Yorkshire carol *Christians Awake!* On Christmas morning she found the stocking she had hung by her bed filled with an orange, some nuts and a shiny sovereign. That was the time she missed Mima most. But she had to dress quickly in her best dress and go along with her father and aunt to the new church.

'They need better heating here!' grumbled Mr Settle. Mary was given her big presents after Christmas dinner: a new golden-haired doll from an aunt who lived in London, a warm cloak with a fur collar from Aunt Clara, and a lovely book from Papa. For tea they had the cake Cook had made, eaten with Wensleydale cheese. After tea she read the first story from the book to Griselda, Lucy, and the new doll. What should she call her? She was pondering this when her father said:

'Next Christmas we must have a magic lantern.'

Clara wondered whether he would remember. It was she who had bought the book he had given his daughter. 'You know better than I do what she'd like,' he'd said.

On Boxing Day Aunt Clara took Mary out for a walk. It was too cold to stay out long, but as they trudged back home down the lane, she said:

'I have something to ask you.' Mary looked up from the ground where she was looking for a conker that a farm boy might have dropped in October. 'Now you are nearly seven, I'd like it if you called me Aunt Clara. You see, Yeranty was your Mima's name for me and nobody else understands it.'

Mary stopped stock still in her tracks.

'It was the name she used for me when you were a baby, dear,' added Clara, taking her hand.

Mary looked puzzled. Yeranty *was* her name. Mima had said so.

'I know your Mima called me that and you thought it was my real name,' her aunt went on, understanding what was going though the child's head, 'but only you and Mima knew it. Mima will always call me Yeranty when she talks to you, I expect, but I think *you* had better call me Aunt Clara, or else other people won't know who you mean!'

'But you are still Yeranty?' asked Mary, puzzled.

'Well of course I am the same person, dear, but it was just Mima's way of talking.'

Mary suddenly 'heard' Mima saying the word and her eyes filled with tears.

Oh dear, what have I done now? Clara wondered.

'If I talk to Mima I can still call you Yeranty, can't I? I shall see Mima again soon, shan't I?'

If her aunt had said Mima would still call her Yeranty that must mean she would come back one day – but when?

'Of course you will see her again. She'll come back to see her mother – but not for a time. She'll be very busy at present with her new little house. You haven't written to her, have you?'

'We sent her the Christmas card,' Mary reminded her. Somehow the idea of writing to Mima, which she had so wanted to do at first, now only made her feel miserable. She dreaded having to tell her about the beads.

'Yes, so we did,' said Clara cheerfully. 'Well, you can practise your new writing when you have had a few lessons with Miss Hartley. Won't that be a nice surprise for Mima? A real letter. You said you were going to write to her.'

'She hasn't written to me,' said Mary. Had she expected a letter immediately? wondered Clara.

At first, her beloved nanny had been so often in Mary's thoughts that one might have said she was never out of them. But after the party at The Nest her new friends had slightly assuaged her sorrow. Mima was a person you wanted to hug and on whose lap you wanted to sit, not really a person you wanted to write things to, though she would write to her soon.

In February she and Tilly would have their seventh birthdays. Tilly said that seven was not *quite* grown up but reported that her big sister Lottie called it a 'good age'. Mary was excited, partly because, now that Christmas had come and gone, in the New Year, which Aunt said was next week, she was to begin to attend the classes at The Nest with Miss Hartley. There would just be the four of them at first, herself and Tilly and Liddy, with Edwin the only boy. Yeranty had arranged it all.

'I'll call you "Auntie" now, ' she said, 'That's what Tilly called her aunt.'

With that, 'Yeranty' had to be contented.

PART TWO

MISS WATSON

CHAPTER FOUR

The little class assembled every morning at nine o'clock in the schoolroom at The Nest. At first, Hodgson took Mary over but after two or three weeks Yeranty agreed that Mary would be allowed to walk through her own garden, and through the little gate to the lane, cross the lane and go through the gate in the high wall. If it was snowing or raining heavily, or in a high wind, she could be taken in the trap the long way round.

The schoolroom was on the first floor of The Nest, at the back, next to where Tilly said their night nurseries had once been. It was now quite a cosy room with a big black fireplace, and a table for Miss Hartley and four little desks in two rows of two. There was a book-case full of story-books, as well as what Miss Hartley called 'textbooks'. The bookcase was topped by a globe, and there was a blackboard on legs and a tall cupboard with all they needed for work – chalk and slates to practise doing pothooks, and pencils and paper and exercise books. Mary was to use pen and ink when Miss Hartley was satisfied she could write well enough.

Mary sniffed the air. It was a smell she couldn't place until she realized it was a mixture of the stuff Mima used to put on her chest when she had a cough and the smell of the slate-pencils they were to use on their slates. There were holes at the top right-hand corner of the little desks. Miss Hartley said, 'That's for your inkwell when you are ready to use ink.'

That first morning Mary was given a slate like Tilly's. Her friend never ceased to complain about the horrible noise the slate-pencil made.

'We are old enough to give up slate-pencils for ordinary pencils,' Tilly said. 'Liddy had a pencil before she was seven.'

'Then we shall see in February,' said Miss Hartley. 'If you make good progress, Mary, you may have a special exercise-book for your pothooks.'

There were books with big letters of the alphabet, which you copied on to special paper with lines ruled like a musical stave, so that you learned to write perfect copper-plate. Yeranty, whom Mary had ended up calling called Aunt rather than Auntie, had taught Mary her letters before she was five and found her an apt pupil, so Mary was already hoping, as soon as she saw the books on the shelves in the schoolroom, that they would be able to read the story-books she saw there.

Miss Hartley began the following day to read to them from a book called *Grimm's Fairy Tales*. Her aunt had read her one or two of the Andersen fairy stories and Mary had loved *The Snow Queen*.

Miss Hartley listened to them all read. Only Edwin read better than she did, Mary thought. Miss Hartley did not instruct her pupils in religion, but Clara had felt it necessary to educate her niece in the events of the Old Testament, until she might join a class of the Anglican Sunday school. A handsome new church had just been built in the village and there was already a small class for children over eight. Some ordinary village children went to these classes, but most of them went to chapel. Mary was surprised to discover that the Crowthers were chapel too. Tilly and Liddy were taken to the little town two miles away to attend the Methodist Sunday school whose classes started when you were four. Miss Hartley had told Aunt Clara that she thought the Crowther girls were learning enough scripture for the time being, so she would confine her reading to non-religious themes.

'One day I hope you girls will go to school in Woolsford,' she said later that week. 'A new school for girls has just been founded there. But you can't go until you write and read and cipher well enough.'

'Is there a boys' school there for Edwin as well?' Mary asked. Edwin looked self-conscious, which was unusual for him.

'Edwin will be prepared for Uppingham or Giggleswick,' said Miss Hartley. Liddy and her sister muttered the latter name under their breath, and Liddy said 'It's a giggly name,' as they both dissolved in hysterical laughter.

'Well, your brothers went there,' said Miss Hartley. It was always at the end of the lessons that she talked to them about life in general and treated them as if they were rational beings. Mary began to look forward to school and it helped her to stop thinking about Mima. Her father was relieved that his daughter liked The Nest schoolroom so much, even if Miss Eleanor Hartley was said to be a sort of Modern Woman. At home, Mary sometimes read to him from some of the stories in the new *Little Folks' Annual* he had given her for Christmas, which Aunt Clara had of course chosen. If he had time on a Saturday afternoon he would listen and smile at the adventures of Sir Percy Vere and Lady Mabel.

In the afternoons at The Nest the children took turns to read aloud from their various primers, but the morning classes consisted chiefly of arithmetic and composition. Mary found keeping up with arithmetic was harder than reading and writing. She and Tilly practised their pothooks together, whilst Edwin already wrote in a tiny little hand and was really clever at calculation. She was not so keen on this but eventually began to manage tens and units. Pounds, shillings and pence, tons, hundredweights, stones, pounds, and ounces, and rods poles and perches took longer, not to speak of furlongs, and worried Mary most. Why was a sovereign also called a pound, the same word as for the weight? Edwin said a gold sovereign must once have weighed a pound. Why was a crown not the same as a sovereign if the Queen's head was on it? Half crowns and florins were not so difficult to fit in because distant relations had given her them from time to time and at Christmas she had received a whole crown from an uncle. She could manage shillings and sixpences, threepenny bits, halfpennies and farthings more easily because she had saved them up in a money-box. But as for a golden guinea, she had never seen one.

William Settle was often tired when Mary asked him to help her, and she stopped asking him when Clara told her he needed to rest. The village people were used to seeing him walk slowly down to the station to catch the train to Woolsford. He had had one bout of bronchitis and Dr Horsfall had told him to wrap up well and mixed him a tonic. But he was more and more bound up with work. The firm was not doing too well at present. He dreaded Fridays, for Friday was wage day and he had had to put some of his workers on to half days, trade was so bad. He managed to get to his Masonic meetings from time to time but hardly ever visited friends in their homes. Of course, since Maria had died he visited less, feeling out of place at the houses of the couples with whom they had exchanged jolly musical evenings. There had been singing and the playing of various instruments until quite late sometimes and he had enjoyed them, but for the last few years even music had failed to cheer him up.

The great day of the seventh birthday of the two Best Friends was soon upon them. Both had been born on Candlemas Day.

'Please may I have Tilly here for tea on my birthday?' Mary had begged.

'You may, so long as I can arrange it with Mrs Crowther. She may have other plans for Tilly's birthday. But if you have Tilly you must have Liddy and Edwin too.'

Privately, Clara rather dreaded having to amuse four children, but she need not have worried. As a little group they were used to amusing themselves between morning and afternoon school, and Edwin was hardly a difficult boy. After their midday bread and cheese in The Nest kitchen they were all allowed to walk in the grounds and were used to playing together. There were quarrels sometimes but they did not last long.

Mary was overcome by the size of the gardens at the Crowthers'. There was even a little lake as well as several large conservatories. It was a beautiful place, but she wanted to show Tilly her own house. She had never had little friends for tea before. Aunt Clara said you invited people, and then they invited you back. She 'owed' the Crowthers for their party. Mary thought, oh, good! If Tilly comes here next week I shall be invited to go to The Nest again for tea. It would not be the same as going for lessons. She and Tilly wanted to have the schoolroom to themselves, to talk about their secrets.

Mary received a birthday card from Mima, a picture of some roses with a little verse, 'With all my love Mima' and many kisses. It took pride of place on the morning-room chimneypiece with other cards from relatives.

After school that Thursday afternoon the guests walked over to Mary's and now they were all seated round the table in the morning room at Cliff House. Clara had asked Mary to 'be mother' and hand round the plate of bread and butter and the dish of jam as soon as Annie came in with glasses of milk for them all. The Crowther girls and Edwin appeared quite at home and were behaving very well, she thought.

When the maid came in, she served Aunt Clara with a cup of tea from a cup and saucer painted with pink roses.

Liddy said politely 'That's very pretty, Mrs Settle.'

'No, I am not Mrs Settle. I am Mrs Demaine,' said Clara. 'Mary would not think to tell you.'

'We are having some of Mama's relations to stay,' said Tilly. Her mother had taught them that it was polite to make conversation. Edwin was silent, wondering how many sandwiches they were each allowed.

'I suppose you have many aunts and uncles?' enquired Clara, hoping the child would not construe this as too personal a remark. She was so out of touch with English provincial society and the way most young people were brought up. When she had been a child in the 1840s children had owned fewer clothes and toys but their parents had perhaps had a more direct way of talking. Her own mother had been a young girl in the Regency, when manners were so much more relaxed. Clara brought her thoughts back to the present moment with an effort.

She really didn't know much about the Crowthers except that they were rich, that Mrs Crowther was a Methodist and that they were friendly people.

Lydia said now, 'Our mama has lots of relations. Father doesn't have so many but they are always coming to stay!'

'With parasols,' said Tilly. 'They like our park and the lake.'

'Have you ever sailed a boat on the lake?' asked Edwin.

'The boys have a skiff,' said Lydia, 'but we aren't allowed it yet. We sailed our little boats there last summer but we got wet and Father forbade us to do it in case we got drowned.'

'Is it very deep even at the edge?'

Just then Cook came in bearing Mary's birthday cake on a tall china stand. There were seven candles on the white and pink icing. Clara had been hoping that her brother might be able to join them and had waited until she was sure he was not coming, but Cook clearly thought she had waited long enough. The children all stopped talking to exclaim, 'Happy birthday, Mary!'

'Hip-hip-hurrah!' said Edwin.

Mary stood up, took a deep breath and blew out all but one candle.

'Jolly good,' said Tilly.

'That's slang,' said her sister.

'I don't care – many happy returns!'

They all clapped. Clara thought they must have had many experiences of birthdays with all those elder sisters and brothers. She cut five slices of the cake, which was a plum-cake, and Mary handed them round.

'Can we play guess who?' asked Edwin. 'I mean after tea.'

'Oh let's play hunt the thimble!' said Liddy.

They looked expectantly at Clara. She gathered her thoughts. 'There are not enough of you for Oranges and Lemons or Postman's Knock, and Ring-a-Ring-o'-Roses is too babyish. Mary can take you up to her nursery and show you her games and toys and then you can decide what to play.'

'Oh yes – I can show you my Noah's Ark,' said Mary, flushed with the success of her first tea-party.

'Have you any playing cards?' asked Edwin.

'There is Snakes and Ladders, and we have Happy Families,' said Clara. ' I shall leave you to devise some quiet games.' After all, Edwin and Lydia were nine, quite old enough in her opinion to play without need of supervision. She was quite tired from her unaccustomed efforts.

'Do you have a rocking-horse?'

'Or a Jack-in-the-Box?'

'I have a music-box—'

'I wish it wasn't raining – we could play in the garden – have you a ball?'

'Our sisters play croquet . . .'

'It's nearly time for marbles.'

What a lot of energy they all had, but they were good children, well brought up.

When they had eaten up all the food and drunk most of the milk, Clara got up.

'Take your guests upstairs, Mary. I'll look in now and again,' and she left them on the stairs to the nursery.

Mary had set out her Noah's Ark, and there was the Jack-in-the-Box on the shelf, and her music-box that told the time. Her dolls, Griselda and Lucy and the new Goldilocks doll were neatly arranged on a rug, and the miniature tea was set out on a little table. The tiddly-winks board was on the floor, her books on a special shelf.

'Oh, you are lucky to have it all to yourself!' cried Liddy. Edwin was busy looking at the books and Tilly at the dolls.

'I don't have a rocking-horse or a doll's house,' said Mary apologetically.

Liddy was trying out a top.

'Let's do the guessing game,' said Edwin, turning round.

'How do you play that?'

'Oh, it's silly – it's like I Spy,' said Liddy.

'You do it, Edwin,' said Mary, 'and Liddy can play with my paint-box if she wants.'

'There isn't any water.'

'Well, with my little tea set then.'

'No, I'll play Edwin's guessing game if he lets us play hunt the thimble after that.'

'You think of an object or a person and then each person asks a question about it that needs the answer 'yes' or 'no', and the first to guess what it is or who it is has the next turn.'

'You start then,' said Mary.

'Right. I've thought of something.'

'Is it a thing?'

'No.'

'Is it a person?'

'Yes.'

'Is it male or female?'

'You can't ask that.'

'Why?'

'Because I can't say yes or no to it.'

'Well then,' Liddy was impatient, 'is it a boy?'

'No.'

'Is it a lady?' Tilly asked.

'No.'

'Is it a man?' asked Mary.

'No.'

'Is it a girl?'

'Yes.'

'Is she pretty?' asked Liddy mischievously.

'Yes,' replied Edwin.

'Is it Tilly?' asked Mary.

'No.'

'Is it Liddy?' asked Mary, puzzled.

'No!'

'Is it her birthday today?' asked Liddy.

'Yes!'

Mary was amazed. They were all laughing and pointing at her. Edwin thought she was pretty. He was being kind because it was her birthday.

After this, they had another round, but as Liddy had chosen Miss Hartley nobody guessed until Mary asked, 'Is she very clever?'

The game turned into a conversation. Tilly said she liked playing whips and tops and skittles best but her sister said that was for boys.

'Well, it's better than old gardening,' said Tilly.

'I like gardening,' said Liddy. 'Father has let me have a little patch of my own.'

'I hate needlework,' Mary said, putting into words for the first time her feelings about sewing. Having friends who were all so talkative made you think more about what you liked and disliked.

'I like jigsaws,' said Edwin. 'And card games.'

'Oh, I like playing Snap and Happy Families best,' said Liddy. 'But Mother won't let us play Beggar my Neighbour. Now, can we play hunt the thimble?'

'There isn't anywhere much to hide it,' said Edwin. 'Unless we go in the garden, and it's raining. Have you Snakes and Ladders, Mary?'

Yes, she had, and when Clara came up about half an hour later she found them all absorbed. It had grown quite dark as they played.

'There's the doctor's carriage for you, Edwin,' she said. 'And he's going to drop the girls at The Nest.'

'Oh, is it time?' exclaimed Tilly. 'I wish I could stay here!'

William Settle was in the hall as they left. He shook hands with Edwin and smiled at the girls. Mary waved them all goodbye.

All William said to Clara was. 'Can you believe it – Woolsford is having its first tramway opened tomorrow. They are all talking about it.'

'Really?' answered Clara. 'Well, your daughter appears to have enjoyed herself today – and the other children too. I feel quite exhausted.' But she spoke in a satisfied tone of voice. Mary came back into the hall.

'Did you enjoy having your friends, dear?'

'Oh, yes, thank you, Yer – Aunt.' said Mary, 'It was *lovely.*'

'Well, as it's your birthday, Annie will clear up the nursery for you and you can get to bed.'

Lucky bairns, thought Annie, the parlour-maid, as she cleared up the games and toys. She wound up the music-box and put away the animals in the ark. No penny toys for them, she muttered, which was not quite fair for Mary had only a penny a week pocket-money and the toys had all been presents from relations who pitied the little semi-orphan.

Annie shook the money-box and sighed.

We are on pensils now, wrote Mary, *and aunty is reding me a book about a doll caled Maria Poppet. Tilly is reding Her Benny and she will lend it me soon. I do hope you are quite well. I love you but I will see you soon and I send you kisses from Mary.*

Clara thought it better not to correct the misspellings and made sure that Mary's letter to Mima was posted to Burnley.

Mary sometimes walked near the lake on her way back to the lane. She knew her way quite well now and often wanted to linger and look round. In the distance there was a little summer-house but Tilly said it was forbidden to the children because they might make a mess there and it was being 'refurbished' for next summer. At first Annie always met Mary at the gate but now that she was used to the walk Aunt Clara allowed her to walk all the way home alone. Over the wall on the Cliff House side were fields with cows belonging to Farmer Hoyle and she had been forbidden to venture there 'in case there was a bull'.

One March afternoon Mary glimpsed some of Mr Crowther's cousins walking slowly along by the lake in the grounds of The Nest. There were two ladies, very elegantly dressed with perky bustles, and a gentleman wearing a bowler-hat and striped trousers. This particular afternoon a brisk wind had arisen and she saw the ladies turn back to the house, holding on to their hats. Miss Hartley was coming out of a door at the side that led to the lane further up. If you came by carriage to the house you went down a long drive that came out by what had been the old turnpike road to the village.

Miss Hartley appeared to enjoy walking and did not wear the sort of hat you would need to hold on in a wind. Mary knew she travelled backwards and forwards on the train to Woolsford. It was the same train that Mary's father took to his work in the opposite direction. In Woolsford the governess had an aged parent. Anyway, that was what Mr Crowther must have called the governess's mother, because Tilly had asked her once if she had one and Miss Hartley had smiled and answered, 'If you mean my mother, Tilly, yes, but it is not polite to ask personal questions.' You could see she was not really cross. The railway station was quite near and Mary could sometimes hear the whistle of a train as it came through the tunnel that went under the road.

The morning after she had glimpsed Mr Crowther's relations, Mary said to Tilly, 'I saw some ladies walking near the lake on my way home yesterday. Are those your cousins?'

Tilly said they were but they were not staying long this time. 'Mother says we are not to bother them,' said Liddy.

Aunt Clara, mindful of her religious duty was now seeing that Mary went to church. Occasionally she took her there, but she preferred evensong herself, so Mary was often taken by Hodgson the housemaid, or Annie. Mima had taken her once or twice in the past. Now, not every Sunday, but what Clara called high days and holy days Mary attended the new St Matthew's.

Easter Day was on 9 April that year so they were still in Lent, and the fourth Sunday in Lent was Mothering Sunday. As Mary had no mother this was perhaps an unfortunate Sunday to have chosen, but it was a popular day with the servants, most of whom were from village families and who, even if they were 'chapel', went home that day with little presents for their female parents.

Mary was sitting at the side with Annie that Sunday when she saw two young ladies come in and sit behind the curtain that was kept for special families. Aunt would have none of this, saying Christians should sit in the same place together. Mary wondered who these ladies were. One of them was quite tall and was dressed in green velvet. She was wearing a little flowery hat.

'I think they're from The Nest,' she whispered to Annie, who said 'Shush,' but looked all the same.

'The Crowthers are Methodys,' she said. She was a Primitive Methodist herself so knew what she was talking about. If her job at Cliff House involved taking Mr Settle's little lass to the village church, it could not be helped. Her own father called the Church of England services 'the vicar's capers' and she had been brought up to dislike Anglican flummeries. But at least it was better than washing up on a Sunday.

'Tilly has some ladies staying,' whispered Mary. Annie quelled her with another look and shoved the hymn book under her nose.

Mary could see the Green Lady quite well and thought she looked sad. She felt sad herself because that morning she had been thinking about her mother and about Mima. She didn't specially connect Mima with going to church, except for the wedding, and that had been in another church over at Sholey, but she did wish Mima were here with her instead of Annie.

After the hymn the vicar began to talk about mothers. Mary didn't understand all he said. She thought they ought to have a special Sunday for people without them. Perhaps some of these people in church had, like her, mothers who had died?

Some days, like today, she could not help thinking about Mima leaving her. She hoped she would have an answer to her letter soon. Whenever she was dressing Griselda, and talking to her, she thought of Mima, because Mima had made her. Liddy had called Griselda a rag doll but Mary thought of her as a Mima doll. She never talked about Mima to Liddy, only sometimes to Tilly. Staring at the ladies now when they stood for the hymns behind their curtain she thought about Mima looking after her and her looking after Griselda. 'Looking after' was what mothers did. Perhaps the lady cousin from The Nest had no mother? Mary thought she looked very beautiful as well as sad. She looked, as far as Mary could see, just like her own mother looked on the portrait that her father was always looking at. The other lady accompanying her did not look old enough to be anyone's mother. Tilly said her own mother had so much to do she hadn't much time for looking after them. She did a lot of charity work, Tilly said. Mary wasn't sure what that was.

'Wake up,' said Annie, poking her in the ribs.

'I wasn't asleep, I was thinking,' said Mary indignantly. 'I was thinking about Mima looking after me.'

Annie looked cross when she said this and gave a sigh.

'You're old enough to look after yourself,' she said. Mary wanted to say, well then, I could go to church by myself, couldn't I? But she decided, better not. She did not especially like church, except for the organ music. It was hard trying to concentrate to say your prayers. She knew by heart the prayers the other people in church all said together but she wanted to pray to Mima like she did sometimes in bed at home. They all moved out, pew by pew, just then.

'Does your aunt tell you to curtsy to the vicar?' asked Annie.

'I don't think so.'

When they arrived outside the church porch where the vicar was standing with his curate, Annie decided that she would not drop a curtsy to him either. She was a good chapel Christian and that meant you didn't curtsy unless you were forced. The vicar smiled at Mary, and then they were away. Annie took a big breath of air and said, 'Well, time for dinner,' and immediately looked more cheerful.

That afternoon Aunt Clara asked her what the service had been about. Mary was reading the book Tilly had lent her called *Her Benny*. Clara thought even the strictest Sabbatarians might think it suitable for a Sunday. She had had a quick look at it and seen it was about poor little street-urchins and a saintly child.

Mary looked up reluctantly. 'It was about mothers – but I thought about Mima instead,' she answered. She looked away. Clara saw how quickly she wanted to change the subject. 'I saw the ladies who stay at The Nest,' Mary added. 'Tilly doesn't like them. She says they are always cross.'

'I thought she had got over her,' said Clara to her friend Hannah the following week, 'but I don't think she has.'

'She will always remember her,' replied her friend. 'Children never forget those who loved them.'

'Well, I hope Jemima Green will reply soon to her letter.'

'She'll have plenty other things to do, but I feel sure she will, eventually,' said Hannah.

'You know the other day, I mentioned the difficult situation we had been faced with, to the doctor's wife. I asked her if she thought children got over separation. I believe she thought I was very peculiar worrying about that sort of thing. She's a funny sort of mother for that nice boy Edwin to have.'

'For some people, children are not supposed to have feelings,' said Hannah, 'but Mary will be all right – she's got you.'

Now she was seven years old Mary read whatever she could get her hands on, for now she loved reading stories more than anything in the world.

'She ought to learn to do something that gets her out more in the fresh air,' said Clara to her friend one afternoon. Hannah Hardcastle now came over almost every week from Woolsford. Since her mother's death her day was her own, and she had been left a small competence from the estate of her father. Clara found her a great comfort and could not help wishing that she had as much freedom as her friend. She loved her niece but it would be years before Mary was old enough not to need her.

'Well, why not buy her a few seeds and teach her how to plant them in the garden,' suggested Hannah, who was a practical kind of woman.

Miss Hartley had had a similar idea but it had been Liddy, not Mary, who had taken it up with zest.

'Next autumn I shall give you each a daffodil bulb,' the governess had said, 'And you will see how the flower appears in the spring if you water it well. You will find that easier than gardening, Mary.' Nature study was one of the lessons Miss Hartley gave, along with globes and history, and of course reading, writing and arithmetic. Mary thought, I shall grow a daffodil for Mima – I hope I shan't forget when autumn comes.

One April morning there was an envelope waiting on Mary's plate at breakfast time. It was addressed to Miss Mary Settle, and it was franked 'Burnley'. As it was a Saturday, Aunt Clara said Mary might read it as soon as she had finished her breakfast. Mary took the letter and held it close to her chest.

'You know who it's from?' said Clara.

'Please can I take it to my bedroom?' Mary asked, 'I want to read it all by myself.'

The child looked so excited.

'Hurry up with your porridge then.'

Mary sat on her little bed and opened the letter. It was written on lined paper and was not long.

Dear little Mary – I am sorry I have not written before I was so pleased to get your letter as we often think about you. I have been very busy setting up our house Burnley is quite a nice place and Sam is doing right well here. I hop you are being a good girl I am sure you are I shall visit you if your dad will let me when I come over to see my fambly. I will let Yeranty know when but it will not be just yet. I hop you are enjoying your lessons – I know you will be a good scholard.

Don't forget your Mima and I send you kisses and a big hug.

There followed a long line of kisses, which Mary counted. There were twelve. In a funny way she found the letter rather disappointing. In Mary's head during the day Mima seemed far away; at night in bed she returned and was felt to be closer. How she wished she could go and see her, all by herself!

'How long is it since Mima's wedding?' she asked Clara at lunch-time when she brought down the letter to show her aunt.

'About, let me see, five months,' answered Clara, smiling over the letter and its spelling and lack of punctuation. But the girl wrote a fair hand for someone who had only a Sunday School education and started work at the age of twelve.

'I thought it was a lot longer ago than that. I shall give her my daffodil. Miss Hartley says we are to plant one each, but it will be a long time before they are ready. I could grow some flowers for when she visits us?'

'I don't think she will be coming just yet.' said Clara, 'But flowers would be ready by summer. You will have to work hard in the garden.'

She was pleased that Mary appeared to have 'got over' the worst part of the separation. It was always at the beginning you missed someone the most. The child's idea of time was perhaps still sketchy, though at least she could envisage 'next autumn'.

Mary took the letter over to The Nest on the following Monday to show Tilly. Tilly did not take a great deal of interest in it except to say, 'Our old Nanny never writes, not even to Mother. Mother says you forget things when you are old,' she added.

'Well, Mima is not old,' replied Mary.

For a few weeks after the letter arrived, Mary would dream about Mima and would wake up glowing with happiness. Then the happy feelings would fade away and she would even wonder if it was her fault that Mima had gone away. If she was lucky she would hear Mima's voice from somewhere inside herself saying, 'It wasn't your fault your Mam died, ducky.' That was something Mima had said once or twice to her in the past when Mary had confessed her fears, and if it wasn't her fault *then*, it wasn't her fault about Mima either, was it? Getting up and getting dressed and preparing for her walk over to Tilly's would take her mind away from her dream and she would even forget it for weeks. But she didn't reply to Mima for some time.

Spring came along that year a little tardily. It was always late in that cold place. The lilac, already out in Kew Gardens, arrived in Yorkshire only in late May. At The Nest they abandoned the paint box and the music box and the rocking horse – a ride on it had been allowed in winter as a reward for good work – and instead played with their skipping ropes, and hoops, and skittles, and balls. Edwin had an iron hoop, the girls wooden ones. They took out their garden spades. Mary found digging hard work. You had to be so patient to see any result. She planted some clary, which Miss Hartley said had lovely coloured 'leaf bracts'. Mima had not visited and was not expected yet. She wanted to grow something for her. She might have success with flowers if Liddy helped her?

Miss Hartley gave fewer spelling bees and more what she called tree walks now, when she would point out the elms and the beeches and the oaks. Leaf collecting would come later. There was less needlework too, which pleased Mary. On Saturday mornings she and Tilly took their dolls for walks or held dolls' picnics, and sometimes Edwin would come round as well. He had a passion for making paper boats to sail on the lake and for flying his kite in the windy skies. The older unmarried daughters in the Crowther clan, Daisy and Lottie, marked out a croquet lawn for the summer, and the skiff was painted by Marshall ready to be rowed on the lake. There was always so much going on at The Nest, especially when the two big boys, John and William, were home from school. On Saturdays, Liddy and Tilly were allowed to walk to the village, which was only a stone's throw away from The Nest's front lodge gate on the roadside, and Mary would go along with them to spend her Saturday penny at the sweet shop. Clara insisted that the shining silver sixpence her father gave her each week was put into her money box, but the penny was hers to spend as she liked. There were penny toys in the shop and Lucky Bags for a halfpenny, filled with what Clara called rubbishy sweets but which the shopkeeper called 'spice'.

About this time Mary started to have piano lessons, given by an old lady called Miss Cordingley who lived at the other end of the village. Tilly had already begun there. It was hard work, what with minims and semi-breves and rests and scales, but Mary persevered. Her father said, 'Your dear mother played the instrument so well,' and it was so unusual for him to mention her that Mary felt obliged to make a big effort. Father's cough, which had been bad in winter when he had had bronchitis, did not disappear even when the warm weather came.

CHAPTER FIVE

Mary was growing steadily. She was still a skinny child but had more colour in her cheeks and was sleeping better. When Clara looked at her she saw the slightly wavy hair was getting darker and the eyes a deeper hazel. The eyes and the hair and the straight little nose resembled her dead mother's, but Mary's skin was darker. She was always busy and active now. Not for the first time Clara thanked heaven for the Crowthers and their brood who had helped on Mary's growing enjoyment of life. Edwin was to leave them for his prep school the following year, but before that, before Mary was eight, there was all the summer to enjoy.

Clara decided not to take her to the coast again in August herself but to try to persuade her brother to take her to Bridlington. William did not look well and certainly needed a holiday. Her efforts were in vain. Even when she threatened she might take a few days away with Hannah, but without Mary, for a little rest cure in Harrogate, he still refused. She had thought this might sway him, but it did not. Neither would he agree to their all going away together. Well then, she would fulfil her half serious threat. Annie along with Cook was quite capable of looking after Mary and her father for a few days without her own presence in the house. Perhaps then he would make more effort to talk to his daughter.

Clara returned refreshed. Mary had spent most of the time with Tilly, and said, 'Father was always at work or busy with Mr Gordon so we tried not to disturb him'. She was a thoughtful child but if she had been a little more of a nuisance he might have got to know her better. Hamish Gordon was his elderly Works Manager, an important person in Mary's eyes and in Clara's a great help to her brother.

In September another child joined the little schoolroom. Mercy Miller, the daughter of a lawyer who had come from Leeds to live in

72

the village, was a large blonde girl with at first little to say for herself. Mary and Tilly tried to make her feel at home at the same time as finding her tedious. In spite of their efforts they succeeded in arousing only what they imagined was a sulky silence from the newcomer. To Tilly's disgust Mercy accompanied the Crowther girls to their dancing classes. Mary had pleaded not to have to attend them for the time being and Clara sympathized. She herself had not enjoyed dancing.

An autumn of leaf pressing and stamp collecting – and more piano lessons was to follow. One afternoon a week Miss Hartley organized what she called her Interest Afternoon. Mary started a scrap album of pretty pictures and pressed flowers, on whose pages she had also started to write a story about a girl called Matilda, which flattered Tilly.

Miss Hartley gave them some bulbs, which had to be watered regularly and kept in a dark cupboard. After a few days Mary had thought the soil round her bulb was too dry so decided to water it every other day, and never forgot. She had looked forward optimistically to a big yellow daffodil. When the day came for the bulbs to be taken into the light, the bulbs belonging to Edwin and Tilly and Liddy had a strong green shoot and the beginnings of a flower, but Mary's had not even tried to grow. The soil was all clayey. Miss Hartley dug the bulb out again.

'You have over-watered it Mary,' she said, 'You tended it too often.'

'I thought it was too dry. I wanted it to grow quickly.' She was heartbroken. Miss Hartley was sympathetic. She realized Mary was a tender hearted child. She knew from Clara that Mary had had to say goodbye the previous year to the nanny who had been with her since she was a babe in arms. Eleanor Hartley thought, bulbs are like children, they need to be 'watered', but do not need to be watched all the time. Still, it was a fault on the right side.

'It is better than letting it die from thirst,' she added now.

'I forgot to water mine ever so often!' said Tilly, whose daffodil was blooming.

'Well, you were just lucky,' said Miss Hartley.

'Mary can have mine if she wants,' offered Edwin.

'No, thank you,' said Mary. It was kind of him but she couldn't give Mima Edwin's bulb if she came on a visit.

If it was pouring down that autumn, which it frequently was, they played battledore and shuttlecock for exercise, in the big hall where, such a long time ago Mary felt, the Christmas party had taken place. Miss Hartley also encouraged a Quiet Hour for reading, which was naturally Mary's favourite lesson, indeed not a 'lesson' at all since she was such a bookworm.

Her favourite stories that year were Mrs Molesworth's *Cuckoo Clock*, and *Carrots*. Aunt Clara sometimes bought her *Aunt Judy's Magazine* as well as *Little Folks*, and Mary devoured the stories there by Mrs Ewing. *Daddy Darwin's Dovecote* was her favourite for a long time. Tilly had many sad books that her sisters had been given as Sunday school prizes and she lent them to Mary to read. To enjoy Mrs Ewing you had to read her slowly, Mary thought, because some of the words were hard, but on the other hand she had finished *Christie's Old Organ*, *Her Benny*, *Jessica's First Prayer* and *Froggy's Little Brother* in a day or so. They were easy to read but very, very sad. The children in these stories were always poor, and often ill and weak, and there was a lot about heaven and Jesus, although at the beginning of the stories many of the story-book children did not know about God at all.

Mary thought how lucky she was not to be poor, and to feel quite well. It made her wonder for the first time whether her mother was really there in heaven. Mima had always told her that she had gone there, but she knew now there was no way of getting there unless you died. After reading *Jessica*, Mary asked her aunt if perhaps her mother might have preferred her to die too, so they could see each other in heaven.

'Certainly not,' replied Clara. 'Your mama would have wanted you as strong and healthy as possible.'

Aunt Clara sometimes read Mary's books herself. There was quite a lot about Jesus in Mrs Ewing as well, but not all the children were well-behaved.

'I think Mrs Ewing very good,' she said. 'Did you know she used to live in Yorkshire? My friend Mrs Hardcastle's sister-in-law lived in Sheffield as a child, and Mrs Ewing's family lived quite near. She was not called Ewing then but Gatty and her mama was a writer too. Hannah told me she is also a very good water-colourist – *and* a great gardener!'

Mary was thrilled to receive this information but depressed about the gardening. Girls often turned out to be good at it, and she was not. The clary seeds had struggled up but then disappeared. It was not until her eighth birthday the following February that a new book arrived for her as a present from Clara, and this time it was even better than anything she had ever read before. It was called *Little Women* and was by an American lady. Mary began to read it on a snowy February Saturday and begged to be allowed to read it on Sunday too. Some children were not allowed to read anything but the Bible and *The Pilgrim's Progress* on Sundays but Aunt Clara, having conceded the street-urchin books, was not too strict about that sort of thing.

'You can go to church with me first and then you may read it in the afternoon.'

In church Mary thought about heaven and said a prayer for her mother. She added one for Mima too, though Mima was not in heaven, but in Burnley. She had finished her story about Matilda, so perhaps now she would write a story about Mima?

Liddy had come down to the schoolroom one March morning with a book called *Black Beauty* under her arm.

'You must read this!' she exclaimed.

It was so unusual for Liddy to read stories, she usually preferred gardening and dancing and riding on her pony, that Mary wondered what the book was.

'It's all about a horse and it's *so* sad,' explained Liddy. Just then Miss Hartley arrived from the station to start the lesson so Mary had to wait to discover more at noon.

The children were now given a small meal at a table in the kitchen before going out to play in the grounds. The afternoon's activities began at half past one and it was whilst waiting for Liddy to appear that Mary, walking down a long corridor at the back of the house on her way to the kitchen, heard the rustle of a skirt and at the same time caught a whiff of scent. She turned round and saw a young woman coming out of a door on the side. She had been told not to stare, and the lady took no notice of her, but Mary felt sure it was one of the cousins she had glimpsed in church a year ago. She forgot about the book and sat down with Tilly.

Miss Hartley took her luncheon with the children and said grace, her unusual *Benedictus Benedicat* that Edwin said was Latin.

'Put the book away now, Liddy,' said the governess. Liddy put the book on a chair but still looked dreamy.

'Are your father's relations staying here again?' Mary whispered to Tilly as they were served with mutton and potatoes.

Tilly groaned. 'Miss Watson and cousin and his friend are. We avoid them. They are on their way to Manchester.'

Mary wondered why they avoided them.

'Why do you want to know?' asked Tilly with her mouth full.

'Manners!' said Miss Hartley wearily and got up to confer with the cook about the pudding.

'I think I saw the ladies before, in church,' said Mary, 'and they were walking round the lake last year.'

'They are awfully smart,' said Liddy, 'but only Stacey is here this year. The other one is getting married—'

'Her cousin Lavinia,' said Tilly.

Miss Hartley returned, saying, ' Sponge pudding today – we are lucky.'

Mary said, 'I thought the one I saw was very pretty.'

'Lavinia is quite nice,' said Liddy.

'Who are you talking about?' asked Mercy who did not usually contribute much to the conversation but who had been listening.

'Oh, it's our father's relations – we are always having people to stay,' said Tilly. 'If it were summer, Alfred – that's the other cousin – might row us out on the lake. He promised last year but nothing came of it.'

'I don't like Stacey,' said Liddy. 'Can I go and read my book before afternoon lessons, *please* Miss Hartley?'

'I am delighted you are reading a book,' said Miss Hartley drily. 'When we have all finished you may read for twenty minutes.'

Mercy ate very fast as usual, odd for a girl who was so slow of speech. Mary wanted to go and see if she could find the young lady again so, usually a slow eater, she raced though her own pudding. When they all got out again, Liddy disappeared.

Edwin said, 'Let's play tag. Bags I start!' and Mary felt obliged to join in. Tilly went off then to see her tortoise.

On the way back in and up to the schoolroom Mary saw an open door on the half landing. She peeped through it. It led into what looked like a little sitting-room. There were so many large rooms at The Nest but this one was quite small, with low chairs in flowery chintz, and lace curtains, and tables her Aunt Clara called 'jardinairs' with large-leaved plants. There were lots of little paintings on the walls and the statuette of a woman in a turban. The back of a person's head was visible over the top of a chair that was facing the window. The hair was dark and piled high. It must be the Stacey lady. Mary remained staring into the room for a. few minutes. She had never seen inside this room before. The lady did not appear to have realized there was anyone at the door and Mary crept away. What would she have said if Stacey – what a strange name – had seen her? Perhaps she would be in church again and then she would be able to have a good look at her.

Next Sunday Clara was surprised when her niece asked if she was going to church. She had never been an assiduous churchgoer but had felt it right for Mary to learn her prayers and understand what religion was about. Of most importance were good works, which she supposed the Crowthers and the authors of Jessica and Christie and Benny were also concerned with. Mary's question about heaven had worried her a little. Was it right for an eight-year-old Protestant child to be worrying over such things? Those pious books Mary had read were all very well, but the religious sentiments were surely overdone for a child reader. It was right that her niece should understand how the poor lived, but tales of the wretched offspring of drunkards were disturbing. She was glad that Mary had preferred the certainly religious Mrs Ewing to the latest of Tilly's loans, which were always concerned with ragamuffins. Probably Methodist books, she thought.

It was Mrs Crowther who was religious; her husband did not live in an overtly 'Methodist' fashion. The family appeared to have enough money to live much more ostentatiously than they actually did. It was to their credit that they lived quite simply, even in such a large mansion as The Nest, and Mary was lucky to know them. Yet they had no taste, or what she knew her dead husband would have regarded as taste. Eleanor Hartley was probably of the same opinion. Sometimes Mary brought back titbits of the governess's remarks and she could see that Mrs Crowther, busy with her good works, was relieved to have her children's minds in touch with a more elevated 'taste,' even if the possessor of that taste might be an unusually 'advanced' woman.

Now Mary was talking about a mysterious lady who was staying at The Nest. The child certainly had an imagination. She also possessed, Clara realized, a romantic nature and needed someone to love. Clara did not flatter herself that she could ever be the object of Mary's love in the way Mima had been; it was enough that she was there to look after her. She had heard the child once say to her dolls, 'I shall stay with you and look after you *for ever*.' She was a faithful child.

But why did she particularly want to go to church the following Sunday? She supposed she would eventually learn the reason.

She replied, 'Yes, of course if you want to – what about going to evensong? For a treat?'

'Oh,' Mary looked uncomfortable. 'I think I would rather go to matins, Aunt.'

To matins they went.

The ancient canon who was the vicar of the church was even more inaudible that morning. Clara read her Book of Common Prayer for the Sunday two weeks before Easter, which was quite early, at the end of March that year. Next Sunday, Palm Sunday would have been a better choice. She ought to have known that. She had never been a communicant member of the Church of England. Her mother, and William's, like so many Yorkshire folk, had been a Dissenter. But Mary's own mother had been a pious Anglican so she had felt they owed Mary an upbringing in that faith. Clara's thoughts strayed idly . . . there must have been 'mixed marriages' in the Crowther dynasty if, as Mary had reported last year, Mr Crowther's relations attended this church when they were staying at The Nest.

Just then she felt Mary's attention sharpen. She had been staring round the church, looking at the dark ruby-red windows, but now as they stood up for a hymn she saw her look over in the direction of the velvet curtain that separated two rows of pews on the right side of the nave. There were two heads visible now as they too stood, one male, one female. Mary was looking so intently that she took the child's attention to her hymn-book by thrusting her own in front of her. Mary dropped her glance and joined in the singing of 'Forty Days and Forty Nights'.

Afterwards, as they went out she saw Mary turn her head to observe the two people who were going out by another door at the back.

As she and Mary shuffled along the line of home going worshippers she whispered, 'Who were you staring at?' never one to suppress her curiosity.

Mary whispered back, 'It's Tilly's cousins – I saw one of them before.'

As they came to the porch they saw the two young people join in the crowd at the church gate from a side path.

'She's called Stacey,' offered Mary as they turned down the lane to walk home. It was a clear fine breezy day, already with the scent of spring in the air, and they saw the two figures hurrying on ahead of them, returning to The Nest the quick way.

'Liddy says Stacey is very pretty but very stand-offish and she is going back to Manchester on Tuesday. Is Manchester in Lancashire, like Burnley?'

'Why, yes, it is. Have you met these relations at The Nest yourself?' Clara was never clear how much the children were allowed to roam round the great house and its grounds. There always appeared to be visitors there, or meetings of Mrs Crowther's Ladies' Guild.

'Tilly says she is a friend of their sister but Lottie is not at home at the moment. I haven't spoken to – to Stacey – but I have seen her upstairs.' She did not mention that she had stared at her from behind the door of the little sitting-room.

The way the young woman dressed, and the way she walked, thought Clara, as they almost caught them up before the turning to Cliff House, made her into a fashion plate. Her walk was slow, her upper back straight but with a slight twist of the hips. You did not see women like that very often in the village. The young man was twirling a walking stick.

'He is called Richard,' volunteered Mary in a low voice. 'Tilly says he is quite friendly.'

'And the lady?'

Mary thought for a while. 'I think she is very beautiful. Did my mama look like that?'

'Well I haven't met the young lady face to face,' said Clara.

'They come every year, Tilly says. They might have a garden party next year at The Nest. Perhaps Mrs Crowther will invite you.'

'Your father and I don't visit much,' said Clara. 'Papa is always busy and does not care to entertain.'

'Well, *we* could give a party next Christmas!'

'Parties are a good deal of work, Mary,' replied her aunt. 'I have quite enough to do housekeeping and ordering and shopping and overseeing the maids.' Mary knew there was always a lot of regular cleaning going on in the house. Aunt was always busy too, like her father.

Now that Mary was a little older Clara found she was sometimes tempted to talk to the child as if she was an adult. She had always been what people called unconventional but she must not bring up Mary to feel everything was a burden, or on the other hand to despise the provinces. Mary was what some folk might call an old-fashioned child. It was the way she spoke and the earnestness of her demeanour. Miss Eleanor Hartley might perhaps give her advice. It was time she called to ask how the child was getting on at the little school. Indeed, Miss Hartley was probably the only woman in the locality, apart from dear Hannah in Woolsford, who might understand her, and Hannah was no radical woman, it was just that she had known her all her life.

'I shall do some water-colours this summer if the weather ever holds long enough for me to sketch in the garden,' she said brightly. 'Painting can be such a solace.'

Mary's glimpse of the remote Stacey was to be her only one that year. Instead, at the end of July, there came at last on a visit, at last, Mary's dear Mima, now Mrs Sutcliffe, and with a dear little baby boy, Bobby Sutcliffe, who was almost a year old.

Edwin was about to leave Miss Hartley's class at The Nest to start at his prep school in the following September. Three events took place during that last week of July, two at The Nest, and one at Cliff House.

Miss Hartley had asked permission for her charges to have a picnic in the grounds of The Nest on Edwin's last afternoon, and had also sent a message to Clara and to Mercy Miller's mother.

'I shall be available to discuss the children's work at five o'clock on the last day of term.'

She had already had a chat with Mrs Crowther, which was easier said than done, for that lady was off almost every morning to Calderbrigg or to Woolsford to attend some meeting or committee connected with the Chapel of which she was a trustee. She was only too delighted to leave the responsibility of her daughters' progress to the governess. Her elder girls had not had the benefit of such an efficient teacher and had consequently found themselves ill-equipped to converse with the right type of serious-minded young businessmen with whom their future lay, she hoped. She was pleased to hear that Lydia was a good practical child with healthy outdoor interests and a tolerable knowledge of arithmetic and composition, though her spelling needed attention, and that Matilda was a kind, capable and friendly child who was not frightened of responsibility.

Most of what Miss Hartley had to say about Edwin was known only to her and Edwin's father, Dr Horsfall. He had come himself to The Nest for a short interview with her when she had expressed a wish that Edwin keep up with his interest in languages. He was a clever boy but she knew his father had destined him for medicine. Mary had forgotten about her 'report', as Edwin called it, and was determined to enjoy the afternoon picnic. They were all sorry that Edwin was going away. Why should boys have to go to boarding-school? Most girls were not expected to. Edwin was half sorry, half excited, to be doing something different. He knew there were new subjects he would soon have to master.

Miss Hartley had one of the Crowther maids set down the picnic implements on a rug on the far side of the small lake. Plates and glasses were unpacked on a snowy cloth and the food carried in a hamper by Miss Hartley, helped by Edwin. Mrs Crowther had been invited to attend but had to decline. There was a missionary come to Halifax to speak that very afternoon, an obligatory meeting she could not avoid.

It was a beautifully hot day with a slight breeze ruffling the surface of the little stretch of water, which they now saw from an unusual angle. Lingering in the air was the smell of the hay harvest, for hay was cut late in this northern clime. The sky was for once cloudless.

Edwin however looked gloomy.

'Race you round the lake!' shouted Liddy, who thought she was a better runner than Edwin.

Edwin said, 'I'd rather have a drink of lemonade if I may, Miss Hartley?'

Mercy got up. '*I'll* race you Liddy,' she said. Lydia's face expressed both astonishment and disdain.

'You will all run to the lake and back – running all the way round the lake is too far on such a hot day. But I am afraid there will be no prizes,' said Miss Hartley quickly, realizing that Mercy had better be indulged. It would be awkward when Edwin had left them, for he managed to keep the peace in an odd sort of way. We need more pupils, she thought. But I must also speak to Mary's aunt about her education.

'No handicaps,' she said. 'To the lake and back and then we shall have a peaceful tea.'

When she had lined up all five children on the path behind, waiting for her signal, she paused for a moment, and then: 'Ready, steady, go!'

Mary ran without looking at the others. She was quite quick because she was thin. Mercy, next to her and very much heavier and taller, set off at a thumping pace like a dog released from a trap.

Edwin ran slowly but steadily and was obviously not out of breath when he turned. Tilly plodded on along by Mary's side, not caring who won the silly race. Liddy arrived back at exactly the same moment as Mercy but both the girls were out of breath. Edwin had arrived before them. He said coolly, 'I'd rather a longer race, really,' before sitting down on the rug.

Mary and Tilly had come up last together, smiling. They turned towards each other and held hands.

'That was very well run, the lot of you,' said Miss Hartley. 'Now, some lemonade.'

'They don't let girls run at my sister's school,' said Mercy. The race appeared to have released her tongue.

'You are a good runner,' said the governess.

'May I take off my stockings,' asked Tilly 'I am so hot.'

'We are all hot,' said Edwin. 'At least girls have cotton dresses.'

'You will have to play rugby,' said Liddy. 'At my brothers' school they play as much as they work.'

'Well it is a good thing to remain healthy,' said Miss Hartley. She was at ease with her little band. It would not last. In a few years they would all be so different.

They stayed out until almost five o'clock. As she washed her hands before leaving, Mary saw her aunt's pony and trap on the drive. She had forgotten that Aunt Clara was to have a few words with her teacher before they all broke up.

Tilly came into the little washroom, saying, 'You are to wait with me in the garden. Miss Hartley wants to talk to your aunt. She's here.'

'Yes, I know.'

'She said they wouldn't be long.'

'What did she say about you to your mother?' asked Mary curiously.

'I don't know. Mother never said. I suppose she would say, "Tilly must work harder." '

'She will say I should be neater,' said Mary.

Mercy came in just then.

'Are you going away on holiday?' asked Tilly.

'No – we shall go to London to see my grandmother,' said Mercy.

'Let's all say goodbye to Edwin, shall we?' suggested Tilly.

Mary felt really sorry that he was leaving the class. He had been so helpful ever since that first time at The Nest when she had lost her beads. He was clever too and kept her up to the mark.

Miss Hartley and Clara were together in the schoolroom and the governess was not saying Mary should be neater.

'So you see, she is such a bright child that I do think she should go to a larger school.'

'But she has no sisters to go with. Which school were you thinking of?'

'I know that a school has just opened in Woolsford – quite near my own home as a matter of fact. The train from Lightholme is very reliable. When she is just a little older perhaps? Will you think about it?'

'If she could go with her friend,' said Clara.

'Tilly?'

'Yes, they get along so well together.'

'It might be hard to persuade Mrs Crowther to send Tilly,' said Miss Hartley, lowering her voice. 'But perhaps both Tilly and Liddy might. May I mention to my employer that you are considering sending Mary one day – perhaps when she is ten or eleven?'

Clara could see that a will of iron was hidden under the governess's pleasant manner. She was right though. Mary ought to be properly educated. But the expense?

'You may say that I am considering speaking to her father about it for the future,' answered Clara. 'But what will you do if all your pupils depart?'

'Oh, I have often thought I might just as well teach in Woolsford – they might open a department at this new school for the younger children. As I have said, Mary is doing well, but she is a clever child who needs direction. I wish she might have the benefit of well-qualified teachers one day!'

Clara was thinking, if I were younger and had never married, I might have become like Miss Hartley. What energy she has.

On the way home, after they had all waved to Edwin who was for once going home in his father's carriage, Clara said to Mary, 'Your teacher is very pleased with you.'

'We had a lovely time by the lake – and Tilly and I ran the race together – it was a lovely day. What did she say? That I should be neater?'

'I'm sure you should – but she never said anything about that, just that you are doing very well.'

The second post had arrived whilst Clara was out and there was a letter in the writing of Jemima Sutcliffe on the hallstand. Clara saw it first and revealed its contents only as Mary prepared for bed after

83

her bread and milk. She looked healthily tired.

'Guess who is coming to see you tomorrow – the first day of your holidays.'

Mary looked blank.

'Your Mima is here in the village with her mother and will call round tomorrow – and she has a surprise for you.'

Mary stared at her. 'What?'

'Mima will be here tomorrow.'

Mary looked shocked.

It took her several moments to take in what Aunt Clara had just said. She felt strange, as if there was something wrong about the news. Mima coming?

It had been such a nice day, school finishing for the holidays, and Tilly and she racing together, and now she suddenly felt sad, and she did not understand why.

'Aren't you pleased?' asked Clara.

Mary stared at her. She felt uneasy. When Clara said good-night and left her to go to sleep, Mary was thinking, I wish Mima were here all the time like she used to be. But when she comes tomorrow she won't know about school and Tilly and Miss Hartley and she might feel upset.

It had been a tiring day for Clara. What with the message from Jemima, and the heat, and waiting to see Miss Hartley, and Mary looking so strange at the good news. But she realized, when she thought about it over a glass of sherry, that Mary's upset was quite natural. She did understand, better than Mary could, that she had changed in the last two and half years and that she had probably felt guilty over excluding Mima and thoughts of Mima from her everyday life, which she had had to do in order to get over parting from her.

Mima however was a sensible girl and Clara did not doubt she would find a way round the difficulty. It was perhaps not an ideal time to make this visit. Leaving it a little longer would have allowed Mary to be thoroughly weaned from her substitute mama, but doubtless it was better got over. One day Mary would be old enough to feel only gratitude, without feeling guilty and still perhaps deep down a little angry over her Mima's abandoning her.

In the event, what might have been a disaster was saved by the 'surprise'.

Clara had told Mima that she was a visitor now and to ring at the front door when she called the next afternoon. The first Mary had heard from upstairs where she had been having her hair brushed by Annie was a: 'Well I never – isn't he lovely!' from Cook, who was coming back from the shops. Mary rushed to the banister and peeped down, feeling suddenly shy.

And there was Mima, her Mima, with a little baby boy in her arms.

'That's the surprise,' said Aunt Clara softly, and she went down the stairs hand in hand with Mary.

On seeing them, Mima put the baby into Annie's arms, opened her own arms and cried 'Mary! Here I am, love!'

Mary rushed to her and the baby started yelling and Mary said, 'Is he yours?' and Mima said, 'He's my Bobby, aren't you, love, and took the baby back and showed him to the little girl.

Mary said, 'Can I hold him?'

She felt both sad and happy, and it was obvious that Mima did too for she was smiling although there were tears in her eyes. Clara said, 'I'll leave you together,' and went to order tea.

After that, a vigorous eleven-month-old baby who has just learned how to crawl leaves little opportunity for either peaceful chat or sorrowful reminiscence.

'Now I've got Bobby to look after, but you'll always be my little lass,' whispered Mima and gave Mary a big kiss. Mary kissed her back. Strangely enough she felt very grown up as they sat on the sofa until Bobby wanted to jump off it.

When you got married you had babies, Mary knew that. Mima looked happy, though she looked different as well, fatter.

'Eh, I remember when you were his age,' said Mima taking the bull by the horns. 'You didn't crawl so quick – but you were about the same size.'

Mary was entranced. It was clear that Bobby needed Mima and Mima alone. She felt old and grown up, especially when Bobby smiled at her and she held his fat little hands. Then he crawled round the room and Mary went after him, which made him laugh. Clara heard them and knew that Mima had worked her magic. It would be hard when she left.

'And tell me what you've been doing – how you're getting on at The Nest,' said Mima in a comparatively quiet moment.

'Miss Hartley is all right and my best friend is Tilly and we have lots of lessons. Did you get my letter?'

'Aye I did – and I'm sorry I hadn't time to answer it but Sam had the chance to come over to see his old boss, so I said I'd come along of him to see my Mam – and you. Well, Mary you've grown, lass.'

Annie came in with a tray – tea for Mima and Clara and milk for Mary.

'It's right kind of Yeranty to give me a cup,' said Mima to Mary.

Mary didn't know whether to say she didn't call her that now, but Clara overheard as she came in and just smiled. She knew that her brother would not have invited the young woman into the small sitting-room, but the afternoons were her province and Mima was more than a servant.

'When you've had your tea I thought you might like to see the old nursery again. We've had it repainted – but there are some of Mary's old toys there that your baby might like,' she said.

'Do you mind if I give him a drink of water first?' asked Mima. 'It's a hot day and he gets right thirsty. I can get it from the kitchen.'

She produced a little cup with a bone handle from a capacious bag.

'Oh, let me get it,' said Mary.

When she was out of the room Clara said, 'She's got over your going, I think, though I know she still misses you – but she's a strong character and her new friends at The Nest have done her a power of good.'

'And how nice she writes. I knew she'd be all right in the end,' said Mima. 'I miss her too but the little one – well, it's a busy life.' She did not add that another baby was expected at Christmas. Yeranty wasn't the sort of person you could tell that to but she might whisper it to Mary.

'My, how she's grown!' she said again. Then she recollected herself. 'We never gave you the photograph that man took of us all at the feast,' she said. 'Mam had to wait for it at Toothill's. I've brought it to show you – there was only one copy – so I thought if you didn't mind I'd like to keep it for our album.'

Mary returned with a cup of water on a tray and was shown the precious photograph of a solemn-looking threesome, Mary in front, Sam and Mima behind her, all of them in front of what looked like a big tree.

'It's true – you *have* grown,' said Clara.

Mary thought she looked like a very little girl. She hardly recognized herself.

'Thank you for showing us,' said Clara. 'Mary would be pleased to be in your album, wouldn't you, dear?'

Mary said. '*You* look different too, Mima.' She couldn't put her finger on what had changed.

Mima put the photograph back in an envelope in her big bag that contained her purse, a bottle for Bobby, a clean face-cloth and a small parcel, and Mary began to play peek-a-boo with the little boy. She felt a bit shy of Mima now.

'Her governess thinks she should go to a girls' high school when she's ten or eleven,' confided Clara. She felt she could say that to Jemima Green who, although uneducated, would feel that only the best should be Mary's. And also, though the woman had been technically a servant, paid a weekly wage by her brother, she had shared Mary's first six years in a way nobody else had.

'I knitted her a pair of gloves for her next birthday,' said Mima. 'It was while I was knitting for Bobby but I didn't want to post them. I thought, I'll take them with me and she can have them on her next birthday. I hope they'll be big enough.'

She fished inside the big bag and presented Clara with a small parcel wrapped in tissue. The baby saw all this and made a grab for the parcel.

'Now, Bobby, behave yourself.'

Clara hastily put the present under a cushion. The baby set up a wailing.

'You give him the drink,' said Mima to Mary.

Mary bent down and tried to pick up the large baby but he was too heavy for her. Mima seized him, and placed him on Mary's lap, saying proudly, 'He can drink from a cup now.'

Mary felt the warm heavy little body and liked the sensation. He dribbled a lot but drank the water all up.

'Oh, I wish I could look after him!' she said. 'I don't know any other babies.'

Mima thought she looked a real little mother.

When the time came for the two to leave, Mima pushing a little cart with high sides that Sam had made, it was still warm, and the air in the garden was heavy with the scent of roses. Mary impulsively picked a pink rose and said shyly,

'Please have it, Mima, and you can press it in a book.'

'I've still got your ring!' said Mima, making Mary remember the beads, but they didn't seem to matter so much now. Mary held out the rose and looked at Mima with big round eyes. The baby saved the day once again, trying to stand up holding his mother's long skirt.

'May Bobby have a nasturtium to hold?' Mary asked her. What a thoughtful child she was, and so grown up.

The way Mary had given Mima the rose spoke volumes – it was what you might call a sadly resigned gesture, thought Clara.

Mima put the child down on the path and gave Mary a big hug.

'There now – I'll come again – can't say when exactly but I'm sure you'll be so big I shan't recognize you!'

'You *will* recognize me Mima, won't you?' said Mary.'

'I was teasing,' Mima replied, scooping up Bobby who wanted to crawl on the path.

'Oh, I forgot,' she said, as she took hold of the pram. 'Sam sends his regards and if you are ever over in Burnley, you know who'd like to see you even if you're a grown up lady by then!'

CHAPTER SIX

By the time Clara had presented the red gloves to Mary on her ninth birthday the following February, Mima's visit seemed to have taken place years ago. Classes at The Nest were still interesting but Mary and Tilly missed the presence of Edwin. Without him they both felt less cheerful. Liddy refused to play with them and went off with Mercy Miller saying they were babyish. Mary did not like Mercy. During lessons Mercy would whisper behind her hand to Liddy. Liddy would not reveal what they were talking about even to her sister. She said it was a secret. Tilly said their secrets were silly. Mary was puzzled. She had the feeling the secrets might not be pleasant ones. Even Miss Hartley noticed how 'thick' Liddy and Mercy were and often told Mercy to turn round and get on with her work, though not really in a cross voice. Mercy did not work very hard but Miss Hartley sighed more over Liddy's handwriting and arithmetic.

Well, if Liddy and Mercy did not want their company, Tilly and Mary pretended they did not care and spent a lot of time talking about the books they were reading. They also wrote little notes to each other, which they would hand over when lessons were over for the day. Both of them read the story of *Jan of the Windmill*, which Tilly had been given for Christmas. Mary lent her friend *The Water Babies*, a present from her father, and they also devoured *A Peep behind the Scenes*. Mary had read *Little Women* three times and for her birthday in February Aunt Clara gave Mary *Little Women Grown Up* which some people called *Good Wives*. If *Black Beauty* had made both her and Tilly cry, the death of Beth now elicited even more tears.

'It's so sad,' said Mary to Aunt Clara's anxious enquiries when she found her niece crying over it one Saturday afternoon in April.

'Well, it's only a story,' said Clara. 'Go and find Tilly and see if you may go for a walk round the lake. It's a lovely day and you can't spend all your time with your nose in a book.'

This became the pattern of Mary's Saturdays. She would go over to The Nest to find Tilly or Tilly would come over and meet her in the lane and they would 'explore'. Aunt Clara had no objection to their exploring the grounds provided they told her if they intended to leave the grounds of The Nest and walk to the village. Hodgson and Annie both intimated that young ladies should spend more time at home sewing. They did not say this to her aunt, only to Mary. Mary very much disliked sewing even if you could use coloured silks for embroidery, and she was not a young lady either.

One Saturday afternoon in May, Tilly was to accompany her mother and sisters to a sale of work at the Calderbrigg chapel for which, much to Tilly's disgust, they had been asked to make penholders and pin-cushions. Mary was not invited. The Crowther children were to be honoured guests at the event, and Mary, as a non-chapel-goer, could not join them. She decided to go for a walk by herself round the lake. Aunt Clara need not know that Tilly was not with her.

This was to be a very important afternoon for Mary. Tilly had mentioned that there were to be some of her parents' friends staying over at The Nest and that they would be attending the chapel sale of work. Mary did not expect that there would be anyone interesting. She had seen the Crowther carriage go smartly along the drive on its way to the big gates on the road. She turned into the lane at the back and ran down the grassy slope towards the lake. On level ground she picked a few flowers – milkmaids, and large daisies that had escaped from the garden, to make a bunch for Clara, as a peace-offering should her aunt discover she had been alone. Someone else, a lady with an open parasol, was walking alone round the lake on the far side. It was a figure that appeared strangely familiar.

Mary stopped suddenly. She was sure it was Stacey, the lady she had glimpsed in church and at The Nest, but Tilly had not said that she might be one of the weekend visitors.

Dare she catch her up and speak to her? The lady was walking very slowly and as Mary watched her she approached the summer-house and sat down on a bench inside. She might as well pass by the little summer-house? She could say *good afternoon*. She walked along the edge of the lake by the laurel-bushes and the rhododendrons and the headstone of the dog's grave that Tilly had once shown her, and wandered in the direction of the summer-house though it disappeared for a moment behind the tiny island in the lake. Tilly said Miss

Hartley's pupils would be allowed to take the skiff to the island when they could all swim.

Mary's feet dragged a little when she found herself only a few yards from the summer-house, and she stopped for a minute and looked back. Then she felt a prickle on the back of her neck and was sure that the person sitting on the bench was looking at her. She turned round and approached her.

Yes, it *was* Stacey Watson, she could have recognized her anywhere. There was an old notice on one of the walls of the lane that said TRESPASSERS WILL BE PROSECUTED. The lady might think she was trespassing. She must be polite.

'Good afternoon, Miss Watson,' she said. The lady was sitting motionlessly, staring at her, but now she looked startled.

'Who are you?' she asked.

'I am a friend of Tilly,' said Mary, 'and she lets me walk round here.'

'Really? Does your mother let you wander alone?' asked Miss Watson in a sharp voice.

'My mother is dead,' said Mary, and then felt uncomfortable. 'My aunt knows I play here with Tilly, but this afternoon Tilly has gone to the chapel sale of work in Calderbrigg.'

'Indeed,' said Miss Watson. 'How do you know my name?'

'Tilly told me,' said Mary. She did not like to say she had already seen her in church and on the lane. It might sound a bit rude, as though she had been spying on her.

'And what are *you* called?'

'Mary Settle. I live over there.' She pointed behind her to the lane. 'At Cliff House. I have lessons here with Tilly.'

'Well, sit down and amuse me,' said the lady.

Close to, she looked about the same age as Tilly's sister Lottie who, Mary knew, was to have her twenty-first birthday next year. Mary wondered why she had not accompanied the family to the sale of work, but it must be because she went to church, not chapel.

'They wanted me to go along with them,' said Miss Watson, 'But I do not care for such things.'

'You have to take things you have made – like needle-cases,' said Mary.

'Well I do not make needle-cases,' said Miss Watson. 'How old are you, Mary?'

'I'm nine – like Tilly.'

'And you are great friends?'

'Oh yes – she is my *best* friend.'

'You share her governess?'

'Yes – we have Miss Hartley.'

Miss Watson yawned behind her hand. There was a silence.

'It's so warm, I think I shall go in,' she said. Mary wanted to ask her how long she was staying at The Nest. She was a very beautiful person, she thought. Her hair was dark and her face very smooth. The hat she was wearing today was one of straw with a purple flower on the brim.

Miss Watson got up. 'I expect the others will be back soon.'

She put up the parasol, which was lying on the bench next to her.

'It is important that the sun does not burn your face,' she said very seriously. 'Remember that.'

She stood up. Mary got up too. Should she curtsy, shake hands?

'Goodbye then, Mary, I expect I may see you at The Nest before I return home.'

Mary was thrilled. Would the lady tell Mrs Crowther she had met a strange girl in the grounds? No, she didn't think she would, and in any case she knew her name, and Mrs Crowther would surely not mind that she came over to The Nest by herself?

Stacey Watson walked away holding her pale-mauve parasol stiffly above her head. She did not look back once. Mary made her way home in a daze.

On Monday Mary asked Tilly about the sale of work.

'Oh, there was a concert,' replied Tilly. 'There were a lot of poor children who sang very well. Mother was pleased.'

'Quiet now, children,' said Miss Hartley. 'I have something to tell you.'

There was a shuffling of feet. Liddy looked out of the window. Mercy sniggered and Tilly looked embarrassed. Mary looked up expectantly.

'We are to have a visitor this morning who would like to see the work you are doing. Just carry on as usual. Get out your arithmetic exercise-books. Remember, last week we were adding and subtracting fractions. Today I shall teach you how to multiply and divide them.'

'At least it's not hundredweights and tons,' muttered Liddy.

'Or rods, poles and perches,' giggled Mercy.

Mary rather liked the idea of rods and poles and perches and always imagined a man, probably a gardener, striding along with a long pole, which he stood upright. A big bird then perched on the pole and . . .

92

'Mary, you are wool-gathering,' said Miss Hartley. 'I asked you a question. We have to revise last week's work if we are to learn about what more we can do with fractions. Now we shall go through the addition of one third and one quarter. Would you come to the blackboard?'

Mary's arithmetic was not bad, certainly better than Tilly's. She recollected herself, went up to the blackboard and took the chalk Miss Hartley handed to her.

'Now what do we write underneath?' asked the governess when Mary had carefully written 1 over 3 and 1 over 4.

'The lowest common denominator,' said Mary remembering the strange phrase.

'And what is that?'

'Er – twelve,' replied Mary.

'Yes, we can divide twelve by both three and four so we put a twelve underneath and then what do we do? Tilly?'

'I'm sorry, I've forgotten.'

'Mercy then?'

'Divide twelve by three which makes four and then divide it by four which makes three,' answered Mercy who was not apparently paying much attention.

'What next? Liddy?'

'Add three and four,' whispered Mercy.

'Add three and four,' repeated Liddy.

'Which makes?'

'Seven,' said Liddy, frowning.

'Seven over twelve then, so the answer is. . . ?'

'Seven twelfths,' said Mary and wrote the answer on the blackboard.

'So one third and one quarter make seven twelfths? Liddy?'

'Yes, I think so.'

'You only *think* so? Are you quite sure?'

'Yes,' said Liddy, with a glance at Mercy.

'Here are a few more sums for you to practise in your exercise books. Then I shall show you how to multiply and divide the same two numbers.'

They were all bent over their work when there was a tap at the door. It opened and Mrs Crowther stood there with someone else behind her. It was a rare occurrence for Mrs Crowther to attend a class, but yesterday she had thought her bored guest might see the children at work.

Mary looked up as Stacey Watson entered the room. Today she was wearing a sky-blue cotton gown. Why would she want to see the schoolroom?

Mrs Crowther more or less pushed her in as Miss Hartley, a trifle pink-cheeked, stood up.

'Would you like to sit down? There is a chair at the back. Tilly – please show your guest.'

'Thank you,' said Stacey graciously as she was led to a chair at the back. Miss Hartley got up then and spoke in a low voice to her visitor, which betrayed none of the annoyance she was feeling.

'They are learning fractions this morning. I'm afraid you will not find it very interesting.'

'It's true my interests are more *historical*,' replied Stacey.

'Well, we shall have some history this afternoon.'

Miss Hartley went back to her seat and the girls tried to appear as if they were concentrating. Mary was agog and excited. It was wonderful to see the lady again so soon. She must show her best work to her, especially if she came to listen to history. If only she had still been at the blackboard when Miss Watson came in.

Miss Hartley wondered whether the young woman was just bored.

Liddy and Mercy were giggling again.

'Shush,' said Miss Hartley. 'I shall go through your notebooks in a moment but first I shall explain how to multiply a third by a quarter, and then how to divide it.'

Stacey Watson gave the appearance of hanging on her every word.

The governess went on with her explanation, drawing the procedures on the blackboard. Tilly was then asked up to try to multiply three quarters by one third and made a mess of it, confusing the addition with the multiplication.

'Cancel out the two threes,' said the governess, 'then multiply across, and you will have' – she went up to the blackboard – 'One quarter. Remember that. In fractions *of* means *multiply*. A third of three quarters is one quarter, is it not?'

'I never understood that,' said a voice at the back. 'You make it sound so simple!'

Did she wish to attempt a sum herself? Miss Hartley wondered sardonically.

'Now we shall have to leave the division until tomorrow,' she said, a faint smile on her lips.

'You turn it upside down to divide,' said Mercy in a bored voice.

'You may go out now, children,' said the governess.

Mary looked back at Miss Watson, who was looking at her. She smiled, and Miss Watson surely smiled back?

Miss Hartley gathered up her books and waited for her guest to follow her. Mary could not linger any longer. She must discuss the visitor with Tilly, for she had not yet mentioned her Saturday meeting.

Tilly however did not seem to want a long talk about Stacey Watson.

'I don't like her,' she stated. 'I heard Mother tell Father she had done her best to make Miss Watson feel at home, but Miss Watson never wanted to talk to her. She wouldn't come with us on Saturday to chapel, and she never says anything to me. I don't know why she bothers coming here.'

Now was Mary's chance to tell her friend about her own exciting Saturday adventure but now she didn't want to. Instead, she said, 'I saw her in church last year so perhaps if she's church she wouldn't want to visit chapel?'

Tilly said, 'Lottie told Jim she only went to church to walk back with our cousin Cedric!'

Mary thought how exciting it must be to live in a family with so many interesting things to talk about.

'I wonder why she wanted to see us with Miss Hartley,' she ventured.

'Oh, that was Mother's idea and she couldn't say "No", though Lottie said she was furious. She said that Mother wanted to encourage her to become a governess.'

'Well she seemed to like being with us. She was smiling.'

'She's going home tomorrow, thank goodness. I quite liked her last year but she's not been at all friendly this time.'

'I think she is very beautiful though,' said Mary.

Miss Watson did not visit the schoolroom in the afternoon. Mary kept looking out of the window to see if she was walking in the garden but there was no sight of her. She was convinced that Miss Watson was unhappy. She might have some terrible secret, or be like Meg in *Little Women* who was in love with a young man, and be frightened of telling anyone about it. Perhaps Miss Watson was really in love with Tilly's brother Jim. During the afternoon lesson, which Miss Hartley changed to geography instead of history, maybe because Miss Watson was not there, Mary thought about being a governess. She might rather like to be one. Aunt Clara said that governesses had usually 'fallen on hard times' and needed the money. Father was always talking about money to Mr Gordon, so possibly one day she would need to be one herself. Miss Hartley had once told them that ladies' colleges had been opened in Cambridge and Oxford where girls might go when they were about eighteen and learn just as men did. Miss Hartley was too old to do that, she supposed. Were men ever governesses? On the way home that afternoon Mary hung back a little in case Stacey Watson appeared. She would tell Tilly one day that Miss Watson knew she was her best friend.

She found she was day-dreaming about Miss Watson over her tea, was imagining looking after her and making her less lonely and unhappy. She did not know how she knew but she was sure that Stacey Watson was unhappy.

As time went by, Mary's day-dreams became more vivid since they now involved the beautiful Miss Watson. She dared not ask Tilly if and when the young lady might visit The Nest again, for she was shy of revealing these exciting new feelings. It would be her special secret. The only person she might tell would be Mima. Miss Watson's not being there allowed her to make up stories about her, and in these stories Mary gave herself a starring part. She imagined long conversations by the lake, and invented a long drama which involved skating on the lake, and saving the lady from drowning. That she could not swim did not seem to matter, for in the stories you told yourself you might do anything. Once, she had made up tales about her dolls but it was much more satisfactory to think about a real person you might look after. In the meantime real life went on much as usual.

Stacey did not visit The Nest again that year. At Christmas, Mary's father had a bad bout of bronchitis that weakened him. He was warned by Dr Horsfall to take things more easily. Around the time of Mary's tenth birthday Miss Hartley spoke once again to Clara about the possibility of Mary's attending the new school in Woolsford. Clara did not want to worry her brother too much at this time and decided to wait until the summer to have a word with him. She knew that Mary would be much happier in a new school if she could be accompanied by Tilly, yet even Liddy, who was older, was still being taught by a governess. Would Mr and Mrs Crowther think Woolsford Girls' High School a good idea? Mercy Miller was a different proposition. Clara knew Mary did not like the child and would not want to leave The Nest, and Tilly, to go to Woolsford with Mercy. It was quite likely however that Mercy's father would want his daughter to go to school. He was a professional man and the school catered mainly, according to Hannah, who had made enquiries, for the daughters of such men. Clara shied away from discussing plans with Mercy's mother, whom she did not know very well. She would discuss the school with Mrs Crowther after she had spoken to William. Thus matters rested until the summer of Mary's eleventh year. It was William who reopened the subject. Dr Horsfall must have frightened him for in the month of June he began to try to return home a little earlier from work. His chest appeared to have settled down though he looked tired.

'I ought to take a little walk with Mary now and then,' he said. 'I don't seem to have had time for my daily constitutional for some time.'

It was in fact years since he had walked for pleasure, so Clara agreed heartily with his suggestion. It was a lovely summer, beautiful in the early morning and just the right temperature for a walk in the evening.

Mary was surprised when after breakfast one morning, just as she was getting ready for her walk over to The Nest, her head full of whether perhaps this weekend Stacey Watson might come for a visit – Tilly had mentioned something of the sort – her father said, 'Come for a little stroll with me, dear, after work. Would you like that? We might go over to the farm.'

'Oh,yes, they're making hay over in the field behind the lake at The Nest – we might watch them.'

She had been going to suggest they helped Farmer Hoyle but then realized her father would not want to do that. He kept his distance from the farmer and his workers, though she had noticed that Tilly's father always talked to him.

She was waiting for him in the garden after her tea and before his supper. She still did not come down to eat with her father and aunt at seven o'clock but had her high tea at five and in summer often played in the garden afterwards.

It was a golden evening when they set off together. He was wearing his panama hat and had taken his walking-stick from the hall. Mary was wearing her old calico school-dress so it would not matter if she climbed walls or pushed though long grass. She had taken off her pinafore and brushed her hair in his honour. One of her day-dreams – one she had discarded – had been that her father might meet Miss Watson and fall in love with her. It had not been satisfactory because she had quickly realized that Miss Watson would then be her stepmother, who might be expected to 'look after' her. She certainly did not want a stepmother, and as far as Miss Watson was concerned she knew that she herself would rather do the 'looking after'. Miss Watson was not the sort of lady who would enjoy looking after people; she was sure of that.

'You can lead the way,' said her father, suddenly jovial. Why did he so seldom want to be with her? They walked across the small field that adjoined the Hall garden, in the direction of her usual walk to the lane. But then Mary turned left, where there was a slight rise in the land, with the walls of The Nest on the other side behind long grass. The farm was down further on their left in a dell with fields rising from it. When Hoyle made hay on the other side of the wall he took his cart across through a five-barred gate and went on to the old pastureland abutting The Nest.

'I was told that all this land once belonged to the farm,' her father said, puffing a little.

'Are you tired?' Mary asked him anxiously.

'No, no – I'm just not used to walking on a lane rather than a road. Your mother used to walk here, you know. She loved to climb the slope and look back though the trees to The Nest – that was when other folk lived there. They owned Cliff House too – and let it out before they sold it to me. Old Walker had a lot of brass at one time but his son didn't want to go on living here – went abroad, I think.'

They both stopped now at the stile at the top and leaned against the wall. Mary was fascinated. Her father had never mentioned her mother to her like this before. As if she had been just an ordinary woman who liked going for walks. Even walks that needed a bit of a climb. She couldn't have been an invalid then, could she? Mary wanted to ask him, 'Did I kill Mama?' but her tongue could not form those words. There was the tiniest breeze, and the sun was still golden and the beech trees the brightest, freshest green.

'She used to gather bluebells down there.' He pointed down the slope on the farmer's side of the wall where there was a little copse. 'When we had her picture painted she asked the painter to put blue-bells in the background. Have you noticed?'

He was talking to her as if she was a grown-up. If only she could grow up quickly now and then he might be like this all the time. There was so much she wanted to ask him about her mother.

'Aye, well,' he said, recollecting himself. 'I wanted to ask you if you'd like to go to school in Woolsford next year. Clara – your aunt – says your Miss Hartley says you're a clever lass. I'm sorry I haven't met her myself – left all that to your aunt – but I've nothing against a lass learning a bit more than they used to – and – I think I could manage it.' She knew he meant manage to find the money. But would Tilly go as well?

'Doctor Horsfall's niece – older than the lad you went to school with—'

'You mean Edwin's cousin Mildred,' supplied Mary.

'Aye, well, Horsfall tells me she goes to the new school in Woolsford your aunt's friend Mrs Hardcastle told us about – and your teacher said something too, I believe—'

'I *would* like to go to school,' said Mary, 'If Tilly – Matilda – could come too.'

'Ah, Matilda – that would be one of Mr Crowther's girls?'

'Yes – my best friend.'

'Well, I don't know about that but I expect your aunt could make enquiries.'

'Some girls the Crowthers know go away to boarding-school,' said Mary.'

'I don't think I agree with that,' he said, wiping his brow with a large pocket-handkerchief.

'No,' she said hurriedly, 'I don't want to go away, Father, but I'd like to – learn things – if Tilly was there too.'

'Well, we'll see,' he said, 'I think we've come far enough – we've to walk back.'

They walked back together companionably, not saying much now. Mary was thrilled. He seemed quite a different person from the father she was used to.

It was a golden evening; she was sure she'd remember it. Her father talking to her like this was such a – such a – treat. She smiled up at him and on an impulse put her hand in his.

Mary *was* to remember that walk with her father taken when she was eleven years old.

Afterwards, Aunt Clara had said she hoped he'd do it more often. But it was not repeated. Business soon took over again and William did not go with his daughter and sister and Mrs Hardcastle later that summer for a few days in Ilkley. On Clara's urging he did however speak to Miss Hartley in July. It turned out she had already taken it upon herself to advise the Crowthers to send their daughters to Woolsford High School in the New Year. She had been offered a post there herself to teach the younger children the following spring, and the Crowthers realized they would have to make new arrangements for their youngest daughters in any case. Nothing was said to the Crowther children or Mary about this for the time being, but Mary sensed something was in the wind.

In the autumn of 1886 Mary was not thinking so much about a new school. Her thoughts were concentrated upon Miss Stacey Watson, for Tilly had informed her that the young woman was about to make a flying visit to The Nest.

'Miss Watson's going to marry a man called Richard Jowett – Lottie told me,' Tilly confided to Mary one Monday morning. Mary was agog. 'I thought you'd like to know,' Tilly went on, 'She's coming over with her "fi-an-say" on Saturday.'

Tilly was not unobservant and had realized her friend was fascinated by their father's difficult cousin.

'Her what?'

'It's what they call it when they're engaged to be married,' Tilly explained. 'Ages ago, before my sister Florence got married, they called Basil her fi-an-say – and then he was her husband.'

'Will she be staying long?' asked Mary, hoping she might sneak over the wall and see her.

'I don't know.'

Liddy, overhearing them, said, 'Mother says Richard Jowett is very nice. They'll only come for the week-end, 'cos they're going to visit his mother in York.'

Mary haunted The Nest on the following Saturday but saw nobody. She continued to think of Stacey Watson almost every night before going to sleep. In private she called Miss Watson her Dream Queen. On the Saturday night she sent herself to sleep imagining that she was asked to be a special maid or companion to the lady when she was married. She would look after her baby if she had one and watch over her. . . .

Miss Watson was not in church on the Sunday morning; perhaps this Richard was not the young man who had been with her before? On Sunday afternoon Mary told Clara that Tilly wanted her to go over for tea, knowing that her aunt would not check, and that her father had gone to see Hamish Gordon, even though it was the Lord's Day.

She could hide behind the bushes in the large Nest gardens or under the trees that grew around the lake. She *must* try to see her again. The idea of her getting married had brought back the feelings she had had when Mima got wed, and although she did not know Miss Watson the way she had known Mima, she still felt vaguely upset. Tilly had said they were to honeymoon abroad and Mercy Miller had giggled.

A mellow sun was bathing everything in its warm low beams that afternoon when she set off for her pretended tea-party. Once over the wall she lingered among the beech trees that had not yet lost all their leaves and were still a mingled green and gold. In the distance she could see several people walking up and down on the lawn in front of the conservatories and could even hear their voices. The autumn sunshine had got everyone outside. Tilly and her sister were not there. They would be at Sunday school, she thought. Mr Crowther was walking with a friend. It was odd watching them when they did not know she was there and it made her feel slightly uncomfortable.

But then a lady and a man came out of a little side-door and strolled round to the back of the house.

It was Miss Watson – she would know her anywhere. Mary walked round by the trees to that end of the mansion and waited. From here she could see the summer-house set back just a little on the slope to the lake. Perhaps the couple would go and sit there.

Nothing happened for a very long time, at least twenty minutes, and she was just thinking about going back home when she heard a voice from over in the direction of the conservatory. A young man appeared. He seemed to be pleading with the person inside for he had one shoulder up and an arm stretched out before him, the palm of his hand curved as he spoke. Mary, whose hearing was excellent, distinctly heard: ' No – leave me – I need a rest – you get on my nerves.'

The man backed out of the greenhouse. He stood there continuing to speak, waited and then turned and walked slowly back out of the conservatory to the house door. After a few minutes Stacey Watson came out. She adjusted her hair and picked a speck off her coat-dress. This time she was not holding a parasol. She walked quite quickly in the direction of the lake. Now was Mary's opportunity. She slid down the slope to the summer-house and sneaked inside. It still smelled a little damp after the previous week's rain. She had not long to wait for she heard the tittuping of heeled shoes on the stone-flagged path, their owner now walking in the direction of the little summer-house. Then there stood Miss Watson, looking over the lake and murmuring something to herself. Mary was now hoping she would not turn round and see her. It was too late. Stacey twirled her skirt, turned and came face to face with Mary, who continued to sit on the summer-house bench.

'What are *you* doing here?' asked Miss Watson in an astonished voice.

'I came for a walk,' said Mary weakly. 'I was feeling a bit – tired so I thought I might just rest a minute – but I'm going now.'

She stood up.

The lady did not look cross, which Mary had expected, but amused.

'You appear to haunt the place,' she said and sat down herself.

Now Mary wanted to say that she knew Miss Watson was to be married but her throat was so dry she could not get out a word. She swallowed.

'Do they know you are here?' asked Stacey, tilting her head towards the house.

Mary took a long look at her. It would be the last time she'd ever see her, she thought and this sight would be the one she must remember when she wanted to think about her.

At last she said, ' No – I was just on a walk.'

'I saw you doing your sums,' said Stacey conversationally.

'Yes.' Then in a rush Mary went on, 'I hope you will be happy – Tilly told me . . .'

The lady looked at her long and hard. 'How old are you now?'

'I'm eleven. Please don't tell Mrs Crowther I was here. I just wanted to see you but my aunt will be wondering where I am.'

Her voice trailed away. Miss Watson looked at her and said, 'It can be our secret then.'

Her words made Mary feel overjoyed.

'Well, I suppose I had better find my fiancé,' said Stacey, and got up.'

She seems like a girl, thought Mary, not like a lady about to be married. As far as people about to be married were concerned she had only her memory of Mima to go by and Mima had appeared *much* older. She wondered what this 'fiancé' was like. He must have been the man in the conservatory.

The lady put out her hand. She was not wearing gloves so Mary took it and shook it awkwardly. 'There – you have wished me luck. I shall tell Richard our secret – nobody else.'

'Was that the gentleman you were talking to?'

'Little Miss Curiosity! You were spying on us!'

'No, I wasn't – I only wanted to see *you*—'

'Well, now you have, and I shall go in and have a cup of tea.'

Mary looked down at the ground and then up at her and what she saw was an expression she could not put a name to. Then the lady laughed.

'Off you go. Thank you for taking such an interest in my welfare.'

The lady turned on her heel and walked quite quickly away.

Mary was thus dismissed.

For the Christmas of 1886 Mary received a copy of *Through the Looking Glass*. She had tried to read *Alice in Wonderland* when she was eight but had not found it easy. This book was much nicer; perhaps it was because she was older, though parts of it puzzled her. She liked the White Knight best, though curiously enough his song made her feel sad, unlike Alice in the book.

It had been decided that in the New Year Mary and the two Crowther girls, along with Mercy Miller, would start at Woolsford High School. The decision seemed very sudden to Mary, who did not know her father and aunt had been over one evening to see Tilly and Liddy's father. By the time she and Tilly had their twelfth birthdays in February they would be genuine schoolgirls.

'Mrs Crowther tells me that Tilly and Liddy will probably go away to boarding school in a year or two,' Aunt Clara said. Mary did not want to think about that. Perhaps it would never happen. For the present, Tilly would be in the same form as Mary. Girls were however divided into smaller classes for some of the lessons, and she was to discover that Mercy Miller would – unfortunately – be with her all the time, whilst Tilly would not. For the first weeks of the spring term all three were to take the train to the city accompanied by a servant from The Nest, and were to be met in Woolsford by Aunt Clara's friend Mrs Hardcastle. Hannah had willingly offered her services to make sure they were all put on the horse bus that went up the hill to the school. After a few weeks they would be allowed to make the journey by themselves.

It was all a great adventure.

Miss Hartley did not teach them any longer; she had started to teach some younger classes at the school. Everything was strange and new. Mary thought she would never get used to it all, but by the summer she could not imagine not being a high school girl. Alas for Mary, the syllabus would for the time being include needlework lessons, but she was put in the class that started French and Latin, which made up for her bad marks in sewing.

Mary was shooting up in height that year, though she was still not tall. When Mima Sutcliffe's mother, Mrs Green, died, Mima came over for her funeral in the summer and visited Cliff House again, as she had promised. She declared that very soon Mary would be taller than she was. She had brought two children with her this time, Bobby, who was now nearly five, and his little sister, Louise Mary.

'The "Mary's" after you, love,' said Mima.

As Mary cuddled the little girl, she saw Mima looking at her carefully. She knew that Mima had not forgotten that she had once cuddled *her* like that. *She* had not forgotten either.

When Mary was thirteen, Tilly and Liddy left Woolsford High School for a boarding-school near Harrogate, but Mary still saw Tilly in the holidays, and they wrote to each other in term-time. She did miss going over to The Nest. Tilly was still her best friend, and Tilly reciprocated, in spite of all her smart new friends. *You will always be my best friend, Mary*, she wrote.

One day in the summer holidays of 1888 when they had gone for a walk together in the grounds of The Nest and were sitting by the lake, Tilly told her casually that Stacey Watson, or rather Stacey Jowett, who had been married less than two years, had had some disagreement with her husband and had gone back to live in Southport.

Mary still thought about Miss Watson, her Dream Queen, and could still remember how she had felt in those days, even if she had only been a little girl then not a fourth-form schoolgirl. She cherished especially the memory of that autumn Sunday when she had gone over to The Nest and seen the young man with Miss Watson outside the conservatory, making that curious pleading gesture. That was before the couple were married, of course.

Tilly added only, 'Mother says it was a mismatch.' Mary was puzzled. What could people do if they married the wrong person?

Later that year autumn winds raged across the moors and there were even floods down in Calderbrigg. Mary and Tilly were back once more at their different schools when William Settle, who had been recently diagnosed with angina pectoris, the 'business man's disease', had a sudden heart attack at work. There was nothing anyone could do, and he died from a second attack a week or so later.

This was the effective end of Mary's childhood.

PART THREE

YOUTH AND MARRIAGE

CHAPTER SEVEN

The will had been read and William buried in the old churchyard. Clara explained to a bemused Mary why she thought it better for them to move away for a time. William Settle had left very little liquid cash, the firm having gone from bad to worse, but Cliff House was left to Mary, her property once she was twenty-one. It had been her dead mother's money that had partly paid for it, and it was not mortgaged. Clara suggested she might let the place as a good source of income, and move to a terrace house in Woolsford. She had her own investments and would pay for whatever Mary needed until she attained her majority, but Lightholme was a popular place for successful businessmen, and so they would have no difficulty in finding tenants.

'We might as well have some money coming in whilst we can. I could just manage financially, but I don't think it would be sensible for us to stay here,' said Clara to Hannah Hardcastle. 'I shall be sorry to lose the servants but they were here mainly on my brother's behalf.'

'Letting will bring in a nice source of income for you and you can always sell when you reach your majority. It would be much more convenient for your school too,' she said to Mary.

Mary was still listlessly overcome by the shock of her father's sudden death and knew it was up to her aunt to make the decisions, so, much against her inclination, she agreed.

Clara added, 'Of course one day it might be more sensible, possibly more fun, and certainly cheaper to live abroad!'

Mary realized that her aunt wanted and needed a change, and if they moved to Woolsford Clara would be nearer her friend Hannah.

They moved in 1889 to one of a terrace of stone-built houses in quite a pleasant part of Woolsford, exchanging the peace of the village, its woods and fields, for the crowded streets of the city.

Clara took her niece abroad for the first time when she was sixteen. During that summer of 1891 they went for the whole of Mary's school holidays to Cauterets, a spa town, or rather village, in the Pyrenees, catering mainly for walkers and climbers and adventurous souls. They stayed however at the well-established Hotel d'Angleterre, a most impressive place. Prices were so much cheaper in France. Clara had fond memories of the hotel, a new establishment when she had stayed there with her husband years before. They had taken the waters and had gone on long walks.

Mary realized that this was the life that best suited her aunt. Now that she was no longer a little girl she had begun to understand her better. Clara was hoping to reassure herself that her niece might one day enjoy a more permanent life in France.

They returned the following summer to the mountains, accompanied this time by Hannah Hardcastle, and stayed a few days in Lourdes on the way back, before finding a pension in Pau, not far way, a beautiful old town that boasted a university.

Mary had only one more year of school, during which she would sit the Oxford Senior examination. She was enjoying her studies, especially literature, but she knew she was lucky to have the opportunity to sample a different way of life, a way of life she felt certain her father would never have countenanced.

Her teachers at the high school were hoping she would try for a place at Oxford or Cambridge after she had passed her matriculation examination. Clara was willing for her niece to continue her studies but Mary knew it would cost less if she studied nearer home. They were not poor, but her aunt's resources, even with the addition of the income from letting out Cliff House, could not be expected to cover three years of university life. The income would eventually be her own but only when she was twenty-one. When she left school she might read and learn by herself, study what took her fancy, or go to college a little nearer home. She was grateful to Clara for all she had done for her and she did not want to go on being a burden.

Not long after they had arrived for the first time in Pau, Clara had discovered the existence of lectures and classes which Mary might one day join.

'I believe they offer literature and history to foreigners – mostly English girls,' her aunt had said. She was already dreaming of staying on the following year, once Mary's schooldays were over. Hannah, who was taking tea with them in the front drawing-room of the terrace house, added that from Pau you might spend the summer on the coast in Biarritz. She knew her friend would not insist that Mary stayed in France after she had left school but it was clear that was what she would prefer. Once Mary attained her majority and received the income from Cliff House, things would be different. Clara had devoted herself to her niece for many years and deserved a change.

Mary did want to see more of the world, feeling she did not know enough about it to make decisions at present, and Clara held the purse strings for the time being. From things Tilly had told her, Mary realized that her aunt had been regarded by Lightholme people as independent. In the eyes of some, Mary had been brought up in a rather eccentric way.

'Well, she may be eccentric but she doesn't treat me as a child,' Mary had replied.

'I think you are lucky,' said Tilly.

'She keeps saying that one day I'll be able to decide for myself what I want to do,' Mary went on. 'I believe she will let me, but I don't want to be selfish.'

'I wonder what I'd want to do if I were given the chance,' mused Tilly. 'I suppose I'd like to marry a wonderful man.'

They both laughed then looked at each other shyly.

'I hadn't really thought as far ahead as that!' Mary said.

Mary divined that Clara, although not the sort of woman who would want to have her married off, might be relieved if she did find a husband. Mary did not want to look so far ahead.

By the summer of 1893, when she was eighteen, Mary learned she had passed her examination with honours. They had gone for the second time to Pau, staying at the Pension Mimosa, but this time they were not to remain in the town for the month of August. They were to spend some weeks on the coast, in Biarritz, and might eventually stay in Paris before returning to England.

Biarritz was a town frequented by the very rich, but also by more ordinary people like themselves, both French and foreign. Mary was packing for the seaside, wondering how smart visitors to such a cosmopolitan place had to be, when the lady in charge at the pension sent a servant up to their rooms with a letter.

The envelope was addressed to Mlle Mary Settle, Pension Mimosa, Pau, (Hautes Pyrénées) France, except that Tilly Crowther's spelling was somewhat erratic. Fortunately, the postman was used to deciphering English misspellings. Pau was full of English people, had an English church, an English bookshop and an English library, and even so was, according to Clara Demaine, not an expensive place.

Mary was sitting at the window. She had opened the shutters and had been looking down on the cobbled square. They were not far from the castle; it was really a beautiful town. Tilly's letters were always a treat and Mary made herself pause before opening and savouring them. She wished they could stay on in the town. She did not truly want to be off again, however great the attractions of sea air on the Atlantic coast. Would it have an English bookshop, or a circulating library? Would everybody be very smart and expect her to look fashionable? One part of her wanted to meet new people; another part wanted to be left alone. But there they'd be till September at least. When they would return home to England was even more uncertain. It was lucky Tilly had written when she had, otherwise the letter might have languished all summer in Pau.

Mary unfolded the letter, written in Tilly's large looping hand. They had never stopped writing to each other, even after Tilly had gone to boarding-school and they had stopped seeing each other daily. Mary had written ecstatically to Tilly from the mountains on her first visit to France. She remembered writing: *Aunt is looking happier every day*. Later letters had gone into detailed descriptions of this south-west corner of France, including Lourdes. When they had seen each other again on Mary's return that year Tilly had listened, with big eyes. She confessed to Mary that she worried lest her residence in France might lead her friend into Roman Catholicism. Mary assured her there was no danger, but did not elaborate, her own religious beliefs now being uncertain. Tilly had stuck to her family non-conformity.

Mary sat on for a moment, the letter in her hand, feeling a little nostalgic, not for the busy manufacturing town, but for Lightholme, and The Nest. What would she be doing at home if she returned? Would she be expected to settle down: pay visits, go to dances, flirt with young men? Tennis was all the rage now – was she missing out on a normal social life? She had learned to play tennis at the high school though she had never been much good at it.

She looked down again at Tilly's letter. She'd reply before they went off to Biarritz.

The Ways of Love

Dear Mary

I do wish you were here to talk to, as it is very boring here. No Liddy at home. She is off to stay with Mother's sister to help with her garden and I am moping at The Nest. Oh, I would just love to come and see you but the family think France is a dangerous place where they eat frogs and still worship Napoleon. (And idols, added Mary, mentally putting herself into Tilly's mind.)

Your new tenants are quite a young couple with no children – I can't imagine why they need such a big place, tho' the lady is very fashionable and gives musical parties. Mother says they are 'flighty' but I don't think she means that literally. I believe the man is some relation of Mercy M's father. I saw Mercy last week and she said she was going to stay with a cousin in Hereford and made a face. I think she has become more human though she always looks so miserable. I have not met anyone new recently but there was a nice minister taking evening chapel last week who kept staring at me. I wondered if I was wearing an unsuitable hat. Perhaps I was imagining his stare.

They say that both Wynteredge Hall and another hall further up beyond Owram are to change hands. Father is agitated about trade – as usual. Liddy says she has met a parson (Anglican) who grows wonderful roses and she is going to steal some cuttings to grow for Uncle.

I must confess I do get a trifle bored here so you must excuse this boring letter. Don't you sometimes just want what our old parlour maid used to call 'A bit of fun'?

Mary spent a few moments thinking of all she wanted to tell her friend in reply. What was it they said? she asked herself irrelevantly – 'Sweet seventeen and never been kissed'? She reckoned Tilly was the sort of girl who got married young and had heaps of children. Like her mother, except you could not imagine Mrs Crowther wanting 'fun'. Still, Tilly's parents, if not eccentric had certainly been more free-spirited with their children than most, in spite of their strong religious convictions. She was glad she had not had a mother like Mercy Miller's who was a flibbertigibbet, or one like her friend Edith's at the high school who forbade her to go on a horse bus, or to knit on a Sunday.

Thinking of the school reminded her she ought to write to Miss Hartley when she had replied to Tilly. Miss Hartley had urged her to take her studies further in a more disciplined way. You would think she would have approved of her accompanying Aunt Clara on her peregrinations, but she had said, 'You could waste years just visiting places and reading in a desultory way.'

Clara had looked rather guilty on overhearing this. Clara, however, had been married, had possibly made a husband her life's work though to the newly critical Mary this did not appear very likely. In any case, her aunt had never worked. Might she once have wanted to? Clara said ladies were in a difficult position. You could not always depend on dividends, and Cliff House cost a lot to run. She reiterated this at every opportunity, and was probably right.

One or two years over here in this delicious country would not make it irrevocably too late to go to college, would it? Last February, Miss Hartley, invited to tea in Woolsford, had kept saying, 'You'll be twenty-one in three years – and then you will have to decide what you want to do. . . .'

And here she was, eighteen and still with no clear plans. Eleanor Hartley had mooted the idea that Mary might one day start a school herself for those people in Lightholme who wanted their children well taught. The idea had interested Mary but she would need more qualifications to do that. She wanted to do something useful with her life but was not sure what. She told herself she was lazy – but she did like to read and learn. She liked children too. At present, though, she was interested in observing things on her travels as well as reading: learning rather than teaching. What did she know that was worth handing on? There were girls at school who would have to work, and most of them, like her friend Edith Wadsworth, would attend the City Training College, or the Yorkshire College in Leeds if they were not sure about teaching. Some older girls came back after they had begun to teach the children of the poor with stories of horrendous conditions and rioting boys.

She picked up Tilly's letter again and reread it. Tilly knew she did not care to see Cliff House in the hands of others but knew also that Mary might not have been happy continuing to go there without occupation. She turned her thoughts away from such gloomy subjects and set herself to amusing Tilly.

She took up her pen:

I like the travel and enjoy speaking French though it is a strong accent down here. I feel sure Aunt Clara will decide to stay on in France indefinitely so I expect I shall start the classes here in Pau in the autumn. I told you about these classes for foreigners, which you

can attend when you are eighteen? I see some very ancient-looking
'students' walking in the direction of the Faculté *or sitting in the*
cafés. I tried to see what one of them was reading and was glad to see
it was a novel – and one I am sure they'd disapprove of at home!

She scribbled on in this way and covered several pages, which she
managed to get to the post before they went off by train and carriage
to Biarritz.

Oh, it was so deliciously hot! Too hot for Clara who retired every
afternoon for her siesta with the blinds drawn. Clara had always said,
'I just can't stand Yorkshire weather,' so Mary had expected the heat
would suit her and was at first worried lest she herself would find
such heat made her wilt. But no – it was the other way round. She
blossomed in the sun.

'You are young,' said Clara, 'and have the advantage of adjusting
your internal temperature more easily. It is we older mortals who find
it tiring.'

Mary noticed that the shops were shut for two hours at midday
and some did not reopen before four o'clock. The fashionable
beaches were almost deserted then, though more ordinary folk went
in the bathing-machines at all hours.

Her aunt and Hannah did not mind her going for little walks on
the shore or the promenade and Mary did not always accompany
them on their walks. She was not lonely in her own company. How
could she be? It was wonderful to feel the sun turning her face and
hands brown. She did wish she could take off more layers of clothes
and advance into the sea like a mermaid.

The sea had many moods and was always audible: if she woke in
the night it was the Atlantic rollers she heard regularly breaking on
the beaches, or during one or two nights, when the daytime skies had
been overcast, roaring and crashing on the rocks. By morning,
though, the storm had passed and the sea was blue again, the sky that
paler blue that reminded her of the colour of her dead father's eyes.

Young ladies were not expected, however, to go for long walks by
themselves, so she compromised by visiting the English bookshop
and the circulating library whenever they were open in the afternoon.
The casino had cool rooms if even a young person became over-
heated, and she would meet Clara and Hannah later on its terrace.
They had no idea how far she walked, being too hot to investigate.

Such freedom was wonderful. No horse buses or carts to obstruct your progress down the vastly long promenade, and very often the tiniest breeze from the sea to cool your skin. There were small clusters of ladies on the Grande Plage too, well-shaded by their umbrellas and parasols, and nobody appeared to take much notice of her. Dotted all over this part of the beach were little tents on small poles with chairs placed under them, and children everywhere, digging and busily making secret castles or gathering pebbles or squabbling, their parents observing them from their tents or deckchairs with attached awnings. She noticed several older ladies walking alone, their umbrellas usually up. Under the awning of the casino there were tables and waiters and cool drinks. It was all so – civilized – she thought.

She felt a different person when she was by herself, felt she had begun to be that different person about two years ago. Or perhaps, she mused, looking at an English newspaper on a stand, she was now aware that she *was* a person. She even felt it when she was in their hotel, not one of the grand palaces overlooking the sea, or on the Avenue Victoria, but a smaller and quite dignified building down a street where many Russians appeared to live. The Hotel d'Angleterre, as in Cauterets, was the best hotel where all the crowned heads stayed, where princes and princesses and aristocrats led their usually sequestered but occasionally public lives. Another 'grand hotel' was the one built on the foundations of the palace built by the third Napoleon for his wife the Empress Eugénie some forty or so years earlier.

What Mary enjoyed most was to walk a little further back from the esplanade to the end of the town, nearer the lighthouse, where there were streets housing quite ordinary people, and small shops selling fruit and vegetables that to her smelled pungently delicious. As she walked along, she would think about herself. Previously she had not thought about herself so often, had taken herself for granted. As far as she could remember, her thoughts had been full of places, objects, other people, not of herself being in those places or with those people, or seeing those things and reacting to them. It had been a little different where a few people had been concerned; she had certainly had feelings about her feelings when Mima had left her, and even about Miss Watson long ago; perhaps they had been the beginnings of self-consciousness.

Tilly she had always taken for granted, as she had her Aunt Clara.

This strong new feeling was that she was a separate person living quite independently of others. Feelings had once appeared inevitable, had happened to her, not self-consciously been put into motion. Now she felt she might influence her own feelings. Was it to do with putting yourself in the place of other people, as you did when reading a novel? Love was maybe the connecting link between the old Mary and this new Mary. And her childhood seemed to be another country. In reality of course she *was* now in another country. Perhaps it was this that had made her much more aware of herself?

Clara had said to her only the day before, when they had met downstairs in the hotel vestibule after she had been out to get her aunt a paper, 'Why you look quite grown up – I hardly recognized you as you came through the door.'

Could she try to explain her thoughts to Tilly? She had rushed that last letter to her, but it was not fair to bore other people; it would have to be her journal. She had so many impressions to record, so many new ideas about the world and herself, but she'd need hours and hours to write them all down.

One afternoon she decided to wander as far as the English bookshop where both French and English books were on sale. Nobody knew her there. Outside the shop there was a slight slope downwards in the direction of the square in front of the casino, where one or two stiffly dressed bearded gentlemen in square straw hats were strolling slowly along by themselves. The ladies always held parasols and bags and usually moved in groups. She saw many such people walking along the esplanade in front of the Grande Plage. Further on towards the lighthouse there were younger people with little children who ran along ahead, continually called back by their mothers. She always wondered where all the people came from, what their ordinary lives were like, what occupations they followed. They could not be poor or they would not be able to afford such a holiday. There *were* poor people; she had seen them in those more ordinary streets, but not poor in the way factory children were in the cold inhospitable streets of a northern city.

Before she went into the shop she looked down at the town spread before her. By the port on the other side of the town, under the tamarisk trees, the fishing boats would be drawn up, always the object of holidaymakers' interested observation. She might stroll down there herself tomorrow, might even persuade her aunt to accompany her in the cool of the evening.

117

She pulled herself together. She must not wool-gather.

She went into the shop, whose bell pinged. The shutters were half-drawn at the front, where a middle-aged lady at the till was surreptitiously reading. Another customer came up to pay and Mary saw that the book was a romance by Ouida. Outside the other window were the same stiffly dressed people walking down the slope to the sea, or toiling slowly upwards.

The English novels were at the back of the shop for the benefit not only of travellers from England but also for those French people who liked to read in English. She had already guessed there were several retired *professeurs* staying in the town. They were probably on holiday from Pau.

English novels were too much of a temptation; she ought not to spend her small allowance on them. She could borrow similar ones from the circulating library a little further away, nearer the church in the old town. If she could find nothing that took her fancy here she'd have a look there, and might also find something suitable for her aunt and Hannah too. Clara could read French quite well although her accent was very English. I ought to be reading French novels in any case, thought Mary. It was sheer laziness that made her browse among English books when she was supposed to be improving her French. She moved to the back of the shop where she knew there were English and French classics as well as the latest books, mainly novels.

There weren't many people in the shop this afternoon – too hot for the older people, she supposed. One customer was a tall angular lady buried in *The Life of Charlotte Brontë*. That brought Mary up with a start. Here she was, so far from home, but between those covers was the story of one Englishwoman who had herself left England for a time, over fifty years ago. Miss Hardcastle might like the book for her birthday. Hannah was an inveterate reader, usually of Sir Walter Scott or Harrison Ainsworth. For such a simple, no-nonsense sort of person she had a very romantic taste in fiction.

An old man with an eyeglass was reading a book whose title she could not decipher. A younger man was burrowing in the shelves below where she had not yet ventured herself on her previous visit. Maybe there were bargains there? Old books nobody wanted? Perhaps she might find Mrs Ewing's *Six to Sixteen*, which she would love to reread. Was she becoming nostalgic for England? She was so fond of her native language.

She put her bag down and knelt down to look under the table where books were in piles, their titles facing the wrong way for any possible purchaser. She slid one from the top of the nearest pile and uncoiled herself.

It had no jacket, but opening it revealed a slim volume of verse by one Algernon Charles Swinburne. She began to read a poem with the title *The Forsaken Garden*, and was immediately entranced. Would it cost very much? There was no price marked inside. She put it down on the table, sure she had heard of this poet. He had not been recommended at school, so maybe she had read his name in a newspaper review. Oh dear! she ought not to buy this, had better look for some French verse.

She left the book on the table. She must give herself a constant stern reminder that she was here to improve her knowledge of French. They had studied Lamartine and Victor Hugo at school but no French poet more recent than those. She'd ask the lady assistant at the cash desk if she had any publishers' lists. Verse would be just the thing to read in the warm evenings, which were always interrupted by large meals and short walks. Verse could be read quickly at first and then you could read it over and over again. It did not take up much space either, and the language of French poetry might be more accessible than catalogues of nouns like those she had struggled through in a novel by Balzac. Ordinary daily vocabulary was even harder. They hadn't taught her about laundry and ironing and carriage fares at school. She was an ignoramus.

She looked longingly at the English book, and took it up again. This was what she really wanted to read.

She could sense that the young man who was now standing nearby was looking at her. He looked quite French but when he opened his mouth it was to ask her in English:

'Excuse me, I think you have dropped a glove?'

'What?' she asked, startled.

He handed her one of the net gloves she had taken off when she began to grope under the table. Gloves were such a nuisance.

'Oh – thank you.'

He was a man of about thirty with a cloud of dark-brown hair. His voice had been pleasant.

'Do you like Swinburne?' he went on.

'How did you know what I was reading?'

He laughed. 'I know the book – in fact I have a copy at home.'

119

How did he know *she* was English? Was it so obvious?

'There's all sorts under there,' he said pointing under the table. 'Probably been there for years. I don't imagine most visitors come here very often.'

'I'd never read any Swinburne before,' she confessed. 'I mean, I've heard of him – it's a lovely poem, *The Forsaken Garden*.'

'Yes, it is. Do you like the modern writers?'

'I don't know them very well. I like earlier poets – Keats, Shelley, some Wordsworth . . .'

'Not Browning ? I thought all women liked bits of Browning. Or Meredith?'

'I haven't read enough to say – I find Browning's poems difficult.'

'They're all mad on Byron here,' he said gloomily, picking up a book she saw he must have laid down earlier.

'I used to love Byron's lyrics – I still do,' said Mary.

She had bought them in a bookshop in Woolsford. What fun it was talking to a young man who knew about poets. As far as she could see, the two of them were now the only customers. The thin lady and the man with the monocle must have gone out.

'I saw you here the other day,' he said, and he spoke quite naturally, but not as if he cared one way or the other.

'Yes, though we only arrived the week before last. I can't afford to buy much. We go to the circulating library for novels. It's not as good as the one in Pau.'

'I know – it's full of Ouida. A few Trollope, but no *Mill on the Floss*, no *Madding Crowd*.'

'I know.'

'You know France well? Are you studying here?'

'I know it a little. I came first two years ago, with my aunt, and again last year. I'm hoping to learn to speak better French in Pau – they have classes at the university there.'

'Well, perhaps we shall see you at the circulating library one day. I'm here with my friend. We were doing a walking tour in the mountains but it rained a good deal and so we thought it was time for some civilization. Now we're too lazy to leave.'

She laughed. He had pronounced the word 'civilization' the French way and sounded ironic.

'Stephen Waterhouse,' he said and put out his hand.

She shook it. 'Mary Settle.'

'I must be off,' he said, 'or my friend Laurence will be getting impatient. I hope we shall meet again – good luck with finding a nice book.'

He bowed, smiled, and took himself off to the lady at the cash desk.

She supposed she had acted with what they called 'impropriety', talking freely to an unknown man, but how interesting it had been. She found herself hoping she might indeed see him again. Most visitors went to the open-air concerts held in the gardens in front of the Palace Hotel. She might go there with Aunt Clara and Hannah. It would be pleasant to extend her acquaintance. Clara was not a stickler for convention but Mary decided she ought not to say anything about this meeting unless she saw the young man again.

She waited until he had gone out of the shop before going up to the assistant. She decided not to ask about *Six to Sixteen* – it would be an excuse to go to the circulating library again. And she had better find some George Eliot and Thomas Hardy. Out of the window she saw that the young man Stephen Waterhouse – now *that* was a northern surname – had crossed the road to walk up the hill.

She took up the Swinburne and paid for her purchase. Two francs. She was being extravagant, but she felt pleased and a little exhilarated. Who was it the young man reminded her of? A grown-up Edwin, perhaps? She had lost touch with Edwin, though Tilly still saw him around the village during his vacations.

She gave a suitably edited account of her afternoon to Clara and Hannah over dinner and added that she might walk to the library in the morning.

'You can find us something to read,' said Hannah.

'Why not come with me?' asked Mary dutifully. If she was going to see that young man again she might as well see if he acknowledged her when she was with her aunt or Hannah.

'We'll see – depends how hot it is,' said Clara.

The two of them really preferred to sit in their deckchairs in a walled garden at the back of their small hotel, or walk slowly in the direction of the casino and sit with a lady-like drink under an awning in a café on the promenade. It never bothered either of them that they were unaccompanied by men. Widowhood was a very comfortable undemanding state, thought Mary, not for the first time. Even if she was only eighteen – just 'out', she supposed, if she had been the sort of girl who 'came out' – she felt the word spinster was embarrassing. She was not called that yet, but a year ago the word would never have occurred to her. Aunt did not realize how she longed for mixed company. In spite of having married Mr Demaine, Clara always said that marriage did not make most women free and independent. *Her* marriage was different, she implied. To Mary its origins were shrouded in mystery. That Mr Demaine had been a painter, she knew, but was shy of asking more. Had her young aunt *eloped* with him? Looking at her aunt she found it hard to believe. He had been much older than Clara, she did know that. Mary had decided some time ago that men and women were not equals in marriage. She would marry a man only if he let her go on feeling free.

Once, when a similar conversation had taken place between herself and Tilly, her friend had pointed out that once you had children you chose not to be free.

If you did not marry, wondered Mary, could you easily live the way you wanted? What about love? It was a dilemma.

After dinner that night, Mary began another letter to Tilly. A letter had been waiting for her here at the hotel, not in answer to her own but because Tilly was off to visit her mother's younger sister, who had many children.

I know I shall be expected to play with them and I enjoy that but I shan't have any time to myself, she had written. She had added her address, and in a postscript had written:

Did I tell you about Edwin Horsfall's safety bicycle? He is the first person we know who has bought one or had it bought for him. He looks so comical sitting up straight on the saddle with a serious expression on his face. He says it's a 'Rover', and I must say he has made me long to ride one myself. Can you see me in the saddle? Have you seen any bicycles in France? Edwin sent you his kind regards and is to continue his medical studies in Edinburgh in October.

Mary smiled over all this. Edwin had not changed, must still be the studious but self-assured person he had always been and as he had been when she had last seen him, before they left for France a year ago and Mary was on a visit to Tilly at The Nest.

She started to write:

A young Englishman actually spoke to me this afternoon in the bookshop here. I was by myself and I suppose people might have called him cheeky, but I liked the way he talked. He knew about books. I am now reading Swinburne and I shall copy out for you part of a poem I like. If ever people stopped living at The Nest I could imagine the garden would be like the one in the poem.

Clara came up then to suggest a short stroll on the promenade in the moonlight and Mary blotted her letter to finish the next day.

She persuaded both her aunt and Hannah to walk to the English library the following morning, hoping she might see Mr Waterhouse on the way, or at the library, but they saw nobody resembling a young Englishman.

An envelope addressed to Mrs C. Demaine was awaiting Clara at the hotel when they returned. Clara opened it in her room and came in excitedly to Mary who was standing in a dream at her window, looking over the sea.

'There's to be a reception at the English vice-consul's. We are all invited to a tea-party. They must keep a register of the arrival of English people.' She looked down at the embossed card in her hand. 'Would you care to go?'

She didn't have much choice, thought Mary, but a tea-party would be something to look forward to. Would the Englishmen go to such an event? Then she checked and scolded herself for allowing her silly imagination to run riot.

CHAPTER EIGHT

The very next day, Mary and the two middle-aged ladies were walking back from the centre of the town along a narrow cobbled street when they passed two young men in straw hats. Mary recognized Stephen Waterhouse. He hesitated for a moment as he passed them, then he raised his hat. She saw him turn to his friend and say something, and then the other young man also raised his hat.

Mary said 'Good-morning.'

Aunt looked astonished as the two men replied with a cheerful 'Good-morning,' before crossing to the other side of the street.

'Who are they? ' asked Clara.' Do you know them?'

Mary answered casually, 'Oh, I saw one of them in the bookshop yesterday. They are English. One of them chatted to me there.'

'Well, if they are English perhaps we shall see them at the vice-consul's reception next week.'

Mary said no more but felt proud if obscurely guilty that a young man – nay, two young men – had greeted her.

During the following week Clara and Hannah hired a carriage to see the sights, mostly the villas and châteaux too far away to visit on foot, or on the other side of town. They also took a carriage to the old port where whalers used to land in the past. They saw many large villas on the way, and on a hill behind, some in the course of construction. The coachman pointed out the great Villa Marbella in its gardens, and spoke of a castle to be built by a baron. They were suitably impressed, and went on to be shown the Villa Les Trois Fontaines.

'In the English style,' said their guide.

So many villas, so many châteaux, and so many of them owned by or tenanted by rich Englishmen . . . 'Milords' and 'Sirs' apparently abounded. Mary began to feel rather tired of it all.

A new casino was to be built and owned by the town – oh, the whole town was going to be even bigger and grander.

Clara and Hannah visited the *Thermes Salins*, which had been opened only that summer. It was a most peculiar building, a mixture of an Arabian palace and a Scottish castle. Mary insisted she had no desire to receive thermal treatment there, or take the waters. Her aunt and Hannah went off for a whole day of mudbaths and strange potions and returned looking distinctly washed out. Mary had not admitted to exhaustion but still felt a little mental indigestion after all the visiting and cataloguing of villas and châteaux.

On the Sunday they attended St Andrew's church, which apart from a handful of Americans had an almost completely English congregation. Mary looked for Mr Waterhouse but there was no sign of him or his friend at the service. She would have liked to visit a Catholic church, finding the relentless Englishness of the town tedious. It was not that kind of England she missed. Why did the English have to import their own styles and churches to a place like this? It was not as if Biarritz was part of the Queen's empire!

The English reception was to be given by a certain Mr Reginald Paget, the vice-consul, in yet another enormous villa they had been shown with great pride at the edge of town. Its name, Toki-Ederra, was clearly Basque, and made Mary long to visit the hinterland to the east and south in the direction of Spain, to see the Basque farms and villages. The only thing in the town she had not done and which she would rather like to do, was to cross the new high iron bridge, built only six years before over a stretch of sea across to one of the off-shore rocks. This rock was named Le Rocher de la Vierge, and a statue of the Virgin had been placed on its summit by fishermen who attributed their miraculous survival in a fierce storm to the interces-sion of the Virgin Mary. Apparently, the sea could be extremely rough, though not usually in the summer season. She wondered what the place would be like in winter with the Atlantic pounding its coast-line.

She decided after this week of sight-seeing that she really preferred to stay in the mountains. Rich people, not to mention crowned heads, in villas and châteaux did not interest her. If you could find out what they were thinking and understand how they lived it would be interesting, but just to gape at rather ugly buildings, however much they had cost, was wearisome. On the other hand she loved the climate and the language, and wished she could make herself invisible, to explore further by herself.

She did not want to appear ungrateful to her aunt so tried to look as if she was enjoying herself. She looked forward to the tea party, in the faint hope that Stephen Waterhouse and his friend might attend.

There they were, the young men. There was Mr Waterhouse, at the head of a long line of people crowding the stairs that led to the first floor reception room of the Villa Toki-Ederra. They were all waiting to be greeted by the vice-consul, Mr Paget, a short rather plump Scotsman, who was standing in the room beyond with his wife. Thick carpets covered the reception rooms; red and golden-yellow tapestries were hanging on the walls.

The Villa Toki-Ederra perched high up on the cliffs, overlooking the mountains and the sea. Clara's party had been a little late arriving, having found it difficult to hire a carriage to go to the other end of town at the same time as all the other English visitors who needed one. The people who had already been greeted by Mr Paget were now making their way back down the double staircase to sit in the garden under a sort of canvas canopy. Yet others were wandering round the reception rooms.

Mary was near enough now to hear a flunkey announce 'Mr Waterhouse and' – she strained to catch the name – it sounded like 'Mr Laurence.' The men were shaking hands before turning to join others who had been invited to make themselves at home in the vast place.

Stephen Waterhouse, catching sight of Mary in the queue behind them, said something to his friend, a tall, fair man, and they waited until the three ladies had been introduced to the consul before coming up to them.

Stephen spoke to Mary: 'Do please introduce us to your family,' he said politely. To Clara and Hannah he added, 'I made the acquaintance of Miss Settle in the bookshop.' (Fancy remembering her name!)

'Stephen Waterhouse,' he enunciated, and bowed. The other man smiled and said, 'Laurence Noble,' and bowed even more urbanely. Aunt and Hannah looked quite pleased to be thus addressed.

'This is my aunt, Mrs Demaine,' said Mary, hoping she did not sound too nervous, 'and her friend Mrs Hardcastle.'

They both inclined their heads graciously.

Laurence Noble shook hands with Mary and said, 'May we get you all some tea? You must be tired waiting all this time. There are chairs in the garden.'

'That would indeed be welcome,' said Clara, and they made their way downstairs.

Stephen whispered to Mary, 'I never imagined there were so many English in the place. It only needs the Queen!' Mary giggled.

'The Queen was here in this very villa four years ago,' said Laurence, turning to her and smiling.

They went into the garden, and before going off in search of tea which was being distributed from a large urn in a very un-French fashion, Stephen turned to Mary saying, 'Not a very forsaken garden, this one, unfortunately.'

Aunt and Hannah disposed themselves on chairs at a small table and the men went in the direction of the urn and the china cups.

'How pleasant,' said Clara. 'I suppose they were the young men whom we saw the other day in the street when we were on our way back from the Jardin Publique?'

'Yes, Aunt—'

'How nice to have someone looking after us!' sighed Hannah.

Mary felt they were pleased to meet new people, and was quite proud of herself that it was all her doing. Aunt was not the sort of woman to fuss too much over her speaking to a young man in a shop, trusting her, she guessed, to know whether a young man was 'presentable'. These two appeared eminently so, for when they returned they were again extremely polite, asking the older women for their impressions of the place before talking in an amusing fashion of their own experiences.

'We didn't intend to come here,' said Laurence Noble, who was an excessively handsome man. 'But it was easy to reach and we were tired of tramping round the mountains. We shall be off soon to explore the Basque hinterland, and perhaps go into Spain – before England, home and duty call us.'

'Oh I'd love to see some of the countryside!' exclaimed Mary before realizing she might sound as though she was inviting herself to join them. Men could just go where the fancy took them. Of course these men were not boys, and were old enough to please themselves.

'You can reach St Jean de Luz by train,' added Laurence, 'The church where Louis the Fourteenth was married is in the town, I believe.'

'Really?' murmured Hannah, 'How very interesting.'

Hannah had read many historical novels of that period and began an interesting conversation with Laurence Noble who was *au fait* with history as well as with aesthetic objects from the past. The two men really were an extremely well-informed pair.

'Have you been across the bridge to the Rocher de la Vierge?' Stephen asked Mary.

'That's the one thing I do want to do before we leave,' she answered. 'Aunt and Hannah are good walkers but suffer from vertigo and neither fancies walking on a bridge over the raging torrents. I am sure they have got the wrong impression.'

'We could take you,' said Laurence, overhearing. He turned to Clara. 'If you have not yet visited it, would you not like to be accompanied over the little bridge to the famous rock at the end of the promontory?'

'*Little* bridge?' said Clara, 'No, I don't fancy that. But I expect Mary would like to go – there is so much we have not yet seen here. It has been too hot to walk far.'

Many middle-aged and elderly English people were chatting in small groups in the garden and Laurence said, 'Don't let us monopolize you – I'm sure there must be people you know here?'

'No – none,' said Hannah forthrightly.

'There was one lady we saw in Harrogate last year and then again at the post office here yesterday,' objected Clara, 'but I never come abroad to meet our compatriots – this event is unusual – we could not refuse an invitation to see a Villa like such as this.'

'You have travelled extensively?' asked Laurence.

'In my youth,' replied Clara. 'I spent a lot of time in Italy and France when my husband was alive.'

'You mentioned Harrogate,' pursued the young man. 'Then you must be from the north of England?'

'Yes indeed, I was born in Woolsford,' replied Clara, 'but I lived in London and abroad until I returned to Yorkshire when my niece was a child.'

Mary felt her aunt was about to expatiate upon the history of her life, and intervened hastily.

'I need to improve my French,' she said. 'Being with English people all the time one just does not get the practice.'

'Suitably chastised!' said Laurence.

'Oh, I did not mean it like that—'

'He is teasing you,' said Stephen. 'We find the same. We like to leave the "shores of Albion" for a time but find our French does not extend to interesting conversations with train drivers or waiters.' They all laughed.

Then Laurence said, 'Shall we take a look around the gardens and the house?'

'We shall stay here. It would be nice for Mary if you would accompany her,' said Clara. She meant both of them, of course. It would not do for just one young man to be seen at such a formal reception alone with a young lady. Bookshops were different. Mary would have liked to wander around with Stephen, and look out over the sea, and waited for him possibly to quote from a poem, but two people were better than no one, so she got up and the three of them began to walk round the extensive gardens, one man on each side of Mary.

'Laurence hails from Yorkshire too,' said Stephen.

'Yes, I am just about to take the tenancy of a wonderful old house – originally Jacobean, I am assured.'

'We have let our own house,' said Mary, 'But it is not Jacobean – only just over a hundred years old.'

'There are tennis courts here – look,' said Laurence. Behind the house they could see a grass court and many outbuildings. The villa itself had five storeys and was built in what Laurence explained was *le style Basque*.

'They say it's a comfortable place to live in,' he added. He appeared interested and knowledgeable about architecture, and she felt he would know all about furnishings too.

'And what a view!' she said, when they had turned and walked to the edge of the garden where a wall overhung the cliff itself. 'Would you want to rent a place like this?' she asked Laurence.

'If I were a millionaire, perhaps,' he replied seriously. 'But you'd need a vast staff!'

'I don't think I'd like to live here permanently,' said Mary. 'I love France and I wish we might *eat* the French way at home, and that we had as much sun and light – but . . .'

She stopped, feeling she was saying too much about her own opinions.

'But your heart is in England?' said Laurence.

Stephen said, 'Well, so is yours, old boy – *I'm* the wandering minstrel, not you. Would you really like to walk over the bridge to the Rocher de la Vierge, Mary?'

'Yes, I would.'

'We could go with you if you like,' said Stephen.

'And if you want to see the Basque countryside or St Jean de Luz, there is a train that goes by one or two of the villages – your aunt might like to take that?' said Laurence.

Vistas of enjoyment opened up before Mary. Yet the men were soon to be off on their further travels, and she'd soon be back being a dutiful niece again, in Pau. Were the men a little bored themselves, or did they just like female company?

'I took my sister to Paris last spring,' said Stephen, as if in answer. 'But she got married this year.'

'He has to put up with me instead now,' said his friend. Mary wondered which one was the real driving force of the friendship. If only Tilly were there with them to make a foursome. But she did not yet know what Mr Waterhouse and Mr Noble – or rather Stephen and Laurence – did for a living, or anything about them, really. Even so, she trusted them. They were interesting and lively and she did hope they might perhaps meet again in England one day. But when would that be?

'I'd love to walk over the bridge to the rock with you,' she said again, and thought she sounded quite bold, 'And if Aunt will agree we could go and see a little of the Basque countryside. They say it's very green and pretty.'

'No sooner said than done,' said Stephen. 'We'll persuade her. What about going to the rock tomorrow?'

They came back to the two ladies who were sitting there happily, their teacups drained. Laurence fetched them each another cup, and whilst he was doing this Stephen suggested a visit to the Rocher de la Vierge the following morning. The ladies could wait on the shore – there were chairs in shelters near where the bridge started and he and Laurence would see Mary safely over and back.

Mary was looking at his dark eyes as he spoke. They had a friendly expression.

'It's most kind of you,' said Clara. 'I'm afraid my niece must be a little lonely sometimes with no young people to talk to.'

Mary smiled. She had not actually felt lonely, but it was always more fun to see the sights along with other people if their tastes were compatible with one's own, and she was certain Stephen's were. She was not so sure about Laurence. He might be rather impulsive, she thought, mixing silence with sudden bursts of conversation.

They all left the villa after the two ladies had walked round the garden again and left their cards on the silver salver in the downstairs dining-room where other ladies, and a few gentlemen, none of them young, were taking their leave. Mr Noble and Mr Waterhouse agreed to meet them at their hotel the following morning to take a carriage to the rock, reached from a promontory at the end of the older quarter of the town, a little distant from the part they knew best.

'Well, you have made a conquest!' said Hannah to Mary after they had all come down for dinner that evening.

'Really, dear,' said Clara to her friend. Then to Mary, 'Which one did you like best?'

She could be surprisingly direct sometimes and Mary felt embarrassed.

Hannah answered, 'Oh I thought Mr Noble such a handsome young man!'

'And Mary?' asked Clara studying the menu which was always presented to them before they sat down so there would be ample time for the cook to prepare their choice.

'Stephen – Mr Waterhouse – is a great reader,' Mary answered.

'Perhaps the other one is too. What do they do for a living at home? I think Mr Noble might be a barrister.'

'I don't know,' answered Mary. 'They are both amusing – I had the idea that Laurence – he's from Yorkshire, you know – might be in business, not in the law. He has taken a lease on a house in the West Riding.'

'Well, how very interesting,' said Clara. 'Thank you, I shall have the mussels tonight.'

Mary was thinking that she liked both men. The other day in the bookshop was the first time she had really had a proper conversation with a young man, and now she had chatted to two. It was possibly easier to make friends abroad, where protocol was not so rigidly followed. Not that she came from the kind of family where things were very formal or strict but she wondered what her headmistress would think of her striking up acquaintance so quickly.

'They are not so very young,' she said aloud. 'I should think they are at least thirty!'

'Well, that is young,' said Clara.

'They surely can't be married?' said Hannah.

'I wouldn't know about that!' said Clara, taking a sip of the delightful Jurasson wine they all liked so much. 'Men can leave their wives behind at home, you know!'

Mary felt the conversation was what Miss Smith, her teacher, would have called indecorous, but she replied, 'I am sure Mr Waterhouse is unmarried!'

'You had better make sure,' said Hannah darkly.

Mary was nonplussed. Did older ladies always assume you talked to men with an ulterior motive? That men talked to a young woman with thoughts of marriage in their heads? It was ludicrous, and she resolved to put a stop to it immediately.

'I thought them both the sort of people one might be *friends* with, she said. 'Stephen – Mr Waterhouse – reminded me a little of Edwin at home.'

Of all people, her independent Aunt Clara would surely approve of friendship between the sexes. Mary was well aware of the talk of the 'New Woman' and how hard it was for young women to be taken seriously.

'Mary is a serious person,' said Clara firmly, admonishing Hannah, who was enjoying her fish, 'and all that matters is that she meets young people of equal seriousness.'

Both young men arrived in a carriage at ten o'clock next morning to fetch the little party to go to the rock. Mary was determined to appear cool and collected although excitement was rippling through her.

The two Englishmen were extremely attentive, fetching Clara her shawl, which she had left in the lobby, and making conversation with Hannah who was inclined to gush. Stephen smiled at Mary, and Laurence, turning to her, said:

'It is not all that high, the bridge, and it's a nice summer day. Have you seen the Eiffel Tower –or been up to the first level?'

'We hope to stay in Paris on the way home,' said Mary. 'I have seen pictures of the tower – indeed I thought this bridge had perhaps been constructed by Monsieur Eiffel.'

Laurence put her right about this, and Stephen asked:

'How long do you plan to stay in Pau?'

'I suppose till next year – to avoid the Yorkshire winter.'

'Won't you be homesick?' asked Stephen as their carriage took a turn in the direction of the centre of the town.

'I haven 't been homesick yet – I do miss my friend Tilly a little. I wouldn't want to stay in France for ever.'

She wanted to ask how long the two men were to stay away from England but thought it might appear forward. Stephen said, 'You must visit the Louvre – I had to spend quite a few days to take it all in.'

'Ah, here we are,' exclaimed Laurence.

There was a path leading down to the entrance to the bridge, crowded with people. They alighted and walked down. The rock was not so very far distant now, and the bridge was quite wide and solid, larger than she had expected from the pictures, certainly not swaying in the fresh breeze from what must be the Atlantic.

Clara was studying the guidebook and looked up, saying, 'There used at first to be a wooden bridge. But the Emperor wanted to build a rampart against the sea and join up all the rocks and make a new port but the sea was too powerful . . .'

They could see several other rocks now.

'Then they built a passage through the biggest rock,' Clara went on.

She was translating from French. Mary wanted to get on to the bridge and talk to Stephen. The ladies said they would sit there on a bench and watch the sea.

'It is built from a "*bloc de grès nummulitique*", whatever that is,' Clara said to Hannah, who did not appear very interested.

It was Stephen who was chatting to Mary as they walked towards the iron bridge, along with scores of other people with the same idea.

Laurence strode on ahead.

'It must be quite frightening in the dark if there is a storm,' said Mary.

People were walking through a covered passage, one behind the other, Mary behind Stephen. The two of them got to the end of the bridge and then saw where Napoleon the Third had tunnelled through the rock to transport all the stones he needed to build his dykes against the sea, and join up the rocks. There was now a wonderful view of sea and town, a few fishing boats in the distance.

On the top of the rock above them reigned the statue of the Virgin.

'You're not a Catholic, are you?' asked Laurence, who had arrived there before them and was looking up at the statue, a rather pained expression on his face.

'No, I'm not.'

'Well, there are some recusants left in Yorkshire – though I suppose it's the country of dissenters.'

Mary wanted to ask him if he was religious but it sounded an odd question, as his own had been. They stared up at the statue and she said,

'I'm not against statues – I suppose it helps the mariners to feel someone is on their side.'

'It is not a very ancient statue,' said Laurence.

'No – I can see that.'

'If you went in some of the old churches you'd find some really old ones – we saw some very old chapels in the mountains, especially on the other side of Spain in Catalonia – quite simple sculptures and frescoes but very impressive,' said Stephen.

'I don't know much about architecture,' confessed Mary, 'but I think York Minster is the most beautiful building I've ever seen.'

'Oh, I do so agree,' said Stephen.

'Most of the urban churches have been restored,' said Laurence. 'Or completely rebuilt.'

Mary felt that her opinions were taken seriously. Both the men treated her as grown up and it was a novel feeling for her. But they were so knowledgeable.

Laurence walked round to the end of the bridge, and Stephen and Mary stood together looking out over the sea. She stole a glance at his profile, a sharp nose, hair blowing over his forehead in the breeze. He turned towards her just then and looked at her, and she felt something like an electrical circuit make a connection up between them. He carried on looking at her, and she thought he was going to say something, but he did not, and then Laurence came up to them and broke the magic.

The three of them made their way back from the rock along the iron bridge, and Mary had such an urge to take Stephen's hand it quite frightened her. She looked down at the sea again and then at the whole town set before them. Laurence turned and gazed back at the rock and its statue.

'The Virgin on the Rock,' he said, 'Like the Leonardo painting – but not so lovely.' Stephen was silent.

Aunt Clara and Hannah were waiting to hear their impressions before they all walked slowly back along the street to the town centre.

Mary told Clara about the train that went to St Jean de Luz. 'Do let's go there,' she said.

Laurence added, 'We were going there ourselves – it's not far, you can get there and back in one day.'

Mary did not want to suggest they all went on the same day but Stephen said, with a glance at his friend, 'We hoped to go on Tuesday. If you are still going to be here, would you care to go along with us?'

Clara and Hannah murmured that they would think about it. Mary did hope they would agree.

Laurence then said he knew of a fish restaurant not far away and what about some luncheon?

Over the meal Mary learned that the two men had been at school together. Stephen lived in London and had read for the bar but did not enjoy his work although he helped his father with legal research. He was thinking of moving into Sussex and taking up farming with his brother. Laurence had inherited a business from his father in the north. It was clear that neither was married. Mary wondered whether they might be 'eternal bachelors'. They both however paid her attention, and Mary knew that Stephen was looking at her when he thought nobody noticed.

'She is an attractive young woman,' said Clara to her friend that night in the privacy of their suite.

Mary was reading in her room but kept finding her thoughts straying to the men. She found them both interesting but it was Stephen's face and bearing that preoccupied her. His cast of mind was, she decided, more like her own – and she had never had a young man look at her like that before. She could admit that Laurence was better-looking in a conventional sense, but he appeared almost too knowledgeable, and made her feel her own lack of deep knowledge of so many things. He must know many young women. With Stephen she felt much easier, in spite of the attraction, because on another level from the personal, she could talk about books with him. Yet both of them had paid her serious attention, a novel experience for her.

Clara and Hannah were discussing much the same thing.

'They are both delightful young men,' sighed Hannah.

'Mary has not met many young men,' replied Clara. 'Fortunately she is a very natural sort of young woman and does not flirt, so she is lucky to have met some young people who are serious-minded.'

'My father used to say,' said Hannah, 'that women expected too much of men!'

135

'Well, they are always bound to be disappointed then!'

Mary felt she had learned much about herself from her conversations that day. It was queer how talking to people made you see yourself a little differently. What she wanted was for someone to define herself to herself, at the same time as she tested out her opinions. Would she now begin to learn how to get on with the opposite sex?

It would be such a pity not to see the two again, especially Stephen, after they had left Biarritz.

Mary had made up her mind to go to a French church the following Sunday, so once Clara and Hannah had gone off to attend matins in the English St Andrew's, she went to a small Catholic church near the vegetable shops. Here she found a mass was taking place both in French and in a strange language she realized was Basque. She stood at the back and listened.

She was back before Clara and Hannah returned, but told them where she had been, and that she had discovered that in the afternoon there were to be processions in the town of villagers from the surrounding countryside, and from further afield in the country of the Basques. They came every year to Biarritz on the Sunday nearest to the Assumption. She persuaded them to go and have a look, and they walked down in the afternoon to the Grande Plage and into the centre of the town to watch. Mary could not helping looking round to see if Stephen was there but there was no sign of either man.

The whole place was crowded with what looked like complete families all in their colourful costumes of red, green, and white, with red and green scarves. The sound of their shouting and singing was everywhere. It was a harsh, strange, even outlandish language, she thought, as she had first heard it in church that morning, full of Ks and Zs. She must ask the men how the language came to be. They were the sort of people who would be sure to know. It turned out that there had been a religious procession from the church of St Martin, the patron saint of Biarritz, and now all the worshippers had joined the Biarrots (as they had learned the inhabitants of Biarritz were called). All the cafés were open, and the sound of a country band floated over in the slight breeze. This town was theirs, belonged to them. What did they think of the worldly foreigners? Had some of them come over the frontier from Spain, where far more of the Basques lived?

On their way back from the celebrations the women sat down for a moment to listen to the town band, a slightly more sophisticated affair, playing in front of the Hôtel du Palais. There were crowds there and on the 'Empress's Beach'. Mary recalled one of the tunes. Her French teacher at Woolsford High School had taught them the song, *A la Claire Fontaine*. Remembering the words, she wished Stephen Waterhouse was listening with her: *'Jamais je ne t'oubliérai'*.

She castigated herself for these yearningly romantic feelings.

She felt more cheerful the following morning when a note was delivered to their hotel from Mr Noble and Mr Waterhouse, suggesting that unless they heard from them before evening they would meet them at the station at ten o'clock on Tuesday morning when there would be a train to St Jean de Luz that would pass through some of the pretty hinterland south of the town to the fishing port. It was not a long journey.

CHAPTER NINE

Mary was never to forget that Tuesday. It stood out in her memory as a day of happiness. She saw through the train windows the 'back country' with its green fields and delicious woods of oaks and beeches and poplars. Everything natural was green. They glimpsed distant farms and old houses and it made her realize how much she missed the countryside. She would never be completely at home in a town, least of all such a glittering place as Biarritz. Her Yorkshire moors and dales had charm as well as wildness.

During conversation on the train she learned that the house Mr Noble was to rent was only a few miles away from Lightholme, and that he knew the district well. She was delighted, but would have been even more thrilled if it had been Mr Waterhouse who was to live there. Clara, listening to them all chattering away as if they had known each other for years, thought how good it was to be young.

The town, with its square, and its beautiful houses, 'built,' said Clara, reading from the guide book, 'from the profits of piracy,' had a much older feel than Biarritz. They were overawed by the sumptuous gold of the baroque altarpiece in the church of St Jean Baptiste where the Sun King had wed his Spanish bride. Mary and Stephen sat in silent contemplation, whilst Laurence Noble prowled round the Stations of the Cross, looking at it, he said, from an aesthetic point of view.

After they had walked to the bridge to look over at the little harbour with its fishing-boats rocking in the blue, and then walked back to the beach, Mary felt her cup of happiness overflowing.

'I wish we were staying here – it's a simpler place,' she remarked to Stephen.

'A child of nature!' teased Laurence.

'A Rousseauist,' said Stephen. 'But I feel it will soon be another fashionable watering-place.'

'Oh, no!' exclaimed Mary. 'It's just that I like to see unspoilt woods and farms and fields,' she added.

'Isn't the sea enough?'

'Oh, I love the sea – I suppose if there were a beach at home as well, it would be perfection.'

Laurence said, 'Then there'd be hordes of visitors. You can't like Woolsford very much.'

'No – except for the free library and the market, but then we are so near Ilkley and Wharfedale.'

'Or Shipley Glen?' suggested Laurence with a faint smile, naming a local beauty spot, notorious for the lascivious activities of the populace about which Mary was not supposed to know.

Clara and Hannah came up then.

'We'd like to see the house where the king stayed – and his bride's house too,' said Clara, 'When you've all had your fill of the sea.' The sea was reminding Mary now of the Yorkshire coast. It must be the fishing-boats, she decided. No cliffs here. Laurence was still thinking about England too.

'There's always Blackpool,' he suggested, as they all walked back through the town, admiring the houses with their arched windows and the shady tree-lined walks.

'I was there last time I was in Lancashire on business,' he explained. 'It was *very* cold.'

Here in south-west France it was certainly not cold. They decided to drink fresh crushed lemon-juice in a small *auberge* from which they could admire the houses Clara wanted to see.

'We went bathing on Sunday,' said Stephen. 'We avoided all those crowds – they went on celebrating all day and half the night.'

'So we had a moonlight swim,' added Laurence.

How lucky they were, thought Mary. If she and Tilly were here together, it would be bathing machines and fuss. She would wager the men had not attended *Les Thermes Salins* either. It was women who were always worrying about their health.

'We were there too in the afternoon watching the processions, ' said Clara.' Was the sea cool at night-time?'

'Quite cold, actually – a north-west wind – very bracing,' replied Laurence. Mary laughed. 'Bracing' was such an *English* word, she thought.

'I have been told it is very stormy in winter,' said Hannah.

'Well, the season finishes in October,' said Stephen. 'Not like Nice

139

or Cannes. Will you be staying on after that?'

'Oh, we'll be here till September and then we shall go back to Pau,' Clara answered. 'We thought of staying in Paris in on the way back home.'

The men had been everywhere, knew Paris well.

'*Très chic* – but only in some quarters,' said Laurence.

Stephen made a face.

'Fashionable life doesn't interest you, then?' Mary asked him boldly.

'I'd rather haunt the Latin Quarter,' said Stephen. 'Laurence here is the *bon viveur.*'

'There are some stunners in Paris,' added Laurence airily. 'Ah, Paris! *Quelle belle époque là-bas!*'

Hannah looked puzzled.

'Same people who come here, I expect,' said Stephen. 'Live in old châteaux, and then build new ones. I hear they are planning a new casino too – it's the church of Biarritz.'

'You mean they worship money?'

'Money and luck.'

'I liked the little church I visited on Sunday,' Mary said. 'A Catholic one.'

'I suppose one might have mystical experiences as well there as anywhere,' said Stephen.

'Mary has them in woods and fields,' teased Laurence.

She enjoyed their badinage, as she had never been the object of it before. Unlike most Englishmen the men were willing to talk about most things, even religion, in a light-heartedly critical way, without paying lip service to conventional pieties. Neither was solemn, but she had noticed they had different reactions to beauty. Laurence clearly appreciated beautiful objects and was a deep mine of information about architecture. Stephen was not forthcoming about his reactions to the sights of this pretty little harbour-town and its history, but Mary guessed he was taking it all in and deciding how he would describe it in future. Just as she was.

They would see them again before the men left to visit Lourdes at the end of the week. Their reactions to that town would certainly be fascinating, she thought.

It had been a most successful day. On their return they said *aux revoirs* at the station before the women took a short carriage-ride back to 'Espoir'.

Dressing for dinner, Clara said to her friend, 'My impression is that the young man is ready to settle down. He looks as if he might have been the wild-oats type to me.'

Hannah tittered. 'You mean Mr Waterhouse? Your niece is certainly taken with him.'

'No, I meant Mr Noble,' replied Clara.

Hannah looked surprised.

'Men don't usually like young women who want to talk about beauty and books and paintings,' said Clara, after a pause.

'Mary is certainly an ideas girl, but Mr Waterhouse seems similar,' said Hannah.

'Mark my words, she has made an impression on Mr Noble', said Clara and added mysteriously, 'Theo would have enjoyed today.'

She did not often allude to her deceased painter husband. Hannah had always been a little in awe of Theo Demaine.

'Perhaps Mary ought not to reveal her enthusiasms so readily?' suggested Hannah.

'I agree – we don't want her heart to be broken.'

Meanwhile the 'enthusiastic' girl was reliving her day as she put on her best evening skirt and blouse. The walking had given colour to her cheeks and a sparkle to her eye. She did wish her aunt would invite her new friends to partake of a farewell supper at Espoir before they left, but decided not to hint at it, for she was aware that young ladies of her age were regarded as very susceptible, and were expected to preserve a certain aloofness in order to retain their charm. It is all nonsense, she thought. If Laurence Noble was to live near Owram he might invite his friend to stay with him in Yorkshire. But she would still be in France.

She found she was trying to visualize Stephen's features, and discovering she could not recreate his face in her mind's eye. It was easy to see Tilly's or even her dead father's features, but far back in her mind she remembered not being able to see Mima when she had first gone away all those years ago, or Miss Watson. This startled her. She had loved Mima, and had what they called a *grande passion* for Stacey Watson. Laurence she *could* see – his fairness, his height, his extremely bright blue eyes. Stephen's darker skin and brown eyes evaded her in detail, yet she could hear his voice as well as she could hear the faintly northern tinge in Laurence Noble's intonations.

The farewells were eventually short. Before the men went off to Lourdes they met Mary and the two ladies for a cup of coffee on the esplanade. Aunt Clara was asked by Stephen if he might have their address in Pau, 'in case I pass through – you never know.'

Mary wanted to say she would write to him but dared not ask for an English address. Hannah saved the day by flourishing a smart blue-and-gold address book and writing down both the men's addresses. *Ridge Hill nr Halifax, Yorkshire*, was Laurence's. The other was

Redcliffe Close, Brompton, London SW.

After their departure Mary felt flat and lonely, unsure she would ever recover her spirits.

They returned to Pau in mid September, by which time Mary was not sorry to leave Biarritz. It had not been the same without the Englishmen. Where was Stephen Waterhouse now, she wondered, as they struggled up the stairs to their rooms in the Pension Mimosa. Would she ever see him again?

The day after their return, a day with a faint whiff of autumn in the air, even in this southern city, a letter arrived for her with a London postmark. So he was back. Aunt Clara had not been there when Madame Lefèvre brought up the post, and Mary was disinclined to tell her of the letter's arrival. How could she begin? *Oh, by the way, I heard from Mr Waterhouse?*

She opened the envelope with shaking hands.

It was a nice letter. They had stayed in Bourges on their way north, to see the cathedral, and then Paris, but only to see some new paintings, and then Laurence had wanted to see Rouen but they had not stayed there long.

I am back in London now and Laurence is busy furnishing the old house that he has rented unfurnished. He asked me when we parted to send his kind regards. 'Tell Mary not to stay too long in France,' he said. 'She would be an adornment to Yorkshire society!' I am helping my father at present in his office in Paternoster Row and may go over to Dublin soon where I have cousins. I am trying to write a few pieces for The Westminster Gazette as I have a friend who works for this journal. I am also reading a lot of new stuff – I feel there is a new spirit around, in poetry anyway, not to speak of the New Woman. My own spirits were a little low on return – I seem to have done so little – I'm sure you would cheer me up, though I ought to be able to cheer myself up, knowing as I do how lucky I am

*compared with most people in this world. Do write – Yours ever, with
fond regards, Stephen.*

Well!

He sounded quite different in his letter from the cheerful friend of
Biarritz. She pondered long her reply. No good telling him of her own
problems about how she should live her life, and she could scarcely
answer him with a description of the ache in her own heart. She might
reply amusingly and perhaps cheer him up that way. But would that
be her real self?

She wrote back, describing her pleasant surroundings, but also
her opinion of the ridiculous fashions worn by some English ladies
in Pau, and the lack of youthful company. She put more effort into
this letter than into her preparation for her French lessons at the
French class in Pau. They were to study the poetry of Leconte de
Lisle and the stories of Mérimée, for neither of which she had
much enthusiasm, though she tried her best to appreciate them.
All the other students were ladies who knew each other, two of
them American. The professor was an erudite but less than
enthralling teacher. She learned more French from talking to
Mme Lefèvre. The real French students were all in the university
quarter of the spacious old town and although it was not far away
she never came across them socially. It was a great disappointment
so far.

She went back to the English circulating library and borrowed
Great Expectations and *North and South*.

'Do you have the novels of Mr Thomas Hardy?' she enquired of
the honorary librarian, a lady of uncertain age whose job it was to
dispense English culture to the English inhabitants of Pau. The lady
looked astounded.

'I believe we have *The Woodlanders*,' she said faintly after consult-
ing the book in which she inscribed the names of borrowers. 'But Mr
Adolphus Messenger has it at present.'

'Then may I please have it next? You have not *The Return of the
Native* or *Far from the Madding Crowd*?'

The lady shook her head.

'Or *Tess of the d'Urbervilles*?' said Mary daringly, knowing of its
reputation.

'Oh no. You might find that in Paris, I expect,' replied the
honorary librarian, pronouncing Paris with a curl of the lip as if it

was a sink of iniquity. She added, 'We have his *best* work.' Mary wondered who chose the novels.

Back at the pension she plunged into Mrs Gaskell and Dickens and had to wait two months for *The Woodlanders*, which turned up at Christmas. A strange sort of Christmas, and Mary felt restless and dissatisfied. She had had no reply from Stephen and was worried he might be ill.

In her feelings of isolation Mary would often carry on conversations with her old rag doll Griselda whom she had with her, having placed it – or 'her' as she still thought of the doll – a little shame-facedly in one of her suitcases, to remind her of home. The best thing would be to write to Tilly, but there were matters she could not really talk about to her best friend. She knew it was peculiar to hold mental communion with a doll, yet after all many women kept the favourite toys of their childhood, didn't they?

They were to return to England a month or two after her nineteenth birthday. Clara needed to see her bank-manager, wishing to change some of her investments, and Hannah had heard from her cousin who had been staying in Hannah's Woolsford home, and now wished to leave the smoky city and move to Menston.

'It is all most provoking,' said Clara.

Mary wished they could go back not to Woolsford but to Cliff House. Only two more years and she would own it outright. But Clara did not want to move back there and money was needed to run the place, even without a servant or two.

Mary resolved to find out more details of her financial situation and at the same time prepare herself for more serious literary studies. She knew she was now too late to prepare for Cambridge, but she might perhaps go to Bedford College in London if she had another year to work for the entrance examination. She felt so much more ready now to undertake some further study. Pau had made up her mind for her. Changing her mind now would probably upset her aunt. It would cost less to attend the Yorkshire College in Leeds as a day student, and maybe she already had the qualifications to go there.

She finished *The Woodlanders*, a sad story that made her think a good deal about the nature of love. She tried not to imagine Stephen Waterhouse in the shape of Giles Winterbourne – whom he did not resemble in the least. She hoped she did not resemble Grace.

She sent her season's greetings to all her friends at home and to Mima and her little family, and received cards from Tilly and the

Crowthers and one or two other English school-friends. At the New Year there arrived a little card from Laurence Noble – the picture of an old gabled house.

They were to return by Paris and stay there for a whirlwind tour of galleries and sights. Theo Demaine's stepbrother was to meet them there and one of the American girls was to travel with them to meet her parents in the capital. Mary knew she should feel excited and full of anticipation but she did not. At last she would see the *Mona Lisa* and the *Winged Victory*, but she felt inadequate, a little numb, when she finally stood before them. What did she really want? She was young and healthy enough, and usually optimistic, but Paris in February surprised them all with its extreme cold, and there had been no further word from Stephen. Why should there be? He would write eventually, as a *friend*, she was sure. Wasn't that what she had wanted him to be? Yet a few smiles from the men who were also sampling culture in the Louvre and La Sainte Chapelle momentarily lifted her heart – just a little. She decided she needed occupation, had been content for too long to sip idly at 'culture' on her travels. What use was she in the world? Tilly wrote that Mercy Miller was learning to be a lady typewriter, much to the disgust of her mother but 'her father has not forbidden her to do it.'

They all arrived back in Woolsford in a late Northern spring. Despite the smoke and the grime and the cold winds, the solidity of the place strengthened Mary's resolution. She would continue her private reading, make enquiries at the Yorkshire College about enrolment in the autumn, and at the same time ask Miss Hartley, who was still teaching, if there was any prospect of her giving French conversation lessons to the younger girls at the school. Clara knew that Mary did not wish to travel abroad again for the time being and said nothing against her new plans. She had changed her mind about further study, which was the prerogative of the young. Clara suspected she would have liked to go further afield but did not want to be a financial burden. France had unsettled her. If Mary persisted in this idea of a studying in Leeds she might perhaps stay with the Crowthers, for she intended to go to Italy with Hannah in the autumn.

She mentioned this to Mary, who said, 'Oh, there are halls of residence, you know.'

Mary gave her first French lesson at the beginning of June to Class

Two of Woolsford High School. They were a group of ten-year-olds, and she was surprised to discover that the little girls gave every appearance of interest, even pleasure. She enjoyed herself too. The pupils had been hand-picked to profit from the lesson and those less zealous had been excluded, but even so Mary felt a sense of achievement.

Tilly was to visit her the following afternoon for tea, after shopping in Manningham. It was on a warm June morning that the postman's second delivery brought a letter to number 3 Deal Terrace addressed to Miss Mary Settle. She did not recognize the writing at first. She had been in the kitchen, attempting to bake a few buns for Tilly's tea, something she found more difficult than getting little girls to repeat French words. They had found a new general servant but she could not come until the following week so Mary was doing what she could. She wiped her hands and blew the flour from the recipe book.

The letter was from Laurence Noble. He asked how she was, how were Mrs Demaine and Mrs Hardcastle keeping, and would they all care to visit him now that he had organized his house to his satisfaction? *I am even thinking of buying it freehold from the present owner, so pleasant is its position.*

Mary was astonished. She had not thought to hear from Laurence again. He added a short postscript:

Stephen is still on a visit to his Irish cousins in Dublin and asks to be remembered to you all. He seems to enjoy Dublin literary life though he is supposed to be there on his father's legal business. Do come and see me in my 'Wuthering Heights' – I can send a carriage to meet you at Halifax station if you care to travel there by train on Wednesday afternoon. The train leaves Woolsford at 2.30 – there is only one change. I shall send you back in the carriage. Let me know if this date does not suit and do please suggest another Wednesday – it is to be my At Home day.
Laurence J. Noble.

When she was shown the letter, Clara said, 'How nice of him – would you like to go over next Wednesday?'

Mary supposed she would.

CHAPTER TEN

The travellers were met at the railway station in Halifax by Laurence's carriage, and the further journey to Ridge Hill, the old hall about three miles from the town, was accomplished without too much difficulty. As they approached the place Mary realized they could have come upon it from the east without travelling to Halifax first. The hills were however fairly steep, and Laurence had probably not wanted to spoil his carriage or his coachman's temper by coming to it directly from Woolsford.

Looking in one direction you would never have guessed how close you were to an industrial town. The house was at the end of a lane a mile from the main road, near a small village, and looked isolated, but when you reached the top of the rise you saw that another newer house was its neighbour. There was a farm in the nearer distance, and pastures were spread lower down the High Shipden valley, but the moors were nearer than they had been in Lightholme. From the back of the house the more distant view would be bleak.

The carriage went through a carved-stone gate into a large cobbled courtyard with stabling. She glimpsed a path on one side by a dry-stone wall that probably stretched down to a garden; the place made her feel it had all once belonged just to trees and wind.

Ridge Hill Hall was built in a mixture of styles. The front and one side was a 'Halifax house' with gables and timberwork and mullions, but the back was much more recently built.

They were ushered into a comfortable low-beamed sitting-room on the ground floor that led directly to one of the front doors. The floors were stone under many dark-red rugs; there was an inglenook that looked genuine, and a fireplace piled with a glowing wood fire. Mary was thinking that the whole room was what used to be called a 'hall'. The interior of the house must have been

147

considerably altered in the years since it was built.

Once they were all settled comfortably, Laurence began to talk about the place, telling them he had decided to buy the freehold. Mary wondered whether he wanted to be regarded as eccentric squire rather than successful businessman.

'How old *is* the house in fact?' she asked.

'Ah, you suspect it is a bit of a fraud,' he replied with a laugh. 'The original house is where we are sitting. My father altered it round at the back to make it more commodious and comfortable.'

'Your father?' she exclaimed, with surprise.

'Yes, Father bought it about forty years ago when he married, and we lived here for a year or two in my childhood. Then he let it out when he moved to Luddenden, to be nearer his worsted-spinning mill on that side of town. It was my mother who found this house too cold and high up and preferred a stone house built in the fifties. I found that ugly – we could never agree. There are some wonderful old houses round here, you know – one not far away from here is three storeys high – Scout Hall – a semi-ruin on the moor, in the middle of nowhere – a family still lives in part of it!'

'Yes, I've heard of that one,' said Mary, 'But there is a folly too, isn't there, Castle Carr, one that people think is ancient but is only about forty years old?'

'You are interested in buildings?'

'Yes – very – if they have a history to them. I like to know who lived there – Shibden Hall, for example. But I find attempts to make a house look old, when it is not, very creepy – I wouldn't like to be alone at Castle Carr at night!'

'I'll take you there one day,' offered Laurence. 'Meanwhile I shall show you all round here and see what you think.'

A woman in a large white apron, covering an ample lap and reaching to her ankles, arrived pushing a table on wheels before her. On it were placed a blue teapot, blue china cups and saucers, and small plates. Mary presumed the woman to be the housekeeper. Was Laurence Noble a rich man? The thought was disconcerting. She wondered if his mother was still alive. The housekeeper went out and returned immediately with a large dish of home-baked scones, butter, jam, and cream, which she placed carefully on a side table.

As if answering Mary's unspoken question, Laurence went on,

'That is Mrs Kershaw – she was Father's housekeeper and stayed on with Mother after Father died a few years ago. Mother died last year. Now this is a better tea than anything in Biarritz! Though it is not really what they mean by 'tea' in Yorkshire, is it? I do take High Tea sometimes though, when I am at home.' She noticed he'd said 'they' not 'we' for Yorkshire people.

The conversation became general – their further travels in France, more details about the house with a description of Laurence's 'programme of works' as he called it, his plan to make it shipshape. The tenants had ruined the woodwork and let grass grow in the courtyard.

'Do you work at your father's mill?' asked Clara, curious as to how he spent his time.

'I keep an overall eye on it. I may not be cut out for textiles but I suppose my father's example showed me how not to make mistakes – the sort of machinery to invest in, that sort of thing.'

Mary supposed he must make hearty profits to live as he did. She had heard the term 'gentleman farmer' and thought Laurence seemed more like a 'gentleman mill-owner' if such a thing existed. He went on talking in a tone of enthusiasm about what she supposed were his real interests. She had glimpsed a wall of books in the room adjoining this one, and there were pictures on the wall she was sure he had chosen.

'I also employ a good manager. I like living here, you see. Business has many ups and downs but existence up here in the North is not as expensive as down South.'

'Did you live in London?' Clara asked.

'Yes, for a time, before my father died. He wanted me to take over, so I did as he wished and came back to live in the town.'

Mary was thinking how different he was, here in his own place. In an alcove at one side of the fireplace was an upright piano. She wondered if he played. If he did he would play well, she was sure. But if he were really good, wouldn't he have a grand piano?

He saw her looking at a picture on the wall on the other side of the large hearth, and said,

'Painting and architecture are my greatest interests. Do you like my little landscape? He painted it in Scotland and this was the sketch for the one the Manchester gallery bought a year or two ago.'

She was sure the sketch was by Millais. He saw her wondering, and went on, 'The oil would be extremely expensive but you can some-times pick up smaller paintings at auctions if you know where to look.'

Mary plucked up her courage and said, 'It is a Millais, isn't it?' She was not sure, but felt she was right.

He looked surprised. 'Quite correct!'

'I loved that big picture of his – it must have been painted when he was a young man – ages ago. I saw a reproduction once. It was called *Autumn Leaves* and there were three girls in a field – it looked like the late afternoon – November probably – and there was a great pile of leaves ready for burning and the children had been gathering them in a basket. Is that in Manchester too?'

'How well you remember it!' he exclaimed. 'It must have been painted nearly forty years ago.'

'Well, it was because one of the girls – the one in the middle – looked so like my friend Tilly!'

'I think I know the picture you mean,' said Clara, wiping her lips carefully with a snowy napkin.

Mrs Hardcastle looked mystified. 'Do you mean Sir John Millais?' she asked.

'Yes, dear. Theo met him once – they were of an age,' replied Clara. 'Of course that was long before I was married.'

Mary knew that Mr Demaine had been much older than her aunt.

'He changed his style after he became so rich and famous,' added Clara.

'How interesting that your husband knew him,' Laurence murmured. He got up. 'Would you all like to see my little library?'

Clara evinced polite interest, Mary pleasure. It was clearly Mary to whom Laurence wished to show his books as he took them round his various bookcases crawling up the wall and the shelves of volumes in the adjoining-room.

She noticed *The Picture of Dorian Gray*, some Ruskin and Pater, and various novels, ones she had read, like *Henry Esmond* and others she had not, like Kinglake's *Eothen*. He had other books on travel in The Middle East and she wondered how much travelling he had indulged in. He seemed to be not only a connoisseur of pictures, and to have a knowledge of architecture but also to be interested in many other things – if you went by his books. Swinburne was most likely on his shelves too. No women writers though, apart from Charlotte Brontë. No Hardy either, not to mention *Jude the Obscure*, but she supposed that would be too much to hope for.

'Do you play the instrument?' Hannah Hardcastle was asking him, indicating the piano.

'Not well, I'm afraid,' replied Laurence. 'Would you like to see the garden? I'm afraid everything is still at sixes and sevens but I am enjoying planning it.'

Was there nothing he did not know about? Was he an expert on women too?

Once out in the garden Mary looked over the outer wall at the lane that ran along parallel to it. Over on the horizon, looking south-westwards, she realized she recognized the silhouette of a hill. When she had seen it from Cliff House it had looked slightly different.

'Why!' she said in surprise, 'that must be Lightholme over in that direction. That's where we live – lived. It's nearer than I thought. My house is still there.'

'Yes, Lightholme is about three or four miles away in the other direction from the way you came,' he replied.

'It's home country,' she said simply, and suddenly felt terribly sad.

There was her old home. Across a mile or so of fields, and then another mile down the hill and along the old Turnpike Road that went in the direction of Leeds, and there she would be. Why had she not yet visited it again?

Laurence must have guessed she was upset for he said, 'Have you not been there to oversee your tenants? I always think it a good idea to see how things are going on. People can be so careless!'

Clara overheard and said with a swift look at her niece, 'Yes, we must visit soon. We have been so busy, you know.'

Mary said nothing then, but on the way back to Woolsford, this time in the carriage, which was to take them all the way home, Hannah made a tactless remark:

'I suppose you could always sell Cliff House.'

Clara looked annoyed. It was none of her friend's business and there were two more years before Mary came of age.

Mary said mildly, 'Oh, I do hope I shall be able to live there again one day.' Inside, she felt rebellious. She disliked living in Woolsford in spite of its concerts and its new park. But she was old enough to understand that she was already nostalgic for her own childhood, and berated herself for this. Hannah pursued the subject in a roundabout way by saying, 'I do think Ridge Hill such an interesting house!'

'But hard to run, I'd imagine,' said Clara. 'He doesn't appear to have all that many servants.'

'Yes, it's a lovely old house,' said Mary, but did not sound very enthusiastic. It was true that Ridge Hill was a house of much greater

151

antiquity than Cliff House but you couldn't help preferring the one you knew, and at present she was thinking of her childhood home.

'You must invite him back to Woolsford to tea,' suggested Clara.

Mary was wishing wistfully that Ridge Hill belonged to Stephen Waterhouse and that it had been Stephen rather than Laurence who had invited them. From what Laurence had said about his friend it was obvious that Stephen was a less 'rooted' person than Laurence Or perhaps not so well off. Stephen probably didn't care about houses and gardens, even if he had appeared to when they were in Biarritz. Was *she* a 'rooted' person? She hadn't thought of it like that, but supposed she must be if she felt such longing for Lightholme. Was it a good thing to want to belong to a place?

She had been impressed by Laurence's *savoir-faire* and his knowledge of so much: books, pictures, gardens, furniture, but wondered why he wanted to impress her aunt. It did not occur to her that he might be intent upon impressing *her*. She supposed they must invite him back to take tea in Woolsford. It was true that there was little intellectual stimulation there. Aunt Clara had done her best, but could not provide her with more than she already had. Her aunt had taken her abroad, allowed her more freedom than most other young women of her acquaintance, whose parents thought about nothing but getting their daughters married off.

She must get herself educated; it was up to her. She wished now that she had taken the idea of going to university more seriously last year. Both Laurence and Stephen had been to Oxford. Well, she would definitely apply to join a general degree course in literary studies at the Yorkshire College in Leeds for the next academic year. She was perfectly qualified. She would speak to Miss Hartley about it.

With this resolve, she made an effort to join in the conversation that evening. After she had gone up to her room to read Hannah said to Clara, 'Did you see the way he looked at her? I do believe he is smitten!'

Clara was annoyed with the way her friend expressed herself. Hannah had always loved to gossip and could not help coming out with her speculations. Clara had of course noticed the way Laurence Noble looked at Mary, but had also decided he was the sort of man who might have sudden enthusiasms for people as well as things. She had also registered that Mary was oblivious to his glances and that the girl was still thinking about the *other* young man.

Over the next few weeks Mary spoke to Miss Hartley and wrote to the Yorkshire College. The reply came swiftly in the form of a prospectus. She must be more specific about the course she wished to follow and then apply for it. Mary pored over the syllabus for a general arts degree and calculated the tuition fees. When Laurence Noble came to tea she would tell him of her plans. Meanwhile, she wrote to Stephen. It was a difficult letter to write and she was not sure she should write to him at all, but she decided it was better to take the risk. If he did not want to reply, he need not. By now he had perhaps returned to London but as she did not know his address in Ireland she wrote *Please Forward* on the envelope. She imagined that the two friends might write to each other and that Laurence might even mention their visit to Ridge Hall.

In her letter she described her feelings about Woolsford, brought him up to date with her latest reading and asked him whether he was enjoying whatever he was doing in Dublin. She added that she had decided to study for at least two years in Leeds, and almost as a post-script said they had been over to Laurence's house and been shown round his domain. How might she end her letter? She would like to write *Yours affectionately* or even *Fondest regards*, but did not wish to embarrass him. Why could you not tell a young man you liked him? Young men were not prevented by convention from telling girls what they thought of them.

She sat back and waited for a reply from Stephen and from the college. Slightly warmer weather arrived and Clara was talking about a visit to the coast. Mary introduced the subject of her projected studies again and showed her aunt the letter from the college.

'If you are sure, dear?' said Clara. 'You have at least two years to improve yourself, I suppose.'

Mary was aware that Clara wanted to spend another year or two in Italy or France, perhaps in a different spa town, but felt that this would just be marking time, as far as she was concerned.

'I could look after the house for you if you decided to go abroad,' she suggested. 'And the tuition fees are not very high if I live at home.'

'I'm not worried about the money,' said Clara.

'I can repay it when I get my money from the rents,' continued Mary, in a firmer tone than she had intended, 'And if they will have me at the school I can teach more lessons, and save up a bit.'

Clara voiced her misgivings to Hannah.

'She doesn't think of a different kind of future for herself. Of course, she's only nineteen,' said Hannah.

'She will meet other young men at the College,' said Clara.

'But it would be a pity not to encourage Mr Noble!'

'She's young and will meet many young people – we mustn't count our chickens!' said Clara, thinking she must sound rather vulgar, though Hannah wouldn't think so. Really, Mary seemed to have no idea of her own attractions.

Laurence came to tea not long after this conversation and Mary behaved very circumspectly. She had just had a reply from Stephen who said how nice it was that Laurence was living so near to Woolsford. He himself was still in Dublin, writing for a magazine there. Ostensibly he was collecting some material for his father at Trinity College on the application of the law as interpreted in Ireland. He went into a few details about the Irish judiciary system.

Mary sensed that this letter was to fend off any subtle enquiries about his feelings. Not that she thought she had overstepped the mark in her earlier missives. She was allowed to discuss his work and his writing, but quite obviously he was demarcating their relationship. She was hurt, but resolved to forget any silly dreams she had had. It would not be easy.

Laurence was an entirely different kettle of fish. He exclaimed with pleasure over some of her not very good water-colours, said he would lend her any books she could not get at the new City Library or the Mechanics' Institute and hoped they might all make an excursion to the Dales when summer really arrived.

She was thinking that he really seemed to like her, and felt both surprised and discomfited. She was determined however to tell him about her plans for study.

'A very good idea!' he said heartily. 'One can never lose anything the more knowledge one acquires. I shall take a great interest in what you do.'

She thought, I suppose he is good looking if you like tall fair men. He appeared to have much more vitality than he had evinced in France. His hand lingered in hers when he left. She could scarcely refuse to see him again. She must talk to Tilly about him.

Tilly often came over to Woolsford when she had shopping to do for her mother at Brown Muff's, the department store, and they would meet in a little ladies' room there. Tilly enjoyed shopping, and there was plenty to see and buy in Woolsford: jewellers, drapers, furnishing shops, bookshops, not to mention the great indoor market.

'I know Aunt and Hannah think he is 'sweet' on me,' she confided to her friend a little disingenuously on one of these outings. 'But what can I do about it? I like him, and he is very sophisticated – but I want to learn more, and grow up a bit, you know!'

Tilly giggled. 'He sounds topping,' she said. 'You don't have to do anything, Mary.'

'But shouldn't I discourage him? Though I'm not certain that he really is interested in me – in that way, you know. I feel sure he's known lots and lots of young women.'

'Most men want to settle down in the end – and you said he was about thirty. I don't mean you should think of him like that, but it's what usually happens, isn't it.'

'What if you are a New Woman?'

'I don't know anything about New Women,' said Tilly. 'I just wish I met more nice young men. There's Edwin of course, and I'm very fond of him but I can't think of him as anything but a *friend*.'

'I'd rather men were friends,' said Mary, thinking, well, that's not quite true, she hadn't really wanted Stephen Waterhouse as just a friend, had she? But even if you fell in love with a man, wouldn't you want him as a friend first? That's how people started off. She had no experience of men but she did know what love was like. Perhaps you changed your mind about young men when love got all mixed up in it.

'Men play by *their* rules,' said Tilly. 'I do know that. I suppose some women want their own rules, but look what happens to them. Men make all the running and we just have to accept it.'

'I just wish I could find someone who feels as I do about life,' said Mary, 'But it's mostly women who feel that.'

Over the next three years she was often to remember these words.

Mary enrolled at the Yorkshire College to study Literature and began her course of study in the October of 1894. Most men preferred to study mathematics or science, so there were mainly young women on the same course as herself. She returned home each day on the train and spent her weekends in study. Occasionally, however, and more often as time went on, Laurence came over to see her on a Saturday. He said he had to be in Woolsford on business, and most of the offices were still busy on Saturday afternoons. Sometimes, early on a Friday evening when he could not visit on the

Saturday, he would meet her outside the college in Leeds and take her back to Woolsford to attend a concert at the St George's Hall. Or they would wander around the shops, which were always open till late. Mary enjoyed the music, but wished she could live in Leeds in the college digs and be more independent. But she did not want to be a further drain on Clara's resources, and it was cheaper to live at home until she could touch her own money from the tenants' rents.

Laurence never tried to embrace her, but would look at her with a fixed expression she at first found disconcerting and then grew to discount. What did he want from her? He apparently enjoyed her company, and she became used to his, without ever feeling she understood him. He also spent a good deal of time over in Manchester on Tuesdays and Wednesdays each week. More 'business', she assumed. Clara was always curious as to how Laurence spent his days and evenings. Did he follow a way of life similar to that which her brother William had enjoyed when he was younger? Mary saw no evidence of it. Clara remembered William telling her how he had used to spend evenings with friends in Lightholme or other villages, till quite late on Saturdays, singing or playing musical instruments. He had attended masonic balls and supper parties, and had attended church regularly, even if most of his time had been spent at work in the office of his mill. Of course, William had been married, and had a partner to accompany him to the houses of mutual friends. All that gay provincial life had sadly fallen away after his wife's death. But Laurence did not seem to fraternize much with other families either in Ridge Hill or in other villages nearby, or in town. Neither did Mary know how much time he actually spent at work. She assumed he would go in on Friday afternoons to oversee the wages being paid, but he had a good Mill manager.

For his leisure, however, he clearly needed a wife, thought Clara. Yet he appeared quite content. She observed his courting of Mary but said nothing to her niece. Indeed they rarely spoke of Laurence, and Clara decided that Mary took his visits as a matter of course.

Stephen had not written to Mary again except once, at Christmas, and she knew better than to ask Laurence for his friend's news. All that was over, or rather had never started.

Mary felt restless; the only thing that seemed to keep her tethered to reality was her work. She was enjoying her literary studies. They had begun with translations of Aristotle's *Poetics*, and Longinus's *On the Sublime* and then Schiller on aesthetics, and she had had to write essays on the meaning of art, specifically literature. She enjoyed all this. It was completely detached from her day-to-day life, and yet she had to offer her own thoughts and conclusions. In her second year she would study great works of English literature – Chaucer and Spenser and Milton. Should she carry on her studies for one final year? She was undecided.

She never forgot Lightholme and Cliff House and went over occasionally to see the tenants, with Tilly in attendance. But she did not enjoy her visits. The house felt alien, full of other people's belongings, and she had begun to realize that even the money her father had been able to leave her would not be enough to refurbish it and run the house properly if she wanted to go back to live in the whole of it.

She was twenty-one in the February of her second year at the college. There were decisions to make, signatures needed, to finalize her inheritance, and along with her aunt she went to see the solicitor about it all. She had to wait until everything was finalized, but she would retain the freehold of Cliff House, keeping tenants for the time being and putting the income from them into her new bank account. Later, she must buy stocks and get the best possible dividends, said her aunt. Clara decided she must consult Laurence about these future financial arrangements. He would surely give good advice.

One day at the end of the summer term of her second year, Laurence came over to the house in Woolsford. Clara left him alone with Mary for a time.

'Aunt wants your advice – but I suppose I'm the one who needs it, Laurence,' Mary said.

'Then I must ask you if you intend to continue with a final year in Leeds,' he replied.

As this was the Shakespeare year, Mary had decided she would stay on and sit for the degree. Her mind was being stretched and she was getting good marks.

'Yes, I think I can manage it,' she replied. 'I shall have my own money very soon –it's about the money that we need your advice.'

Laurence looked grave, making Mary feel nervous.

'If you are to finish the course, then I shall spend more time in Manchester till you have done so.'

He paused. 'I was going to ask you if you would care to marry me, Mary. But I don't want to get in the way of your own work. This will give you time to think about it.'

'*Marry* you?' she replied, stunned.

'Yes. I believe I love you, Mary. I've waited a long time to feel sure – so I can wait another year, I expect! Anyway, I have this business to complete over the other side of the Pennines, so I shall be away a good deal during this next year. This will give you time to consider.'

She was amazed; he had appeared so unromantic – except for those long indecipherable 'looks'. And yet was not his way of proposing to a woman a trifle unromantic?

'I can see you did not realize,' he added. 'Well, I am quite prepared to wait until you have finished your studies.'

Did he mean wait for her to marry him or wait for her to decide whether she wanted to? She was all at sea. Marriage was said to be in the mind of all young ladies but she had thought Laurence just enjoyed her company.

'I didn't know . . .' she got out.

He smiled and took her hand. 'That is part of your charm,' he said.

She said, more firmly now, 'Will you write to me – whilst you are away?'

She was thinking, he could always have written to me about his feelings if he had wanted to, given me some idea of his thoughts. Young men did write love letters, didn't they? Laurence was not a shy man. Did he just feel it was time for him to marry? Or had he been extra scrupulous, wanting her to taste the pleasures of study and freedom?

'Say nothing to your aunt. Wait a year – can you do that?'

Now he must be in earnest!

Gracious, Laurence was what she realized many young women would think of as a 'coup'. Well, she didn't want to get engaged, but it was true, when she began to think about it, that here was being presented a direction to her life. She had thought she would find a post in some school, or would spend happy days thinking and reading. Marriage might put paid to all that. But it was a chance – something actually happening, rather than a figment of her own imagination. She had so often longed, on the days when work had seemed heavy and pointless for, Something to Happen.

They agreed that nothing would be said to her family and she promised she would think about his proposal. It would certainly make it easier to sort out Cliff House – perhaps relinquish it for ever? No! Laurence kissed her hand.

Aunt Clara came in when Mary was standing awkwardly looking out of the window and Laurence had seated himself in the armchair, for all the world like a husband.

As the talk veered to property and money, Mary was being forced to reconsider her desire to live again in her old home. *If* she married Laurence – but what was she thinking of? – she would not be living in Lightholme. Laurence had bought his own lovely old house. All it needed was a mistress. He did not need her money. Now that he had asked her – not that she was going to accept – things became clearer. Oh, if only it had been Stephen who was proposing to her. She suppressed this ignoble thought. It was better not to marry than marry the wrong man, wasn't it?

And yet . . . marriage meant children, and she had always wanted children. The thought made her blush inwardly. If only she had an objective adviser who would understand her conflicting feelings. But the possible adviser had just made his own feelings clear. This man, she thought, as Clara discussed wills and shares and tenants and Mary's finances – this man said he *loved* her. Did he feel for her as *she* had felt for others, as a child and later? She could not imagine that, but wasn't it what she had always wanted, what all girls were said to want?

Mima had loved her and she had loved Mima. Papa must have loved her too, a little, for she had loved him, if not in the way she had loved Mima. She had certainly loved Miss Watson. In the way of a schoolgirl, perhaps, but it had been a real feeling.

She had certainly fallen in love with Stephen Waterhouse, however stupidly. As Laurence Noble may have guessed. Could she ever be in love with Laurence? Was it necessary to be in love with the man who asked you to marry him? Should she not say, 'yes' to life rather than to literature?

Maybe her feelings would be clearer in a year. She must not let her wretched mind analyse and dissect so much. She knew she needed to feel secure. Her life had in many ways been safe, but she knew she needed inner security. Would any reasonably nice man suffice? Or nobody? Did she want nobody? She did not feel romantic about Laurence but she found him attractive, and perhaps that would do. As far as her admittedly small amount of experience went, she already knew that love encompassed many different feelings. She did not say anything to her aunt when Laurence had gone, having given them advice about investments and contracts and tenants. She would wait for him to broach the subject of his proposal. When he thought the time was ripe he would surely ask her to decide when to inform

Clara. If he were rejected he would probably not want Clara to know. They did not have to ask anyone's permission to marry. But it was odd sitting there with it all unsaid. He did not stay on in the evening after his tea.

I want to love, not just 'be loved', she said to herself in the middle of the night when she woke from a strange dream whose contours were in her mind but whose content had evaporated on waking.

'I loved Mima because Mima loved me,' she thought as she lay there in her narrow bed in her room at the top of the terrace house, the sound of the just waking day beneath her in the street. But Mima went away. Stacey Watson didn't 'love' me. Neither did Stephen. Laurence says he does. *I must believe him.*

Would his feelings be enough to weight the scales on his side so that she might think about him seriously? Would he be the right man to spend her life with?

She need not make her mind up for a year. Why not ten years? she asked herself sleepily, and returned to sleep, not this time to dream.

When she woke again the sun was streaming through the curtains and she thought, Laurence knows a lot about pictures and books and buildings and music. Stephen Waterhouse knew about those things too. Did most women accept a man who said he loved them?

I must trust him, she decided; must believe him when he says he loves me. Laurence was a physically attractive man, a clever man. She still could not help being honest with herself though and acknowledging that she could have felt differently about Stephen Waterhouse – and possibly others. She had hardly known Stephen and it had all come to nothing, been in her own head, but she was certain her feelings had been genuine. Perhaps you could not be a good wife and make a good husband out of a romantic feeling. What about shared tastes?

From her inexperience of men and her fairly sheltered youth Mary could not help being puzzled about the value of physical attraction. Obviously, Laurence found *her* attractive. Had she liked Stephen because she had perhaps wrongly sensed that he liked her physical presence? Or was that just a way nature had of making a woman fall in love? She had acknowledged the force of the physical attraction she had found immediately in Stephen. Had she mistaken that for the possibility of love? Did it proceed out of the same need as the desire for love? Wanting to be close to a man who felt as you did, a man with whom you might go hand in hand towards the same horizon . . . was that a chimera?

When she had stood looking out over the Atlantic with Stephen close to her, she had felt herself physically attracted to him, a novel sensation. She had liked him from the start, but afterwards, most of all she had felt a kind of yearning. Stephen could not have felt that or he would have wanted to see her again. Laurence seemed to want to see her quite often, but he did not appear to yearn for her. Why was it that women could not set these things in motion, and had to wait for men to declare themselves?

All this went round and round in her head. Where were the answers to such questions? If, one day, she did not accept a man who had feelings for her, would she be left lonely? Lonely, and childless.

She had always imagined she would have children; the certainty seemed to have been with her ever since Mima had given her the doll Griselda. When she was a little girl, the doll had been her baby, but it had also always recalled Mima, for whom she had felt such a strong love. When Mima had gone away, that love too had been associated with unhappy yearning. Even as a child, after the first shock she had not stormed or raged, had just felt terribly sad and abandoned. Her present state of mind, the unrequited feelings she found she still had for Stephen Waterhouse, resembled her old grief, though they had far less cause. She was grown up, had not known the young man for very long, but she *had* thought there had been in his eyes a definite, if faint, interest in her. Well, that was not to be. Why could she not stop thinking abut him?

If Laurence felt about her the way she had felt for Miss Watson when she was young and untried, she felt rather sorry for him. He did not truly know her, even if he thought he did, maybe that was why he was attracted. But neither had she really *known* Stephen Waterhouse for that matter. She had known Mima. Oh, yes, the child she had been had truly loved Mima Green, as she would have loved her mother – and mothers should never go away. In her dreams, Mima sometimes came back and her feelings were so powerful words could not describe them adequately. They were bliss, she thought. True happiness. . . but now she must grow up, and try to accept that she could never be the first to move in matters of love.

It was also true that she still wanted something to happen. Perhaps everybody did when they were young. Aunt Clara was always saying she wanted everything to stay the same, but Mary did not think she meant that she did not want her niece to marry. *Would* she accept one day to share her life with Laurence Noble? Would that be the grown-up, the sensible thing to do?

She decided to talk to Tilly again about Laurence. The next opportunity would be when she went over on a visit to the Crowthers at The Nest the following Saturday. Laurence was to be away in Manchester on that mysterious business of his.

'But you said you didn't love him,' objected Tilly when Mary told her about Laurence asking her to marry him.

'That doesn't apparently matter at the moment – anyway, he did not ask me whether I did or didn't. People's feelings can change, I suppose, and he is just giving me the opportunity to have a year to think about it.'

'I wouldn't need a year to make up my mind. If I loved someone, I'd *know*,' said Tilly.

'It's not really about that, though. I've realized that if a man says he loves you, you mightn't know straightaway if you'd want to marry him, and in the meantime you might learn to love him.'

As she said the words they sounded prim and hollow. 'Just because *he* feels for *you*.'

'Is that what you think most girls have to do?'

'It was you who said that, Tilly! I'm sure your sisters accepted their husbands because they were courted by them. You see, I don't know if I could do it – I meant only, that was the way women behaved, not that I wanted to be like that myself. I just don't know, Tilly. I like him, and I suppose he is very eligible! I'm sure people would call him a great catch – but that part of it rather puts me off.'

'I never thought you were as keen on getting married as all that, Mary.'

'No, I'm not – but how else is one to live? If only I could be sure of doing the right thing. What if nobody else ever asked me?'

She knew as she said this that she must try to be strong on her own behalf.

'He's given you a year to make up your mind,' said Tilly. 'If I were you I'd just wait and see.'

In this way matters rested, and the next time Mary saw her friend, some weeks later, she did not mention Laurence's proposal.

They were walking the old way down the lane from The Nest in the direction of Cliff House but had turned towards the farm, for Mary had said that for the time being she did not care to go and look at her old house. For some reason her memories of Stacey Watson were in her mind, and she asked idly, 'What happened to that Miss Watson?'

'Oh, there was a great scandal after she left her husband. He divorced her, you know. Then we think she married again – but nobody really knows.'

Mary was thinking, *she* must have married the wrong man – maybe she's happier now. Perhaps even Stacey Watson had changed. Perhaps everybody went on changing and that was why people needed to get married: to stop themselves acting upon their changes and following their fickle hearts. It was rather depressing. Except that she guessed Stacey Watson had possibly not taken her marriage vows very seriously in the first place. Now why should she think that?

'If I got married, I'd be faithful – there wouldn't be any point otherwise,' she said aloud, and Tilly, walking ahead, looked round at her and said, 'Yes, so would I.'

Mary sickened herself with interrogations during the following year. What would she really like best to do? Her first answer was: *Continue studying, and try to write*. But she was not sure she had enough talent to put all her eggs in one basket. It was her last year at the Yorkshire College and a busy one as far as her studies were concerned. Marriage might be an exciting alternative that would not stop her continuing to study – or starting to write. Laurence had always stated that he liked independent women, and she did want to be a 'New Woman'.

If she married Laurence she could not go to live in Cliff House, but must sell it, or continue to rent it out. She still felt strongly that she wanted to hold on to her old home. A husband might be offended that a wife wished to hold on to property of her own but perhaps she could make it a condition of marriage? She could say that it would be better to receive a regular income from the house than to have a large amount of capital, for she had read that the stock market was always fluctuating. Her father had always said that land was the best investment. It was not that she had a good business sense, which was what she hoped Laurence might think; just that she had an atavistic feeling for a house and a place.

It took her all year to get used to thinking about marriage.

PART FOUR

MARRIAGE

CHAPTER ELEVEN

It was the idea of marriage, rather than marriage to Laurence in particular, that preoccupied Mary during the first half of the following year. This was strange, but she reckoned that once she had thought about why she wanted to get married, she could consider whether she would be doing right by Laurence. She found her thoughts jumping off in all directions, her feelings still in turmoil. It would be easier to rely on Laurence's judgement, and he had not asked her to fall in love with him! Did he expect her to? Was he 'in love' with her?

Her final literature examinations took place in June; they were a relief from worrying about the future. She did well, but nobody urged her to continue her studies. Most of the women who had passed either became teachers or got married.

Once she had jumped the hurdle of the general arts degree Mary decided to concentrate upon Laurence, continuing to rely on the fact that he said he loved her, and because he loved her, wanted to marry her. It took her some time to make up her mind what to do, as she gave herself a severe talking to. Sometimes she felt she was revising for an examination. Was she looking for security? Probably. Did she fear that things did not last, and people did not stay? Yes. But Aunt Clara and Tilly had remained part of her life, hadn't they? Perhaps the trouble was that he had said he 'loved' her. Did love last?

Over and above all this was the strong desire to repay the love she had received as a child from Mima to a child of her own. She had no doubts about wanting a child.

She did not want to stay for ever with Clara and Hannah in Woolsford. To live alone at Cliff House would be what she would really like to do, but it was a daunting prospect and one she could not afford without at least one family of tenants. If she stayed with her aunt she might have to spend the rest of her youth trailing round

European spa towns. She could find work teaching children, like Eleanor Hartley ... Yes that was what she ought to do.... But then she thought, 'I'd rather bring up children of my own!' If she rejected Laurence's proposal, who else would ever ask her? Come come, she said to herself, you know how you dislike women who think they are on the shelf at twenty and here you are at only twenty-two – and a man wants you!

She had enjoyed the little teaching she had undertaken, having found herself capable of enjoying the company of certain children, but she had enjoyed her further studies even more.

All her thoughts seemed to cancel each other out. The thought of Stephen Waterhouse or someone like him was still lurking in her heart. If Stephen had wanted to pursue her she would have had no hesitation. But he had not.

Before she exhausted the pros and cons of what she realized was an excessively rational way of proceeding, she felt she must try to understand Laurence better. When they met over the next week or two she tried to do this – and found him both more interesting and more baffling.

When he said that he was not a religious believer but that he believed in keeping up *les convenances*, she felt uneasy. She was still not sure what she believed, but felt she was young enough not to settle for religion as social glue. She wished she might have undergone a dramatic conversion, become a Methodist like the Crowthers, or a Catholic, or even a steady middle-of-the-road Anglican. She wished she had studied more philosophy and theology, but knew that a leap of faith would not be likely as the result.

She appreciated Laurence's taste and knowledge, and trusted his experience, but was frequently driven to wonder *why* he should want to marry her. It must be that he had fallen in love. She could understand that in the abstract, but she knew herself too well, she thought, to think that he really understood her. Did she delude herself even here?

After all this she suddenly thought she must be mad, and decided to have done with it and to accept him.

Upon which matters moved swiftly.

Laurence did not appear surprised when she told him, over a cup of coffee at Spinks' restaurant in Woolsford, that, yes, she would marry him. He looked mildly gratified and even, she thought, relieved, and went on to suggest that a quiet church wedding in the city might suit them both. He had several business matters to conclude over the next few weeks but saw no reason to delay after this. Mary would have been quite happy to marry at the office of the civil registry, except that Aunt Clara might be owed, or might expect, something more traditional.

Mary therefore agreed, and told him she had never dreamed of a big wedding for herself in a large church full of relatives. The only wedding she remembered was Mima's, and remembering it still brought tears to her eyes. She had never been able to unburden herself to Laurence about all that was in her heart concerning Mima.

Laurence Noble and Mary Settle were married in October 1897 at a quiet ceremony in a small church in Woolsford. Mary felt it was all a dream. Clara and Hannah were the chief guests; Tilly was there, of course, and Liddy, and a cousin of Laurence, with a few of her own more distant Settle and Dyson relatives, along with Edith Wadsworth and other friends from the Yorkshire College.

Mary had written to invite 'Mrs Jemima Sutcliffe', but Mima had just had a miscarriage and had been told to rest. She wrote Mary a letter full of love, and hopes for her happiness. It was the one thing that made Mary pause, as if she was deluding Mima into a false belief about her feelings for Laurence. She had not wanted Stephen Waterhouse to be invited and Laurence had not mentioned him as a guest, so she had not either. Another business friend of Laurence, called James Walshaw, whom Mary had met only once, was asked as best man.

Afterwards, Mary and Laurence took a sleeping car on the night train to Kings Cross, a hansom to Victoria Station, and then the Dover train to Paris where they remained for only one night, followed by a long train journey to the northern Italian lakes. They were to stay for a month on their honeymoon in Gardone and then go on to Como.

Laurence made love to Mary for the first time in Italy, both of them having been too exhausted to do anything but sleep whilst at the Hôtel Meurice on the rue de Rivoli. Mary found lovemaking rather pleasantly overwhelming at first, if not quite the revelation she had expected. Laurence seemed used to it, and was a considerate lover, but she found it difficult to distinguish any romantic passion he might be feeling from ordinary masculine lust. She had no standard of comparison, so presumed this was something common to the male sex.

She came swiftly to the conclusion that her husband was more attracted to her body than to her mind – which surprised her. She could not help feeling pleased that he should find her an object of desire, if rather dismayed that he appeared to take less emotional or intellectual interest in her than formerly.

She adjusted to making a new life for herself as she waited to be in what Hannah Hardcastle called an 'interesting condition', which everyone said was, after all, the right true end of their regular love-making.

There was plenty to do in the house after she had made friends with the housekeeper, Mrs Kershaw, who was apparently still to carry on working for them at Ridge Hill. She also bought a bicycle which, in spite of the hills, she much enjoyed riding round the district. In Woolsford she would not have dared to ride among all the traffic of horses and trams, but here she could ride up and down to the nearest village and round the lanes if not right into town. Owning it gave her a wonderful sense of freedom. She had never enjoyed driving a pony and trap, and even now disliked having to take the carriage for shopping. Laurence kept a carriage and a trap, old Harry Forbes doubling as gardener and coachman.

The first year of their marriage passed, and then the second, and still she was not 'expecting', in spite of Laurence's lovemaking. If not quite so frequent as at first it was regular enough during those first two years. She supposed that babies did not come just when you wanted them. Laurence still appeared to find her attractive, though she wished that she could talk to him more about the things that interested her. At least they both had time to pursue their own interests.

When they celebrated their second wedding anniversary in the autumn of 1899 she had become a little more anxious. As that year drew to a close she wondered whether Laurence was as worried about it as she was. He had never evinced the great desire for a child that she had always nourished. She did not broach the matter but waited for him to do so, felt embarrassed as well as sad. By the third anniversary of their wedding, she was attempting to resign herself to being barren, and Laurence was more and more occupied by his business connections, often tired when he returned home.

One day, towards the end of 1900, when she was tidying up a bookshelf, she discovered a letter. It fell out of a book of the plays of Ibsen, including *The Doll's House*, which she had read in her own copy when she was at college.

The writing on the envelope was in the familiar hand of Stephen Waterhouse, the date the late spring of the year they had all returned to England from Biarritz. She could not resist opening it and reading it. The address was in Surrey, so he must have written it before he went over to Ireland. She had kept his last letter to her in an old music-case, reluctant to let it go, along with two or three letters from Mima, and some from Tilly, received in France, not wanting to destroy bits of her past when she moved to Ridge Hill.

15 May 1894

Dear Laurie

Your letter amazed me. What can I say, I who have no hopes at present of being able to offer a young woman a home or a future? You know my financial situation, and it has not improved, nor is it likely to, for some time. I had become very fond of the little woman, tho' I would not think her yet quite ready yet for what my sister calls 'settling down', and I would not be able to – alas – for some time. There are human possibilities for someone so young that it would be wrong to deprive anyone of, before she grew up and knew her own mind. I cannot see that forcing the matter would do any good, though I know your temperament is such that it would seem to you to be the best course of action.

If we lived in more rational times it would not be necessary to confuse love with this 'settling down', at least not until girls had reached years of discretion, though I expect they would not agree! Their lives are shorter than ours, as far as what they believe their real destinies to be, and we men must not wait too long if we are to make them happy.

I hoped by the age I now am to have done enough to provide for a foyer *but it is one of the drawbacks of the life I lead that no woman could be expected to share it just yet. I had hoped to make a friend of her, and then, who knows, perhaps one day, if she loved me, and had no other offers, and my affairs were in better shape, to enter into a more serious state of affairs. I had no idea that you were so attracted to her. I suppose it would be a sensible way of putting an end to your other entanglement – at least I hope so.*

I can't stop you because I can't offer her anything solid myself –

171

except my love – and you can offer your hand. I only hope you love
her. I wish you well. . . .

Mary read on, horrified and disturbed. Stephen Waterhouse had felt
he might love her but had given her up to a friend whose finances
were on a better footing. Had Laurence been asking for his permission or his opinion? She had never imagined that she was the first
woman he had loved but she did wonder about the 'entanglement'.

She put the letter back in the book and made sure the book did not
appear to have been recently consulted. She would tell nobody about
what she had found.

She woke in the night disturbed by the fear that perhaps
Laurence's carelessness might mean that he did not really care now
if she did come upon it. But that was absurd. Worse was her realization that if Stephen had been a little in love with her he could have
taken steps to test her own feelings. What had she cared for
'prospects'? She had thought her own feelings for Stephen
completely unrequited, so she had suppressed them. She had had
three years to explore those human possibilities that Stephen had
mentioned, three years when Stephen might have got to know her!
Laurence must have expected her to agree to marry him much
earlier, but he had waited, she must give him credit for that. It was all
her own fault; she had had the courage to pursue her studies, but not
the courage to wait longer before she decided to marry the – richer –
man who said he loved her.

That was of course what all women were supposed to do – respond
to a man's love – wasn't it? Never to dare to be the prime mover.

From Mary's diary:

3 April 1901

I have decided to try to put my thoughts in order – yet again. I was
thinking how Laurence likes things to be done properly. It runs
counter to any affection he might have pretended he had for la vie
de Bohème, *or the creative life of the mind, which I found attractive.*
The time of my marriage now seems centuries ago though it is only
three and a half years. I should not have married <u>anyone</u> when I was
so young, I mean for Laurence's sake as much as my own. There was
no compulsion on me to marry but I suppose if I had not I might be

172

abroad with Clara, where I can't help thinking I might have met SW again . . . but that is foolish and I try not to think about it. I might have been teaching, though, and keeping the Manningham house going. Instead, I enjoy the fruits of my husband's father's past labour, along with his own, and the labour of countless operatives. Should I feel guilty about that? Laurence is down at the mill today as it is wage-day – Friday – and he is also to confer with the manager he appointed a year ago to keep an eye on everything when L is absent. He turns out to be the son of Father's old manager, Hamish Gordon.

5 April

L says trade is very bad at present. I was thinking that my husband has good taste, I mean for things like furniture. I hope mine has improved since I got married. Apart from overseeing accounts, and those of a now-deceased partner of his father in Leeds, and buying machinery L now goes every Wednesday to York or Leeds to attend auctions, where he bids for pictures and furniture, but he does not often come home with much. In the evenings we both read, and I sometimes do my piano practice if I think Laurence is not listening, or try to paint, using the sketches I did last summer.

As we are not church members, or do not attend very often – unlike most manufacturers from around here Laurence is not a Methodist – our circle is rather restricted. We have stopped going to dances in Elland, which we did when we were first married, but we still go now and then into Woolsford to concerts, now that the train there is direct.

I have the garden to oversee but I am not a gifted gardener, and must write again to Liddy for advice. There is always plenty to do in the house, and I have improved my knowledge of cooking, but I know I ought to be doing something more suited to my talents. Tilly thinks I am lucky in many ways, so why am I discontented? Is it only because I have no child? Tilly has not much spare cash now that she is married to the Reverend George Ramsden, her Congregational minister, and they have their little Maisie. Tilly has the best gift in the world, a child.

The death and funeral of the old Queen, that took up so much space in the newspapers in January and February, and the proclamation of King Edward –even in Calderbrigg where we went to listen – are now thankfully over, but the newspapers are full of this disastrous Transvaal war which is costing the country dear. I am so very much against this campaign.

A beautiful day today. We deserve it, after a very cold March with 25 degrees of frost. I enjoyed the snow earlier in the year but there were such hard frosts in January too, and bitter north-east winds, and then fog, to make everything worse. Last winter Laurence said we might go this year to Mentone or Cadenabbia to avoid the worst of the Yorkshire winter but he has never mentioned it again, I suppose because trade is not doing too well. I can't summon up any enthusiasm for travel at present. I have become an old stick-in-the-mud at twenty-six. I only hope L is happy. Recently he has seemed more than a little distracted. There were many problems with the mill earlier this year and they had to put some of the workers on half time.

6 April

Today I noticed for the first time this year a tender faint film of green: the trees beginning to dress for summer. And then straightaway there came to my mind the idea of a beautiful young tree being like a lovely young woman putting on a silk chemise of pale eau de nil and a thin underskirt, and then standing looking out at the moor from the window of the boudoir. The boudoir would be at the back of the house on the top floor . . . I cannot seem to stop day-dreaming.

We have a new neighbour whom we have not yet met officially. I have seen her recently in the garden of Birch Wood from the bottom of the lane that skirts both our gardens when I have been in the carriage on my way home from shopping in town. The other day I saw her in the distance over the wall at the side of our garden. Yesterday Laurence said that I must drop our card at Birch Wood and ask her to visit us. His manager thinks he may have once met her husband. Convention will have it that a new neighbour must first be invited as guest to one's own home before she can be said to have joined our local society. Even here we follow protocol. At least, Laurence's, so I suppose my, rank of provincial life must do so, although I wish it was different and that we could all be as free as the birds that alight wherever they wish both in our garden and hers. . . .'

The journal was becoming a repository for her dissatisfactions and she did not admire herself for this. Through the window of the little top room, her 'eyrie' at the back of the house, the room where she did her reading and what Laurence called her 'scribbles', she could see slow-moving clouds over the distant moor. There were such splendid skies in this part of the world. In spring, as now, the clouds chased

174

each other all over the wide heavens, but at night, all seasons alike, when the stars came out the sky was like a great reel of black velvet dotted with sequins . . . or the moon would shine as if behind gauze, wreathed in cream-coloured veils of cloud.

Mary shook her head to banish more reverie. She must try to think what she ought to be doing. Telling Mrs Kershaw what to buy for the rest of the week, she supposed, or buying some of it herself at the covered market in town. She enjoyed visiting this market, as there was a bookshop there. The market and the shops in town were open till quite late in the evening.

She very much wanted to get to know the new neighbour, said by the village grocer to be a widow, a Mrs Hart. Perhaps she would turn out to be a congenial new friend, for she missed female company. It had taken her some time to realize that she had little truly in common with Laurence, who might be up to date in cultural matters but did not enjoy the simpler pleasures of life – flowers, new novels. Just being alive, thought Mary, having your own ideas, trying to write and paint, even pottering around. Of course he played the piano a lot better than she ever would. His general standards were so high, she had decided, because he was not a creative person but an interpreter or an aesthete. This realization also made her feel guilty. She missed the rush of high feelings – of ecstasy and joy, even the yearning that had accompanied her adolescence.

She was growing older, she supposed, but could you never share these things? She feared not. She must be what Eleanor Hartley had once taxed her with being – a dilettante. She made a new resolve to try and make the best of what she had – a husband who was attentive, and a pleasant, if fairly uneventful life.

There was still plenty time for her to have a child. Perhaps she would be able to conceive if she thought about it less often.

The following Monday she judged a good day to leave their card at Birch Wood. She walked down the lane and round to the gate of the their neighbour's house, in the wall on the far side of the entrance to their own drive. Birch Wood was set back only a little and when she pushed the gate open she saw the garden was much neglected.

The house had been empty for some time and was nowhere near as old as their own, having been built only about fifty years previously, when businessmen had begun to colonize the surrounding area of the rapidly growing town. When she had first come to Ridge Hill,

Birch Wood had been tenanted by the family of a Scots power-loom engineer who had soon moved on to a better job in Woolsford.

She pushed the gate shut, which made a protesting squeak, and went up to a green door at the side of the house which looked as if it had been painted a little more recently than the gate. She pulled on the bell that was hanging outside this door and waited for a maid to answer it. No maid did, but there was the sound of footsteps and then a woman's low voice said, 'Who is there?'

This was awkward. If the woman was the owner she could not give a servant the card to leave in the hall, as one usually did, to be picked up later by the mistress of the house.

'It's your next door neighbour,' she said, sounding rather silly in her own ears.

'Wait a moment – would you please go round to the front door?'

Mary felt even more stupid. Perhaps this was the housekeeper, though the accent sounded more like that of a fairly educated woman.

'It's only to leave our card, I can put it though your letterbox.'

'No, I'll come through.'

Mary walked round to the front, passing a bay window on the way, and found a larger door. It had no letterbox. There was the sound of bolts being pushed back. She would just hand in the visiting card and depart.

The woman who opened the door and stood in the half darkness of the hall was wearing a long *peignoir* and looked slightly dishevelled. She was about thirty-seven or eight with long dark hair that had not been dressed that day.

'I'm sorry to disturb you – I'm Mary Noble from next door – I just brought our card with an invitation to come over for tea on Thursday,' she stammered. 'I'm sorry,' she said again, and wondered why she should apologize. 'Perhaps your maid did not hear me ring.'

'I have no maid at present,' said the woman and put out her hand. 'Anastasia Hart,' she said.

Mary took the proffered hand and shook it.

'Then I'll be off – do try to come . . .'

'I expect I may,' said the woman. 'I don't know anyone round here.' She took the card. 'Thank you.'

Mary waited a moment, before saying, 'Do let me know if there's anything I can do to help you – our housekeeper may know someone who would work for you. . . .'

The woman was scrutinizing her. 'You are very young,' she said finally. Then, 'I believe somebody told me a Mr Noble lived in the next house – but I have not got out much yet.'

'Well, I must be going. I – we – shall hope – hope to see you on Thursday. I'm sorry it is such short notice. . . .'

The woman did not move to shut the door but went on looking at her closely. Mary could not help wondering if she was perhaps ill.

Then Mrs Hart gave a faint smile, and said, 'Goodbye, then.'

Mary turned and walked away. She heard the door being bolted as she walked down the drive.

The woman had been good-looking, but pale and had a rather tragic air about her. At the same time, Mary was thinking, why should I think that? Have I ever seen her before?

She told Laurence of the meeting when he returned that evening.

'I hope she will accept – she looked in need of company,' she said. 'And, you know, I'm sure I have met her before!'

Laurence, who had listened in an absent-minded way to Mary's description of her afternoon, now looked up and said quite sharply, 'Met her before – but where? I don't believe she comes from round here – at least that is what my manager said the other day. I believe he met her husband in Manchester.'

'Perhaps I am mistaken, then,' said Mary.

But when she woke in the night it was with a sudden stab of recognition.

She knew who the lady was.

Anastasia? 'Stacey'? Surely, Miss Watson?

Older by how many years? Fifteen, sixteen?

Changed, but still beautiful.

Mary resolved to say nothing to anyone unless the lady chose to reveal herself as the one-time Stacey Watson. Tilly had said, hadn't she, that she had married again? That must be her second husband then, if she was a widow. But how should the grocer know? She looked forward to Mrs Hart's reply with a mixture of impatience and a tinge of quite irrational dread.

The answer came in a flowery hand:

Mrs Anastasia Hart thanks Mrs Noble for her kind invitation and will be pleased to come over to Ridge Hill for tea on Thursday the eleventh.

Would she recognize her? A little girl would have changed more than a grown woman, though Stacey herself, if it were she, had changed a good deal too. But the light had been poor. Perhaps she was wrong and had confected an old memory out of a stranger?

Mary looked forward to Thursday but she was also strangely anxious. Ought she to find out more about her before she asked her if they had met before? Miss Watson might not remember a little girl from so long ago. She might be mistaken and the woman bear only a slight resemblance to 'Stacey'. She'd like to be sure, and she could not sit and stare at her visitor, ask personal questions, without appearing rude, or at the very least nosy. The lady might not wish to reveal that she had been married and subsequently divorced. Should she mention that the rumour was she was a widow?

On the morning of the proposed visit, before Laurence left the house, she said,

'Did Mr Gordon tell you Mrs Hart was a widow?'

'I don't believe so – why?'

'Because if she's the woman I met when I was a child I heard later that her husband divorced her!' said Mary robustly.

Laurence looked a little shocked.

'I hope you will be tactful then,' he said as he went into the porch.

As if I am not always tactful, thought his wife. She was only a neighbour after all. Yet she was very curious about her. She was nervous on the morning of the visit when she went into the kitchen to ask Mrs Kershaw to set a little table in the small sitting-room at three o'clock, and then personally inspected one of plum-cakes the housekeeper had baked at Christmas. Mrs Kershaw always made her feel nervous. Mary had imagined the woman would want to retire soon to live with her sister in Leeds, but nothing had been said. She must be over sixty. Mary enjoyed the housekeeper's cooking and did rely upon her when she had to entertain, but she made her feel inadequate.

She changed into a dark-blue afternoon gown, one she rarely wore but one that Laurence liked. As she looked at herself in the glass, she wished her husband could join them at the tea party.

She was ready in the sitting-room, trying to read a book, when the bell went at four o'clock. She heard Ethel, the new parlour-maid, welcome the guest, heard their steps in the hall, and then the sitting-room door was opened by Ethel with a flourish. Mary rose and advanced towards Mrs Hart, who stood there, unsmiling, dressed in a long black tea-gown. Perhaps she too was feeling nervous. Mary felt a compulsion to put her guest at her ease, and as was her habit when she wanted to be welcoming chattered haphazardly. A seat was found for the visitor by the fire, and the table trolley on wheels was wheeled in by Ethel, who took a good look at the visitor as she handed round cups and plates.

'How comfortable you have it here,' sighed Mrs Hart. 'My own house is so cold.' She was looking around with interest.

Mary handed her a cup of hot tea, enquiring, 'Have you found a servant yet?'

Mrs Hart sighed. 'I'm afraid that my reduced circumstances mean that I can afford only one maid. But Mrs Robinson, an old companion of my stepmother's, may come to help me.'

She set her cup down carefully. Mary waited, in case the reduced circumstances were explained, but when no explanation was forthcoming, she said: 'Will you take some cake, Mrs Hart?'

'Thank you.'

Mary passed her a pretty little plate painted with a bluebird, on which a piece of plum-cake rested. Mrs Hart looked at the plate and said, 'How pretty.'

'Yes, it is from a set that belonged to my husband's mother.'

'I don't suppose you needed to buy many new things when you came here,' said Mrs Hart. 'I was told that your husband's family had lived here. But *you* can't be very old!'

Mary was a little nonplussed, but said, 'Do you know this part of the country then? I heard you had come over from Manchester.'

'I know the town a little – I stayed near here years ago.'

Now was Mary's chance, but for some reason she was reluctant to take it. She postponed what she wanted to ask, saying instead, 'I used to live not very far from here when I was a child.'

'You met your husband here, then?'

'No – that is – we met for the first time abroad – but by then I had been living in Woolsford for several years.'

She saw that Mrs Hart was just as curious about her as she was about her visitor.

Mary took a mouthful from her piece of cake and watched as Mrs Hart nibbled at her own, before Anastasia asked in a polite voice:

'Oh, where did you live before Woolsford, then?'

Now that Mary had got the question to come from Mrs Hart she would soon be able to ask her what she wanted. She wished she could say, I thought you were wonderful – and you are still a beautiful woman, though you look so much older. . . .

'I lived at Cliff House in Lightholme,' she began.

'Lightholme? I believe I once visited there.' She stopped, and appeared reluctant to continue.

Mary pounced. 'We lived in the next house to The Nest – where my friend Tilly lived. In fact I'm sure that I have met you before – it must be fifteen or sixteen years ago. . . .'

Mrs Hart said in a faint voice, 'That was where a cousin of mine lived, as far as I remember . . . but I don't remember you.'

'I'd only be a child then,' said Mary, determined not to reveal that she remembered her guest quite well. She was now sure from the expression on her face that Anastasia Hart remembered the summer of her engagement.

'Tilly Crowther was – is – my best friend,' she added.

'I do believe I remember a child I met there one summer, a friend of the Crowther girls,' said Anastasia slowly.

'Yes, Mary Settle – that was my name.' You came to The Nest when I was eight, she thought, and again when I was nine, and I saw you with your fiancé when I was eleven, and I never forgot you. As if she could ever have forgotten her day-dreams, but there was no reason for Anastasia Hart or Stacey Watson to remember her. Except that the last time, when she was eleven, it had been just before Stacey married her young man, a time of life a woman must remember well.

Perhaps she ought not to remind the former Miss Watson of it, but she could not help saying aloud:

'I once sat in the summer-house at The Nest with a lady called Stacey Watson.'

She would pretend she had heard nothing of the subsequent fate of her marriage, though surely Anastasia must guess that Tilly would have told her. Instead, she added, 'I believe my husband's manager, Alex Gordon, mentioned that he had met your husband.' She said nothing about the grocer and the widowhood.

Mrs Hart looked at her sharply but did not reply for a moment, obviously wondering how much she wished to reveal to this new Mary.

Mary decided to put her out of her misery and said, 'It must be hard for you to be here alone – do let me know if there is anything I can do for you.'

As she spoke, she remembered exactly how she had felt when,

little more than a child, she had been fascinated by this woman and, in some curious way, had wanted to look after her. There was still something compelling about Anastasia Hart. Now that she was grown-up, Mary could see that men must have found Miss Watson attractive, just as she felt sure they would find Mrs Hart attractive too, in spite of her having lost the bloom of youth.

'Mrs Noble . . .' the other woman began.

'Do call me Mary,' said Mary impulsively. 'I always think of you as Stacey,' she added. 'It was Tilly Crowther who used to call you that.'

Anastasia Rose Watson she remembered Tilly enunciating, adding *We call her Stacey*, as if to cut her down to family size.

'Really? How is Tilly?' asked Anastasia.

'She is well – she is married and living in Leeds. They have a little girl.'

She wanted to add: I envy her that. I wonder if *you* have any children, she thought. But she guessed that children would never have been part of Mrs Hart's plans for life. Looking at her, she noticed for the first time that there were tiny lines around her eyes. How old would the old Stacey be now? She could not have been much more than twenty-one when she had stayed that last time at The Nest, and she must have been about ten or eleven years older than herself.

'May I call you Anastasia, Mrs Hart?' she asked her boldly.

Mrs Hart looked at Mary with an expression that Mary could not decipher. Was it amusement, or slight disdain, or annoyance? Then she must have decided that Mary meant well, for she smiled, though Mary sensed it had cost her an effort to do so.

'Do, please, Mary,' she said.

After this, the conversation did not revert to the past except when Anastasia rose to go and asked, with every appearance of nonchalance that did not fool Mary in the least:

'Do you ever go over to The Nest now?'

'Not since Tilly got married,' replied Mary. 'But I go occasionally to Cliff House, my old home. I have tenants there and must check from time to time that all is well.'

'You have a place of your own then? How does your husband like that?'

Mary sensed the bitterness behind her words and assumed she must have or have had a husband who disliked independent women.

'Oh,' she replied lightly, 'I think Laurence is quite pleased I haven't sold it – yet. He knows I was happy there as a child.'

Anastasia glanced at her watch. After a mutual exchange of commonplaces, she left.

'I hesitate to ask you over to take tea with me,' she said as she went out. 'I still have to get the place to rights.'

'Don't worry about that,' answered Mary, 'You must come over again soon – one evening perhaps – and if there is anything you need, do ask me.'

Shortly afterwards, Anastasia departed, leaving a faint scent of *chypre* in the room.

Mary felt just as puzzled and intrigued by her as ever.

As they ate their supper that evening she said to Laurence,' I was right – I *had* met our neighbour before.'

'Really?'

'Yes, at Tilly's when I was a child – I saw her three times over the years and never forgot her!'

'What was she doing at The Nest?' asked Laurence, looking interested.

'She was a cousin of Mr Crowther and used to come to stay. Mrs Crowther once sent her into the schoolroom to watch us at work. I think she found her rather hard to entertain. But the last time I saw her was just before she married –I even saw the fiancé.'

Mary was not going to tell her husband about her old schoolgirl feelings for Stacey Watson. It was a precious memory and one she thought it best to keep to herself. Especially from the new Mrs Hart, who might think her silly.

'What did you think of her this afternoon?'

'She has not changed a great deal in looks, though I did not recognize her definitely at first. Today I had the impression of a rather sad woman – though I'd imagine she could be difficult.'

'Well, if she *has* just been widowed she would not look very cheerful.'

'She never said anything about that. She *must* have been married more than once – I didn't ask her anything about being widowed, but if she is, it must be the second husband, since Tilly told me she had been divorced from the first one, the one who stayed at The Nest.'

'How unusual. Well, I suppose we might discover the truth one day. Did you ask her to come over again?'

'Yes, I did – perhaps we could have a little dinner party soon. She told me that she could not entertain us because as she was renting her house it was still all at sixes and sevens. She was looking for a maid, but now she thinks an old friend of her stepmother may come over to live with her.'

'Let's wait until it's a bit warmer in the garden,' said Laurence, who was not a devotee of the entertaining of local people as guests, being too fearful of being caught up in what he called the politics of 'Dumbletown'.

'Yes, it would be nice to have a garden supper, though one can never predict the weather. I might ask her round again before then.'

Over pudding, she remarked, 'I wonder how your Mr Gordon met her husband. I suppose he often used to go over to Manchester for you?'

'Alexander used to know Manchester well,' replied Laurence. 'But now that our old office over there is shut down he won't have been over the Pennines recently. He must have met him some time ago.'

'I wonder if she decided to come here because she wanted a new life and knew the district in the past?'

'I've no idea,' said Laurence.

Mary was thinking *over the Pennines* sounded romantic, bringing visions of wild moors. It made her wonder how Jemima and her family were keeping in Burnley, which was the nearest town to their part of Yorkshire. She must go over soon to see her again. It was almost twenty years now since Mima had left Cliff House, and her two children were almost grown up. She had never had another after the miscarriage at the time of Mary's wedding.

If *she* had had a child in the first year of her marriage it would be three this year.

How time flew.

Thinking about The Nest brought it all back.

Clara was back on the Continent with Hannah and they had now announced their intention of staying in Baden for at least a year. They had been in Montecatini, a small Italian spa town, and now wanted a change.

Tilly was busy being a housewife and mother in Leeds and was expecting another baby later in the year.

Not for the first time in the last two years, but more intensely than before, Mary felt lonely. Usually she had plenty to do and was used to a rich inner life that came from a mixture of reading, what she called her 'early morning thoughts', and the observations she made on the walks she took in the district, sometimes with Laurence but usually by herself.

She took little real pleasure in looking after the house except for knowing she had at least tried to do her best. In spite of being old and interesting and in parts beautiful, Mary never felt it was *her* house. Laurence had brought her to *his* house. Running a home and a household was necessary work and it usually had to take precedence, but it was not her personal choice. She often found herself dreaming of another home, but was never sure if it was the old Cliff House or somewhere she had imagined.

As for the garden, she liked that better and felt it belonged a little more to her than the house, perhaps because Laurence had done little to it. He liked planning the shape of gardens but knew scarcely any names of flowers, nor did he take any interest in them. Mary told him that a walled garden was very fashionable at present and persuaded him to allow her to ask Harry Forbes to demarcate a plot for her at the end of a small lawn at the side of the house near one of the outer walls. The gardener-cum-coachman had come in to help out the previous owner years ago and was pleased that she took an interest. She called this plot her 'secret garden', and grew rambler roses up one of the south walls, which Laurence was persuaded to admire.

She would wake up in the morning with a feeling of something missing, a feeling that was not quite unhappiness. She did not know what name to give it. She was sad about their not having a child, but she still enjoyed spending time alone, so long as Laurence appeared reasonably content, which she had come to doubt and did not know how to deal with. He appeared self-sufficient, but she worried over the lack of genuine intimacy between them. Might it just be her imagination? On the other hand, if it existed it must be her fault. He had never said he needed more of her, and had formerly appeared satisfied. *Did* he still find her attractive? He had used to tell her she was, and she had decided it had been primarily her physical attributes – and her youth – that had attracted him to her. She supposed that they were now just used to each other. Other couples of their acquaintance had had to adjust to the presence of children. Perhaps Laurence felt the lack more than he let on, yet he often said he was not a great lover of children.

She felt no particular physical need, but occasionally dreamed of a different sort of lover, though she did not imagine she could ever be unfaithful. She no longer wished she might see Stephen Waterhouse again, and would be embarrassed if he knew she had seen that letter from him to her future husband.

The lack she felt in her life must be the result of an over-active imagination, of thinking what might be, but was not. That she was not completely fulfilled and would perhaps never be completely happy, must be the fault of her own temperament. Was she at all suited to marriage? Had she let Laurence down in some way? She had so often asked herself why she had thought it necessary to marry as soon as she had finished her college studies. It must have been because she wanted to be like other women, regarded as 'ordinary'.

But I *am* quite ordinary! she thought.

She had feared being left high and dry with Clara, had thought Laurence presented a much more exciting prospect. But most young women did not ask themselves, *Why marry?* did they? Rather, *Why ever not?*

All her present introspection ended only in her feeling subtly guilty. She did not feel 'grown up'. She continued to write in her journal about these major lacks in her life.

She was invited to spend a day with Tilly in Leeds the week after meeting Mrs Hart. Tilly would cheer her up. Laurence was busy and she would much rather talk to Tilly alone, though you could not say you were alone in the presence of the lively two-and-a-half-year-old Maisie.

She took the train and then a tram to Tilly's house, a large shabby manse in Headingley. Tilly's husband George was a big shambling man who resembled his house. Mary did not know him well but liked what she knew, sensing his kindness. Tilly had married him in what Mrs Crowther had considered unseemly haste. But Tilly was happy. You could see how happy, even in the middle of the chaos of the meal-table and in spite of confessing she did often feel weary.

She greeted Mary, who had arrived just in time for a hasty lunch. The Ramsdens had only one servant, a slatternly-looking girl called Aggie who served them mutton and rice-pudding. Little Maisie was encouraged to eat with the grown-ups before Aggie took her out for a walk. 'The minister', as Mary always thought of him, ate his lunch more quickly than Mary had ever seen anyone eat a substantial meal, and then dashed off for a busy afternoon of visiting chapel folk.

Now that she could see for herself the life Tilly had chosen, refusing any financial help from her father, and soon to have another call upon her time with a coming second baby, she still envied her. Might that have been her own life if she and Laurence had had children?

No, Laurence would never have lived the life of Tilly's husband; he was far too dependent upon his creature comforts. Was she the same? I've been spoilt, she decided.

Maisie skipped out at two o'clock dragging Aggie behind her. Mary and Tilly went to sit by the fire in a little drawing-room.

'Bliss!' said Tilly, sitting down heavily. 'Since she was eighteen months old Maisie has never had an afternoon nap like most children.'

Mary said, 'You never have any time to yourself, do you? But you look happy.'

'I just don't have time to think about it,' said Tilly simply. 'But I suppose I am – very happy.'

'I do envy you.'

Tilly knew that no reason had been found for her friend's inability to become pregnant and knew how it was upsetting her.

She said, 'You have compensations – peace and quiet, to begin with.'

'Yes, I know. Maisie is so interesting, though, isn't she? I do like children of that age.'

This was balm to a mother and they spent the next half-hour with Tilly recounting some of the amusing things little Maisie had said and done. Mary decided to tell Tilly about the latest manifestation of Stacey Watson which she had been storing up to tell her when the opportunity arose.

Tilly was fascinated. 'Well, well! – I must ask Mother what she knows. I wonder if they know she's back living three or four miles away from The Nest.'

'I would say she hasn't told anyone – it was just a fluke that I recognized her.'

'I told you that she'd married again. I seem to remember some rumour – it was a year or two ago and Father didn't want to say anything about it to me, even though I was married – that she and the second husband had separated. Not divorced, though.'

'Well, the grocer says she's a widow,' said Mary. 'Though the lady herself never mentioned it.'

'She must be a Merry Widow, then? Oh dear, as a minister's wife I mustn't say such things!'

They both laughed, but then Mary said, 'I do wonder if this separated husband really has died. What was he called?'

'I can't remember. I'll ask Liddy when I write to her. Would you like a cup of tea before Maisie comes back?'

'Yes, please, then I'll have to go home,' Mary replied with a sigh.

Tilly looked at her with a little puzzled look.

They sat on quietly, sipping tea, and for a few moments Mary felt she was a child again.

When she left she felt both rejuvenated and less than satisfied with her own lot.

CHAPTER TWELVE

'**M**ight we give a little party in the garden one evening?' Mary asked Laurence at the end of May. 'We've owed hospitality to a few people for ages – and we still haven't had Mrs Hart over here in the evening.'

It was Mrs Hart she really wanted to see. It had indeed been a year since she had done more than have female friends or neighbours for morning coffee. Laurence didn't object to this as he imagined women liked exchanging recipes. Unlike so many comfortable mill-owners he did not enjoy evening parties which in this part of Yorkshire usually included music of one sort or another, in his opinion badly played or sung.

'If she'd wanted to see us she could have asked us over,' he said.

Mary had glimpsed Anastasia Hart once or twice in town, accompanied by an elderly woman whom she presumed was the old friend of her stepmother Mrs Hart had mentioned, come to help her housekeep.

One day through a gap in the fence at the side of their garden Mary had seen her in the distance lying in a hammock under a tree. She had made no effort to repay Mary's call.

Laurence finally agreed reluctantly to give an evening party for about a dozen people. There would be champagne, and Mrs Kershaw would cook two plump capons to eat cold, along with white wine. They would finish with strawberries and cream.

Mary invited four couples of their acquaintance, along with Mr Alex Gordon the mill manager, who was a bachelor, and of course Anastasia Hart.

Would she accept?

'You must invite her personally,' his wife said. 'I'm sure she would

188

like to meet *you*. Take the invitation round yourself. You haven't even seen her yet!'

Laurence said he had done as Mary asked the following evening on his way back from work, and reported there was a dragon by the name of Mrs Robinson who had answered the door. He had introduced himself to Mrs Hart. He seemed ill at ease and Mary wondered if Anastasia had been offhand.

'Oh, I think she will accept,' he said.

In the cool of the evening of a perfect day in early June, Mary gave her party. A long trestle-table had been taken out under the trees and over it Mrs Kershaw had spread a vast snowy-white linen cloth, another of Laurence's mother's household goods. Mr Forbes's son Ronald, who sang tenor in the church choir, had been asked to preside over the champagne. The best Noble crystal glass was produced from cupboards Mary had never properly explored, and the best silver cutlery displayed.

Why did she not do this sort of thing more often? Because Laurence never suggested it. She must have been half-asleep in the first years of her marriage not to have seen such entertaining as quite normal, and not beyond her.

The two most interesting couples were on holiday abroad but almost everyone else had accepted. She wished now that she had invited Edith Wadsworth and Rebecca Wilkinson from college, with whom she had kept in touch. They were both still unmarried, but she feared lest they might now find her too *bourgeoise*. She suspected she was projecting her own feelings on to them.

Two middle-aged couples from the town accepted, one of whom, the Pyrahs, Laurence said he had promised some time ago a look at his house. The other couple consisted of his accountant, Mr Hubert Moon, accompanied by his wife Florence. Two younger couples also accepted, the Brooks and the Rhodes. Mary knew Marcus and Maria Brook, an intensely musical pair who had once invited them to a private concert, which she had much enjoyed. The Rhodes were nondescript people with very loud voices, children of some old friends of Laurence's mother.

The party was going well when Anastasia arrived. Living the nearest, she arrived the last, just after Laurence's manager, Mr Alexander Gordon. He was a pawky Scot who looked very like his father whom Mary remembered seeing years before conferring with her own father at Cliff House. Gordon worked very hard for Laurence. Would he say he had already met Mrs Hart when she introduced them? Or had it only been her husband he had met? He gave a stiff bow but said nothing.

Anastasia looked very lovely in a slinky high-necked dress of brown silk. She had fixed a red velvet comb in her dark hair, and was obviously used to being the cynosure of all eyes.

'You have already met Laurence,' said Mary, as her husband came up.

'Yes, indeed – so kind of you to invite me personally, Mr Noble,' she murmured, accepting a glass of champagne and then turning back to Alex Gordon.

Mary went up to her husband who had moved away, and whispered,

'Do talk to Mrs Hart. Gordon must not monopolize her!'

If I were a man I'd fall in love with her, thought Mary, admiring the dress and the white arms and aware of that lingering *Chypre*-like scent that seemed to hover like an invisible cloud around the woman. Mrs Hart would most likely consider the other guests very boring, apart from the Brooks.

I ought to have made more of an effort to get to know younger people, Mary was thinking. There were some cheerful families who lived not far away but Laurence said they were noisy. They could surely not be as noisy as the Rhodes, who came from further off, somewhere near Spenborough. At present they were regaling the Pyrahs, who looked solemn and interested, with gossip about their new town council. Mary talked to Mr Moon, who at least spoke intelligently. Mrs Moon was talking to Maria Brook, and Marcus Brook had just joined the Pyrahs, adroitly turning the conversation round to the latest concert of his town chamber orchestra.

Flitting from one couple to another, introducing those who had not met before, seeing that Ronald Forbes went round with the champagne and filled up glasses, and making an effort to talk to each of their guests, Mary found she needed a second glass of champagne herself. The first was certainly helping her make small talk to these disparate people. Had she put them at their ease, the duty of a good hostess? Oh, she did wish she'd invited Rebecca or Edith. Of course Tilly and her husband would have been even better, but Tilly was expecting a baby any minute, and they found it difficult to get away in any case.

Thankfully, Marcus Brooks came up to her just then and she always enjoyed talking to him. She was about to introduce him to Anastasia who was now sitting down, still with Mr Gordon, when Mrs Kershaw appeared at her elbow. It was about eight o'clock and she was asking in an urgent whisper whether it was time to serve the chicken.

'Yes, please do.'

She looked round for Laurence but he seemed to have vanished. Chairs had been brought from inside and placed under the trees and Mary shepherded the Brooks and the Moons and made sure they were ready to be served by Ethel, who was combining the roles of house- and parlour-maid.

How very much easier it would be to have them all go up and help themselves to a plate of food. But that would be too informal, she supposed. As she drained her second glass and then helped Mrs Kershaw and Ethel to serve the food, she saw Laurence, now back and standing next to Ronald Forbes who was holding a bucket of ice. Mrs Rhodes was exclaiming, 'Oh dear, I shall be quite tipsy.'

Anastasia strolled slowly up to the table with Alex Gordon and turned to speak to Laurence. She had shadows underneath her eyes when you looked at her closely. Mary wanted nothing better than to talk to her, but first had to see that everyone had a seat, a snowy napkin and a plate of food.

'It's a lovely picnic,' Maria Brook said to her, and smiled. Mary took her own drink and food, though she did not feel very hungry, and joined Anastasia and Laurence and Mr Gordon, who were now seated at a slight distance away from the others. It was not going to be easy to introduce Anastasia to the other guests if Laurence did not think it necessary. Mary listened to their talk, which seemed to be about a mutual acquaintance in Manchester. She had done her bit. Everyone was eating and drinking and chatting. Now she could relax.

Anastasia was picking at her chicken but appeared to have enjoyed a glass or two of champagne, for she was a little flushed.

'So original,' she said to Laurence. 'Quite like a Bohemian party! Did your wife tell you that she and I met years ago? Isn't that a strange coincidence?'

Mary did not think it all that strange, since the lady's relatives lived quite near.

Laurence said, 'Yes, she did mention it.'

Mary murmured that it seemed a long time ago but that she

remembered her very well. Anastasia went on, giving a peculiar emphasis to her next words, 'I was known as Stacey in those days. Nobody calls me that now!'

Mary had the sudden feeling that she was still a schoolgirl and that her party – it was hers really, for Laurence had taken little interest in it except for providing the dullest of the guests – was regarded as a childish attempt to please the grown-ups, was really more like a picnic by the side of the lake at The Nest. She said without thinking:

'Oh, we had such fun at The Nest – where you stayed, Mrs Hart – Anastasia. It was before I had to go to live in Woolsford. I do so miss Lightholme!'

The champagne must have unloosened her tongue, for she sounded rather too intense in her own ears.

'Aye, my father liked that part of the world,' said Alex Gordon, rolling his 'r's. He seemed determined to be pleasant. 'Mrs Noble's father had a lovely house near the place where you used to stay, Mrs Hart. Did you never see it?' he asked.

'It was nothing like so grand as The Nest,' said Mary. 'Didn't you think that was a beautiful house, Mrs Hart?'

'You and your husband have this wonderful old house and yet you still miss your old home?' She sounded amused.

Had she been rude to Laurence, saying she still missed Lightholme? She did, though. Perhaps Anastasia thought she did not appreciate Ridge Hill.

'Oh yes, this is an unusual house. But I suppose we always look back to where we lived as children and see it as somewhere special.'

'Nostalgia,' said Laurence, looking at Mrs Hart.

But what Mary was really feeling was nostalgia for her old self, not just the desire to be back at Cliff House. Laurence knew that she did appreciate his – their –house but was aware she still missed Lightholme. He knew nothing about her old passion for this woman.

'*This* house has far more history,' Mary said. 'One's childhood home – well that's different – childhood itself holds a different kind of history.'

'But it was The Nest – that was its name, wasn't it? – that you liked best?' asked Anastasia. As though she could have forgotten its name! 'Better than your own home?'

'Well, for different reasons.' replied Mary.

'I believe you said the other day when I called on you that you had once enjoyed a holiday in the very place where my wife and I met?'

Laurence interposed, turning to Mrs Hart. He wanted to change the subject.

'Oh, I believe I did, yes. Did you go to France often, Mary?' asked Mrs Hart.

'I accompanied my aunt several times – it was in Biarritz that Laurence and I first met. He was there with – a friend of his.'

'I have never travelled abroad,' put in Mr Gordon, proffering his glass to Ronald who was now gliding round with a bottle of cold Chablis. 'Aye, bonnie Scotland is where I go for my holidays – such as they are.'

'I'm sure you are always kept very busy, Mr Gordon,' said Anastasia, and the way she spoke convinced Mary she must remember meeting him before. Did she come from a manufacturing family? I know so little about her, she thought. Tilly never said much about her family background.

'Your father was *so* hard-working – when he used to work for Father,' she said to Alex Gordon.

'How strange! Another coincidence!' said Anastasia playfully.

'Not really, Mrs Hart. There are few engineers who do the work my old pa did – and Mrs Noble's father – Mr Settle – had a mill similar to Mr Noble's, but weaving not spinning.'

Mary sensed that although Laurence was saying little he had his attention upon Mrs Hart. Both of them addressed remarks to anyone but the other, as if they did not approve of each other. She wanted Laurence to like her Miss Watson, and for Stacey to like him.

'When we have finished our supper I could show you the rest of the garden,' she said to Mrs Hart and Mr Gordon.

'It is better planted than mine,' said Anastasia.

'But of course you are only renting,' said Alex.

'Alas – and probably not after the summer,' she said.

'You are thinking of moving, then?' asked Laurence.

'Yes – since my husband died so recently I have been very up and down in spirits but now I think I shall go back to Cheshire where my family used to live.'

So she really was a widow.

Laurence looked as if he wanted to say something else to her but after a moment he turned away. The other guests were now cheerfully chatting to each other, wine and food having done their work well.

Mary eventually persuaded Anastasia Hart to stroll round the garden with her. She kept off the past as a subject of conversation, and showed Anastasia her walled garden, but not the gap in the fence from which she had glimpsed her.

'I remember you always liked walking in gardens!' said Anastasia, with a long look.

Carriages came early for the two Rhodes, as their journey was quite a long one. Mr and Mrs Moon and Mr and Mrs Pyrah left half an hour afterwards. The Brooks said they were walking home, since the evening was so lovely, the air warm. Mr Gordon had arrived on his bicycle but said he would wheel it 'hame', as he had imbibed so freely. Mary thought him a little boring, a little complacent, but a sensible man.

Anastasia said, 'How frightfully peculiar he is!' when he had gone and she was being helped into her cloak by Laurence.

'Laurence will see you home,' Mary said to Anastasia.

'Well, it is not very far is it!' But Laurence said he would be pleased to do so.

Mary went into the kitchens to congratulate Mrs Kershaw and Ethel who had already washed up and were putting away the plate and glass. Ron Forbes was bringing in the chairs.

'Thank you – the food was very good. I must try to cook it myself next time,' she said to Mrs Kershaw.

'Mr Laurence has never been a great one for entertaining,' said Mrs Kershaw. 'Leastways, I expect he might have been when he lived elsewhere.'

Mary said 'Good-night,' went up to her bedroom and looked out of the window in the moonlight before she drew the curtains.

She was already in bed and had almost fallen asleep when Laurence came in. She sat up with a start.

'It was a good party, wasn't it?' she said.

'Oh, yes. Very successful.'

He turned down the flame in the gas mantle.

'You don't like her – Mrs Hart – do you?' she asked him as he wound his watch.

'Why do you think that?'

'Just a feeling I had. She is so good-looking! I'd imagine any man would fall for her. If I were a man I'm sure *I* would – as they say – 'fancy' her.'

'Really, Mary.'

He sounded annoyed rather than amused, but soon appeared to fall asleep. Mary, having been woken up just on the borders of sleep could not now fall asleep again. The champagne and the wine, which had seemed at first to make her feel relaxed, were now making her mind work more quickly. She slept at last in the early hours.

After the party nothing much seemed to happen. Mary kept hoping that Anastasia would invite her *chez elle*, and was surprised that she did not. One would have thought common politeness would insist upon a return of hospitality. She would have liked to ask her to come over again, but that would be rude if the woman obviously saw no point in their meeting again. No, she would not ask her.

One afternoon she saw Anastasia in town coming out of a shop in The Arcade, where a mixture of rather expensive little stores sold such items as silks for needlework, knitting-wool, or raffia for basket-making, much patronized by middle class ladies. Anastasia did not see her, so Mary made no attempt to engage her in conversation and saw her walk away slowly as if she were weary. A hansom was waiting at the side of the street near the entrance to The Arcade, with a middle-aged lady in it.

June, her favourite month, was over; July came and went with the most intense heat Mary had ever experienced in Yorkshire. She loved it but Laurence did not, and appeared much preoccupied. Mary guessed that business was not going well and almost plucked up courage to ask Alex Gordon's advice but was worried lest Laurence might think her interfering.

He made no suggestion that they should go on holiday before summer was over, so she told herself that if he had said nothing by the middle of August she would ask him directly if anything was the matter. She occupied herself reading, playing the piano, sketching and gardening, and took over some of the cooking for the week when Mrs Kershaw went on her annual holiday, leaving Ethel in the kitchen.

She also went over twice to Leeds to see Tilly who had had her second child, a little boy, but who was taking longer than usual to recover, having caught some type of infection. Maternity always made Mary feel anxious; she supposed it was the result of her mother's having died shortly after she was born. Tilly's baby was fine; it was Tilly who needed more help.

'I could come to stay, and help you with running the house if you like,' she said on her first visit. Tilly was now feeling a little better but was told to rest in the afternoons, which was impossible with a young baby and little Maisie to look after.

'No, Mary dear, I must get over it by myself. I would accept if I really thought I could not manage, but George has found me some help. His youngest sister has just finished her schooling. She's bright and strong and isn't needed for a time at home, so he's asked her to come next week. I had no time to tell you – I couldn't even to find the time to write you a short note . . .'

'I was going to offer to take little Maisie for a week at Ridge Hill,' said Mary.

'Perhaps next year, when she's a little older. She hasn't been away from home without me yet – and you have to be careful not to give an older child the feeling she's in the way with a new baby around.'

Mary thought how sensible Tilly was, and how competent. She liked talking about babies and their problems with her old friend.

She had not broached with Laurence the idea of Maisie staying with them at Ridge Hill, had feared he might be less than enthusiastic. She left Tilly, feeling much relieved, and on her second visit was pleased to see her friend looking more robust, and a strapping girl playing with Maisie.

They were already into early September and Mary had still not asked her husband how the business was getting on. One evening when Laurence was working late she gathered some flowers for the little drawing-room. She arranged them, and then sat down for a while looking out of the window, before going out into the garden again. The flowers in the herbaceous borders smelt heavy and sweet, especially the nicotiana and the phlox, and she found herself recalling the *Chypre* scent Anastasia had worn.

She thought she heard voices over the wall in the next garden. It would be that Mrs Robinson, she presumed, talking to her mistress. Through the gap in the wall, feeling rather guilty that she was looking through it at a woman who clearly wanted nothing to do with her, she saw Anastasia in the distance, wearing a flowered cape, looking less *svelte* than usual. She was walking slowly towards the conservatory at the back of her house. She had not yet gone to her brother's in Cheshire then. Would she be off soon? She had the impression the woman was not well. My imagination running away with me again, I suppose, she thought.

The next morning she was sorting some books in her little eyrie at the top of the house when Ethel came panting up the stairs.

'Mum, there's the lady from next door to see you – I've let her into the room.'

Ethel always referred to the sitting-room as 'the Room'.

'You mean the older lady, Mrs Robinson?' asked Mary, getting up from the floor where she had been putting some of her old favourites on to a lower shelf.

'Nay – it's that Mrs Hart. She just said, "Tell your mistress Mrs Hart would like to see her".'

'All right, Ethel, I'll come down.'

What could Anastasia want at this hour of the morning? Still clutching a duster she went downstairs, preceded by Ethel.

Anastasia was sitting on a sofa. She looked up.

'Don't get up – do make yourself comfortable – I'm glad Ethel found you a chair – it's ages since we met – how are you?' gabbled Mary and cast the duster on to a table.

Anastasia said, 'I'm sorry we have not been able to invite anyone round – the time passes so quickly – but I came to say that next week my companion Mrs Robinson and I are to return to see to matters connected with my husband in Manchester.' She was not going to family in Cheshire then. 'I've decided not to come back here – so I shall be terminating the tenancy,' Anastasia went on hurriedly, not looking at her.

'I'm sorry to hear that,' said Mary. 'I'd hoped we could get to know each other better. Is there anything I can do to help? You must have a lot of packing.'

She sounded to herself as if she was speaking disjointedly, but Anastasia was the one who faltered a little as she went on:

'I came to ask you if you would like to come round tomorrow at about four o'clock for a cup of tea? I know it's very short notice, but recently I have not been too well.'

'I'm sorry,' Mary said again.

Indeed, Anastasia did look unhealthily flushed, her eyes heavier than the last time she had been at Ridge Hill more than two months previously. How time flew.

'Laurence will be sorry to hear you are going away,' Mary added politely. 'But I'd love to come over tomorrow. Can I give you a cup of coffee before you go?'

'Oh – no. No, thank you. I must get back to the sorting out and packing – Mrs Robinson is suffering from the heat.'

She rose to go. Mary saw her out. Ethel had disappeared into the kitchen.

She was puzzled. Why had Mrs Hart felt the need to ask her round just when she was about to leave?

She was soon to discover.

At four o'clock the next day Mary presented herself at the front door of Birch Wood. It was another hot afternoon, one of those summer afternoons rare in the north of England, but which, if you liked hot weather, and Mary did, were even more beautiful for their rarity. She hoped that it would not end, as so many really hot English days did, in dark skies and thunder. She had put on a simple flowery cotton blouse with puffed sleeves, belted into a wide flared skirt. A bit out of date, but Mary abhorred fashion on her own account and would never wish to compete with Anastasia. As she went out of the porch she grabbed her old straw boater. It was quite exciting to be summoned by her long-ago crush. Did the idol know she had once fascinated an eleven-year-old girl?

Stacey Hart opened the door herself and stood aside to allow her guest in. Her eyes looked slightly red-rimmed, her face pale and a little sweaty.

All she said was, 'Mrs Robinson is lying down – it is too hot for her.' The weather did not appear to suit her any more than her companion. 'I thought I owed you an explanation,' she said as she gestured Mary to sit down before a table on which teetered a tray with a small teapot and two cups and saucers.

'I'm afraid I have no milk – I don't take it myself and in this heat it goes sour very quickly.'

She wobbled a stream of rather dark-looking tea into one of the cups. Mary took hers and waited. As Anastasia was preparing to sit, Mary noticed her thickened waistline, more obvious today as she was wearing a long dress of plain cream-coloured cotton. Could it be. . . ?

But her husband was dead, wasn't he?

Perhaps guessing her thoughts, although Mary did not think she had given away her reaction, Anastasia said, and it was as if she had learned a lesson by heart,

'My husband's death at the end of March was very sudden. I decided to get away as soon as I could.'

Mary waited.

'It was such a shock that I wanted to start afresh somewhere else. I did not know then that I was –that I was – expecting. I am returning home now, since I am told I am to expect a baby at the end of the year!'

Mary said involuntarily, 'Oh how wonderful! I'm sure it will help to make up for your previous loss. . . .'

Various emotions appeared to struggle on Anastasia's face as she said now in a cooler voice, as if her news was anything but wonderful, 'I must confess that it has been a great shock.'

How long had she known? No such knowledge had appeared to be upsetting her on the occasion of Mary's supper party at the beginning of June.

'How will you manage? Will someone come to help you with the packing, and accompany you on the journey?'

'I have Florence – Mrs Robinson, and I did not bring many suitcases. I left most of my personal items at home.'

She mustn't have been sure how long she was going to rent the house.

'I came only for a temporary change after all my – upsets,' added Anastasia, seeing Mary look surprised. 'I have packed my big trunk to send on ahead – we leave next Thursday.'

The memory of Tilly's words, *She had separated from her second husband too*, were suddenly in Mary's head. Had Mr Hart really died suddenly, earlier in the year, as Anastasia had just said? She did not believe her.

Why could she not have said that before, if that were true?

Was he still alive, but estranged from her? Had he made her do something against her will? A baby would not be such a happy event if that were true. She believed her about the child, though. It was obvious this afternoon.

Mary remembered how she had once decided that children would never have played any part in this woman's plans. It made her feel sorry for the person who was sitting before her now like a statue, looking not at her visitor but out of the window. Hard on the heels of this feeling Mary felt sorry for herself. What an unfair world if a woman like Anastasia Hart could find herself with child when she, who so longed for a baby, should be barren.

'Do you want me to tell my husband,' she asked. 'I feel sure he could help you with the journey. It is such very hot weather and he is used to trains and travel.'

'Oh, please don't concern yourself,' said Anastasia half-heartedly. 'But I can tell him, surely?'

Anastasia shrugged her shoulders. 'Will you take more tea?' she asked, as if this part of the interview was now over. But Mary was made of sterner stuff.

'If your family can't help you, I feel sure you should not be carrying things in your . . . condition. At least Laurence can convey you and your companion to the station in our carriage.'

'There are porters,' Anastasia answered feebly, just as the door opened and a small fat woman came in.

'This is my . . . friend. Florence Robinson,' said Anastasia. 'Flo, here is Mrs Noble insisting we are aided on our travels on Thursday by Mr Noble. I have told her we shall be quite able to manage by ourselves.'

'Well, isn't that kind,' said the small woman coming up and helping herself to a cup of tea. 'If Mr Noble wants to help us, I'm sure we should accept.'

She looked up at Anastasia over her teacup and some message seemed to be passing between them.

'I shall suggest it tonight,' said Mary. 'And now I must be going.'

'Well, I suppose we must say goodbye, then,' said Anastasia. Mary hesitated. She would like to tell her now how much she had been impressed by her when she was a girl – it might cheer her up, for she looked perfectly wretched. But Anastasia rose and extended her hand and she felt dismissed.

Mary needed too to think over the coming event, as they always called childbirth, alone. Anastasia Hart was no longer young. She'd be about thirty-seven, and giving birth to a first child at that age might not be easy, might even be dangerous?

As she took her leave, she was aware that Mrs Robinson was giving her a long scrutiny. What a curious couple they were. Anastasia had said her companion had been 'a friend of my stepmother'. Had her own mother died? She must ask Tilly more about the Watson family; she'd write to her with this news.

Over supper that evening – cold fish, no pudding, but grapes for dessert, as it was so hot, Mary told her husband Mrs Hart's surprising news and broached the subject of his helping her get on the train.

'You might even combine it with one of your auction afternoons,' she said brightly. 'If they leave early, you could accompany them to Manchester, see they got on the right train to wherever it is they live, and then have the rest of the day to spend the way you liked. There are auctions on Thursdays in York, aren't there, so perhaps it's a day for auctions in Manchester too?'

'I could ask Alex Gordon to help her,' said Laurence, 'I'm busy at present with a big new order – I can't afford to waste time. You never know when another will turn up.' He was spending more time at the mill than usual.

'No, Laurence, I think you must help them. She has been our neighbour now for some time – it's the least we can do to help the poor woman.'

In the end, he said, 'Well if you insist, I will ask them if they would like my help.'

'Why not go over after supper? I told them I would ask you, and she may think you won't unless you tell her straight away.'

Over coffee Mary began to speak of her doubts about Anastasia's story.

Laurence had lit a cigar and as he was drawing on it, she said, 'I think it all very odd, for you know – I remember telling you that Tilly once told me Anastasia had separated not only from her first husband but also from her second. And she is expecting a baby at the end of the year but she says her husband died in March!'

'Your friend may have got the story wrong,' suggested Laurence.

'Perhaps your Mr Gordon might have heard more about her?'

'I doubt it – in any case Alex is no gossip. It's not really our business, is it?' He sighed. 'I'll do as you wish and offer my services to our neighbour. Thursday, you said?'

'Yes, but you could go over now and sort it out?'

'I'll call in on my way to work tomorrow,' said Laurence, and disappeared behind his newspaper.

Thus it was arranged. The next evening Laurence returned home with the information that he had presented himself to Mrs Hart and Mrs Robinson that morning before he left for work in town, and they were now agreed he could see them to the station in his carriage on Thursday.

Mary had deliberately refrained from calling at Birch Wood during the day.

Next morning she told him, 'I shall go round to say goodbye today, and then I shall not be in the way tomorrow. I hope they have purchased their tickets?'

'Certainly,' said Laurence, and that was that.

When Mary knocked at the back door that afternoon Mrs Robinson answered it.

'She is resting,' she said when she saw Mary.

'Please say I came to say goodbye and to wish her well. My husband will be round at eight o'clock tomorrow morning with our carriage.'

'So kind,' murmured Florence Robinson, 'And now you must excuse me.'

Really, they were both so unfriendly, thought Mary, feeling a little disappointed that she might never see Anastasia face to face again. But if that was what the lady wanted, she must accept that she could do no more. She urged Laurence when he returned home to ascertain their new address in Lancashire.

'Shall you take them there? I thought you might – and then go on to the auction rooms, You said you needed a new desk – or, rather, an old one.' She smiled.

'No, no – I shall do that at the autumn sales in October. Apparently they need help only for getting into the train. I am told someone will be there waiting for them on arrival.'

Laurence asked Forbes, who doubled as chauffeur, to have the carriage taken round early to the Birch Wood front drive on Thursday morning. Mary thought how considerate her husband was, once he had decided to help.

It was another hot day. Dressed in his linen suit Laurence was ready to call on Anastasia and her companion by eight o'clock. He had calculated it would take some time to load the carriage before proceeding to the town station.

Mary wanted to help, but he said, 'I'm sure there is nothing for you to do.' Agreeing that goodbyes had already been said, Mary waited half an hour before she heard the crunch of wheels turning out of the gate. From the window of her eyrie she saw the carriage turn down the lane.

So that is that, she thought, yet she felt curiously certain that she had not seen the last of Anastasia Hart.

CHAPTER THIRTEEN

L aurence returned home that evening after work looking hot and dusty. When Mary asked him how things had gone on at the station he said, 'Oh, I saw them off and gave the keys of Birch Wood to Widdop, the agent in town. She asked me if I would.'

'Did she give you the address of wherever it is she's gone – was it Didsbury? I suppose you remembered to ask for it?'

'Yes, they asked me to send on any letters. They've gone to some other suburb of Manchester, near Prestwich, I believe.'

'I hardly saw her, but I shall miss her,' said Mary. 'It would have been so nice to have a baby living next door.'

Laurence did not reply to this and Mary went on, 'I'd like to write to her – see how she's going on . . .'

'I believe Mrs Robinson said they would be looking for a better house eventually – but the temporary address they gave me would do for the present.'

'Then you must give it to me. I can readdress any letters that come for her as well.'

Mary wrote to Anastasia a week later but by the end of the month there was still no reply. On the other hand, nobody had written to Birch Wood for Mrs Hart either. She did hope the next residents, whoever they were, would buy the place rather than rent it. She was feeling terribly isolated. If only someone like Tilly could live next door. As a Free Church minister, Tilly's husband was unlikely ever to have enough money to do so.

Mary wrote to Tilly about the puzzle over Anastasia's husband. She knew Tilly would not have much time for writing letters but she looked forward to a reply eventually. Laurence had announced that Ridge Hill was to have a telephone installed the following year. He already possessed one at the Mill. A little exchange was being built, with an operator trained for the Ridge Hill district, which would include them. Tilly had no telephone as yet, but her husband needed one, and how pleasant it might be one day to be able to speak to her old friend. You could scarcely believe how many new inventions were being put into use everywhere – telephones, 'motor' cars with 'internal combustion' engines. . . .

At the end of the month Tilly replied to Mary's letter.

I have asked Mother about Mrs Hart. Ma is now more willing to tell me things since I became a mother of two! She told me there was a scandal after both Stacey's marriages. She thinks this second husband was called Quintin, and was the cause of her previous divorce! You may remember the young man who stayed here, her first husband, Richard Jowett, whom she married about six months after her visit. I believe you once told me you'd seen him in the distance. She must have been about twenty-two at the time. Well, apparently, it was Mr Jowett who divorced her. She married the adulterer, Quintin Hart, I suppose, but there was some later scandal because the second husband – Quintin that is – left her too! He didn't divorce her, just separated from her. Left her to stew in her own juice, I expect. She must have met yet another man and had another affair. My mother didn't know anything about Mr Hart's death but Stacey was definitely still married to him. Ma was really upset by the whole saga.

Nobody in our family or Father's has ever been divorced or separated, but my mother did say that Stacey lost her mother when she was about thirteen, and her father married again, but the stepmother didn't get on with her, though apparently getting on well with her brother. Ma has no idea of course that Mrs Hart has been living only a few miles from The Nest! Shall I tell her? I think better not, don't you? Of course, in spite of Mother being quite 'progressive', she blames the woman, not the man – or men.

Mary pondered all this. Anastasia had lost her mother at an impressionable age, and another woman had replaced her. Would she have been different if she had not had a stepmother?

The weather at the beginning of October was mild and mellow. The town was lacking water and Laurence reported many mills were not working because of the lack of rain. Even so, an autumn like this was Mary's favourite season; the low golden rays of the sun would soon be replaced by colder, windier weather. As she walked slowly in the garden, enjoying the light, and the heavenly blue of the mild skies, and the apples ripening on the trees, she kept thinking how it would be an ideal time to be expecting a baby. She could almost imagine it was herself and not Anastasia who was ripening in the sun, full of harvest promise.

In October she received a sad letter from Mima in Burnley. Her husband, Sam Sutcliffe, had died suddenly. Their two children, Bobby and Louise, were fortunately both in work. The boy had been apprenticed to his father and would soon be ready to take over at the smithy, helped by Sam's old assistant. Louise had been working at a milliner's for some time and was already courting a decent lad of whom Mima approved. She wrote that she had found temporary work till Christmas, going over to help with a family who were about to emigrate to Canada. Louise did not want to leave Burnley, but Mima often wished that she herself might take up work away for a time, in a house where she could live in and make a new life for herself now that her children were grown.

Immediately she read this, Mary wondered whether Mima was still hoping her old charge would eventually have a baby of her own whom she might one day look after. If only she had. She thought of Anastasia. Had she yet arranged for a nursemaid for her coming baby? She could not imagine Mrs Hart would relish the sole charge of a child but she knew nothing of her financial circumstances. Anastasia however would not be an easy employer and Mary would not want to encourage Mima to take a post where she might not happy. Still, the idea might be worth mentioning. She felt she ought to have been of more help to her erstwhile neighbour.

She told her husband that very evening that she had heard from Jemima Sutcliffe who needed a live-in post and might be prevailed upon to work for Mrs Hart, if Mrs Hart ever needed a nanny. Laurence looked surprised, and Mary went on,

'I meant, if she ever wrote to ask us if we knew of a good nurse-maid.'

Laurence replied tartly that Mary must not give herself the job of organizing other people's affairs. This hurt her.

'I was only wanting to help Mima, who will not have much money now,' she replied.

Next morning, she sat down and wrote a long letter to Mima.

*I am so sorry about Sam. I remember him so well and he was one of
the best men I have ever met, salt of the earth, as they say. I wish I
could help you, but as you know there is no child here. If there were,
and you were free, there is nobody on earth I'd rather have to help
look after a child of mine.*

She looked up, realizing there were tears in her eyes that were not
only for Sam Sutcliffe, whom Aunt Clara had always called a 'nature's
gentleman'. She must not give way to easy self-pity. She finished off
the letter, adding that she might be able to let Mima know of a
woman in the New Year. Having written this, she decided she would
go and visit Mima anyway after Christmas. She did so want to see her
again. She had put it off and put it off, hoping that one day she might
have good news, and that Mima would be an honorary grandmother
at last, but she had been embarrassed because a baby had not yet
arrived. She ended:

*I shall enquire about a live-in post for you and I promise to come
over and see you soon whenever it is convenient . . .* adding for
politeness's sake, *Let me know how much notice you would need
for my arrival.*

She thought her Mima would be pleased to see her at any time, but
she must not take her for granted. Her own attempts at a new life,
with her duty to Laurence and the overseeing of Ridge Hill, had
made her neglect her oldest friend.

November arrived, and with it a big change in the weather. Rain fell
heavily, a blessing for the mills, but the cause of bad flooding. Ridge
Hill was high enough up for the fields to be dry. Days alternated
between driving rain and biting frost. Summer seemed to have taken
place in another country, not another season. Mary occupied her time
reading the French novels she had found in Laurence's study, drug-
ging herself with words, for if she had an idle moment she could not
help thinking about Anastasia Hart. She could not imagine the reality of her present existence. She scolded herself for becoming
obsessed with the woman.

One day, Laurence came back from the auction rooms in York
with an antique desk such as he had been coveting for some months.

It was put in a small lobby next to his library, to be polished with his favourite lavender beeswax, whilst it awaited the sorting out and emptying of his old desk. Mary had been promised this for her own papers. She had many journals, and attempts at writing verse, and a collection of the new 'postcards,' and of letters she had not wanted to throw away, as well as all the notes she had taken in France and at college. She had recently begun writing some fairy stories for Tilly's daughter in a large old ledger she had found empty. Laurence had taken the rest of his trade records and mill ledgers from the desk she was to inherit and they were stacked in the lobby. He was busy in town that week so she had polished his new desk for him. The old one was to be taken up to her eyrie.

She went down one afternoon to check that the desk was empty before Forbes took it up for her. It was heavy and was lodged against a wall next to a large bookshelf. She noticed a clutch of papers that had fallen behind the desk, and bent down to pick them up. They were mostly receipts, and she was just putting them into the lobby with the rest of his papers and ledgers when she saw an envelope amongst them with one page of a folded-back letter sticking out of it. She looked at it idly, and then with more interest as she saw the signature: *Florence Robinson.*

She looked at the envelope again – and then took the letter to the table in the library. She had never forgotten the letter she had found in the collection of plays by Ibsen, however much she had wanted to. Laurence was certainly careless with his post.

She opened this one, telling herself she was curious to know if her husband had perhaps had something to do with the estate agent who managed next door.

It was dated 15 January 1901, from 25 Monkswilde Crescent, with no name of a town. Mrs Robinson did not have a very good hand.

Dear Mr Noble,
I am writting to say it is very kind of you to have found Rose a lodging for the time being but I hope not for long. Till they have settled the will ecksetera. She hopes to move away next month but does not tell me everything. I think you should know that she says *she is making a complete break and making a new life but that won't just be up to her will it. I thought I should tell you in case she has not yet done so. Yours respectfully Florence Robinson.*

Mary's legs felt weak. She felt all at sea. Surmise after surmise skidded through her brain.

Rose had been Stacey Watson's second name. She had always known that.

Laurence had known Mrs Hart before she arrived at Birch Wood. How long had he known her? And how well? Why had he not told her, his wife, not betrayed in any way at all that he already knew her? He must have found Birch Wood for her to rent.

Why had he deceived her about that, if nothing else? Mary sat down, still clutching the letter, feeling like an actress who has stumbled into the wrong sort of play.

She must put the envelope back among the other papers that had to be put away in the new desk. She would not mention it, no she would not. She could not believe that Laurence had seen much of Anastasia after her arrival at Birch Wood, but she was puzzled about the baby Anastasia had said she was expecting at the end of December or in early January. Was she deluded? Was she perhaps ill? If her husband had died by January – certainly not in March as Anastasia had told her, he could not possibly be the father of a child to be born at the end of the year. Immediately Mary imagined another shadowy lover and that Laurence had rescued her, decided to help her start a new life. But in that case why had she left Birch Wood? Laurence could clear it all up but she was not going to ask him.

She looked again at the incriminating letter from Florence Robinson, written before Stacey ever arrived next door. No, she would say nothing about it – not tonight, anyway, nothing, just as she had never said anything about Stephen Waterhouse's letter. But she must find out what it was all about.

She made up her mind to confront Alex Gordon at the mill on a day when Laurence would be away. She was about to put the envelope back, wedged among the ledgers, when a gas mantle was lit in the hall and Mrs Kershaw came into the library.

'Oh, I'm sorry – I didn't know you were here. I see you've polished the new desk.'

Mary looked up, stood up, said in a voice that sounded shaky to herself, 'Oh yes – I'm just going up. Perhaps Forbes will move the new desk in here tomorrow?'

Mrs Kershaw did not appear to see anything amiss and Mary grabbed a book she had been reading and slipped in the letter she was still holding as she went out.

Later, she put the letter back among the pile of papers and receipts.

She wished she had dreamed it all.

She felt depressed and anxious. She must talk to Alex Gordon.

After thunder and lightning, the winter weather manifested itself in snow, making the roads to town impassable for a day or two. Laurence was excited by the newspaper reports of Marconi's success in sending words across the Atlantic by his 'wireless telegraphy'. Another new invention come to real life. Mary felt less excited. A telephone line to Tilly would still be wonderful but she could not summon up great enthusiasm for Mr Marconi.

How could Laurence not realize she might have gathered information about Anastasia from Tilly? He didn't notice that she might be preoccupied. She must be an excellent actress. Perhaps she had been acting for years.

As Christmas drew nearer, a time of year about which she still felt a childish excitement, the snow disappeared. There would probably be no white Christmas this year, at least not in Ridge Hill.

Laurence went back to work once the roads were free of snow, and then the opportunity Mary had been waiting for arose. He told her he would take the chance to go over to Woolsford on the 19th, the Thursday before Christmas, to see an export manager whom he had not been able to see earlier on account of the blocked roads. He would be away all day and would be late back that evening.

Mary decided to go to the mill office in town on the day of his absence, under cover of checking the turkey order at the market.

Wednesday was dull and cold. Forbes was stoking up the fires downstairs every day and Mrs Kershaw was preparing to bring out her Christmas cakes and cheese. Mary felt what a waste it was; they ought to be inviting neighbours in to help them enjoy the season. They had not yet been invited back by any of their summer guests, except for the couple from the Spen Valley on a day during the previous week when the carriage could not have got through. She had been relieved, for in her present impatient anxiety she would have found their voices extremely irritating. As for inviting other Christmas guests, Laurence had been adamant. You could not invite people round when they still 'owed' you a party.

How ridiculous, she thought. Yet perhaps she could still invite her old friends from college? Then she felt, no, she was not in the mood for it.

She dressed carefully on Thursday morning and said goodbye to her husband, who went down the lane in the carriage to the town station. Forbes would soon be back, and then she had arranged for him to take her in the trap to the old mill office in town and meet her later at the market when she had done her shopping.

By noon she found herself climbing the steep steps to the door of the office of Noble & Co in a narrow alley off a busy street, half a mile away from the mill itself. After all her contriving, she did hope Alex Gordon would be there.

He was, for when she pulled at the bell she heard a clattering on the stairs that led up to the post room, and he opened the door himself.

'Why, Mrs Noble!' he exclaimed. 'Is anything wrong? Mr Noble has gone into Woolsford today.'

He led her into one of the downstairs rooms, an inner office where buyers and loom engineers and the deputy works manager usually came to discuss business or repairs or wages.

'Yes, I know. That is why I wanted to see you. If you have just a few minutes? I'm sorry I could not let you know beforehand.'

He indicated a large mahogany chair on which she sat down. He perched opposite, upon what must once have been a dining-room chair belonging to Laurence's father.

She was determined not to sound embarrassed and began without preamble.

'I want to ask you something personal. I'm sorry to spring this on you but there is something I really have to know. Just between you and me,' she added.

At this he looked nervous and coughed.

'You may know nothing about it,' she said, 'but I gathered from my husband that you had met our recent neighbour, Mrs Hart's husband, before she came here. You met her too when you were over in Manchester on business, I believe?'

She was thinking that he did not actually look very surprised to be asked, but he did not at first reply. He was obviously waiting to see if there were more.

Mary went on, 'You talked to her at our party if I remember aright?'

'Aye, I remember I did.'

'Well, had you met her before?'

He looked extremely uncomfortable.

210

Mary repeated, 'It is just between you and me, but I want to know anything you can tell me about her. For example, was Mrs Hart living with her husband when he died? I believe he was called Quintin Hart?'

She wanted to ask him how long Laurence had known Anastasia, tell him that she had reason to believe they had known each other before she came to live next door, even that her husband might have arranged for her to do so, but she lacked the courage to put it quite like that. Mr Gordon must not suspect she was curious about Laurence, only about the woman.

In answer to her voiced question, Alex Gordon took on an air of puzzlement, saying, 'Now, how should I know that, Mrs Noble?'

'But it's true you had met the lady?'

'Aye, I had – in Manchester. I had met both the Harts some years ago. As far as I know he died recently.'

She could see he was prevaricating. If *he* had met them, then it must have occurred to Mary that his employer, who, some years ago, often went into Manchester accompanied by his manager, had probably also met her.

'Would that have been last year when he died – or before?'

'It was last year, I believe. I recall I met her again in connection with some stock she held in a firm I had once managed.'

It sounded plausible. Mary decided to use some feminine wiles, in order to try and find out more.

'Mr Gordon,' she began again in a softer voice, 'you remember your father once worked for mine?'

'Of course. He was a fine man, Mr Settle, but my father always said he was a great worrier.'

Like you, she thought he might be implying. She went on, 'Are you sure this Mr Hart is really dead?'

'Oh, aye,' he replied, shocked. 'I'm sure I heard he had died, but I don't recall exactly when.'

She continued to look at him carefully.

'I've a feeling it was last year – last autumn, I believe,' he said.

Did he know about the coming baby? Probably not. He was now, she thought, looking embarrassed, but also relieved. Her suspicions were sealed. If Anastasia was having a baby in December or January then that child must have been conceived around March, by which time Mr Hart, she was now being told, was well and truly dead.

But Anastasia really had been a widow. A 'separated widow', she thought irreverently.

Alex Gordon was still looking shifty. Should she add to his embarrassment? The poor man would always be loyal to his employer, but might he know something about the tenancy of Birch Wood?

He had decided to reassure her, for he cleared his throat and added, 'I had the impression the lady was used to her own way – a wee bit unbalanced – maybe suffering from a wee dose of neurasthenia. She was a woman inclined, I would imagine, to throw herself upon the mercy of a kind heart.'

Mary rose. That was what she wanted to believe herself, but she would enlighten him further. Then he would not dare mention her visit to Laurence.

'Well, Mr Gordon, I am grateful to you for seeing me. However, I am sorry for her, unbalanced or not. She has returned over the Pennines – as you may know.'

'I believe I did hear that.'

Mary put on her warm gloves as she now said briskly, 'Mrs Hart is expecting a child at the end of the year. I thought I might be of help to her.'

The manager, who had risen to see her out, took a step backwards and looked excessively shocked. He blushed to the roots of his sandy hair.

'I can see you did not know. She told me herself.'

'Well, well. A terrible thing,' he muttered, 'and her a widow.' What is the world coming to, were clearly his unspoken words. He looked extremely miserable.

'Please don't mention my visit to anyone,' Mary said as she went out, but she was trembling.

In the carriage home she felt both upset and angry. Alex Gordon was the kind of efficient person who would work for the love of it and remain loyal to a firm. As far as personal matters were concerned he would, like all men, remain loyal to his sex, would always blame the woman. If an employer, or friend of his, arranged, say, to compromise himself by helping a woman, he would hint that the woman was at fault for accepting.

What indeed could she ask Laurence when she was still so much in the dark about Anastasia's life? She decided to give him the benefit of the doubt, for the time being to say nothing. She would act as if she had discovered nothing. She would allow events to decide for her.

If only she could ask Tilly for advice, even if it were not the sort of thing you wanted to give your best friend as a succulent morsel of gossip.

She could write to Stephen Waterhouse: *Tell me if you have heard of Anastasia Hart*, but she was too proud to want him to be the person to whom she told tales.

Pride, however, was not her principal emotion. Laurence loved her, she was sure, but he had hidden something from her. There were always things you did not understand about other people. It was no sin to help a beautiful woman. It was what to do next that was the problem.

What had she once said to her husband?

If I were a man I'd fall in love with Anastasia Hart.

Events were soon to give her actions a direction. Alex Gordon might think her an unlikely benefactor for charity towards the Society for Fallen Women, but he did not know her very well.

Neither, she was beginning to think, did her husband.

The following Monday, the day before Christmas Eve, Mary was surprised by a visit from Maria Brook, the musical friend whom she had not seen since the party in June. Maria could not stay but had come to extend an invitation to an impromptu Christmas Eve concert she and her husband had decided to give the following evening.

'I know it's terribly short notice but we have only just decided to go ahead with it. A cousin from Ilkley has come to stay. He sings really well so we thought we'd invite just a few people round to listen to some piano music and have some carols and songs. We were going to ask you in October but it all fell through when Marcus got bronchitis. Do come – if you have no other arrangements. . . .'

'Oh, I'd love to, but I shall have to ask Laurence. He's busy preparing for final stocktaking at the mill after Christmas. How can I let you know?'

'It doesn't matter –just come along at eight if you can. Couldn't you come by yourself if he can't?'

'He'll have the carriage if he's working late. I'll try to persuade him, but you know . .' she was going to say, *You know what men are like*, but Marcus wasn't like that at all. Mary was used to refusing such invitations. Laurence still thought all local people were tedious, and pronounced that not one of them of them could play an instrument as it should be played. As for the singers . . . he was so critical. Why

213

shouldn't she go by herself? No, she felt she must make the effort to stay at home in case he could come back earlier than he feared would be the case and wished to eat supper with her.

When she retailed the invitation, Laurence said, 'Oh, I'm sorry but we really can't. I shall have to go into work on Christmas Eve, I'm afraid.'

He looked so preoccupied and distant that she did not risk telling him she could perfectly well go alone.

Mary's Diary

27 December

I am so relieved Christmas is over. Mrs K did her best and the food was good and L opened up two bottles of his favourite claret, but I felt so out of sorts, and he had little conversation. The best thing that happened was that when I looked out of the side window as I went up to bed I saw the most wonderful silver moon with a bright halo round it. Now, alas, it is pouring down.

Last night I had a strange dream. Much of it has slipped away now but I think I was at Cliff House – and Father was there, and Aunt Clara, and we were going to have a concert. Then Laurence came into the room and said he had called round with an invitation for me to come on a holiday, which he said my mother had arranged. I said I could not go. Tilly was there too, and Clara said she could go on the holiday but I realized (in the dream) that Father could not really be there because he was dead. It did not seem strange, though, that my mother had sent a message by Laurence. I said 'Oh I will go on holiday with you, Mr Noble.' I was thinking, well, he has invited me, and nobody else has. Clara was smiling. Then Laurence said to Tilly, 'Mrs Settle loves Mary, but she wants her to go abroad.'

'But Mother went away a long time ago!' I cried in the dream, and as I spoke I had a sudden sharp memory of the 'disappearance' of other people. I believe I was thinking of Stacey Watson and Stephen Waterhouse. The dream logic then told me it might be a good idea for me to have a holiday, and I might find them. But Mima came into the room just then. I ran towards her. Just as she was going to scoop me up in her arms the dream finished.

It was such a strange atmosphere, a mixture of decision and indecision.

I woke up wishing I had gone to that concert by myself.

214

Mima sent me a lovely Christmas card. She is managing all right, she says. I had sent her and her children a big box of sweetmeats – candied fruit – and she wrote on the card that they had all loved them, including herself. I do want to visit her soon. The dream has made me feel almost desperate to see her.

L is going into work tomorrow for the big annual stocktaking. I think he is extremely worried about trade. Many mills have closed during the past year. I have the feeling he would like to sell the mill and go to live abroad. Not that he has said anything, but I often catch him looking into space as if he was imagining a different sort of life. I don't think he ever expected to have to devote so much energy to textiles. Before we married, I had the impression that it ran itself, with the help of the manager, and that his father had left a good deal of money, though he has never exactly said how much.

Looking preoccupied, Laurence left the house early in the morning of 28 December for the mill, telling Mary that he would take his supper in town and she need not wait up for him. It was a Saturday, a working day for the weavers, and in the morning even for the mill-owners and managers.

She decided she would spend the morning dusting and resorting all the books she had brought with her from Woolsford four years earlier. She would put them in order on the shelves of the lovely large oak bookcase she had brought from Cliff House to this little room, her eyrie, at the top of the house, reached by a narrow twisty stair. There were books from her childhood here, presents from relations, and from Miss Hartley and Clara, and school books, all her college text-books, and her own purchases over the years from Woolsford and Pau and Paris and even Biarritz. All her favourite reading was here, which had so often solaced her when she had felt dull or despondent. Books had never let her down.

If you stood on a chair you could see out of the mansard window that looked over the garden. Usually though she just looked at the clouds and the wonderful skies. This cold bright morning Mrs Kershaw brought her a bowl of soup and an apple before she went off shopping in town at noon. The sun streamed though the window and Mary was savouring her solitude and making mammoth plans for her future self-education and reading, determined not to think about Anastasia and her mysteries.

She was lucky to have time to herself like this. Poor Tilly never had. She supposed she must be accounted selfish. But it was not her fault, was it, that she had no child to tend? She firmly pushed that thought away too, and blew the dust from Mrs Ewing's *Flat Iron for a Farthing*.

She heard the bell tinkle in the hall downstairs in the kitchen. Ethel was having the weekend off to visit her ailing father and Mrs Kershaw was out, so there was nothing for it but for her to put down her books and go down the two flights of stairs to the front hall. She opened the door.

'Why, Mr Gordon! Is something amiss? Has something happened to Laurence?'

Alex Gordon's face was so long she was envisaging an accident – Laurence in a heap at the bottom of the office stairs, or his hand speared by some wretched machinery. Gordon was always at the office to help with the stocktaking, and remind his employer of matters he might have forgotten.

'No, no, Mrs Noble – he's not had an accident. May I come in?'

'Of course.'

She led him to the smaller sitting-room where Mrs Kershaw had left a well banked-up fire.

'I apologize for arriving in this way,' he began, 'but I thought it was my duty.'

'Please, Mr Gordon, let me make you a cup of tea.'

'I'll not say no!'

He sat down and stared into the fire. Mary went into the pantry and then the kitchen in search of the tea caddy. She busied herself with the kitchen range. A kettle of hot water was always left by the kitchen fire and she took it and boiled it up, found a tray and a teapot, measured out three teaspoonfuls of tea and made the brew. What did he want? She thought of the books waiting for her upstairs.

Alex Gordon was about to enlighten her for he stood up as she brought in the tray. He looked solemn.

'I have been asked to tell you,' he began, 'that Mr Noble has been called away to settle something to do with work.'

'Oh.'

'I have been asked to tell you,' he said again, with heavy emphasis, 'that he may not get back tonight.'

'Oh?'

He said nothing more for a moment so Mary said, 'I see. He told me he might be late. Did something happen at work?'

Gordon took his cup and sipped it slowly.

216

'Aye, well, I thought you ought to know...' he hesitated. 'I debated with myself whether to tell you but – after seeing you last week I thought I must.'

Mary waited.

He reiterated heavily, 'He asked me to tell you he had been called away..'

Couldn't the man get to the point?

'But he did not ask me to tell you,' he continued ponderously, putting his cup carefully on the saucer, 'that he was called over to Manchester.'

Mary's heart missed a beat. 'On account of work?'

'A telegram arrived this morning,' he continued. 'I saw it. But it was not the first one. A telegram arrived just before Christmas also. It was after you had been to the office.'

'Please, Mr Gordon, say what you have to say. What is all this about?'

'He was not called away on account of the firm.'

'No?'

'No, this telegram today told him to go immediately to Prestwich. It was signed Robinson.' He shut his eyes and repeated its contents. ' "Come immediately Prestwich stop R is ill".'

'R' – was that Rose? Had the baby arrived, then?

'The first telegram,' Gordon went on, 'which I saw with my own eyes – was last week from the same individual. I opened it because Mr Noble was out of the office and I deal with all correspondence. It said, "A boy has been born".'

'I was never told,' Mary got out.

'As you will remember, I knew nothing whatever about this ... coming event. After the second telegram arrived today he said he must go to Manchester. He did not tell me why. He asked me to finish the stocktaking and to tell you he was off on business. I have told you all I know.'

Mary's mind was whirling. Two telegrams ... a baby born ... Anastasia ill. ...

He must have decided to go over to Manchester immediately.

Gordon stood up. 'I have done ma duty,' he said. 'Remember my very words to you were that I was asked to tell you he might be away on business. I'll be off back to the office now. I expect he'll be back tomorrow.'

What could she say except 'Thank you?' Messengers were never welcome and she disliked his slightly lugubrious Scottish manner.

He made quickly for the door, crammed his bowler back on his head, wound a scarf round his neck, then hesitated, shook her by the hand and marched off. She could see a hansom cab parked on the drive, and found herself wondering if it would be charged to business expenses.

She knew Anastasia's address in Prestwich; she would surely not have moved again so soon. She would follow Laurence to Manchester and get to the bottom of all this.

Anastasia had had a baby and was ill. That was the main consideration. Childbirth was dangerous. Had she a good doctor? And the baby? How was the baby? A little baby boy!

Mary had a lump in her throat, but she dashed around madly, found a pencil and paper to leave a message for Mrs Kershaw, and decided to ask Forbes to drive her to the station. It was too far to go on her bicycle.

She must pack a small bag. Should she send a telegram? No.

Her feelings were getting all mixed up: fear, excitement, curiosity.

She must help Anastasia. That was her clear obligation. Mental and emotional turmoil could wait. Decisions could wait . . . all the rest could wait.

She went upstairs, left her books as they were, shut the door, went into her bedroom, packed a change of clothes and her purse, and fished in her handkerchief drawer for the inner belt where she kept sovereigns for emergencies. It was her own money from the Yorkshire Bank. She pushed everything into her bag and went down to write the note to Mrs Kershaw. She took her coat and hat, scarf and gloves from their pegs in the hall and just then heard the kitchen door at the back being opened and the sound of voices – Mrs Kershaw and Forbes.

There was no time to be lost. She went down, all ready to go out.

She took the bull by the horns.

'I've been suddenly called away,' she said, 'I'd just written you this,' she held out the paper, 'Mr Gordon called with a message from my husband who has had to go to Manchester. I have decided to go there myself to see Mrs Hart. She is ill.'

She found the half-lie was easy to formulate.

'I expect we shall be back tomorrow – but I'll send you a telegram to let you know. She may need my help. I'm sorry to leave so suddenly.'

Mrs Kershaw stood there for a moment but she had taken it all in.

'I'll see to everything,' she said. 'Don't you worry. Forbes was just about to put the trap away but he'll take you to the station, miss, I mean ma'am.'

'You are an angel!' said Mary wildly. 'She has had a little boy.' With that she went out to Forbes in the courtyard.

She knew the train times. A train at four o'clock, she remembered from Laurence's going to Manchester before they were married. Had he gone direct from Halifax? She'd be there, if her luck held, by eight o'clock and then she could get a hansom cab. . . .

Mrs Kershaw put her basket down when Mary had gone, shook her head, then went to the fire to poke it and sat down for a peaceful cup of tea. It was not her business, was it?

PART FIVE

DECISIONS

CHAPTER FOURTEEN

It turned out to be a tedious journey, at first in a local train to the junction about two miles away. She might just as well have taken a tram. She remembered that Laurence had often made the journey across the Pennines via Huddersfield, and she had forgotten that different companies went on different tracks. But once she was in a second class carriage steaming through the Calder Valley she relaxed, though the window let in acrid smoke. She was alone in the carriage after the first stop and firmly pulled up the window strap when they entered a tunnel. The journey was now only one of some twenty-eight miles, but it was very slow. By four o'clock, darkness had fallen. They would pass through Rochdale, but not Burnley, which was much further north.

She was determined not to sit worrying about whatever might soon await her, so she tried to turn her thoughts to more pleasant things, thought of Mima who had come to see her in Lightholme although she had never yet been to see her in Burnley. Why ever had she not? Maybe she could go there on the way back to Yorkshire by a different route. To make the time pass more quickly she thought about railway journeys abroad. In the Basque country, for instance, bringing back memories that had become both happy and painful. She reflected upon other journeys: the one to Blackpool on the Lancashire coast, whose picture was framed on the carriage wall behind her, a journey taken every summer by families in Lightholme. They went there for 'wakes week', but she had never been to this Mecca of the popular imagination herself, and knew parts of France and Italy better than the coastal resorts of her own country. Other thoughts pushed in again then. . . .

She was beginning to feel that she had been confined in a small space called marriage, always waiting for her husband to return home. He had not even wanted to go abroad for the past two summers. She had relied on books and nature and music to keep her going. As she sat alone in the corner of the small stuffy carriage, she began to wonder if she had taken several wrong turnings in life that were too late to go back on now. She should have gone to Cambridge or London, or stayed on to do more study in Leeds. She should have qualified herself for work, stopped worrying about marriage and babies ... stopped wishing Stephen Waterhouse would fall in love with her. She might have met Laurence, but decided to remain a spinster working woman like Eleanor Hartley.

It all came back to Laurence, and then her mind would turn to babies. She would think about Tilly instead. But her thoughts were drawn back to Stacey Watson, who seemed much more real to her than Anastasia Rose Hart.

Mary sat on, pondering journeys, and the journey of her own life, determined not to speculate upon what she might find when she got to Prestwich. In contrast to her melancholy musings she had the feeling she would know what to do when the time came. She must look to the future. It was no good regretting the past.

After a much longer wait at the station than she had imagined, in a Manchester that seemed a great gloomy place; and after a bumpy journey in a horse cab that took her to a suburb, Mary arrived at the house whose address was on the piece of paper she held in her hand. It was a one of a terrace of tall brick houses built in the middle of the previous century. Only one faint glimmer of light showed though a curtain on the first floor.

Then she heard it – a high-pitched piercing wail.

She pulled on the bell. Nothing happened. She pulled again and this time after several minutes she heard a shuffling step and then a bolt being pulled back.

Mrs Florence Robinson stood there. Mary had come to the right place. She saw the woman look puzzled. Then light must have dawned, and she realized who her visitor was, for her mouth opened. She stepped backwards, did not attempt to close the door, but remained standing there, speechless.

Mary said, 'I am sorry to give you a shock. May I come in?'

There was a pause as her words hung on the air.

'I came to see Anastasia and the baby,' she added. 'I was told the baby had arrived.'

'You'd better come in,' said Florence Robinson, and shut the door behind them.

Mary had not mentioned Laurence, but Mrs Robinson, looking very flustered, said as they stood in the hall, 'Mr Noble is out getting the doctor to visit again.'

'Mrs Hart is not well?'

With a sort of gloomy satisfaction the woman answered, 'Raving. Very bad, very bad.'

'And the baby?'

'Five days old and she can't – or won't – feed him. He's hungry.' She sounded carelessly callous.

She motioned Mary to follow her up the stairs. Mary saw she was wearing down-at-heel carpet-slippers.

There was an aspidistra plant on an *étagère* half way up and when she reached the landing Mary saw a worn patterned carpet running down the middle, and three closed doors, one at the end, the other two next to each other. From behind the door at the end the high-pitched screaming began again.

'It's not what *you*'re used to,' said Mrs Robinson. 'If I may speak for myself, I'm glad you've come. I won't take the responsibility any longer – I told him so. I'm off as soon as the doctor's been again and it's all settled.'

Mary realized that Mrs Robinson must have formerly received her orders from Laurence. When had he started to employ her?

She found she was whispering as she asked, 'Was it a difficult birth? Was she very ill?'

'Yes, it was – I had to get a doctor in – but I told you, she won't feed him,' said the woman flatly. '*He* can't do anything with her. The doctor who came before just told her to get on with it. "Do what the doctor says," I said to her. Now he's gone for another doctor.'

She presumed the woman meant Laurence.

'Can I see her? And the baby?'

'She says she won't see anyone – not that she seems to know what she's saying. She didn't want him to get the doctor again but he took no notice – he's frightened.'

She said this with some satisfaction.

'But the baby. . . ?' Mary asked again.

'I was to deliver him myself – I used to be a midwife but I had to send for a doctor half-way through – as I told you.'

Mary realized that Florence Robinson had been and still was very frightened, otherwise she would not have sent for Laurence. Was she really a midwife? How did Anastasia's stepmother fit into this story?

'My job's done now,' she said. Then again: 'The baby's hungry. They always are after the first three days. I gave him sugar water to begin with.'

'But what about milk?'

'She wouldn't even try to give him suck – says she's not a cow and I must give him a comforter or some water. Now he needs milk, so I gave him some condensed milk from a tin I bought. He didn't like it though and it didn't agree with him. But it's not my responsibility.'

Except for her first start of recognition Mrs Robinson had not evinced the slightest surprise that Mary should be there.

'Where is he? I must see him,' said Mary.

'I told you – he's gone for the doctor—'

'I meant, the baby!'

If only Tilly were there, or could be reached on a telephone. She would know what to do. She remembered Tilly saying something about a baby belonging to a woman in her husband's congregation whose milk failed, and she had given him condensed milk from a tin, which Tilly had said was too rich, just not suitable. Hadn't Tilly told the woman to boil up cow's milk for at least fifteen minutes? She tried to remember. At Ridge Hill, pasteurized milk was delivered to the kitchen – she remembered Mrs Kershaw telling her that. Tilly had once said something too about poor people giving babies 'pobbies' – bread soaked in warm milk – but she must have meant when a baby was being weaned.

All this was going through her head as she followed Mrs Robinson down a long hall and up some stairs.

Mary had seen plenty of babies feeding from bottles. There had always been a Lightholme baby with a bottle in his mouth wheeled round the village in a perambulator. She realized that she was profoundly ignorant about how the milk got there and how often a baby needed it.

'Couldn't we boil up some milk? Have you a feeding-bottle?' she asked.

'I told you – I bought one – and a teat – but the milk gave him colic.'

The screaming from behind the end door was growing louder. Mary marched to the door, opened it, and saw an improvised cradle, a drawer placed on a low bed.

226

'She wouldn't prepare a thing,' said Mrs Robinson.

Mary approached the 'cradle' and saw a tiny creature who had kicked off the covering sheet and was writhing and screaming. It was a piercing sound such as she had never heard before.

She went up to the cradle and took up the little body as if she had been performing such an action all her life, carefully holding up his head and putting him against her left shoulder. He needed wrapping round tightly. At least he was wearing a nappy and a nightdress and there was a loose shawl on the bed, along with a comforter. Better wash that.

She bent down and with her free hand took the sheet that had been kicked off, placed it on the bed, knelt down, laid the baby on it and wrapped it round him firmly as though he were a little papoose. Then she sat on the bed holding him.

'There's some fresh sugar water till the doctor comes,' said Mrs Robinson, who stood like a statue in the doorway. She went on, 'I'm not a nanny,' she said, 'But I put the nappies on him, and provided the shawl. *I* bought the bottle for the water a week or two ago to use till her milk came in. It's downstairs in the kitchen. How was I to know she wouldn't feed him herself?'

'Then you'd better go and fetch it,' said Mary. 'Did you boil the bottle clean? Boil the dummy too.' The woman disappeared downstairs.

Was there not enough money for a proper cradle? What on earth was Anastasia thinking about? She was a selfish woman as Mary knew, but she must be ill to be so neglectful.

When Mrs Robinson returned with a bottle and the dummy, Mary settled the child in the crook of her arm, sprayed a few drops of water from the teat on to her wrist to make sure it was not too hot, and then put the teat in his mouth. At least *somebody* had bought a bottle. He sucked quite strongly. He must be parched. When he had drained the bottle she put him against her shoulder as she had seen Tilly do with her baby, and rubbed his back. She burped him, though it was only water the poor child had taken. He should be having milk. Where could she get some? She put the comforter back in his mouth, and kept him in her arms. He fell silent.

'I shall go in to his mother. Have you told her I am here? Please boil up some more water, and if you have any milk left by the milkman boil that too – for a quarter of an hour – and cover it to let it cool,' she said in a voice she had never heard herself use before. 'When my husband gets back, tell him I am here.'

As the woman went out, she followed her, still holding the baby.

Mrs Robinson went up to the door at the far end of the landing, knocked, opened it, and said, still standing at the threshold, 'Mrs Noble to see you.' She turned and went downstairs, Mary hoped to the kitchen and a clean kettle.

Now what? Mary went into the room, the child against her left shoulder.

The curtains were half-drawn and the light was dim but there was enough light for her to see a bed in the far corner. Slumped against a pillow and bolster was Anastasia Hart.

Mary stared at her in silence for a moment. Then she said, 'I came to see how you were – I will see your baby gets some suitable milk. But hadn't you better feed him yourself?'

'I will not,' croaked Anastasia, not looking up.

Mary went up to her and could see that her eyes were dull.

'Did you have a terrible time?' she asked sympathetically.

'I can't feed him. Mrs Robinson will see to him.'

'She must get some proper milk, then. You are not well. The doctor will be here soon,' Mary said to comfort her.

Anastasia did indeed look ill. When she looked at her closely, even in this half-light, Mary thought her limbs looked floppy.

Suddenly she tried to sit up straighter. 'Why have *you* come?' she gasped. 'Haven't you done enough damage?'

This almost took Mary's breath away but she replied levelly, 'I have come because I was told by Mr Gordon where Laurence could be found, and I was worried. The telegram said you were ill. I also wanted to see your baby.' She held him up.

'Oh, do take him away!'

As if realizing he was the subject of the conversation the baby began to hiccup. Anastasia made no motion towards him. The comforter had fallen out of his mouth so Mary put it back, saying, 'Won't you hold him? He is a lovely little fellow.'

'*You* can look after him,' said Anastasia.

The child began to scream again.

'Willingly. But won't you give him his next bottle?'

'Where is Florence?' asked Anastasia, averting her eyes from Mary and the baby.

'Mrs Robinson has gone down to the kitchen.'

'*You* can feed him if she goes. *I* don't want him. I never wanted a baby.'

Mary thought she had better get it over. 'He is Laurence's child, isn't he?' she asked her.

The woman stared at her and then began to cry hysterically. Had the birth affected her brain? Mary had heard of such things happening. She certainly needed a doctor. She did not look fit to be trusted with her own baby at present.

'I will feed him if he cries again but I'll go back and put him down in his cradle again just now,' Mary said. 'Then you can tell me about it.'

Anastasia went on weeping, and then suddenly stopped, took a big breath and said between clenched teeth:

'Mary Settle! – I knew you would come. *You* can have him – go on, please, please take him – just leave me be!'

As Mary turned to go out, she added in a strange voice, 'You can be his stepmother!'

Rather his nanny, thought Mary.

She went out of the room with the baby and met Mrs Robinson toiling upstairs with a tray on which was the baby's bottle filled with milk.

'Is it boiled?'

'What do you take me for? It's what the milkman brought yesterday – I don't think it's suitable.'

Mary preferred not to answer this, took the bottle, which was warm, but not hot, returned to the small room at the end of the landing again, and settled the baby in his cradle. There was one chair upon which she could sit. She would not go back into Anastasia until the doctor returned.

What a scene. She could hardly believe she was part of it. But here was undoubtedly a real, hungry baby. She had always understood from Tilly that a baby was better off with his mother's milk. Some mothers might find it distasteful, but why should Anastasia not even want to use a feeding bottle? She was surely intelligent enough to know you needed to sterilize milk for a baby.

She began to croon mindlessly: 'Bye-baby baba hush-a-bye baba-bye baby, barba-bye . . .' to the tune of Bye-Baby-Bunting, which she remembered Jemima Green had used to sing to her. 'Bar-baby, Barn-a-bye . . .'

'Barnaby' – that was a nice name for a baby boy. No name had been mentioned and she doubted even thought of. Well, she would call him Barnaby!

Just then she heard the door below open and the sound of male voices mingled with Mrs Robinson's. She stood up and waited. Should she immediately confront Laurence? What had Mrs Robinson told him? Whatever she wanted to ask Laurence, the baby was more important.

She took her courage in both hands and opened the door just as two men were rounding the end of the landing.

'Hello, Laurence,' she said pleasantly.

Mrs Robinson must have told him, for he stopped, looked at her, nodded, and said, 'My wife,' to the young man, who must be the doctor. Then he turned up the gas mantle on the landing and said, 'This way.'

As the doctor turned to greet her, Mary realized with a start that it was a face she knew.

'Why, it's Edwin!' she exclaimed.

It really was Edwin Horsfall. He must be quite recently qualified, following in the steps of his father. What a surprise. Tilly had never told her where he had gone after he had finished his studies.

She said to him, ignoring her husband, 'If you will tell me what to do when you have seen Mrs Hart, the baby is in here and he is still very hungry.'

She felt quite calm. Dr Edwin Horsfall was holding a full milkman's bottle in one hand, his bag in the other. Had they been shopping?

He looked at her in a surprised way, smiled, but said, 'I have some more suitable milk here. It can go in the kitchen to stand in cold water until we are ready to boil it. I've more in my bag.'

'I got Mrs Robinson to boil yesterday's milk up – but this would be better,' replied Mary.

Laurence said, 'The mother is here.' He almost pushed Edwin Horsfall into the room and shut the door behind them.

Mary went back to the baby, who was lying in the cot sucking on his comforter. The bottles must be pasteurized milk.

Why would Anastasia not put her baby to the breast? Mary knew how women managed, for she had observed Tilly, who had made no fuss about it. Who was she herself. though, married but childless, to advise a woman like Anastasia?

Perhaps Edwin Horsfall would be able to get some sense into her. It was not just that Anastasia might be incapable of suckling her baby – that did happen to women – but that she refused to contemplate it.

Surely a new mother would at least make an effort to see that her own child did not starve? If she was so against breast-feeding why had she not prepared bottles and made enquiries about cows' milk? Women like her would have had wet-nurses not so long ago. They still did in France, didn't they, and amongst the English aristocracy?

Mary's indignation quite banished her anger over her husband's duplicity. She went downstairs, found the basement kitchen and stood the bottle of milk in a pan of cold water from the tap. Mrs Robinson was in the sitting-room and saw her pass on her way down the hall.

Mary went back upstairs and saw Doctor Edwin Horsfall coming out of the bedroom. Seeing her at the open door of the little room he came up to her.

'I knew it was you straight away, Edwin.'

'Is Mr Dalrymple your husband? I knew you married a man from Ridge Hill—'

'Mr Dalrymple?'

Well, that was a facer. Laurence must be very eager not to be noticed.

'The man who fetched you is Laurence Noble, my husband,' she said firmly. 'It's all a muddle – and I really don't know what to do.'

'Never mind now,' he said briskly. 'We must boil up some of that milk I brought, and I'll be back with more. I'll get hold of some tomorrow from the dairy. It's the best I can do – the clinic will be shut tomorrow as it's Sunday. Let's deal with the milk I brought with me. Where is the kitchen? You have to boil it freshly each time.'

'She'd got in a tin of condensed milk,' Mary said, 'but I didn't think it was suitable so I asked Mrs Robinson to boil the milk from the old bottle. He hasn't had it yet. I've only just arrived here,' she explained, 'but the kitchen's downstairs in the basement. I have put the milk you brought there. Mrs Robinson is supposed to be looking after Mrs Hart. If he cries again or is sick, what shall I do?'

'You can always let me make up a feed,' said the surprising Edwin, 'if he starts screaming again before I have to go. Mrs Hart certainly needs looking after – your husband came on account of the lady, not the baby! I gathered she would not feed her child. It was my colleague who helped deliver her. He visited the day after the birth, and yesterday. He's off duty today.'

'I was frightened that he might die when he cried so loudly,' she confessed.

'Babies can survive a few days – they always lose a little of their birth weight at first – but this one is really hungry.'

'Mrs Robinson gave him sugar water,' said Mary.

'That was better than nothing.'

The baby opened his eyes and then his mouth, and began to bawl again.

'Barnaby,' she said. 'Hush!'

'We'll warm up some of this milk and fill the bottle. I'll examine him when I've seen to the mother again. Nobody can force her to feed her child, I'm afraid.'

They went down two flights of stairs and into the basement kitchen.

Mary found a small saucepan, which she scrubbed under the tap. She was wondering if Laurence would come downstairs looking for them.

Edwin Horsfall seemed incurious about the situation but Mary saw him look at her surreptitiously. She boiled up on a gas ring half the milk the doctor had brought. Mrs Robinson was nowhere to be seen. Just then they heard from upstairs the sound of the baby crying again.

'I think we'll have enough for the present,' Edwin Horsfall said. 'They take several ounces at each feed.'

He poured the boiled milk into the bottle and placed it into a pan of cold water. She followed him up to the source of the yelling.

'Find a chair to sit on. It's tiring work – and you can feed the baby slowly. His mother will need further medical attention. She ought to go into a nursing home, and she'll need a nursemaid for her baby.'

'Laurence can look after Mrs Hart,' said Mary firmly. 'I can be the nursemaid if you tell me what I should do – what's best to do – for the baby. I don't live here, you know,' she added unnecessarily as the surprising Edwin fetched up a chair, tested the milk, shook the bottle again and plugged it into the infant, who needed no further instruction. Then he handed the bundle of baby and bottle over to her.

'Is ordinary boiled cows' milk all right then?' she asked him as she sat there with the light warm burden on her lap.

'Depends where it comes from. Some probably is, but a lot of milk stands around in bottles and jugs and churns and gets dirty. Some of the milk babies are given is adulterated. I've been working on it in Salford. A medical colleague of mine is patenting powdered milk – but it isn't for sale yet,' he went on. 'They have cleaner milk in Lightholme – and it's pasteurized. Cows would do for him there – though of course it lacks lactose.'

Now he was talking as if to himself, still the serious-minded old Edwin.

She wondered how long he had been working with the poor in Salford. She knew so little about him. Out of all the doctors in the north of England it was a miracle that it was Edwin who had turned up. Dr Horsfall was obviously an expert on infant feeding.

Edwin obviously had a similar thought because he said, 'They would not have bothered with the milk if I hadn't insisted. Thank goodness there's somebody sensible here like you.'

As they sat there and the child went on feeding, she was thinking, Mima would know just what to do . . . I could telegraph Mima and ask her to come. We could go home and look after the baby there – it's all so uncomfortable here. Did Anastasia really live in this awful house? Would she want to keep the baby with her, fed or unfed? She appeared slightly out of her mind.

She could not help other emotions jostling in her own troubled mind – envy rather than jealousy, indignation, even contempt for a man who had must have encouraged a woman to live near him whilst still protesting that he loved his wife. . . . If marriage had not solved his problem for him, he should have left one of them alone. But there was so much about this betrayal that she did not know. Was Anastasia an 'old flame'? She pushed these thoughts away, not before she had noticed that, if she were indeed wronged, her anger was not with Anastasia but with Laurence. She looked down again at the tiny bundle that appeared to be so unwanted, and she knew what *she* wanted to do.

The child drained the bottle, and so Mary burped him again, watched by Edwin, who smiled. What a relief to have someone there who knew what he was doing. But Edwin had always been like that.

'I brought nappies too,' said this practical doctor, and showed her how to put one on. Then, 'I must see to my adult patient now,' he said, and went out of the room.

There was a little nightdress under the cot cover. Mary had never dressed a baby as small as this one and had a struggle putting it on but eventually managed. After this, she wrapped him in the cot blanket for the time being and sat waiting. If Laurence said nothing, then neither would she.

'Barnaby,' she said, 'go to sleep and I shall get another bottle ready and keep it warm.'

233

She heard the sound of raised voices from the bedroom of which the door, like hers, opened on to the landing. Anastasia was shouting:

'No! No! I won't!' Then Laurence's voice, cajoling, low. Mary crept to the door.

'For God's sake get him looked after!' and then noisy weeping. Then she heard the voices of Laurence and Edwin talking. Laurence must have said something to Mrs Robinson who had crept back upstairs, for she heard her say:

'I'm not a baby nurse – I'm not employed to be a nanny neither. If you're taking Mrs Hart away to be looked after *properly*' – she almost spat out the word – 'you must find a nanny and then I can leave.'

Dr Horsfall came out on to the landing and went up to Mary who was leaning against the doorpost.

'I have told your husband – he is I believe the 'guardian' of the lady? – that she needs expert care.'

'But what is the matter with her – why won't she feed her child?' cried Mary in distress.

'Well, it sometimes happens after a birth that a woman rejects her baby. You might say some women aren't in their right minds for a time. She won't improve without rest and treatment for her nerves. She ought to go into a nursing home to rest – I've told your husband. And we must find somewhere for the baby. Apparently she's never changed her mind about refusing to care for him – that's unusual – but I don't think she'll improve in his presence.'

'Let me speak to her,' Mary said.

She must make it clear to Laurence that she could and would help. She got up and went across the landing into the sickroom. Edwin Horsfall stayed by the baby. He began to unwind the sheet and examine him carefully.

In the next room Laurence was sitting by the bed, his head in his hands. Mary felt sorry for him, though she felt sure now that he had duped her. It all seemed so – incredible. But she had never seen Laurence look as he did now. He lifted up his face and she saw it was tear-stained. . . . Her rational husband had wept!

But all this could wait.

He looked at her as she went up to Anastasia, took her hand and began to speak.

'Stacey,' she said, 'will you listen to me? I can help you with the baby if you want. If you think I am not capable by myself, I have my

234

old nanny living in Burnley. Her husband died recently and she wrote to me at Christmas saying she wanted a 'living-in' job for a few months. She's an expert with babies. She would help, I know, and I'm quite prepared to take charge until you feel better. Do you understand? We – I mean Jemima Sutcliffe and I – could look after him at Ridge Hill for the time being.'

'Do *you* understand?' whispered Anastasia, lifting her head from the pillow, her eyes small and shrunken. 'Ask Laurence – *he* doesn't want the charge of a child.'

'He has helped you,' said Mary, and saw her husband flinch.

Anastasia drew herself up, beckoned to Mary and whispered, 'Help me, Mary – Mary Settle! I remember you well.'

In a more normal voice she said to Laurence who was now sitting with bent head.

'Mary Settle looked at me so strangely once. I think she is my fate. Let her have the baby, and take him home. I shan't want him back.' She repeated in a weaker voice, 'I shan't ever want him back,' and stared at Mary again.

Laurence looked anguished. He stood up.

'That's enough, Rose,' he muttered.

'Laurence, may I speak to you for a moment alone?' asked Mary.

She got up, and he followed her on to the landing. Laurence shut the door and the door of the little room in which the doctor was talking softly to the baby, as he looked him over.

Laurence and Mary remained standing.

Mary said quietly, 'You were stocktaking, Laurence. Later we can both do some 'stocktaking'. I have possibly been living in a fool's paradise . . . not any longer. I'm sincere in what I suggest, and Jemima Sutcliffe will come if I ask her to help me look after the child. He may not be your responsibility in the eyes of the law,' she said, 'but he *is* yours, isn't he? You can have him back when she is better.'

She would like to have said: *The child I couldn't give you*, and the words were almost on her tongue, but she held them back. She did not even at this moment want to sound melodramatic. Laurence did not answer her question directly, but said,

'I never needed children, Mary.'

He had guessed the further implication of her words.

'You *love* her, don't you?' Mary said, 'Or you would never have got her into this mess. See she gets well again. You must stay by her – you love *her* – and I can help *you* – and her. Then you can both decide what you want to do.'

'Why should you do this for me or her?' he asked. 'Her sister could adopt him – or a good family would—'

At this Mary's sorrowful fury burst out. 'You dare to suggest that! No, I can look after *your child* until his mother knows what she wants. It's not a good place for him here, and the milk is better at home if she refuses to feed him. He will die if you leave him to her, you know – she didn't even bother to see he was fed at all. She's ill – you can sort out all the rest when she's better.'

'Very well,' he said. He sounded completely defeated.

All her hurt was in her voice as she said, 'We'll talk about it later. We have to see that baby stays alive, Laurence. May I telegraph Mrs Sutcliffe? Will you let me do my best?'

'Very well,' he said again. 'Take him home and I'll follow when I can . . .'

'But what about *her*?'

He looked blank.

'You know, when I was a little girl I fell in love with Stacey Watson – your "Rose",' she said in a quiet voice, 'So I can quite understand *your* loving her – without understanding why you should have married *me*. I could love this baby too – because it is a baby, not because it is yours – or hers.'

The door of the child's room opened and Edwin appeared, putting his stethoscope away.

'The infant is back to sleep again,' he said cheerfully. 'A grand little lad. . . . But I think Mrs Hart must go somewhere tonight. I can find a nursing home for her.'

He opened the door to the other room, just as Mrs Robinson came out agitatedly.

'She has tried to cut her wrist.'

'Oh, no! Oh, my God!' Laurence hurled himself into the bedroom. Mary stayed by the door. Anastasia was lying on the bed, and she could see a jagged piece of glass on the pillow.

'She broke the glass of water,' said Florence Robinson in a shocked but petulant voice. 'Is there a handkerchief you could put round her wrist?'

Edwin Horsfall took over. He looked at the cut. ' The cut is not grave – the intention was,' he said. 'I shall telephone The Haven – it's a well-known nursing home for nervous cases – and see if we can get her in tonight. And I think Mrs Noble should telegraph her old friend and they can take the child somewhere safe.' His father probably remembers Mima, thought Mary.

Edwin had found a bandage in his bag and was binding it round his patient's wrist. 'You'll see to the child, Mary.'

Laurence looked at him, surprised.

'There is enough milk here that I brought with me. Will you be able to manage the journey back home? I can't see any point in Mrs Hart taking the baby with her at present. I'll take the responsibility for this advice.'

'Once I have sent a telegram to Mima, and she's arrived here, we shall go home,' said Mary, looking at Laurence.

'If they can go by train I can send my carriage to meet them,' replied Laurence with an effort, not looking at his wife. 'They can go home tomorrow – or Monday. I will let my housekeeper know.'

Home? thought Mary.

She knew that Ridge Hill could never be her real home again.

An hour or two later, Laurence accompanied Anastasia and the doctor to a small hospital nearby, to await a longer journey on the morrow if The Haven, the nursing home Edwin Horsfall had mentioned, would take her.

All Laurence said to Dr Horsfall before they all left in the ambulance the doctor had summoned was, 'Are you sure Mrs Hart ought not to take the infant with her?'

'I see no point in her present condition,' Edwin had replied drily. 'That is, if she wants him to live?'

Laurence had looked scared and then relieved. He had said nothing further to Mary.

Anastasia was now running a temperature and took no interest in her own departure on a stretcher. There was not even a goodbye from her to her baby. When Laurence did not return, Mary sent Mrs Robinson to buy cotton wool, as there were no more nappies in the house, and to the post office with a telegraph to Mima. She sent a prepaid reply:

Am at 19 Globe Terrace Prestwich with relative's baby. Returning Ridge Hill Monday. Will explain later. Can you come help here or Yorkshire? Love Mary.

All night she wondered at the responsibility she had taken on, and tried not to panic. The thought of Edwin Horsfall helped her to stay calm. *He* thought she was capable, and somebody had to look after 'Barnaby'.

She sat up most of the night in the chair, staring at the tiny creature. It was not because he was Laurence's child, or even Anastasia's, for they were two people she had at present no reason to love, but she felt her insides turning to water when she looked at him, a small stranger in the world. He was so tiny – though the doctor had said he was of normal weight, and he certainly needed loving. Mima, who was no relation to her, had tended her as a baby and loved her, hadn't she?

Mrs Robinson announced her intention of going to bed. Mary dozed fitfully, waking whenever the baby stirred and cried, and the urgent demand for more milk started up again. Having tasted ambrosia, he required a constant supply. When she saw a faint late dawn in the dark window, she took him up and nursed him, and felt they were giving each other warmth.

Now it was Sunday afternoon and she was still alone with the child, waiting to hear from Laurence. Mrs Robinson had done a little more shopping for her in the morning at Mary's insistence, but had just departed in a cab, saying only, as she gave Mary her keys to the rented house, 'You'll regret it.'

Mary was on tenterhooks waiting for a reply from Mima, but before a telegraph boy could arrive, the bell rang and there was Dr Horsfall on the doorstep.

She wanted to ask him, *Am I doing the right thing? Am I being foolish, when people will think I am being unselfish?*

He would not understand what she meant, knowing no details of the situation. He must have some idea, though, because of the way Laurence had been with Anastasia, and the fiction of 'Mr Dalrymple'.

She asked him instead, as she led him into the dingy sitting-room downstairs,

'She will recover, won't she – and take the little one?'

'To speak the truth,' he said, 'I don't know. Physically, yes, but she seems emotionally disturbed. The best thing for the baby at present is for you to look after him.'

'He's asleep upstairs,' said Mary. 'I look in on him every half an hour.'

238

It seemed so odd talking to the grown-up Edwin about a baby, but she realized how sensitive and yet down to earth he was.

He said, 'I come with a message from your husband. He asked me to send a Mrs – Kershaw? – a telegram to say you will arrive tomorrow afternoon with the baby and possibly a nanny. I have done this.'

So it was all to be above board.

'He asked me to book a cab for you to go to Manchester station tomorrow. This I have done. The train is at ten o'clock and will go directly to Dean Junction where your husband has asked for his carriage to meet you. Have you heard from your Mrs Sutcliffe?'

At that very moment there was a peremptory knock at the door and Edwin went to answer it, followed by Mary. There stood a telegraph boy in his uniform.

'Mrs Noble?' he enquired.

'Yes.' She tore open the yellow envelope.

Arriving Manchester 4 pm Sunday and will find my own way Love Mima.

She showed it to Edwin. 'Thank goodness!' she said.

'Now you will be all right. I brought some more milk with me. Tell Mrs Sutcliffe that well-boiled pasteurized cow's milk will suffice when you return. At present he'll take about four ounces per feed but soon he'll want more.'

'How can I thank you enough?'

He brushed aside her thanks, and added, 'Your husband says he has the keys to this house. You can leave the other keys here and he will see Mrs Hart's things are packed. He also said that he has told your housekeeper he will return home himself when he is able.'

'I expect I shall hear from him when Mrs Hart is settled,' Mary said.

'I have arranged for her to stay at The Haven, the nursing home I'm acquainted with.'

'What sort of care does she need? Is she *dying*?'

'No, no – an infection, added to emotional imbalance. She needs rest and care. The birth was a big physical shock – I assume that affected her mental equilibrium. Birth can take some women in that way.' Now he was being a doctor, not Edwin.

'You know a lot about it.'

'Well, so I should. I'm specializing in paediatric medicine – which of course involves mothers. But I don't know what the lady's usual reactions are.'

Did he want her to tell him?

'Did my husband say anything else?'

'No, only that if you need money to buy a layette or anything else you are to use his account.'

She said quickly, 'Did my husband mention someone adopting the child? Or anything like that? My husband is . . .' Edwin shook his head and Mary stopped, overcome, but then took a deep breath and went on more calmly, 'Tell him that I shall take care of this child until Anastasia – Mrs Hart – decides what she wants. She is a widow, you see, and so she is the legal guardian of the baby.'

She had thought that out during the watches of the night. 'Don't say any more now.'

He looked round. 'This isn't a nice place for a new-born baby. There are worse, I know, but if Mrs Hart won't co-operate he'd be far better off elsewhere for the present – somewhere healthier. I blame myself for not following up my colleague's visit last week. He didn't tell me much. It should have been my case but I was away in St Helen's. He thought she'd come round, but he was wrong.' In a different tone of voice, he added, 'I shall come over to see the child – and you –when I next visit my parents. If I may?'

'You know I still own the house at Lightholme? That I have tenants there?'

She had the sudden overpowering feeling that she didn't want to go back to Ridge Hill. Edwin must have seen something in her face, for he said:

'Yes, my father told me. You have been very sensible and kind – and now I must go to another of my cases. Once you get some moral support, you will manage!'

You always used to give me moral support, Edwin, she thought. Even as a boy not much older than herself, he had always had confidence in her.

'Remember me to your aunt,' he said as he got up to leave.

'She is abroad.'

'And to Tilly,' he added, as he went out.

I expect I shall have to write to Clara eventually, thought Mary, when Edwin had gone and she had fed the baby again and cleaned him up. How very much she wanted to tell Tilly what had happened. She dreaded telling Clara.

The rest of the afternoon she kept looking out of the window from the baby's room, waiting for the rattle of cab wheels on the road outside.

She was in the kitchen boiling up some more milk for a quarter of an hour before letting it cool, as Edwin had instructed her, when the bell went.

She went up to the hall, bottle in hand, placed it on the hall table next to an empty pair of antlers that had once held coats and hats, and opened the door.

CHAPTER FIFTEEN

One look at Mima standing there so solidly and Mary could at first utter not one word. Then there was a loud screaming from upstairs.

Mima held on to the bag she was carrying, saying, 'I know that noise!'

Mary got out, 'I was just about to give him this . . .' but Mima picked up the bottle and was immediately off in the direction of the cry. Mary felt relief flood through her. Mima had not asked whose the baby was or what Mary was doing there. Mary followed her upstairs and Mima needed no instructions as to how to deal with a hungry baby. They sat there together in the little room, Mary sitting on the bed, not saying anything at first, the only sound the loud sucking of a teat.

When he had finished Mima held him over her shoulder as she patted his back.

'That's what I do,' said Mary.

'Get a bowl of warmish water, love. Have you cotton wool?'

Mary proffered that and then hurried off to fetch the water. When she returned, Mima rapidly wiped him, put on a square of linen she appeared to have brought with her in her capacious case, and then handed him over to Mary.

'They all need cuddling,' she said.

Mary fetched another chair in from Anastasia's now abandoned bedroom and they both sat down. Mary felt the child's limbs relax. Soon he was asleep.

'I can tell he's one of those good babies,' said Mima. 'Some never stop their yelling even if they're full of milk.'

Mary put him down in his improvised cot. 'Well, it didn't seem like that yesterday!' she said.

She began to try to explain how matters stood. She found it easy to tell Mima about the baby's mother, and her refusal to feed, at which Mima tut-tutted, it was harder to explain her own relationship to the child. What was it exactly? Friend? Stepmother? Aunt? Nanny?

'Let me make us a cup of tea whilst you unpack. There's a bed in the other room – and then I'll tell you the rest,' she said.

Mrs Robinson had stripped her bed and Mary found some thin but clean cotton sheets in a chest of drawers.

She went downstairs to the kitchen to make some tea. She had hardly eaten since the previous day, had asked Mrs Robinson to buy biscuits, but she had forgotten. Now she noticed on the table the brown-paper carrier Edwin had left for her, opened it and found it packed with another feeding-bottle, a teat wrapped in tissue paper, two packets of biscuits, some bananas, six rashers of bacon in grease-proof paper, and six eggs. She heard Mima come downstairs.

'When are we leaving?' Mima asked, once they were sitting at the kitchen table with tea and biscuits.

'There's a cab booked to the station for a train tomorrow morning. Laurence arranged it.'

Mima waited to be told more. Mary went on, 'I found out from the manager at the mill that Laurence had come here to the baby's mother, so I followed him on Saturday. The mother is someone I used to know –a relative of Tilly's at The Nest. For a time she rented the house next door to us but moved away in October. I knew she was expecting a baby, but I had *no idea* at first that the baby's father was certainly my husband! Then I began to suspect that ... that Laurence ...'

'Oh, you poor lass!'

Mary began to speak rapidly.' You see, at present the mother is disturbed – very nervy and hysterical. She's not the kind who would want a baby even if she was happily married, and she just refused to see to him at all. I think Laurence really loves her – I guessed from a letter I found that he had known her before we were married – and then he must have met her again after she was separated from her second husband. *He* died but I'm not sure when ...'

Mima made a clucking sound of disapproval.

'Laurence must have wanted to have her nearer him – or she wanted to be nearer him – I really don't know. They were crazy. Did they think they were going to carry on secretly for ever? Then she found she was pregnant. But there's a lot I'm just guessing. It didn't occur to him I might find out about her and follow him here. All he could think about was her – Anastasia – Mrs Hart. I don't suppose he really cares about the baby. But you see, Mima, when I asked him yesterday if the baby was his, and he didn't contradict me, I thought, if *she* doesn't want him I really want to look after this child.'

'Poor little mite! You did the right thing – maybe they'll come to their senses. How did they think they were going to manage with a baby? Was he going to leave you?'

'I have no idea. I don't think he knew either. The baby's nearly a week old now and he was screaming yesterday – worse than you heard just now. I'd never heard anything like it. Laurence had gone out to fetch a doctor for Mrs Hart. There was a woman companion here too – an awful woman called Mrs Robinson. She claimed to be a midwife, but I'm not sure –if she was, surely she'd have known how to feed a baby? I arrived – and then the doctor arrived and he turned out to be Edwin Horsfall who used to live in Lightholme. It was unbelievable!'

'Well, Mary, you've certainly landed yourself in something!'

'Do you remember Dr Horsfall? Edwin is his son. We both went to the little school at The Nest. He's been absolutely wonderful – though he must think we are *all* mad, me as well.'

'What a carry-on,' said Mima. 'But your husband wants you to look after his by-blow – for the time being?'

'I suggested it. I was so worried that the baby would die if he were left to *them*. He was just crying from hunger all the time. His mother just doesn't care, and Laurence was not doing a thing about it. She told me to take him away with me. You see, I'd wanted to be friends with her when we were neighbours, but I realize now why she didn't want to see much of me! Laurence never let on at all that he knew her! I wouldn't have credited him with being such a good actor.'

'Have they given the bairn a name?' asked Mima.

'I call him Barnaby – they hadn't even given him a name, Mima.'

'You'll get fond of him. Folk do when they care for bairns.'

'I know. I'm already fond of him.'

'They'll have to come to a proper arrangement then. You were right to cut through it all to what mattered most. I mind a lass down Burnley had a bairn she didn't want. He reminded her of the dad – a right bad 'un he was –so her sister took him in. He's a nice little lad now.'

Mima took Mary's hand. 'You were allus a kind little thing,' she said.

'No, it's you who are kind, coming to help me like this. I kept think-ing of how you took me on when I was a baby.'

'Eh, lass I was right pleased to be asked. It's grand to see you again, Mary.'

'I'm sorry it's been so long. I think I've been living in a dream . . . I kept hoping I'd be expecting myself.'

Her voice went flat. Mima squeezed her hand.

'Sometimes it just doesn't happen,' she said. If that was what her husband was like, maybe that was a good thing.

Mary guessed what she was thinking. 'If I'd had a baby he would-n't have gone back to her,' she said. She went on quietly, 'When I knew she'd had the baby and that it was Laurence's, I ought to have been angry. I despise his falsehoods, but I wasn't angry with her. Then, when I saw the baby and saw how she really seemed to loathe him it made me sorry for her. I know how Laurence feels about her.'

'Does yon doctor think she'll recover?'

'Yes – in time.'

'She might want him back?'

'I don't think she will. What can Laurence do? I don't think he'll abandon her.'

'Men often get themselves out of fixes. This Edwin – he thought it better for you to look after the child?'

'Yes, he did, and Laurence has said absolutely nothing else about it except that he will pay for some clothes. I still have to have it out with him.'

'Do you love him? Your husband?' Mima asked her shyly.

'I thought I did. I loved him because he said he loved me, and I thought, he won't leave me, then, since he is so keen to marry me, but I don't think he ever loved me – not the way he did her. I was so stupid. I should never have married him, but Yeranty . . .' she stopped, overcome. Mima took her in her arms.

Mary said, 'I need you as much as the baby needs me, it feels so safe.'

But I'm not a child now, she thought.

'You did right to offer to help,' said Mima. 'You put the fate of the little lad first. Eh – I never forget when you were not much bigger than the bairn upstairs and your dear mam died . . . but maybe your husband will want you as his wife, along with his fancy woman as well by his side.'

'He can't have us both,' said Mary.

'Would *he* be employing me, then?' Mima asked after a pause. The light was fading and it was cold.

'No, Mima, I'm employing you. It's a proper job. I was trying to find one for you, anyway. I was so sorry about Sam. But don't think of it like that—'

'Aye, well it was a right shame. . . .' She sighed, and then went on, 'I'd better get it straight with your husband. He knows you were going to ask me to come along?'

'Oh yes, to stay for as long as you can, or want to. I'd be so grateful. Just show me what to do, will you – like you did for me after my mama died.'

'I'm chuffed it was me you thought of!' said Mima. 'I don't suppose your man can be all that bad if he's stood by her. I mean, I know he's doing wrong but he hasn't abandoned her.'

'No, he's not bad, just weak. I suppose he thought he'd got over her before we married.'

She was thinking: all the time he was courting me he was most likely still seeing her. Such realizations kept popping into her head however much she tried to banish them.

'He loved – loves – her and I can understand that very well. I think she must already have been married for the second time when he first got to know her. But what makes me angry is that when she came to live near us he pretended he didn't even *know* her! If she hadn't come to live at Birch Wood I need never have known at all.'

What would she have done if Laurence had told her?

'He wants to have his cake and eat it,' said Mima briskly. 'Like most men. Now, I'll have to see if yon baby needs anything – a blanket for sure. We'll settle all't rest another day. Let's get you back home first. And I'll stay alert tonight so you can get some sleep. You look right washed out.'

'There now, here's your old comforter,' said Mary when she found the child had kicked off his sheet and was beginning to grizzle.

'I hope it's not wrong to let him go on having the dummy, so long as it's kept clean. Mrs Robinson gave it to him.'

'*You* had one long enough,' replied Mima fondly. 'I mind Yeranty saying "when is that child going to lose her dummy?"'

It was odd to think that once she had been as small as this little creature and Mima had done everything for her. It must be the reason for her wanting to look after little Barnaby.

'Eh, lass, do you rightly know what you might be letting yourself in for?' said Mima.

'Aye,' said Mary, 'I do that.'

She couldn't help smiling.

Mary slept for ten hours; she felt as if she had never properly slept before and savoured waking slowly and deliciously from slumber until, with a sudden start of memory, she realized where she was, and sat up in a panic.

It was all right. Mima had been on duty through the night, and came in just then to report that all was well.

'How I needed a good rest,' said Mary. Mima would not be there to help her for ever; she had better get used to shorter nights and lighter sleep, adjust herself to putting another being before herself.

After that it was all rush and bustle to be ready for the cab. They packed up, tidied the dismal house and left a full coal-scuttle in the grate. Mima produced a long baby-robe from her bag and they wrapped the child in it, and in as many other layers as they could find – a small sheet, and the blanket from the makeshift cot. On and around his head they put a tiny woollen tea cosy they found, which made them both laugh. Mary had brought little with her. If only she had thought ahead, but not in her wildest fantasies had she imagined she would be bringing Anastasia's baby back to Ridge Hill.

Barnaby, as Mima had begun to call him too, took his early-morning bottle well and Mima boiled more milk, filled another bottle ready for the journey, and wrapped it in her spare flannel petticoat. Almost January now, the unkindest month, but fortunately not as cold it might have been on this short winter day, though from the train windows they were to see snow lying on the fields.

The day after tomorrow would be New Year's Day. 1902! A new year for the nurturing of a new life. But first there was the cab journey from the dull Manchester street to the station, and then the train. Mima carried Barnaby, and Mary the paraphernalia of travel and infant necessities. Soon they had crossed into their own county.

'I always like to go home to Yorkshire,' said Mima.

The baby had slept all the way but was now ready for his bottle.

They arrived at the junction. Was it only two days ago – Saturday afternoon – that she had boarded the train there? Impossible!

Almost home now, and Mary saw the familiar carriage waiting in the station yard, Forbes standing by it. She was suddenly nervous.

Had Laurence truly told Forbes and Mrs Kershaw to expect the advent of a baby?

How much might Mrs Kershaw guess? She was an astute woman in many ways and she had not liked their recent neighbour. Mary had seen her unconsciously wrinkle her nose when Mrs Hart's name was mentioned.

Mary had rehearsed her first words to Mrs Kershaw many times over in the train: *Mrs Hart is ill and has asked me to look after her baby for the time being ... this is Mrs Sutcliffe who has to come to help. ...*

What did she think she was doing? Kidnapping a baby? In the cold light of day she could not believe that Anastasia did not want to try to feed and look after her own child.

'I keep thinking there'll be a telegram from his mother awaiting my return, asking me to take him back,' she whispered to Mima.

They were sitting in the carriage now, rugs drawn round them both, the baby snug on Mary's lap with her arms enfolding him. She thought about the relationship she actually had with this baby. It was comically strange, in spite of the solemnity of her undertaking, that she wanted to, and could, fulfil his needs, however imperfectly. He needed her, as once she had needed the woman sitting next to them. It was an awesome overpowering need. Had she always been intended to look after him, however badly the clothes of a guardian angel might fit?

When Forbes met them from the train he had only said, 'I'm told you've taken on a mission of mercy, Mrs Noble?'

Was he being ironical? Did they all guess about Laurence and his neighbour? She resolved to give no hint to him, or to Mrs Kershaw or Ethel, about her husband's part in all the wretched entanglement. They could guess – might eventually ask – but she would leave it to Laurence to extricate himself.

This, and sharing the situation with Mima gave her more peace of mind.

The journey in the carriage from the junction to home was partly on cobblestones, a long journey, but at last they were out of the town on the other side and then had reached the top of Ridge Hill.

The lane came into view: it was as if years had passed since she had left it; she could no longer remember exactly what she had intended to do the last time she had passed down its rutted way.

When they turned down the lane and drove up their own drive

under the bare trees and the one or two conifers, she was quite sure of one thing. Even if Laurence decided to go on living here in the same way as before, she could not, and would not. For as long as she made no further plans, Ridge Hill would have to do, but plans she must make. For the present she had to concentrate on the baby.

Mrs Kershaw was waiting for them in the porch. Mary imagined she saw questions behind her eyes but, whatever were her private thoughts, she had clearly chosen discretion and they were not voiced. Mrs Kershaw had been well trained. Mima was introduced and welcomed, the general situation was explained just as Mary had planned to explain it, and Barnaby was cooed over by Ethel.

The housekeeper knew her job; a little room had been prepared in a dressing-room that led off the bedroom prepared for Mima. On the other side of the baby's room there was another spare bedroom, which Mary intended to occupy. For the time being they would take turns to get up at night. Mrs Kershaw had even produced an ancient cot, had obviously planned its being used one day.

It was almost as if Mary had brought her own baby home, complete with nursemaid, but she tried not to think of it like this. She might not be needed for very long.

It was very cold, and Ethel had lit a fire in both bedroom grates. Ahead were days and, who knew, weeks, of solicitude for an unwanted infant. Mary went down to thank Mrs Kershaw for all she had done, and to tell her all that the doctor had suggested about the milk.

'Ours is pasteurized,' replied the housekeeper. 'Mr Gordon came round. He'll be back here on Thursday. Mr Noble wanted him to make decisions for the time being. He telephoned the works.'

'Good,' Mary replied vaguely, 'I'll speak to him. I expect my husband back sometime in the New Year. He had more business to conduct in Manchester.'

She did not mention Mrs Hart, nor could she say that things would soon return to normal, though Mrs Kershaw might suspect that Laurence's 'business' in Manchester was much the same as it had always been. She looked at her shrewdly but kindly, and Mary left matters at that.

Life with a small baby is much the same everywhere, once there is enough warmth and food and love, and a routine is established, which depends on the temperament of the infant. With the help of Mima, Mary was soon settled into a routine of her own.

'Mrs Kershaw asked me about the baby's mother,' Mima told Mary a day or two later. She often went down to the kitchen to chat and help, and had made a friend of Ethel. 'I think she doesn't like to ask you. I said that the mother was ill, and a bit disturbed in her mind. Was that all right?'

'Of course. He must decide what to say to Mrs Kershaw himself,' Mary replied.

To Alex Gordon on the Thursday, when he was shown into the morning room where a fire was burning brightly, Mary explained a little more. He was told about the nursing home and why his employer's wife had taken charge of the infant.

'Mr Noble will be back next week,' he said.

To this, Mary replied, ' I was not sure about that. He really must have a telephone installed here. My husband has not had time to write to me yet about his plans.'

A letter did arrive, though, the following day.

Little Barnaby was looking slightly fatter, they thought, and the diarrhoea that the milk had at first occasioned was somewhat abated.

Mima also received a letter from her son. He wrote that all was well with them. They could manage, and they hoped she would stay where she was if it were a good position.

Laurence's letter was weird, a mixture of the apologetic and the coldly reasonable. . . . Mrs Hart was no worse – much the same. At the end he wrote:

We have to talk. I am sorry you had to find out like this. I will tell you more when I see you. Perhaps Mrs Kershaw will see that we are not disturbed when I arrive – most likely Tuesday. I hope you have all you need?

To this Mary replied:

It is indeed time we discussed matters. Please tell his mother that little Barnaby, as we have begun to call him, is feeding well . . .

Not that she minds about that, she thought. She added:

I think you have to register the birth within a month. As you are in

Manchester, perhaps you will do that? Will you ask her what she wants him called?

She knew they always put the name of the mother, and Laurence would have to write *widow.* Could he add the father's name? Or would he just be an 'informant'? If Anastasia Hart preferred the child to have a different name, Mary needed to be told. *You might like Barnaby Laurence,* she suggested. Would they want him christened?

Was she being presumptuous? Would Laurence tell her it was none of her business? But it *was* her business! Here was the baby and here was she. Over there were her husband and the baby's mother. How long did they intend her to look after him? She added, after her 'Barnaby Laurence' suggestion: *We need to know how long you want him to stay with us here.*

Did Laurence intend to leave Ridge Hill, take the baby and live with his mistress? Calling Anastasia his mistress was, she supposed, the truth, but it sounded melodramatic. Everything about Anastasia had always been melodramatic, but she didn't believe the woman was acting a part at present. How had the excessively rational Laurence got himself into this mess?

She knew how. Through passion, the kind of passion she had never aroused in him.

The next day she received a letter from one of her tenants, a Mr Hinchliffe-Lister, saying he would soon be obliged to leave his part of Cliff House as his business was to move over to Scotland. This made Mary's heart leap and provided her with a great deal of long hard thinking when she lay sleepless during the night, waiting for the child to wake and cry and require feeding, a change of napkin, and a little 'maternal' comfort.

If Laurence told her he wanted to take the baby and return to live with his 'Rose', or if he wished to return and live with her, as before, without the child, what should she say? She did not think he wanted the child, but she found herself feeling he should not abandon Anastasia now.

She had never come across such a situation before, and felt powerless. It was all up to the man to choose, as usual. But they had to come to some arrangement. What would most young wives do? Take the unfaithful husband back, and shut their eyes to his liaison? The advent of the baby had changed everything, and looking after that baby had already changed her, and she suspected would change her even more in future.

If Anastasia did continue to reject the child, she knew what she would prefer to happen. Mima had guessed what she really wanted.

She would rather have Barnaby than her husband. That was the stark truth. Well, Laurence would rather have Anastasia than her! But had she the strength to leave her pleasant comfortable home and start afresh, with the additional responsibility of a child. Could she take him on for life?

Barnaby still cried quite a lot from colic, especially in the evenings and at night, so that when Laurence arrived the following week she would have been too exhausted to think clearly if it had not been for Mima.

If she made a bargain with her husband to let him have what he seemed to want, which would allow her to do what she so strongly desired, would they both be acting selfishly? Once more, all hung upon Anastasia's own frame of mind, one Mary found incomprehensible, and upon Laurence, and what he wanted to do about his 'Rose'.

She herself had every reason for recrimination. He had neglected her; he had committed adultery. Did he realize that she had recently asked herself whether in her heart of hearts, she had ever truly loved him? He had told her he loved her, and her decision to accept his proposal of marriage had stemmed from that, as she had told Mima. It was Laurence who had not fulfilled his side of the bargain.

'Mrs Kershaw has made us some tea,' said Mary.

Laurence was in the hall at Ridge Hill. He had arrived in the trap with Forbes, and come straight into the house where Mary had been nervously awaiting him, alone in the sitting-room. She came out to him. Would he look at her in the eyes? He had not done so in Prestwich. How absurd it was. Nothing had changed from the countless times she had welcomed him home over the last four years; and yet everything had changed.

He took off his hat and coat, threw them on an old oak chest and followed her into the warm room. She had replenished the coals twenty minutes ago, and a fire was burning brightly.

'It is very cold out,' she said soberly.

They were both awkward, so she plunged in.

'How is Anastasia? If you want to see Barnaby – he's upstairs with Mima.'

'He is well?'

'Fine – just a bit colicky – it's the cows' milk.'

He began to warm his hands by the fire, before turning to face her.

'Please have some tea,' she said hurriedly, and poured him a cup.

He sat down in the armchair opposite hers on the other side of the hearth for all the world as if he had just returned from a long day at the mill. She poured out a cup for herself.

'Did you get my letter?' she asked him.

'Yes, I have done as you suggested,' he said drily. 'I have registered the child, and Rose says she likes the name you chose. I have added Laurence.'

'Is she feeling better?'

'If you mean, is she a little calmer, yes. They have given her something to make her sleep.'

'Have you come to take him away then?' she demanded. Her heart was in her mouth.

He looked surprised. 'No, to discuss the matter with you. There is nothing else we can do at present.'

He looked so depressed and disturbed that Mary said, 'You can be reassured – he is being well cared for. But when she recovers, will she want him?'

'I doubt she will ever want the charge of a child,' he said, and looked at her directly.

Was he thinking of leaving his mistress and returning to live with his wife – and the child?

'What about you, Laurence? I know men don't know how to care for babies – at least most don't – but they come to like the idea of a son of their own.'

He looked puzzled, then surprised, as if it had not yet occurred to him to think along those lines. For a time he said nothing and she waited.

Then he said, 'Perhaps I am a monster but I don't see myself as a father yet. I am doubtless much at fault.'

'Anastasia never wanted children when she was married, did she?' Mary thought she had the right to remind him of Anastasia's previous marriages.

'She had a very unhappy childhood. Her mother neglected her. Her father married again, to give her a mother, I suppose. There was mutual loathing between the two women.'

'So there won't be any step-grandmother wanting little Barnaby then? I thought Florence Robinson was a friend of her stepmother? That's what she once told me.'

'No, Mrs Robinson was a midwife who knew Rose's own mother. That is immaterial now.' He paused. 'She nearly died giving birth,' he said.

'If the birth had gone smoothly, might she have been as happy as most new mothers are? Once she gets back her strength, won't she want him back – and begin to love him? Laurence?'

'If I thought it were true I would take him back to her as soon as she is better, Mary. I knew before how she felt. She spoke of adoption, but she knew her sister-in-law would have nothing to do with her and there was no grandparent left on either side.'

He did not tell her the worst, that Anastasia had often said she hoped the baby would die.

'You suggested an aunt might adopt,' Mary interrupted. 'She must have felt very lonely – except for you.'

'I want the child to be safe, as much as you seem to do,' he said. 'What you did was unexpected, yet I thought you did not act entirely on impulse.'

'Laurence,' Mary began, 'Anastasia Hart is the only person with a legal right to this child. You will both have to choose.'

'Yes.'

'I gather you and she would not wish to bring him up together. You and I might, I suppose, stay together and bring up the little one if she wanted that. It would mean she gave him to you, and you acknowledged him – but never saw *her* again. Is that what you want?'

Would she be willing to do that? She supposed so, if it was the only way of looking after Barnaby. What would happen to Anastasia then?

'You seem more concerned with him than with your marriage,' he said.

'Yes,' she said shortly.

'Well then, you could go on looking after him. It can all be kept quiet as far as society is concerned,' he said.

'As if I care a fig for society!' replied Mary angrily, 'You want to marry her? Why didn't you marry her before? You should never have asked me to marry you.'

'She was married when I first met her, and I was married when we met again,' he replied flatly.

'I gathered as much from Tilly. If it had not been for her coming to live next door I'd have been kept in happy ignorance, wouldn't I?'

He said nothing.

'People don't choose whom they love. It's the way you deceived me that hurts,' she went on, still not willing to press a moral advantage too far.

I have not asked him when exactly he began to see her again after we were married, she said to herself. Was it only just over a year ago that they met 'by accident'? Or did he make love to her again in the first three years of our marriage? I don't want to know. It wouldn't make any difference to how I feel about the baby.

He cleared his throat. 'I do regret living a lie with you – last year. I can't regret my love for Rose.'

She ought to be feeling terrible jealousy, and she did not.

'I deserve to hear the whole story one day,' she said, 'but that won't change what I want to know just now. Are you – or both of you – or is she – going to take the little fellow away?'

He put his cup down on the hearth.

'You are such a Bohemian, Mary, so unconventional. A 'New Woman' – taking the baby – just like that! Marching in and telling me what to do! Admirable, I suppose.'

Was he being ironic?

'A child matters more than anything, Laurence.'

'And now to hint you want to keep him.'

'Yes, if his mother doesn't want him.'

'I suppose what you probably believe is correct. I don't want to leave her . . . and she does not want to look after the child. So.'

The situation had not changed, then – and perhaps he expected opposition. But she must have it out with him now. Laurence could be reasonable – a 'New Man' perhaps?

'What do you want to do? ' she asked him more gently. 'If you don't want to leave her now, what about us?'

He said, 'I know what *you* want!'

Could he possibly be jealous of a *baby*? She looked at him for a moment and then looked into the flames of the fire.

'I wouldn't want to go on living with you, knowing you loved someone else, Laurence. If we'd had children of our own, I think I could, and many women do. I think *marriage* is more about children and sharing your life than about passion.'

He looked uncomfortable.

255

'Of course to have that too would be best. But you love *her*!' she cried.

I understand why, she thought. And I could never abandon that little boy now to a stranger. Aloud, she said, 'He is yours, and you will always be his father. You can't undo that.'

'I know. And you have grounds for divorce. Yet a woman might want to stay married and force a man to a bargain.'

'What kind of bargain, Laurence? The longer I look after the baby, the more I love him.'

He was silent. She guessed he was thinking it was probably not his fault that they had had no child together.

'If she wants *you*, she might still change her mind about Barnaby. Children grow up quickly. In a month – or a year – in five years, even.' Mary's tone of voice betrayed her distress.

'You really do want to keep him for good, don't you?' he said in wonderment. 'It isn't to get even with us?'

'How can you say that? You don't understand. I don't want to get even with anyone. I suppose pragmatists would say that the best thing for that little baby would be for you to marry his mother and bring him up yourselves. You seem certain she won't change her mind.'

'I don't think she ever will. As for marrying – you are a strange wife, encouraging a husband to marry another woman!'

'Then you have never really understood me.'

'Would Mrs Sutcliffe be willing to go on helping you?'

'For as long as I needed her.'

'You would become another Aunt Clara,' he said, not entirely kindly.

Or another Mima, she thought.

'I wanted to return to a child the love I was once given after my own mother died. I so wanted a child of my own. It's too late for us now – even if I could,' she said intensely.

He looked uneasy. 'As you have pointed out,' he said, 'legally he is not mine to dispose of.'

'When she recovers – would she sign papers – make it legal?'

'Legal adoption does not exist in this country,' Laurence said drily.

'An agreement witnessed by a solicitor would surely have some force?'

He got up, walked to the window, cleared his throat and said with his back to her, 'I didn't really come here to talk about the baby. I came to confess my wrongdoing and to ask you for a divorce.'

'I must confess that I knew something was not right. It was partly my fault. I was self-deceived.'

She wanted to hear him say definitively that he would allow her to bring up his son.

At last he said, 'I have not made you happy. I would be happy for you to bring him up. I cannot think of anyone I'd trust more.' He cleared his throat. 'When Rose is mentally recovered I shall tell her that is what I would prefer.'

Mary's heart gave a curious jump. He had paid her the best compliment she had ever had from him.

'I know you will be – are – a good mother, Mary. We shall have to consult a solicitor – I am as aware as you are that one can't 'play stations' with a baby. You would need a promise.'

'You see, I can't be angry with *her*. With you, yes, I feel angry – or I did – but not with her.'

'Well, you are a feminist!' said her husband, not sounding completely cynical. 'I never underestimated your intelligence, Mary. I don't need to tell you that it is an extremely delicate situation as far as the world is concerned.'

He sat down again, and poured himself another cup of tea.

'It will reflect badly upon her – and upon myself – if society gets to know about it. You, however, will be a heroine!'

'Don't talk like that, Laurence. I am not a heroine.'

Laurence went on, 'When she told me about her predicament I had already considered going to live abroad, but how could I be seen publicly to leave you?'

'There is no point in telling me that now, Laurence.' She felt drained, if less nervous. She had never known him be so straightforward with her.

'What did you say to Mrs Kershaw?' he asked.

'If you mean, did I hint that Mr Hart had died a little later than he really did and that your 'Rose' was already expecting when he died, well, I didn't say anything to contradict that. I said she was ill – which she is – and hinted I might 'adopt' the baby. The sticky part will be what we do as a couple.'

Really, they could have got on very well as friends, not lovers, she thought.

'You knew that he had died too soon to be the father of the infant?'

The way he said 'the father of the infant'. How could he so distance himself from his own paternity as if it had had nothing to do with the way he felt about Anastasia?

'Your manager knew, more or less, so I wormed it out of him. I expect Alex Gordon has come to his own conclusions about the paternity of the child. If you both come back to live here when it has all blown over you needn't care too much about *your* reputation, since your wife will be seen to have connived with you!'

Morality apart, Mrs Hart would be ruined without Laurence's protection. It would not, however, be the first time she had been ruined. By now she must be careless of her reputation. Probably her own would soon be in shreds as a complaisant wife.

'I shall tell her what I think best,' he said again. 'You can rely upon me. When she is better I shall tell her how you feel, though she may find it hard to believe.'

If she had the care of Barnaby she would never stop Laurence seeing him. A child must know its father, even if he did not live in the same house. This thought pulled her up with a start. Time to think about that later.

She said, 'You love her so much – a mistress who doesn't even want to look after the child she has had with her lover.'

'You have a right to be bitter.'

'No, I'm not. Just puzzled.'

What sort of wife had Anastasia ever been to anyone? Well, they could live abroad whether he was divorced or not. Mary's mental picture of Paris, or a French watering place, did not contain a small figure in the foreground.

'What if I, the wronged wife, had not come along?' she said, not being able to stop herself now that at last Laurence was being honest with her. 'What would you have done?'

'I don't know.'

I have not been married to you for four years without understanding a little about you, she thought.

'I should have been less naïve four years ago. I trusted you.' Should she confess her discovery of that letter from Stephen?

'I hope you understand I am sorry. If you bring him up, I know *you* well enough to understand that to bring up a child was what you really wanted from your marriage to me.'

'It was not the only thing I wanted, Laurence. I am not the kind of woman who thought of her future only as a mother, but once I was married . . .' her voice trailed off.

'It is what many women want – even most women – if they are honest,' he said.

'I don't think I should have married anyone until I was older and had accomplished more in the world . . . grown up. If people regard me as unselfish and you as selfish, it is not strictly the truth. I could even defend you.'

She thought, real unselfishness means devoting yourself for hours and days and weeks and months and years to a vulnerable person – a child – when you would rather read a book; it is what most women do. She thought of Tilly, and Mima. But *they* most likely didn't want to spend their time with their nose in a book. It would not be easy for her; she might have the worst of both worlds. Most women didn't have a choice, did they.

'I would have had it differently – if I had not met her again,' he said.

He thought, to be brutal, I still want Rose. Mary guessed what he was thinking.

How very different men were from most women. She understood both Laurence's rationality, and the overpowering passion that had flowered in him – a passion that would never have been for her. Not ever.

'So we agree?' she asked, finally.

'Yes – I shall return to Manchester for a week or two and meanwhile you carry on as you have been doing. I'm sure you will have some plans in that head of yours.'

'I shall wait for you to tell me how she is and what she wants, and for you to speak to a solicitor in the meantime.'

Had Edwin told him anything more about what was really the matter with Mrs Hart that accounted for her rejection of the child?

Laurence was in fact still smarting over what the doctor had actually said to him, which he did not intend to tell Mary. Horsfall had implied that responsible men should not give children to 'unbalanced' women. The chap was probably some sort of a feminist himself.

He said, 'I think your old friend the doctor will be discreet, don't you?'

She smiled for the first time that afternoon. 'Does *he* know you are the baby's father?'

'I would imagine so. As he is an old friend of yours, didn't he voice his suspicions to you?'

'Edwin said nothing. He is very professional. He was most kind to me, though.'

She stood up, feeling a little light-headed after this long laying of their cards on the table by both of them.

'And now you must see Barnaby!' she exclaimed.

She called Mima who was waiting upstairs. The baby had been fed and had been asleep, but when Mima brought him down in her arms as they had arranged he began to cry.

'This is Mrs Sutcliffe,' Mary said.

Laurence said stiffly, 'Thank you for coming to help my wife.'

He was clearly a little at a loss, not knowing whether to address Mima as a servant or as a friend of Mary. It was obvious too that he very much disliked the noise of the crying child, though he did his best to conceal it.

'I won't sit down,' said Mima. 'He'll be quieter if I walk up and down with him.'

'Let me take him a moment,' said Mary. Mima placed Barnaby in her arms. Mary put him against her left shoulder and stroked his little stalk of a neck.

'There, there,' she said. 'Look, Laurence, he's a bit fatter, isn't he.'

She turned round so that he could see the little face and held his up his head in her palm.

'He smells so good now!' she said and murmured comforting words to him.

Laurence, trying not to show his lack of interest, even possible distaste, made an effort to look at his son and agreed he looked both pinker and plumper.

Mary kissed the baby's nose and then asked Mima to take him upstairs again.

'It would be a lot harder without Mima,' she said when she had gone out of the room.

She had not been sure if Laurence intended to stay at Ridge Hill that night, but he reiterated very firmly that he must return to his work across the Pennines for the time being and would give Mrs Kershaw her instructions.

'Before you go,' said Mary, 'I had a letter the other day from one set of tenants at Cliff House. They're to leave quite soon. Once things are settled between you and me I want to move there and live in that part of the house. I wanted you to know now so that it's not too much of a shock. I would like to take Barnaby to live at Cliff House.' And you can make up a story for Mrs K, she thought. 'Of course you'd be able to see him whenever you wanted,' she added.

'I did not think you would want to stay long here,' he answered. 'We shall have to see to finances – they will take some time to disentangle. This is still your home – until you choose to leave it.'

He considers he is being generous, thought Mary.

'I shall have the income from the other part of the house,' she said.

He looked doubtful, yet at the same time relieved. He said, 'You needn't worry about money for the child. I shall help with those expenses.'

'Money is always useful,' she replied, thinking, without it whatever would he do, whatever could *I* do? As for Mrs Hart, she had none. To her credit Stacey had not demanded to live in much style in Prestwich. Laurence had obviously paid for that, and for Mrs Robinson. Maybe he had wanted to be careful by not setting Anastasia up in a palace? I am so lucky to have a little money of my own, she thought.

'I couldn't let you go without telling you of my intention.'

'As long as you stay here – am I allowed to stay here too?' he said with a hint of sarcasm.

She coloured and said, 'There are plenty of bedrooms, Laurence.'

'We won't quarrel,' he replied, and went off to speak to Mrs Kershaw.

Dusk had come upon the house and garden; twilight always made Mary feel melancholy and this evening made her feel especially so. She did not regret her long talk with Laurence; time, however, could not be rolled back, and reality was sometimes painful and pitiful. For things to be different, her own mother would have had to live . . . and fate would have had to give her a baby of her own.

Before Laurence left Ridge Hill in the dark of the evening he returned to where Mary was sitting, hesitated, and then shook her hand. She felt exhausted, as well as relieved, when she heard the crunch of his carriage wheels fade away on the gravel. But there was still the possibility of Anastasia changing her mind so she did not allow herself to set her mind completely at rest.

Barnaby cried a good deal that night.

Mary watched over him, and stood at the window with him in her arms, as a cold dawn broke over the hills.

CHAPTER SIXTEEN

Many long letters were to pass from Ridge Hill to Headingley, and to Baden from Ridge Hill and Headingley in the first half of 1902.

Mary started a long letter to Tilly one cold February afternoon.

Ridge Hill
7 February 1902 (Friday)

Dear Tilly

Thank you for your sweet letter. It was so good to get an answer to my disjointed epistle. Mima has gone into town to buy some warmer vests for Barnaby – it is so cold here. I have an hour or two spare this afternoon whilst he is asleep. As you know so well, babies can be unpredictable, and he may wake up any minute, but I think that at six weeks old he is now getting more used to his routine. Mima told me babies were easier after the first few weeks unless they were screamers or always hungry – apparently some are like that! I've found out one has to devote oneself entirely to an infant – no half-measures. Last week he gave us his first smile – I am sure it was not wind, as people always claim it is, for he often does it now when I stare at him! I can't remember exactly all I told you before. Lack of sleep easily makes one disorientated. If it weren't for Mima I'd never have had time some days to wash my hands, never mind write letters, but I am determined to take my share of the work.

I have still not told Aunt Clara! I dread it, but I must do it soon, before someone else tells her. I do hope she will not think me stupid, or saintly. I could bear her anger, not her mistaking my motives. I know I am not a fool, and I am not really being unselfish. It is hard to explain, yet I feel sure I could have carried on as I was, just getting more lonely and self-obsessed, if Laurence had not done what he did.

The Ways of Love

I know he did wrong but you could say that 'God moves in a mysterious way', couldn't you? Or is that blasphemous?

On consideration she crossed out the last two lines and went on:

I felt very lonely during the last year or two without quite realizing that was what it was. I thought it was just not having a baby. What L did was a shock, yet in another way I am not surprised. His never breathing a word to me about his real feelings and what he had been doing all those times in Manchester is what makes me angry. I suppose most people would say, 'He is an adulterer and deserves no pity' – but there are plenty of husbands – and wives – like him who fall in love with someone else.

I now know Laurence had been 'in love' with her before he married me, but he ought to have known me well enough to realize that I might have understood if he had told me when he proposed to me. I can well imagine why a man – or even a woman –might fall in love with the beautiful Anastasia. She is a kind of sorceress with a mysterious attraction for romantic people. I had not thought L romantic, so I did not know him well enough either! I once told him that if I were a man, I could imagine falling in love with Mrs Hart. When I told him that, he just looked annoyed.

You may remember I felt her attraction when I was a child, but I never told him about it. That was wrong of me. He could have taken that opportunity to confess.

Is it stupid to think that people should tell their husband or wife about their present feelings? Everybody thinks you must keep these things secret. If she had not been expecting a baby I think I would have turned a blind eye so long as he had accorded me the same free-dom – not that I was thinking of 'carrying on' with anyone else. If we had had any children ourselves, would I have felt differently? Will men and women one day be able to act more honestly or will that destroy the fabric of society?

There, I have shocked you. Our society cannot condone his way of behaving, but it's not enough just to put a label on it and call it wicked. He did not, I am sure, intend to commit adultery when he married me, and for some time – I don't know how long – he didn't. We are not supposed to sympathise with people who are 'swept off their feet' but I can't help it. He really does love her in the same head-strong, infatuated way one loves when one is very young. I suppose I was blind, but he covered his tracks very well. He truly thought it was all over between him and her when he married me. He married

263

me to 'get over her' – and then met her again.

I would not put it past her to have 'engineered' that reunion. She must have had an unhappy life. I think she will recover from what might be what our medical encyclopaedia calls 'puerperal madness', and get back to normality. She was in a very bad state, a most frightening frame of mind, just could not bear to see the poor baby, never mind feed him. I'm sure Laurence was terrified. But even in her right mind she'd never have wanted to look after a child. She had already told him that, before she had the baby. What he thought she was going to do, I can't imagine –I expect he was just hoping she'd change her mind once she saw the infant. . . .

(Later)

I had to stop there because Barnaby woke up. Laurence has written to me and appears to believe he is still fond of me. I know now he was never in love with me, and he knows I know. When I was twenty I wanted passion – and might have had it with his friend Stephen. I expect some people might consider such a confession shocking.

Possibly I married the wrong man, but I told L that most likely I should not have married at all, certainly not when I was so young, with little experience of men, except from books. Mother-love turns out to be quite different, even if it is adopted mother-love, doesn't it? It has to be absolutely unconditional. Is any adult person really worthy of that? If I am allowed, I shall go on loving and looking after Barnaby. All children need to be loved and looked after.

I have agreed to start divorce proceedings as soon as the law allows, and I shall have to appear 'wronged'. I suppose I am, even if I'm exchanging Laurence for his son. Well, Tilly, truth turns out to be stranger than fiction, doesn't it? All I can do is just wait and see, and pray Mrs Hart does not change her mind – I still dread that. I'd be completely heartbroken if she returned to normal and then changed her mind and took him away. If, God forbid, she wanted him back, I should have to return him, like a parcel – I'm not a kidnapper. You could not bear to be parted from your babies, and it feels as if Barnaby is my baby.

Mima said to me the other day how she suffered when she left me to get married, which of course she wanted to do, all perfectly right and natural. It makes me think that the more women please themselves, the less they please the small children in their care, and this does not appear to apply to men. It makes me wonder too about the New Woman. So long as we don't have the care of a child we can be like men. You are lucky to have your kind husband. I'd wager he could look after a baby as well as a woman if he had to. His saying that it was ' a Christian act' that I did, ' but very rum', made me smile. Everyone will blame poor Anastasia, not Laurence, yet in her own way she was being quite rational. She did not even seem to mind what the child was called, or was indifferent, so L registered his own name as B's second name. The surname is Hart, which is nothing to do with either father or son!

(Feb 9)

Tilly, if things do turn out right, would George christen him? I am unsure about religious matters but I feel the little one ought to have the benefit of the doubt. Your sort of religion is charitable.

Mima is such a help, and reassures me when I fret. She knows several women who bring up a sister's or a friend's child. (They are more 'tribal' than the bourgeoisie!) Ever since I was six I have missed her at the bottom of my heart. Aunt Clara did her best, though she was not a naturally tender person. I think I am becoming more grateful to her for providing a home for me after Mima went away and Father died. Oh dear, I really must write to her.

Mima will stay with me only as long she wants. Her daughter is to marry so she will move back one day to Burnley to help look after any future grandchildren. I shan't be lonely, just busy, when she goes.

I have still not told you of my great plan. I heard from one of my tenants (with a family) when I returned from Manchester, and they are to leave Cliff House very soon. Immediately, I had a clear idea of what I want to do. I cannot go on living here – it is L's house anyway. If I am allowed to keep Barnaby, I shall move back there, taking Mima with me at first, and I intend to live more simply than we do here. I shall have the money from the other tenant and L has insisted he will help with the financial upkeep of the child – who is, after all, his son. I told him I didn't want any other financial help from him. I have another dream of my own for when Barnaby is older – I won't tell you about that yet.

A move will take some months to sort out, but I am determined. I want to be my own mistress there. I never wanted the housekeeper to stay on here, once I got the hang of domesticity and housekeeping. She always made me feel I was not the real mistress of the house. Laurence couldn't understand it. He thought her staying on here would make my life easier, which I suppose it did in a way, yet I felt superfluous – she made me feel about twelve years old.

265

L came back here again last week, and actually stayed three days, so I suppose Anastasia is improving. He said to me in a rather sarcastic way, 'If you do leave here, all you'll miss will be your rambler roses!' I don't know what he has told Mrs K, but I expect she has come to her own conclusions.

Things are very fluid at present and I will let you know when more is decided. If all goes well I shall tell everyone I am to adopt Mrs Hart's child. I said when we got back from Manchester that I was looking after him because Anastasia was ill and couldn't look after him herself, but Mrs K must surely have guessed the identity of Barnaby's father. I did not disillusion her about the date of death of Mr Hart but maybe she is more astute than we know.

You say in your letter that your mother told you recently that your father's cousin, Mrs Watson, Anastasia's mother, neglected her; perhaps even beat her, and that there was some sort of a scandal. I expect your mother took pity on her later, having her to stay and all. Your ma must be becoming more outspoken in her middle age. Fancy her saying 'Stacey Watson always had men around her'. It all comes down to mothers in the end, doesn't it?

(Feb 11)

You will never guess who came over yesterday to see us – Edwin! He was on a visit to his parents in Lightholme so he thought he might see how little Barnaby is doing. Mima remembers Edwin's father. Anyway, Edwin said Barnaby was thriving and that we would be able to add other things to his diet when he is about four months old – not quite 'pobbies', just rusks in milk. We get pasteurized milk from the town. Edwin knows the doctors behind a scheme for sterilizing milk in St Helen's in Lancashire and selling it for two pence to poor mothers. Has this scheme come yet to Leeds? Edwin wants to start this scheme up everywhere – he was in Liverpool helping with it.

He told Mima I was looking well (in spite of my lack of sleep). I am so looking forward to the day when you install a telephone and then I mean to get one at Cliff House. Now I must finish this monster missive and consider what to tell Aunt Clara. Kiss the children for me and give George my kindest regards—

With love from Mary.

The Ways of Love

Ridge Hill
Saturday 15 February 1902

My dear Aunt Clara,
Thank you for your greetings from Baden. You both seem to be enjoying German spa life. I am sorry I have not written a long letter to you since Christmas. I am very well, but so much has been happening here that is difficult to explain. Prepare yourself for a shock. The upshot is that Laurence is in love with another lady whom he has known for some time, indeed knew before he met me in Biarritz. She is a widow, a Mrs Hart, actually a relative of the Crowthers, and she was our neighbour here from last April. I may have mentioned the party we gave in summer at which she was a guest. In October she moved away to Prestwich near Manchester. Just after Christmas I discovered what my husband already knew: that she had given birth to his child at the end of December. He had gone there immediately when he heard she was ill, so I decided to follow him there. I found things very much awry. Mrs Hart was refusing to accept the baby, would not feed him, and Laurence had had to call a doctor. Eventually she was taken to a nursing home.

Well, Aunt, I took over the baby! Nobody else appeared to want him. I telegraphed Jemima Sutcliffe to come over, we brought him here, and here we still are with the little one. He is a boy called Barnaby.

Laurence and I have by now had many long discussions about the best way to proceed. It seems doubtful that Mrs Hart will ever want the child back. She is still in the nursing home, better in mind, and visited daily by my husband when he is staying in Manchester. I am determined now, with Laurence's complete agreement, to take on his child for good.

Well, that is one thing. The other is that Laurence and I have decided to end our marriage. For me, the most important thing is to look after the child, but Laurence has decided he does not want to abandon the child's mother, though he has no wish to take the child himself. We have therefore come to a mutual agreement to divorce, though it will be a lengthy process.

As these events were unrolling I heard from my tenant, Mr Hinchliffe-Lister, that he was to leave Lightholme to go north to Scotland with his family. I intend therefore, if all goes well, to seize upon the chance to return to live at Cliff House with the baby, Barnaby, and with Mima helping me for as long as she wants. Her

267

assistance has been wonderful.

Laurence knows of my intention. We do not quarrel. Although he does not want to look after the child himself, he will help to pay for his upkeep. The situation is, I am aware, a very unusual one, possibly unprecedented. Nevertheless I do assure you that I have never been so curiously content! It has been a tricky and difficult time for us all. My husband intends eventually to take the lady abroad with him.

I know this will be a shock for you, but please do not fret. You took good care of me for many years after Mima left and now I want to take care of someone. Not having a child of our own has been a great grief to me, if not to Laurence. Whenever he wants to see Barnaby, once we are settled at Cliff House, which will be in the not too distant future, God willing, he'll be welcome to visit as the child's father, if not as my husband. I don't believe there will be any scandal, but I shall not care if there is, for I have done nothing wrong. As I shall be living four miles away, the other side of the hill, all that people will be told – in case you are worried –is that my husband has separated from me but that I am bringing up his child.

I feel sufficiently strong to manage all this. I shall be helping out another woman, and bringing up a child whose father prefers it that way. Laurence will be glad, I believe, to know the child will be well looked after, leaving him to look after Mrs Hart. I already love Barnaby. You begin to love a small scrap of humanity and he has begun to smile and coo.

Well, Aunt, I realize all this may upset you but I do beg you to have faith in me and not to worry. The past is over; all that counts now is the present. Please do not feel the need to come rushing home. If you are uneasy, write to Tilly. She knows the whole story. I feel better than I have for years!

Look after yourselves. When you do come back to England I hope to have established my new ménage and you will be very, very welcome at Cliff House. I have not forgotten all you did for me in the past—

Your loving niece,
Mary.

For days Clara and Hannah read Mary's letter over and over again and sat up many nights discussing the news. Clara had at first been horrified. Then she decided to resign herself and blame both Laurence and fate for not giving Mary a baby.

'I get the impression she thinks she should not have married him and is now trying to repair her life,' said Clara. 'She never admitted to us that her marriage was not happy.'

'Many women have a childless marriage. You did yourself,' replied Hannah.

'I never really wanted children – I had quite enough to do looking after my husband. I would have had to put up with it if he had fallen in love with another woman. He did not. She seems to *want* her husband to leave her.'

'He wants to stay with this other woman.'

'What will she be left with, poor child?'

'A baby,' said Hannah simply. '*I* never married but that was always what I wanted!'

Clara looked quite surprised. 'Do you think I ought to go back and see what I can do?' she asked her friend.

'No – I should leave it to blow over. Jemima Green – what's she called now? Sutcliffe? She'll look after Mary.'

'I shall write to her friend Tilly as she suggests,' decided Clara. 'Just to make sure Mary is all right. Tilly is married to a Free Church clergyman so I'm sure we shall get the truth from her.'

'You need not return to England till it has all died down.'

'Are we being very selfish?'

'You are sixty-four Clara. You have your own life to live now – you did a lot for Mary. Are you angry with her?'

'No,' replied Clara simply. 'I just don't have the energy any longer to interfere.'

'I'd love to know more about the other woman!' said Hannah.

16 Wood Terrace Headingley
14 May 1902

Dear Mrs Demaine,
How nice it was to have a letter from you. I am sorry I did not reply earlier, apart from our Easter card, but I must reassure you about Mary. I went over to see her and Mrs Sutcliffe and the baby last week, taking my own little children who were thrilled to hold a real baby. Little Barnaby is flourishing and Mary and her old nanny are two devoted worshippers. Although it is an unusual situation I believe Mary will be all right. She even looks different, quite transfigured, though she is now what she calls 'tethered' to real life with a vengeance. It is a restriction she seems to desire. Fate dealt her a hard blow in one way and yet what it took away

with one hand it gave with the other. Mr Noble was not there. I believe he has taken Mrs Hart to convalesce in Mentone for a few weeks but they will return when she is better and will then discuss whatever the final arrangements are to be.

You ask me to tell you what I know about Mrs Hart and her past. Mary does not want to 'tell tales', so I will tell you all I know. Forgive me if I have to speak of things one does not normally write.

Mary may not have told you that as a child she met my father's cousin Anastasia – 'Stacey' – Watson a few times when she was stay-ing with us at The Nest. Perhaps you may remember Mary mentioning her years ago? She was very impressed by her, for I do remember she could talk of little else. The lady was extremely beau-tiful, but I am afraid that we Crowther children did not like her at all and I like her even less now. I have had scraps of information about her from Mother, and lately from Mary herself. After all, she is the baby's mother, however unnatural a one, and we must pray for her. I think Mary has done the right thing, a good deed. I would not have had the willpower to do it myself. Fortunately my dear husband and I are already blessed with two little ones.

What I tell you is in confidence and with Mary's permission so that you will not think she is leaving Laurence for a mere trifle. She is giving up a very pleasant life at Ridge Hill in that interesting old house because she says she cannot live a lie. Whatever she says now, I am certain she was always a good wife. She debated long and hard whether to marry Mr Noble, spoke of him to me and asked my advice. Perhaps I gave the wrong advice. Laurence appeared much enamoured of her, though it did come to light later that the other gentleman you met in Biarritz was also very attracted to her. My dear friend discovered that Laurence had effectively stopped his friend Mr Stephen Waterhouse from courting her. Waterhouse was a poor man and could not have married for some time. Mary however had found him very much to her taste when they met in Biarritz in '93. You will remember him.

After you all returned to England the following year Mr Noble must have written to his friend to ask his intentions, for he had decided to court Mary and wanted to know if Stephen Waterhouse intended to do the same. Poor Mr W, according to Mary, could not have afforded a wife for some time so Mr Noble decided to proceed. I think from what Mary has told me that he was already in involved with the other lady, who was married (for the second time) to a Mr Quintin Hart, the cause of the rupture she had with her first husband whom she had married in '86. (I do remember that date because it

*was the year she stayed with us for the last time before her wedding!)
He divorced her five years later and she married Mr Hart in 1892.*

*Laurence met her just after this and fell in love with her. Mr Hart
separated from her quite early on in the marriage, and Mr Noble
may have been the cause. Then Mr Noble decided he ought to find
himself a wife. I'd like to think that he made it clear to Mrs Hart that
she was doing wrong, and as he was the cause he must try to put an
end to it. He must have had his eye on Mary as a possible wife when
he invited you all to see his house.*

*Quite when his 'affaire' was broken off, I don't know. He finally
persuaded Mary to marry him in '97, after three years' courtship, as
you will remember. Mary does not now believe she should have
accepted him. Mr Noble met Anastasia Hart again, Mary thinks
early in 1900, though she has not enquired. He realized he was still
attracted to her, and rekindled their liaison. She says they used to
meet in Manchester when he was supposed to be there on business,
and his mill manager, Alex Gordon, knew something about it.*

*Mr Hart died suddenly in the autumn of 1900, making Anastasia
a widow, and then she insisted upon coming to live nearer to
Laurence! In the spring of last year, she prevailed upon him to rent
Birch Wood for her, next door to Ridge Hill. Imagine! Then she realized she was expecting a baby. Laurence was still under her spell but
had not envisaged a baby, and neither had she. Mary thinks she told
him after a summer party they gave at Ridge Hill. He could not
break it off or send her packing immediately – he is not a cad. He
was worried out of his wits, and must have felt very guilty. Mrs Hart
hinted to Mary that her husband had died later than he did, so that
he could have been the father of the coming child, though she had
not lived with him for ages.*

*Well, she could not stay on indefinitely near Mary if they were to
keep the paternity of the child secret. She wanted the child adopted,
or she would reveal all to the unsuspecting Mary. Mr Noble sent her
to a house in Prestwich, (near Manchester), and got a Mrs Robinson,
a cast-off acquaintance of Mrs Hart's mother, to look after her. The
baby arrived around last Christmas.*

*Mary will have told you what has happened since then and that
she is now hoping to go on bringing up her own husband's child. On
return from France Mrs Hart will sign an affidavit to that effect in
the presence of a solicitor. Before that, Mary wants Mrs Hart to see
Barnaby again to make quite sure she will not change her mind
when she has seen how bonny he is.*

I know you are regarded as a strong-minded and independent

271

lady so you will not mind, I hope, that I have spoken to you rather plainly of matters that are not usually discussed by ladies. Mary wanted you to know what she calls the 'facts'. All she can think of at present is whether Anastasia Hart may change her mind and want her baby back. It is a continual fear and until it is settled she will be anxious.

Mary has put everything, all her energy and commitment, into caring for this little scrap. She has taken full responsibility, and the odd thing is that Mr Noble accepts what she has done. I think he realizes how much she wanted a child. She did not act in an irrational manner, for I truly believe that if the baby had been left to Mrs Hart she would have let him die through neglect, such was her attitude. I expect Mr Noble is relieved not to have to do anything more about it. He seems set on waiting for Anastasia to recover and then he says (Mary tells me) that he will go to live abroad with her permanently, thus avoiding any scandal. He must be insanely in love with her.

Mary feels that it was partly her fault that she married him without thinking more deeply why he wanted to marry her. As he is the guilty party he cannot move to divorce her – she has done nothing wrong – but she thinks he ought to marry Mrs Hart. As the law now stands, the child could not be retrospectively legitimized.

Mary has gone into it all. She will have her own solicitor there when Mrs H swears an affidavit and officially hands over the child. The mother, not the father, is the legal possessor of Barnaby because Mrs Hart was not married to Mr Noble. If Mr Hart had not died he would be regarded as the father and therefore the legal parent! I confess I did not know myself that a mother must get permission from her husband even to take her own child abroad. It is very unChristian of me yet I can't help feeling that it is a mercy Quintin Hart died when he did, even if his wife's return to Mr Noble had happened before his death.

Mary has plans to move back to Lightholme and she will tell you all about them eventually. I do earnestly beg you not to return to England just yet. She has my husband's support and mine as well as Mrs Sutcliffe's – even in a curious way her husband's. She will be very happy for you both to come and see her and Barnaby when all is settled. He is a beautiful child.

    I remain

        Yours very sincerely.

        Matilda Ramsden.

In the summer Laurence wrote to Mary from France. Anastasia added a few lines in a faint though stylish hand. This was an odd little communication; certain phrases sounded as though they had been suggested, even dictated, by Laurence.

Villa Soleil, Mentone

Dear Mary Noble,
I have been very ill but am almost better. I have not changed my mind about the boy. I cannot remember much of what happened at Christmas. I ought to say thank you, oughtn't I? We shall come back to England soon so that I can declare to your and my solicitors that you are now the mother of my baby and are to continue in full and sole charge of him. After all, he is your husband's child, and that is what he wants you to do, as well as myself. I shall sign a paper to that effect. Laurie will tell you all the rest of it and then we shall come back here.
   Yours faithfully,
      Anastasia Rose Hart.

Laurence and Mrs Hart stayed on in Mentone until mid-August, before returning to England for a week, to settle matters with the solicitors in Leeds, as Laurence had arranged. Mary and Barnaby were to attend, along with Mrs Sutcliffe as witness. Barnaby was now over eight months old and had been sitting up for over a month. He laughed a good deal nowadays and was unrecognizable as the tiny screamer he had been. Mary was dreading the day Anastasia saw him again, and felt sick with nerves on the morning of the day they were to meet. Mrs Hart could still change her mind, especially as the child was now so attractive and lively.

Mary, with Mima holding Barnaby, was ushered into the office of Woodward & Woodward on Park Row. What an incongruous place for the settling of people's lives, Mary thought. Barnaby had to be present of course. Perhaps she ought to hope he would cry, which would certainly put off his father. He cried little now and was very alert. Mima had put him in the little carry-chair they used for him and she placed that in a large horsehair armchair, and gave him a toy to play with.

The others were late. Mary awaited their arrival with her stomach churning and her heart beating like an imprisoned bird. Before they arrived, the solicitor, an impressive-looking and hearty-sounding man explained he was not Mr Woodward but Mr Sugden. He introduced them to his colleague from another solicitor's office, Mr Marsden, a small, rubicund, middle-aged man who was to represent Mrs Hart, paid for of course by Laurence. Mary had insisted on paying her own fees. What she was to sign and Mima to sign as witness had, in fact, no legal binding but might be called upon if there were ever any dispute in future about the child. Sugden peered over at Barnaby and looked quite surprised that the child regarded him fixedly. Mary realized it was his gold watch chain and spectacles that were attracting Barnaby's gaze. She hoped the meeting would not drag on for too long. They had a carriage coming for them in half an hour to take them the fifteen miles or so back to Ridge Hill.

When Laurence and his mistress came in five minutes later, Mary felt on tenterhooks, mingled with relief that things were at last to be settled. Anastasia was wearing a veil, which she lifted as soon as she sat down. She looked at Mary and then she looked over at the child.

She said, 'He seems quite large.'

Laurence had acknowledged his wife by shaking her hand. Now he looked more carefully at his son.

'A fine boy,' he said.

Mr Sugden cleared his throat and said, 'May we start?' He produced two large sheets of white parchment, written in beautiful copperplate, from which he proceeded to read. It was addressed principally to Anastasia and was full of 'whereas'es' and 'whatosever's.

When he had finished she looked baffled.

'Is it your wish now that Mrs Mary Ellen Noble takes full charge of the infant Barnaby Laurence Hart until he shall reach the age of twenty-one?' he asked.

'Oh, yes, of course,' she said, as if it was very little to do with her.

'Will you read these two papers over and then sign both? One is for you to keep. I shall not need Mr Noble's signature. My colleague will ask Mrs Mary Noble to sign a similar paper.' Anastasia skimmed the paper quickly and nonchalantly.

Laurence watched her, and then said to Mr Sugden, 'As I told you, I should like if possible before my wife signs, to put it on record that the infant is my natural son.'

'This is sworn separately,' said Mr Sugden in a clearly disapproving tone. 'It is on record,' he said, producing another large sheet of parchment, 'that Mr Noble may visit his natural son Barnaby

Laurence Hart whenever he wishes, provided he does not remove him from Mrs Mary Noble's care and provided she is apprised in advance of his intention to visit.'

Mary was reminded of her wedding in Woolsford. Mr Sugden had missed his vocation. He ought to have said, 'Do you take this baby to be your lawful baby to have and to hold in sickness and in health and thereto you pledge your troth?'

'As I wrote to you, I have made some further arrangements,' Mary said to her husband when they had all signed the various papers, and they had been stamped with the seals of the two offices. 'We shall move into Cliff House before the bad weather begins – we hope by the end of October.'

Laurence nodded his head. He appeared to be keeping a tight rein on his feelings.

Just then Barnaby began to shout and wave his hands. He stopped when Anastasia went up to his little chair.

She looked at him closely and said, '*Adieu* – you will be well looked after.'

The baby stared at her and Mary's heart missed a beat. Then he laughed and dribbled and banged his wooden rattle on the side of the chair.

Anastasia adjusted her veil.

Mima gave Barnaby a rusk for the other hand.

Laurence and Mary said their goodbyes.

'I shall be writing to you,' said Laurence. It would be about the divorce, which would be a long-drawn-out matter if she knew anything about lawyers. As the innocent party, Mary must petition.

'You must come over at Christmas or the New Year,' she said in a neutral voice.

And that seemed to be that.

She didn't mention anything about any future plans she might have for Cliff House. She'd already started to redecorate her part of it, and her plans might take years to put into action.

Ridge Hill
15 August 1902

Dearest Yeranty,
The meeting has arranged everything well and now I may breathe a sigh of relief. I could not help feeling sorry for Laurence, and

puzzled by her. When next I write we may have packed up and returned to dear old Cliff House. I assure you that I am not attempting to put the clock back or recreate my own childhood. I just hope and trust that Barnaby will be as happy there as I was – and that was very happy. I know I owe a lot of that to you.

You and Hannah will be very welcome to come and stay there for as long as you wish, once we have sorted out our part of the house. Thank you, again, Aunt, for all you did for me in the past. If I have upset you, please forgive me. I feel, indeed I am sure, that I am doing the right thing. He is a lovely little boy and to bring him up in such a place will be helpful to him as well as to me. Mima will stay on for the time being but will eventually go back to her family. She has been a brick and I could not have managed without her.

As far as my husband is concerned I know he is now with the woman who has meant most to him.

Your loving niece,
Mary.

Mrs Kershaw had known that Mary was to leave Ridge Hill but had made no comment. On the other hand, she was fond of the baby and said, 'I shall miss him.' Mary had told her she was to 'adopt' him and Mrs K had just replied, 'Yes – I see.'

What Laurence had told her, Mary never knew. She was to stay on at Ridge Hill after Mary had gone, along with Ethel, who cried when they finally left.

From Mary's diary

28 December 1902
Holy Innocents' Day

Anastasia was his real love. He could not help falling in love with her. He did wrong in marrying me. It was clearly not Laurence's fault that I did not have a baby, nor his fault that she didn't want his child. I admire him now for sticking with her. Until recently I felt angry that he had once put off Stephen Waterhouse from pursuing his friendship with me. But I might also have blamed Stephen for not having the courage of his convictions. I know he found me attractive! But I didn't marry Laurence for money, or to have an easy life, or for his valuable possessions, or his lovely old house, but because I felt I ought to join the human race and be like other people.

Now all that old knot of feelings has been disentangled. What counts in the end must be trying to do good in small ways. The care of a child is a constant accretion of 'small ways'. . . .

I shall grow climbing roses on the south wall of Cliff House. . . .

Barnaby has just had his first birthday and really enjoyed his cake with one big candle and his new toys. He said 'No!' for the first time the next day! The other words are 'dog' (the farm dog who often comes round here) and 'light' – the Christmas-tree candles. Laurence is not coming over yet. He sent a present – a velvet hat.

I often think about my childhood, now that I live here again.

I remember as I walk around the familiar lanes how I loved my father but was too shy to tell him – or he was too shy to let me. I know how he and Yeranty cared for me. What would I have felt for my own mother if she had lived?

I have had many strong feelings in my life, and have been lucky to have much love given to me. I adored Mima, who introduced me to maternal love, and yearned romantically for young Stacey Watson, who beckoned me in the direction of beauty and glamour. She must have beckoned in the same way to Laurence later. I had begun to feel the same way about Stephen – I certainly felt the power of physical attraction – but it was not to be. All these things are over.

For Tilly I feel enduring friendship. Maybe friends of the same sex are the longest-lasting of all one's relationships?

I wonder whether one is more influenced by such people than by those who guide us on to the paths of reason? Eleanor Hartley and the teachers at the high school and the college showed me the treasures of the mind and extended my thinking powers. Laurence himself pointed to a world of things that I might not have understood without him. Ironically, he made me reconsider my real self.

It is all the past, now that I am caught up and absorbed in a little being who is not yet completely formed and depends on me not only for care and love, but also to display and clarify the world for him.

ENVOI

ENVOI

The Boer War, as it came to be called, was over by May 1903. It had dragged on for almost four years. Mary was more concerned that summer with Barnaby's back molars and his new toddler self. Mima had warned her it was the most tiring time for mothers, but Mary was only twenty-eight and had plenty of energy. She often asked herself how the forty-year-old Anastasia would have managed, even if she had wanted to keep her little boy. She came to realize that Anastasia had seen her at first as a sort of superior maternity nurse, who had arrived to take over the baby. Now she gathered she was seen as a real adoptive mother. As far as the 'nannying' was concerned, well, many rich women did much the same, even if they showed more interest in their infants and did not deny them milk.

What Anastasia really thought about the unfortunate fact that the father of the child was Mary's own husband would never be revealed. Maybe she thought she had a right to Laurence, having laid claim to him before Mary had.

Mary was overjoyed as well as grateful that she could now give herself up to a fond and steady maternal love, a mixture of passionate tenderness – the tenderness she had felt that first night as she watched over the baby – and a separate rush of emotion she had not expected to feel, or believed a woman could feel who had not herself given birth, a queer kind of pride. Her deep well of maternal feelings coalesced with what she had always thought of as her real self. That self could never betray Barnaby. One day he would grow up, as all children must. She trusted it would be as a happy young man.

Tilly often said to her George that because Mary had never known her own mother and had lost Mima, her mother substitute, when she was six, and her father when she was twelve, she might perhaps have expected to lose her husband too?

George said, 'But she knew love – that's what makes the difference.'

George was interested in the theories of the new psychologists and believed that human babies unconsciously absorbed the unconditional love shown to them.

Tilly realized that although Laurence might be in Mary's debt, so she was in his. She said this too to her husband, who was an unusually liberal-minded minister of the Free Church who could not approve of divorce but regretfully thought it might sometimes be the least bad option.

'I suppose Noble has repaid the wrong he did to her,' he would say. 'I wonder if the Christian churches in general will ever countenance divorce. I'm sure it makes a difference if there are no children to consider.'

Mary chatted constantly to Barnaby who was unsurprisingly an early talker. He also had a well-developed sense of humour. For the child of a woman like Anastasia he appeared remarkably well balanced. Mary dared to hope he might have inherited Laurence's brains, but would not be upset if he hadn't.

Early on in their days at Cliff House she had wheeled the little boy in his perambulator to the village shops where they were met only with smiles. When he could toddle, she walked him over to The Nest, to show him where his Aunt Tilly had once lived, and where she herself had once played and been to school. When one of Tilly's brothers came to live there with his young family Mary was invited to call.

'That will make you respectable,' Tilly said, laughing. People from the village who had known her as a child assumed that 'Mary Settle-that-was' had separated from her husband, a not unknown event in the lives of the rich, and that she was bringing up their child alone. She did not try to disabuse them. To Barnaby, when he was older, she would explain that his father lived a long way away with another mama.

One day, in the summer of 1904, as soon as they finally returned from Baden to Woolsford, Clara and Hannah came over to stay in Lightholme. Barnaby was introduced to 'Yeranty', and this time Clara smiled over the name. She appeared to accept her niece's unusual domestic arrangements, though it had taken her a year or two.

The divorce between Laurence and Mary Noble also took time. It was made absolute in 1905.

Laurence married Anastasia once his divorce was through and

they continued to live abroad.

Barnaby had already begun to call Mary 'Mermi'. Since Mima was called by the name he heard Mary call her, for a time he had both a Mermi and a Mima. A 'mama' was not important since he never saw her. He had already accepted Laurence as his father though he saw him only rarely. A 'Daddy Noble' brought Barnaby expensive presents on his twice-yearly visits, and Mary was careful to tell the little boy that the expensive toy was also from his 'Mama Noble'.

From a letter from Laurence to Mary

. . . I thank you for your letter, which in the circumstances seems to me fair. We cannot bury our past but we need not any longer feel obliged to disinter it. The French have a different system from ours: a natural child can be reconnu, *which is what I have done with your help. I am happy to be able to see him now and again, and I hope that if you ever remarry, your future husband will be agreeable to my visiting the boy whom I now consider as your son too.*

The year Barnaby was five, Laurence brought his wife with him to Cliff House for the first and only time. Mary was not sure the visit was a good idea. It was not Anastasia's own idea for sure; Laurence had prevailed upon her. The couple brought with them a large mechanical elephant *Made in Germany*, for which Barnaby showed suitable gratitude towards his father's wife. Anastasia was distantly friendly to her son, like some sort of grown up cousin. After their visit Mary felt obliged to explain to him again that the lady who had visited with his papa was his 'Mama Noble'. She hoped he would remember one day.

A few weeks later, after the Nobles had gone back to France, Barnaby was playing with his elephant, and said suddenly, 'Mermi, you are my mother. Daddy's lady who gave me Jumbo was very pretty but Mama Noble is not a Mermi, is she.'

Mary's great idea had been revealed to Tilly and Mima a year after their return to Cliff House. She was going to organize a schoolroom and teach children there, just as Eleanor Hartley had once done at The Nest. The school would grow as Barnaby grew. Mima helped her at first with these arrangements, which did not come to fruition for a year or two. By then Mima had returned home to enjoy being a grandmother, and Mary felt confident she could manage the garden and her part of the house, with the help of a woman from the village and young John Lightowler to garden and drive the trap. She now had a splendid new bicycle.

But all her plans would not have been so successful without the encouragement of Dr Edwin Horsfall, who had moved back to Lightholme when Barnaby was four, to take up his father's practice, as well as to further his research in Leeds. People trusted Edwin; the parents of possible pupils cast aside any lingering doubts about a divorced woman.

Mary pored over the writings of Dr Froebel, eventually installed a sandpit, and bought several easels and other pieces of equipment. Picture-books and stories had arrived long before, when Mary brought back the contents of her old eyrie at Ridge Hill. She taught Barnaby to read, but read aloud the old favourites of childhood to him, and then to other children. As time went on, newer stories, in books published since Mary's own childhood arrived. The old book-shelves of her father's study having welcomed such favourites as *Black Beauty*, *The Cuckoo Clock*, *A Flat Iron for a Farthing*, and *Treasure Island* now held the stories of Beatrix Potter, *The Wind in the Willows*, and *The Story of the Treasure Seekers*. As Barnaby grew older Mary discovered with him books that boys liked – Kipling, and Rider Haggard and H.G. Wells. She was pleased to be learning new things herself, not least about little boys.

One of her pupils was the daughter of Mercy Miller who had married Frank Gledhill, a wealthy farmer, and who now renewed acquaintance with Mary, much to the latter's surprise. Most of the Crowthers had now left the district, apart from Tilly's brother Jonathan at The Nest, who sent his son and daughter to sit next to Barnaby and little Faith Gledhill.

Mary had come to know Edwin as the best male friend she had always longed for. That he was also a kind and competent man who loved all children, she also realized. He was especially fond of Barnaby. She began to find him very attractive, but it took her longer to realize that he also loved and admired Barnaby's 'Mermi'.

On Barnaby's sixth birthday Edwin asked her to marry him. It took Mary some months to make up her mind to marry again. Her first marriage had made her wary, not of commitment, but of the actual state of matrimony. She finally decided to dismiss her doubts when she understood that she loved Edwin and he loved her with a steady, happy love.

She became Mary Horsfall when she and Edwin were married in a simple Quaker ceremony in the December of the year 1908.

Yeranty moved back to Woolsford for good after her friend Hannah died. She could not be persuaded to move into a small apartment at Cliff House, but to the end of her life she regularly visited them all in Lightholme.

Miss Eleanor Hartley, once she had retired from the high school in Woolsford, lived to a great age and was still, when she was almost eighty, taking the train daily from Woolsford to teach at Cliff House School, proprietor Mrs M.E. Horsfall. It became a larger establishment after the last family of tenants moved away.

Mima lived on in Burnley, the matriarch of a large family. Louise had four daughters, and her brother Bobby, the blacksmith, four sons.

Tilly and her husband went on to have three more children and continued to live in Leeds, where the Revd. George Ramsden was an extremely popular preacher.

Edwin and Mary had no children together, but Edwin was responsible for the health of many poor infants, and Mary for the education of many others, even if most of them were less poor. She offered free education to any promising village girl over the age of twelve, but when only one wished to take advantage of it, since families needed the money their daughters could bring in, she made the schoolroom at Cliff House a place where small children from the village might come on Saturday mornings to listen to stories being read. This was highly successful, and encouraged more children to read. The headmaster of the village National School had no objection; he was pleased anyone took an interest in his pupils out of school.

The fondness Edwin felt for his stepson Barnaby, whom he had known since he was a few days old, was reciprocated by the boy. Barnaby adored him and called him Daddy. Edwin was often busy at his surgery or on home visits, or at meetings concerned with the health of the district, but for Barnaby after the age of seven he was a constant presence. The boy flourished and enjoyed a very happy childhood at Lightholme in those years before war stalked the land.

Mary found that marriage and the teaching and organization of her little school did not detract from the side of her nature she had indulged during the frequent solitude of the last two years of her first marriage. What she was careful to call to Tilly and her husband the 'spiritual' dimension of living, rather than the 'religious', which belonged to her inner world as well as to the world around, became more accessible through bringing up Barnaby. Laying before a child all the pleasures of existence, the sky and the clouds, the trees and the stars, flowers, walks, animals, landscapes and places; introducing him to poems and music and pictures and stories, had extended her own faculties and given her great happiness. Nurturing Barnaby's talents was one way of loving, and this child of a man and a woman, of both of whom she could not deny she had once been fond, was her link to the future.

Edwin was aware that Barnaby might be jealous of his own presence after the years when Mary had been his only 'real' parent, and was always careful to show he accepted the existence of the child's 'other father', the mostly absent 'Papa Noble'. This helped Barnaby, quite a different kind of child from the one his stepfather had been, and he came to admire the man his mother had married. He learned when he was older that Edwin had helped save his own life, and in adolescence realized that Edwin's joining the family had released him from the obligation to worry about his mother. He could be independent with a light heart, knowing the two of them were happy. Edwin was by then Mary's present – and future – reality, and gathered her life together for her in a way she could never have believed possible.

Anastasia died in Mentone in 1912. She never saw her son again after the visit she made when he was four. After her death, Mary and Edwin wrote to Laurence concerning the possible change of Barnaby's surname by deed poll. Laurence might like it changed from Hart to Noble? He was surprisingly lukewarm about this idea, suggesting instead that if the name were changed at all it should be changed to that of Horsfall. This they eventually did.

Except for the tenuous 'keeping in touch' with his son, Laurence stayed away from England until the outbreak of war, leaving his business to be managed by Alex Gordon, who became his partner. They both made a good deal of money during the war with the demand for army greatcoats. After the war, Laurence sold the mill to Alex and returned to France, to live the life of a *rentier* on the Côte d'Azur. He also sold Ridge Hill to Mr Gordon, and Ethel stayed on as Gordon's housekeeper.

Barnaby missed being called up in the Great War by only a year or two; it ended when he was almost seventeen. He loved buildings and paintings from an early age, and went on to study art and design and, later, architecture. In 1929 he married Charlotte, Tilly's youngest child, who was teaching botany at Cliff House School. Along with their baby daughter, Viola Mary, the couple holidayed in France in 1933, and visited Laurence at his villa near Antibes a few months before his death. There they met an old man whom Laurence called 'my dear friend'. He was called Stephen Waterhouse, and showed great interest in Barnaby and in news of his mother. Laurence was more interested in his son's talents for painting and his passion for buildings.

When Viola was seven, war broke out again. There were no more holidays in France, Barnaby was commissioned as a war artist, and his family evacuated back to Yorkshire. Just before the war he and Charlotte had had another child, a son, James Laurence. The school, a refuge for evacuees in the war, closed after it, and the house reverted to family occupation. Mary and Edwin lived there for the rest of their long lives.

Mary's granddaughter Viola, who was Tilly's granddaughter, as well as Anastasia's, inherited both her colouring and her temperament from Anastasia, and was a raven-haired charmer. She also inherited from her father a talent for art, and became a landscape photographer. Unfortunately, her marriage to a Frenchman was not happy; their daughter, Marie-Hélène, stayed with her mother but often spent holidays in France. Viola's brother James stayed on in Lightholme, and it was James who went on living at Cliff House and became in his turn, like his step-grandfather, 'Doctor Horsfall'.

He and his family still live at Cliff House. Much has changed, though the house has not changed very much. The Nest has been demolished and the lake drained. Many houses now stand where the old mansion once stood in its beautiful grounds.

As we know, Viola came back to live near the place where Tilly and Mary, the grandmothers she loved, had grown up, and with which the 'other' grandmother she had been told about had been slightly acquainted.

The Ways of Love

In the nineteen nineties, Marie-Hélène married a Yorkshireman. They named their first daughter Mary Anastasia.